OTTAWA STORIES FROM THE SPRINGS

anishinaabe dibaadjimowinan wodi gaa binjibaamigak
wodi mookodjiwong e zhinikaadek

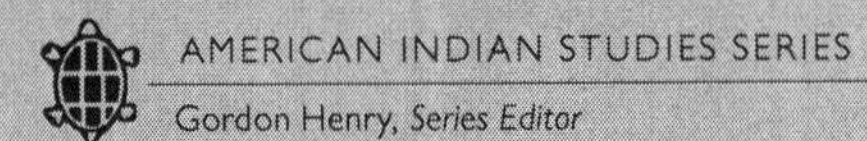

AMERICAN INDIAN STUDIES SERIES

Gordon Henry, *Series Editor*

Bawaajimo: A Dialect of Dreams in Anishinaabe Language and Literature, Margaret Noodin | 978-1-61186-105-1

Centering Anishinaabeg Studies: Understanding the World through Stories, edited by Jill Doerfler, Niigaanwewidam James Sinclair, and Heidi Kiiwetinepinesiik Stark | 978-1-61186-067-2

Document of Expectations, Devon Abbott Mihesuah | 978-1-61186-011-5

Dragonfly Dance, Denise K. Lajimodiere | 978-0-87013-982-6

Facing the Future: The Indian Child Welfare Act at 30, edited by Matthew L. M. Fletcher, Wenona T. Singel, and Kathryn E. Fort | 978-0-87013-860-7

Follow the Blackbirds, Gwen Nell Westerman | 978-1-61186-092-4

The Indian Who Bombed Berlin and Other Stories, Ralph Salisbury | 978-0-87013-847-8

Masculindians: Conversations about Indigenous Manhood, edited by Sam McKegney | 978-1-61186-129-7

Mediating Indianness, edited by Cathy Covell Waegner | 978-1-61186-151-8

The Murder of Joe White: Ojibwe Leadership and Colonialism in Wisconsin, Erik M. Redix | 978-1-61186-145-7

National Monuments, Heid E. Erdrich | 978-0-87013-848-5

Ogimawkwe Mitigwaki (*Queen of the Woods*), Simon Pokagon | 978-0-87013-987-1

Ottawa Stories from the Springs: anishinaabe dibaadjimowinan wodi gaa binjibaamigak wodi mookodjiwong e zhinikaadek, translated and edited by Howard Webkamigad | 978-1-61186-137-2

Plain of Jars and Other Stories, Geary Hobson | 978-0-87013-998-7

Sacred Wilderness, Susan Power | 978-1-61186-111-2

Seeing Red—Hollywood's Pixeled Skins: American Indians and Film, edited by LeAnne Howe, Harvey Markowitz, and Denise K. Cummings | 978-1-61186-081-8

Shedding Skins: Four Sioux Poets, edited by Adrian C. Louis | 978-0-87013-823-2

Stories through Theories/Theories through Stories: North American Indian Writing, Storytelling, and Critique, edited by Gordon D. Henry Jr., Nieves Pascual Soler, and Silvia Martinez-Falquina | 978-0-87013-841-6

That Guy Wolf Dancing, Elizabeth Cook-Lynn | 978-1-61186-138-9

Those Who Belong: Identity, Family, Blood, and Citizenship among the White Earth Anishinaabeg, Jill Doerfler | 978-1-61186-169-3

Visualities: Perspectives on Contemporary American Indian Film and Art, edited by Denise K. Cummings | 978-0-87013-999-4

Writing Home: Indigenous Narratives of Resistance, Michael D. Wilson | 978-0-87013-818-8

OTTAWA STORIES FROM THE SPRINGS

anishinaabe dibaadjimowinan wodi gaa binjibaamigak wodi mookodjiwong e zhinikaadek

Translated and edited by
HOWARD WEBKAMIGAD

Michigan State University Press | East Lansing

♾ The paper used in this publication meets the minimum requirements of ANSI/NISO Z39.48-1992 (R 1997) (Permanence of Paper).

Michigan State University Press
East Lansing, Michigan 48823-5245

Printed and bound in the United States of America.

21 20 19 18 17 16 15 1 2 3 4 5 6 7 8 9 10

LIBRARY OF CONGRESS CATALOGING-IN-PUBLICATION DATA
Ottawa stories from the Springs : anishinaabe dibaadjimowinan wodi gaa binjibaamigak wodi mookodjiwong e zhinikaadek / translated and edited by Howard Webkamigad.
pages cm.—(American Indian studies series)
ISBN 978-1-61186-137-2 (paperback : alkaline paper)—ISBN 978-1-60917-422-4 (PDF) 1. Ojibwa Indians—Folklore. 2. Ottawa Indians—Folklore. 3. Ojibwa Indians—Michigan—Harbor Springs Region—Social life and customs. 4. Ottawa Indians—Michigan—Harbor Springs Region—Social life and customs. 5. Harbor Springs Region (Mich.)—Social life and customs. 6. Ojibwa language—Texts. I. Webkamigad, Howard. II. Title: Anishinaabe dibaadjimowinan wodi gaa binjibaamigak wodi mookodjiwong e zhinikaadek.
E99.C6O87 2014
398.2089'97333—dc23
2014015748

Book design by Charlie Sharp, Sharp Des!gns, Lansing, Michigan
Cover design by Shaun Allshouse, www.shaunallshouse.com
COVER IMAGE: The normally unornamented bag on the cover was customized circa 1881 by an eighteen-year-old Joseph Ettawageshik, who used it to carry the mail along the Lake Michigan shore from Harbor Springs to Good Hart to Cross Village and back. Letters between some of the elders whose voices are heard in *Stories from the Springs* likely were carried in this bag. (Frank Ettawageshik collection, used with permission.)

Michigan State University Press is a member of the Green Press Initiative and is committed to developing and encouraging ecologically responsible publishing practices. For more information about the Green Press Initiative and the use of recycled paper in book publishing, please visit *www.greenpressinitiative.org*.

Visit Michigan State University Press at *www.msupress.org*

Contents

PART 4. CONTEMPORARY STORIES

Note on the Recordings

James M. McClurken

Jane Willets undertook research with the Odawas at Harbor Springs, Michigan, in 1946 when she was a student of anthropology at University of Pennsylvania. Her professor, Frank Speck, had cultivated a relationship at Harbor Springs with Fred Ettawageshik, an artist and community leader. Ettawageshik agreed to help Willets in her fieldwork, collecting information on arts, performance, economy, and community history for a study of culture continuity and change in Little Traverse Odawa communities. During this collaboration, Jane and Fred married and it is their son, Frank Ettawageshik, who introduces the following collection of stories recorded by his mother during the first year of her fieldwork.

Frank's introduction tells the story of his mother's first visit to Harbor Springs. Funded with a grant from the American Philosophical Society, equipped with a wire recorder, and having read the scant anthropological literature on the Tribe, Jane set out to meet Fred and the members of his community. After a long train ride through what seemed like a wilderness, Jane arrived in the lakeside tourist town only to learn that Fred was engaged as a speaker on a Great Lakes cruise. These recordings are a result of this missed connection. Indian Town, the Odawa settlement tucked between sand hills behind Holy Childhood of Jesus Church was a local landmark. Jane found the settlement on her own and set out to meet people in the community. Although she knew no one, Jane made friends with a community elder named Victoria Cooper, a storyteller whose tales are recorded in this collection.

Many of the stories in this collection were told and recorded at Victoria's kitchen table. Victoria allowed Jane to leave her recorder sitting on the kitchen table for several days. People wandered into the kitchen, pressed the record button, and told their stories to Jane's machine. The result is this collection of tales that Odawa people living in the mid-twentieth century told among themselves in their homes away from the tourists. The collection reflects a living cultural tradition in which the narrators repeat old stories about the formation of topographical features, origins of the crops raised in their gardens, morality stories, and etiquette. Sometimes they do so with a modern twist, like placing the traditional cultural hero *Nenibozhoo* aboard a steamship to play jokes on the passengers who filled Harbor Springs each year.

This project was a long time in preparation. I first learned of these recordings as an undergraduate student at William James College, Grand Valley State University, in 1977. Working on an oral history project that aimed to collect stories from Ottawas and Potawatomis living in western Michigan, I reviewed the sparse literature published about Michigan Indians to that date. The American Philosophical Society catalog listed a manuscript Jane coauthored in 1955 with Gertrude Kurath and Fred Ettawageshik titled "Religious Customs of Modern Michigan Algonquins." A yellow-paged Xerox copy of that manuscript still occupies a place on my bookshelf. The catalog also listed wire spools on which these collected stories were recorded. Technology of the time made duplication of the recordings difficult and almost twenty years passed before I could hear their contents.

While working for the Little Traverse Bay Bands tribal reaffirmation project in the late 1980s and early 1990s, I had many opportunities to speak with Jane about her work. I asked about how the information in her recordings was useful to the Tribe's endeavor. Jane told me that Fred had begun translations of the recordings but that events in their lives had prevented him from completing the work. She could remember the people who contributed to the recordings but not their contents. As a surprise for Jane, I contacted the American Philosophical Society to see if I could acquire copies of the voices on the wire spools. The recordings had recently been digitized, cassette tapes were available, and the APS curator graciously allowed me to purchase copies. Jane and I spent several hours listening to the tapes, talking about the peoples' voices, her life in the Little Traverse Odawa community, and her recollections about their contents, but the actual content of the tapes remained inaccessible at the time of her death in 1996.

Howard Webkamigad had tried to teach me Anishinaabemowin as part of my college education in 1977. I failed miserably, but I valued Howard's efforts and our paths crossed several times during the next twenty years. In 2001 the Little Traverse Bay Bands Tribal Council contracted me to conduct enthohistorical work related to the Odawas' traditional use of natural resources within and around the boundaries of the reservation created for them by the 1855 Treaty of Detroit. I immediately thought of Howard as a likely translator. The translations in this book are the results of his excellent work.

Thanks to Michigan State University Press, Jane Willets Ettawageshik's research is receiving the attention it deserves. Hers is the only ethnographic research conducted on the historic Little Traverse Reservation during the mid-twentieth century. The press published her 1955 manuscript as, *The Art of Tradition: Sacred Music, Dance, and Myth of Michigan's Anishinaabe*, 1946–1955, edited by Michael David McNally in 2009. At a time when traditional culture seemed eclipsed by post–World War II modernity, Jane and the people who worked with her helped to collect and preserve the insiders' vision of tribal culture and world view. *Ottawa Stories from the Springs* will allow readers to learn about that culture through the words of the culture-bearers themselves.

Foreword

Frank Ettawageshik

My mother, Jane Willets, often spoke of the endless forests she rode through on the train. Raised in Pennsylvania near Philadelphia and schooled at Barnard College in New York City, she traveled north through Michigan's Lower Peninsula in the early summer of 1946 to do field work for her anthropology master's program at the University of Pennsylvania. Professor Frank Speck was her faculty advisor. Dr. Speck had become friends with my father, Fred Ettawageshik, while my father was working as a lecturer at the 1926 U.S. Sesquicentennial International Exposition held in Philadelphia. My father had attended the Indian School at Carlisle Pennsylvania before serving in the U.S. Army in the First World War. After the war he made a short visit home to Harbor Springs before going back east to work.

My mother chose Northern Michigan for her field work from three possibilities proposed by Dr. Speck. After making her choice, Dr. Speck introduced her by correspondence to his friend Fred. I recently read the letter that my father sent to my mother in response to her inquiry about lodging possibilities and travel arrangements. This was their first correspondence and eventually led to a long life together. As their first child I was named Frank in honor of Dr. Speck.

When my mother completed her long train ride through the wilderness she found that her contact in Harbor Springs was not in town. My father, who had completely forgotten about my mother's pending arrival, was on a trip provided to him by friends who were concerned for him because my grandfather, Joseph Ettawageshik, had died a few weeks before. My aunt Julie Ettawageshik Black helped my mother get settled.

Until my father returned from the trip, my mother was on her own to begin her research. She brought a wire recorder and note pads, and a supply of gifts that she had been advised to present to her prospective interviewees. She was afraid of dogs and nearly every household had them. Her first visit was to the home of Joseph Kishigo in Indian Town on the west end of Harbor Springs below the bluff. She braved the large barking dogs in the front yard and knocked on the door.

Veronica Kishigo Medicine, one of today's tribal elders in Harbor Springs, was the young child who answered the door. Veronica tells me that she wondered who this lady was but remembered being impressed that she had brought gifts. This was the first of many doors she went to and the beginning of several years of recording interviews, storytelling, and songs throughout the Indian community. My mother completed her thesis and received her master's degree. By then she and my father had decided to marry and she made Harbor Springs her permanent home.

The recordings she made were partially used for her master's research. There was much more to do, however. She collaborated with Gertrude Kurath and my father on a significant body of work that resulted in a manuscript finished in 1955, and finally published in 2009 (*The Art of Tradition*, Michigan State University Press). In addition to the published manuscript, however, there are many other of her original wire-recorded interviews in Anishinaabemowin (Odawa language) in the archives at the American Philosophical Society in Philadelphia.

My father translated a few of the recordings in the early 1950s, but most of them still remained untranslated many years later. My father walked on in October 1969 and my mother was starting to feel an urgency to get this task accomplished. We first obtained copies of the recordings on cassette tapes. She made a couple of attempts to get started before finally working with Dr. Jim McClurken in Lansing, Michigan, who made the contact with Howard Webkamigad. Howard's subsequent translations made possible the publication of the volume that you now are holding.

As I was growing up listening to my father tell stories and learning from my mother about her work, I never dreamed what lay in store for my path in life. In 1967, after graduation from High School in Marion, Michigan, I attended the University of Michigan. I then began a pottery business while still in my early twenties and ran a gallery called Pipigwa Pottery. (*Pipigwa* means Sparrow Hawk and was my father's Indian name.) At the same time I started to work in local township government. In 1989, I began working with others at Little Traverse Bay to organize an effort to gain acknowledgement of our tribal government by the United States. Later, in the summer of 1989, I was first elected to the tribal council serving as the vice chairman. I became the tribal chairman in 1991, serving in this capacity until summer of 1999. I subsequently served as chairman from 2003 to 2009.

These years saw the tribal status reaffirmed by the United States in 1994, followed by incredible growth, from three employees to more than 250 by 1999, and nearly 1,000 by 2009. The establishment of administrative programs to provide services for our tribal citizens was an exciting development after years of abject poverty for a large number of our people. One of the many essential components of the research that supported the reaffirmation was the work done by my mother.

And now, with the publication of these transcriptions and translations, a new window is opening up to the minds and stories of the elders from the late 1940s and early 1950s from Harbor Springs. Howard Webkamigad has done an important service to the ancestors and to the present and coming generations. His work has taken recordings that were understandable to only a very few and made them available to a wide audience. A whole new tribal generation will get to read firsthand the words of their ancestors, and the reading public will get a rare chance to share in this experience.

In the cemetery on the bluff in Harbor Springs my mother and father are buried side by side in a plot under spreading maple and oak trees within sight of Little Traverse Bay. At my mother's internment we spoke of her long train ride from Philadelphia to the "ends of the earth" through Michigan in 1946. While each of us seeks to leave our impression on history, on the lives of others, rarely do we get the opportunity to have the continuing impact that the speakers in these recordings will have for the future. The speakers, my mother who recorded them, Jim McClurken who shepherded this project through several years of ups and downs, Howard Webkamigad who transcribed and translated the recordings, and the staff at Michigan State University Press all share in this great accomplishment.

INTRODUCTION

boozhoo,

waabgegek ndoo igoo. makwa ndoodem. wiikwemikooNsing zhinikaadek anishinaabek e danakiiwaat, mii wodi e njibaa yaaN. manidoo minising temigat iwi shkonigan.

Greetings,

My name is Howard Webkamigad. I was born into the Bear Clan. I come from an Anishinaabe community called WiikwemikooNsing. This settlement is a part of the Wikwemikong Unceded Indian Reserve located on Manitoulin Island.

ACKNOWLEDGMENTS

These stories that I have transcribed and translated were recorded around the time I was born. As I understand it, the stories were originally saved as wire recordings, collected somewhere in the area of Harbor Springs, Michigan. The copies of the recordings I listened to were on cassette tapes. The quality of the sound was good for most of the stories. There were some parts where some of the words were difficult to hear, but for the most part the sound was discernible without too much difficulty.

I, for one, learned a lot from these stories. The collection includes stories of history, stories with cultural information, contemporary stories, and legends. I would like to acknowledge several people who helped me with these stories. First, I am thankful for those elders who had the foresight to leave their words imprinted via mechanical means so that someone in the future might hear and understand what they left for us. I also want to thank two of my students, Peggy Hemenway and Ted Holappa, who suggested to James M. McClurken of Michigan State University that I could possibly translate the aforementioned tapes. Thanks to Dr. McClurken for honoring me with the task of transcribing and translating the stories from those tapes. Also, I want to acknowledge my older brothers, Alfred and Henry, both now deceased, for helping me with some of the older words that had fallen into disuse in my generation.

GENERAL COMMENTS

I did not know the amount of work I was getting involved with in taking on this kind of project. The work was tiresome and tedious, but rewarding as well. Transcribing stories is time-consuming when the audio level is good, and even more so when the sound quality is poor. I had to rewind segments of tape countless times, straining to hear the words, and I hope I have captured most of the words as they were uttered by the people who left them those so many years ago. As one storyteller said in a segment of tape, "Ginimaa gonaa wiya daa yaa ge nisastawit" ("Maybe there will be someone around who will understand me"). I was able to understand most of their words.

There are many Anishinaabe people who speak the Anishinaabe language much better than I do. Still, in my years of teaching, I have always had difficulty getting students to maintain an interest in the language. Once, when I had a respected elder come to a class I was teaching, he asked the students if they knew how to say "where" in the Anishinaabe language. The Anishinaabe word I was trying to get my students to use was slightly different than the elder's way of saying "where" in his dialect, and after my students said the word that I had taught them, he abruptly told them that what they were learning was slang. Over half of the class lost interest in learning the Anishinaabe language after that elder's visit. This problem stems from the many dialects of the Anishinaabe language that are still spoken. This aspect of the language is beautiful. It also can be very humorous. There are some speakers who are adamant that their way is the *correct prescribed* way of speaking the Anishinaabe language. When students come with the attitude that their way of speaking is the correct way, it makes for an interesting class.

There are almost as many ways of spelling Anishinaabe words as there are speakers of the language. We have not yet developed a prescribed writing system. Although at a gathering in Toronto, Ontario, sponsored by the Ministry of Education of the Ontario Government in August 1996, there was a consensus that the double vowel method should be used by those of us who were writing and teaching the language, the next step has not occurred—that being a gathering to develop a list of words that are general across dialects and agreeing to spell them one way. For example, to say "bear," some speakers would use "makwa," and others would use "mkwa," while the system I use combines the two by using italics to indicate the variation. I usually write the word as "m*a*kwa," which lets the reader know that they can sound out the italicized *a* if they want to, or they can leave it out, the option is indicated though the spelling of the word is consistent.

I also am not saying that there is a prescribed way of pronouncing words in the Anishinaabe language; there are various dialects of the language. Some call it Ojibwe or Ojibwa or Chippewa; some call it Ottawa; some call it Potawatomi; some even call it a French word, Saulteaux; some call it Atikamek; and some call it a different name in the Anishinaabe language. It is possible that all dialects are a generation away from death. Only older people still speak most of the Anishinaabe language dialects, and more rarely today than forty to four hundred years ago, back when the language was spoken on a daily basis.

We do not have the luxury of denigrating an Anishinaabe speaker's dialect as slang, as the loss of our language is fast approaching. We as speakers have to understand that there are several dialects, and we have to acknowledge them as valid ways of speaking. We have to get our speakers to understand that they may be the Ishi of our language. All dialects are beautiful.

There is also a lot of humor that comes from differences in meaning due to dialects. For example, an Anishinaabe man from southwestern Ontario who is rather stout—not fat or obese, just portly—married an Anishinaabe woman from northwestern Ontario. During the summer months, the man and his wife would return up north to visit her family. One day, during such a visit, the man got up, went to the fridge and opened the door, and announced, "Aapidji go *ndoo* bakade"—"I am very hungry." No sooner had he finished his utterance when his mother-in-law burst out laughing, with tears running down her cheeks. He turned to her and asked what was so funny, and his mother-in-law told him what "Aapidji go *ndoo* bakade" means in their northern community: "I am very skinny." If you look at the two statements, they are related in a sense: if one is hungry long enough, one becomes skinny. It seems clear that for one group, the meaning of the phrase changed over time, whereas for the other group, the meaning stayed the same.

As another example, a woman from northern Manitoba asked me "How are you?" as she is accustomed to asking in her area: "Aaniish naa e zhiyaa yin?" Where I am from, however, we would ask this in one of two ways, the first being "Aaniish naa e zhibimaadizi yin?" though since this might elicit some smart-alecky responses, we tend to use the short form more often: "Aaniish naa?" Where I am from, the phrase she used has acquired a sexual connotation, and it has come to be understood or akin to asking someone if they are in the mood for love. Having had some contact with other dialects, I knew what she was asking me, so I responded appropriately, but other speakers may have been offended by her legitimate question, and they might have made fun of her or even scolded her for misspeaking the language. There are speakers out there who have assumed the mantel of speaking correct Anishinaabe. I have met many of them. However, dialects can make for an interesting and oftentimes humorous exchange. That is the beauty of dialects, thus the beauty of the language.

Very few young people are raised with Anishinaabe as their first language. Most of the people who speak it are approaching old age, so I tell the students to be respectful in approaching someone who may still speak the language. I further caution them that there are many dialects, and what I am trying to teach them is not necessarily how the people in their home community use the language. I try to give them a basic understanding of how the language works, how verbs work, how tenses are made, how plurals are made, and how the personal pronouns work, with a main goal of getting them to say and make up sentences. This is a lot to ask of anyone who has no grasp of the language at all. My classes consist of both those with no language at all and those who are speakers, including some who frown on my dialect. Even though I caution the students about the dialect differences, there are some who will come back after visiting their home community and tell me that they were told that what they were learning was incorrect and I have to remind them of my previous warning. Ah, the joys of teaching.

Another unique characteristic that differs between dialects is the type of objects that are considered animate and inanimate. Now, do not think in terms of English animate and inanimate, because the English dichotomy does not correspond with the animate and inanimate dichotomy in the Anishinaabe language. What is animate in Anishinaabe is not necessarily animate in English, and what is inanimate in English is not necessarily inanimate in Anishinaabe. So the way I try to teach the concept is by defining the Anishinaabe animate as maaba and the Anishinaabe inanimate as maanda.

When I was much younger, a few of us ventured into the United States to find work. We learned of a native community a short distance from the town where we found jobs. One of my friends said to me one day, "Aapidji go nitaa anishinaabemowok gwonda anishinaabek" ("These Anishinaabe people here really speak the language very well"). And I said, slightly chagrined, "Well, what about us?" In our Anishinaabe dialect, we tend to drop certain vowels at certain times but to retain them at other times. In this native community in the United States, the speakers tended to sound out vowel sounds at all times. I guess, in English, we would say they enunciated their words carefully, whereas we did not. But we spoke the language well, as did they. We communicated with these other speakers very well, but they were the older people, and many of them have gone on to the spirit world since we first met them those many years ago. That community now may have less than ten speakers, if any, of the Anishinaabe language.

Another time I met two older men who were visiting our community and who were about the same age as my dad. I think these men hailed from Alberta, or maybe they were from Saskatchewan. I asked them to come to my place to visit my parents. When we got to the house, the men sat down on the couch, and I said to my dad in the language that these two native men were from out west somewhere. The older of the two men spoke very slowly and clearly in his dialect; he told me to slow my speech down so that he could understand me better. My parents and these two men from out west had a good visit, although there were a few instances when they just looked at each other, as some of the words were really different between the two dialects. To them, we spoke too fast. To us, they sounded out the words very well, they enunciated clearly, whereas in our dialect we tend to drop certain vowels at times.

As you read the English translations of the stories, you will notice that I use as many passive-voice sentences as active-voice sentences. As a young student trying to learn English, I was always admonished for using the passive voice in constructing English sentences, as I was told this was not acceptable because it was not the prescribed manner of speaking and writing English. However, in the Anishinaabe language, passive-voice constructions are used equally as much as active-voice constructions. So, subtly albeit overtly, I was taught in my English classes that my language was not acceptable since it uses a good number of passive-voice constructed sentences in everyday language exchanges. For some reason, it became prescribed that the passive voice was a flaw to be frowned upon in the English language. Although the passive voice is prescribed this way in English, it is not necessarily so in the way I try to teach the Anishinaabe language. Thus, the passive voice will appear just as much as the active voice in these translations.

Also, you will note that I do not subscribe to the notion that capital letters begin a sentence. I do use capital letters in my rendering of the Anishinaabe transcriptions, but I use them to denote that the preceding vowel is a nasal vowel. Also, you will see that I only use a period to denote an end of an utterance. This can cause some learners consternation because they have become used to—or, should I say, they have become indoctrinated in—the use of capitals to begin a statement and the use of punctuation marks to end a statement or question. I do use commas and quotation marks, but I have chosen to ignore other conventions. In the Anishinaabe language a question usually begins with a question word, or it has a specific word to let us know that this is a question. However, there are also utterances that have only intonation to tell us that it is a question. This is problematic, as it is sometimes difficult to convey intonation through writing.

No matter what writing system is used, there will be some problems with it. The written form is not an exact replication of the sound or the flow or the tone or the rhythm of the language—and it should not be. It is only a close approximation of the sound of the language.

Toward the end of "The Man Who Caught the White Eagle" the storyteller makes an interesting utterance. To the person who is listening to the audio, he or she would hear the speaker say: "baamaagonsek" or "baamaa gon sek." Loosely translated this means, "when you have killed him/her" or "until he/she is dead" or "after you have caused his/her demise," or something similar. Note that the word for "killing" and the word for the plural "you" is rolled into the "nsek" syllable. However, I wrote the statement "baamaa*mpii* go nis*aa*yek," including the omitted sounds so that the reader can look in an Anishinaabe dictionary and get an idea as to the meaning of the phrase.

This illustrates how much difficulty a learner would have if he or she were working with a dictionary. He or she may be able to pick out the word "baamaa" as meaning "later/after," but he or she may not see any resemblance between any of the other words in the utterance and any words in an Anishinaabe language dictionary. With the system I use, the reader can see what the full word should look and possibly sound like, which may help him or her figure out its meaning more easily in a dictionary. There are many such occurrences as this in the transcriptions of the stories in this text.

This compilation of stories is a good start for someone who wants to learn the language, as it may help him or her discover intricacies and nuances of the language. These stories will not make the reader become fluent. Fluency comes from practice and speaking on a daily basis.

Those who have a copy of the audio for the stories will notice that I have rearranged the stories into categories, so they do not follow the way the stories were on the tapes that I listened to as I transcribed and translated them. First, I compiled the Nenibozhoo stories at the beginning of this text under the section titled "Nenibozhoo Stories." I put stories about Nenibozhoo first, as he is considered by the Anishinaabe people as the first Anishinaabe to live and walk on earth. The next section is titled "Legends and Cultural Stories." These are stories that have a mythical quality to them. Some also have a teaching or moral associated with them as well as a sense of humor. The third section, titled "Historical Stories," relates historical events in the rich history of the Anishinaabe people. The final section deals with stories of recent times, thus I titled these as "Contemporary Stories."

Some of the stories have a combination of historical, mythical, and cultural features, so I sorted them based on what I thought were the major themes in their content. Most of the stories tell us about the Anishinaabe people being on the land in North America since Nenibozhoo's time. For some reason, certain areas of jurisprudence now want the Anishinaabe people to prove that they have been occupiers of certain tracts of land in North America even though, as our stories tell us, we have been here from time immemorial. Such are the convoluted workings of legalizing robbery. The British North America Acts and the United States Constitution were documents drawn up to legitimize an illegitimate takeover of an occupied and already settled land. With all the knowledge the justices surely have accumulated over the years, they have the audacity still to ask us to prove how long we have been here on this land. The stories in this text go a long way in reassuring anyone that we as Anishinaabe people were here in North America long before the newcomers; maybe someday they will honor the truth and acknowledge that fact. I hope the Anishinaabe people will still be speaking the Anishinaabe language when that happens.

. . .

NOTE: Those who have heard the audio version will notice that I did not include certain segments in the written form. I omitted the segment where there seems to a gathering at a home of someone, and there are several conversations going on. Also, I did not include the segment that has the singing of hymns, nor the songs that had drumming and chanting. I was more interested in the stories.

miigwech.

Anishinaabemowin Sounds

VOWEL SOUNDS

Long Vowels

aa makes the sound equivalent to the o in the English words pot and odd
ii makes the sound equivalent to the ea or ee in the English words eat and beet
oo makes the sound equivalent to the o in the English words open and owe
e makes the sound equivalent to the e in the English words met and set

Short Vowels

a makes the sound equivalent to the u in the English words shut and cut
i makes the sound equivalent to the i in the English words sit and bit
o makes the sound equivalent to the oo in the English words cook and good

Nasal Vowels

aaN iiN ooN *eN(heN)* aN

I use the capitalized N to indicate that the preceding vowel is nasalized. The N should not be pronounced when making these sounds. These sounds can be made by pinching one's nose, but that would look funny, so try to make the sound without pinching your nose. The *oo*N is the word for oh, and *eN(heN)* is the affirmative, or the word yes.

PHONEMES

Phonemes are the basic sounds of language, but theoretically they have no meaning. The italicized sound representations below have meaning in the Anishinaabe language, thus theoretically they are not phonemes. The following are some of the phonemes in the Anishinaabe language.

aa	ii	oo	e	a	i	o
baa	bii	boo	be	ba	*bi*	bo
chaa	chii	choo	che	cha	chi	cho
daa	dii	*doo*	*de*	*da*	di	do
gaa	*gii*	goo	*ge*	*ga*	gi	go
jaa	jii	joo	je	ja	ji	jo
kaa	kii	koo	ke	ka	ki	ko
maa	*mii*	moo	me	ma	mi	mo

naa	nii	noo	ne	*na*	*ni*	no
paa	*pii*	poo	pe	pa	pi	po
saa	*sii*	soo	se	*sa*	si	so
taa	tii	*too*	*te*	ta	ti	to
waa	*wii*	woo	we	wa	*wi*	*wo*
yaa	yii	yoo	ye	ya	yi	yo
zaa	zii	zoo	ze	za	zi	zo
shaa	shii	shoo	she	sha	shi	sho
zhaa	zhii	zhoo	zhe	zha	zhi	zho

The italicized letters above represent sounds that have specific meaning in the Anishinaabe language. The *e* represents the present tense in the interrogative and subjunctive and clausal forms. The *bi* is the short form for "zhibi," a location word for the non-living maaba category words; as a prefix it also signifies coming toward someone. The *daa* is a modal, and it represents could, would, or should, depending on the context. The *doo* is the present tense indicator in statements. The *de* is a marker to indicate some possibility, almost, or a nearly sufficient aspect to the situation. The *da* is the third-person definite future tense indicator in statements. The *gaa* is the past tense indicator in the interrogative and subjunctive and clausal forms. The *gii* is the past tense indicator in statements. The *ge* is the definite future tense indicator in the interrogative and subjunctive and clausal forms. The *ga* is the definite future indicator for the first and second persons in statements. The *go* seems to have no meaning but is included in the language to add to the flow of it. The *ji* is a future tense marker adding the meaning of able to or will be able to. The *kaa* is the short form for gaawiin, the Anishinaabe word for no. The *ko* represents the term meaning used to or usually. The *mii* implies then or thus. The *naa* is asking for agreement or assent, and *na* is the question mark indicator used where there otherwise is an absence of question words; the word *na* also calls attention to something or someone like the English expression "Check that out." The *ni* is a prefix that signifies that the person whom the speaker is addressing is leaving. The *pii* is the Anishinaabe word for when (as in time), and it also means at that moment/time. The *sii* is a suffix or an infix that completes a negative sentence. The *sa* is another term that doesn't seem to have any meaning other than to add to the flow of the language, much like *go*, mentioned previously. The *too* represents the verb to put. The *te* is the location word for the maanda (inanimate) category words. The *waa* is the indefinite future tense marker for the interrogative, subjunctive, and clausal forms. The *wii* is the indefinite future indicator in statements. The *wi* is the maanda (inanimate) word identifier; in some dialects it is pronounced as *iw*. The *wo* is the maaba (animate) word identifier; in some dialects it is pronounced as *ow*. The *yaa* is the location word for the living maaba category words. The *zii* is a suffix and an infix that completes a negative sentence. The *zhaa* represents the verb go.

PRONUNCIATION

If the reader practices saying the sounds, he or she will start to feel comfortable saying the words, and thus speaking. My use of italics in the stories is intended to alert the reader that letters are not necessarily sounded out depending on the dialect. Several of these stories include words storytellers did not sound out in full. The word that was most commonly contracted in these recordings was miidash.

I hope you enjoy the stories, and I hope you learn something about the Anishinaabe people.

· PART 1 ·

NENIBOZHOO STORIES

nenibozhoo miinawaa zhiishiibeNik

aa*niish*, ngoding, nenibozhoo gichi niibana zhiishiibeNon gii nisaan. gaa shkwaa biinaat, mii iwi gii nigowaat. shkode gii zhitoot,

> "togowa nga ka*w*e nibaa."

e piichi minozawaat dash ninda, mii iwi jiigi shkodeng gii wiishimot, shkodeng nikeyaa (*doo*) zhidiiyeshing,

> "koowaabam gewe e zhinaagozi yaaN."

e piichi gichi nibaat mii gewe anishinaabek gii bid*a*goshiniwaat, (*doo*) waabimaawaan (*doo*) zaag*a*gaadeshininit zhiishiibeNon, gii kidawaat,

> "togowa mowaadaa gewe."

gaa gidamowaawaat, mii iwi neyaap gii baad*a*kisidowaat kaadeNsan.

gweshkozit nenibozhoo, (*doo*) makowenimaat zhiishiibeNon, aano*w*i (*doo*) zagigaadenaat, gaa*wiin* wiya. (*doo*) gagwetaanigidaaza nenibozhoo.

> "tawa togo*wa*, e zhinaagozi yaaN, gichi wewena gga kinoomawin nonggo*m* iwi gii aagonetaw*a* yin."

miidash, nenibozhoo gii namadabit zhewe shkodeng (*doo*) gichi jaagizo nenibozhoo. gii maadjiib*a*toot, bapiichin dash aanowi (*doo*) giziiwidiza, (*doo*) miskowiinindjii gaye nenibozhoo, aanowi giziindjiishing mitigooNsing. (*doo*) gichi miskowiiwaak*o*ziwok gewiin*a*waa gewe, mii iwi nonggo*m* miskowaabiiminagooNs e *oo*nji zhinikaazawaat.

Nenibozhoo and the Ducks (*CONDENSED VERSION*)

This one time, Nenibozhoo the trickster had killed a great many ducks. After he had cleaned the ducks, he buried them in the ground. Then he built a fire over the area. Nenibozhoo thought to himself,

"I think I will take a nap for a little while."

So while the ducks were cooking, he laid down near the fire with his rear facing toward the fire.

"Watch the ducks my likeness,"

he said. And while he was sound asleep, several natives who happened to be out hunting arrived on the scene and they saw the legs of the ducks sticking out of the ground.

"Let's eat those ducks."

After they had eaten all of the ducks, they then stuck the duck legs back into the ground as they were previously.

So when Nenibozhoo awoke from his nap, his first thought was of the ducks he had cooking, so he grasped at one of the legs and pulled, there was no duck, only the leg. Nenibozhoo became very angry.

"Okay, my likeness, I will now teach you a lesson because you did not follow my directions."

That is when Nenibozhoo sat on the hot coals of the fire, and he severely burned his rear end. Nenibozhoo started to run, and every once in awhile he tried to wipe his burned rear, and when he did, he got his hands all bloody, so he wiped his bloodied hands on some shrubbery as he ran. These shrubs were coated with the blood from his hands, and this is how the red willow came to be, and that is why they are called red willows.

nenibozhoo miinawaa newe zhiishiibeNon

aaniish, mii sa giiyeN gii yaat owo ndo aansookaan, nenibozhoo giiyeN (*doo*) zhinikaaza *owo* sa, *owo* sa waa dibaadjimak nongg*om*. gii giibaadiziiNwi go maaba nenibozhoo, gaa zhizhiyaat go. maanda dash *n*iyiing nibising, mii wodi e bibaa zhaat, (*doo*) bibaa wiigobii*sh*ke giiyeN. ookomison giiyeN (*doo*) bibaa *n*andowaabidamawaan *n*iyiin, wiigobiin. wiigobiish gonaa e daming gonaa, zhaazhag*o* gaa nakaazawaat anishinaabek, wiigobiish, sabaap gaye go gii zhitoowaat, mii go gaa nakaazawaat, wiigobiish. gii zhi-aawaan go zhewe wiigobiishing, yaawaan, sabiin, giigooNon wii n*i*saawaat, wii madozang. e bibaa zhaat wodi, (*doo*) bibaa wiigobii*sh*ket maanda nikeyaa wodi nibisan e ndigowogin, miid*a*sh wodi, gimaapii wodi nim*a*daabiit maaba nenibozhoo, *n*iyiing, waagwaaseNskaak nim*a*daabiit, geget sa giiyeN g*o*naa wodi (*doo*) baatiinawon yaa*w*aan, zhiishiibeNon. aapidji giiyeN go (*doo*) ozaamiiniwon, mii giiyeN go e yaanigokomowaat zhiishiibeNik.

> "geget sa g*o*naa (*doo*) baatiinawok zhiishiibeNik. aaniish iidik ge zhichige yaaNmbaa*n*.",

(*doo*) inendam giiyeN nenibozhoo.

miidash giiyeN miinawaa gii nig*o*piit, noopiming gii nizhaat, wiigobiish nin*a*ndowaabidang. miidash iwi gaa nim*a*kang newe wiigobiishan, mii bezhik gii kchipizot iwi wiigobiish. maanpii gii toot. miidash gimaapii miinawaa gii nim*a*daabii. miidash wodi *n*iyiing, biboonishiwaaning gii nim*a*daabiit. geget sa giiyeN g*o*naa, maanpii d*a*sh giiyeN wiigobiishan gii toonan, zhinda kchipizowining. wewena go gii m*a*shkow*a*pidoon maanda wiigobiishi kchipizowin. miidash iwi, miidash giiyeN aanowi *n*andomaat, zhiishiibeNon.

> "maajaak. maajaak, nshiimeNwidik.",

doo inaan dash giiyeN.

> "nshiimeNwidik maajaak."
> "na gosha nayiinawi*n*d nenibozhoo medwe kidat. g*doo* nandow*e*m*a*goonaa gosha nayiinawi*n*t nenibozhoo, nshiimeNwidik maajaak, (*doo*) kida gosha nayiinawi*n*d *o*wo nenibozhoo. nenibozhoo gosha go *o*wo.",

(*doo*) kidawok sa giiyeN.

Nenibozhoo and the Ducks (*LONG VERSION*)

Well, there is this legend about the one who is known as Nenibozhoo, that is who I am now going to talk about. This one called Nenibozhoo was rather foolish at times as this was one of his attributes. This one time he was going to this one lake and he was going to get basswood. Actually he was looking for the inner bark of the basswood for his grandmother. The Anishinaabe people of long ago used this to make string and to make rope and it was the basswood that they used for this. They also used it to make their nets, so they can gill net the fish, as this is one way they always have fished. As he traveled in the direction where these lakes were located, as he went down toward the lake, he came across an area of birch, and just out there on the lake there were so many ducks swimming about. There were a great many ducks as they covered a great portion of the lake.

"Oh my, there are so many ducks. What could I or should I do?"

this trickster, Nenibozhoo, thought to himself.

Then he ventured inland, he went back into the forest, and he continued to search for the basswood. After a short time, he found the basswood, and he started to make strips, and he used one strip to make a belt that he tied around himself. Then he put many other strips of basswood in this makeshift belt. Then once he had enough basswood, he went back down toward the lake. It was at the place called Ponshewaing, that is where the lake was. He had all this basswood tucked into his makeshift basswood belt, which he was taking to the lake with him. He really tightened this basswood belt so that it would not get loose no matter what he did. When he got to the lake, he tried calling to the ducks.

"Come here my younger siblings,"

he apparently said to them.

"Come here my younger siblings."
"Why it is Nenibozhoo, listen to what he is saying. He is saying we are related to him now, as he is saying, 'Come here my younger siblings.' That has to be him, that Nenibozhoo,"

they supposedly said amongst themselves.

"gaawiin go ginigeN ndaa zhaasii.",

(doo) kidawok sa giiyeN zhiishiibeNik.

mii iidik maaba nenibozhoo (doo) nishkawigot iwi. gaawiin go wiya (doo) bizhaasiiwon aanowi nandomaat.

"maajaan na nshiimeNwidik.",

aanowi kidat, tibewe zhewe e koobiigodinik. mii iidik maaba nenibozhoo gaa zhigoogiit. maanpii wiigobiish gichi niibana gii toon. gii googiit maaba nenibozhoo, wodi dash yaanit gii ninakozhowe. giyegeti giiyeN maanda dash naabit nibiishing maanda dash naabit, mii giiyeN go eta kaadeNsan yaabidanggin, mii gewe yaawaa kaadeNsawaan, owo sa gewe bebaabimishkaadjik gidibiik zhiishiibeNik. besha wodi gii nizhaat, gii nigidiziitang, mii zhinda ninda wiigobiishan kina gii nizagigaadepinaat newe, gii zagigaadepinaat. mii kina go gii nizagipidoot kaadeNsan, wewena go gii takobidoot go. gaawiin iidik gonaa gewiinawaa wii moozhatoowaat iwi takobinindowaa. gimaapiich gii jaaganaanan, ninda niyiin wiigobiishan. mii sa gichi geskana gii mookiset.

"yaa-aa. nenibozhoo gosha nayiinawint maaba.",

(doo) kidawok sa giiyeN, yaawaak, zhiishiibeNik. aapidji giiyeN (doo) nowaatoowok, mii giiyeN go eta, (doo) giinaadiziwok e piichi zegagoowaat nenibozhoon (doo) bimookisenit. gaawiin maamdaa wii gizikewaat, banggiisheN gonaa aanowi gizikewok. miidash giiyeN gwonda yaawaak, zhiishiibeNik, mii go kina go gimaapii gaa zhigizikewaat go, miidash gii mbisaawaat newe nenibozhoon. (doo) ani nichiiwinaagozigoban owo nenibozhoo.

noopiming dash wodi maanda nikeyaa, giyegeti giiyeN (doo) nimbiigoziwok yaawaak, zhiishiibeNik. (doo) mbinaawaat nenibozhoon, (doo) bimiwinaawaat, mipokogoodjininit nenibozhoon, (doo) bimiwinaawaat. aapidji giiyeN go (doo) ninowaatoowok. miidash maanda gonaa, noopiming gonaa, gwodji gonaa, mitigowaakiing gonaa, mii iidik maanda wiigobiish gonaa, eshkam gonaa nowonch gwonda (doo) nizhichigewaat zhiishiibeNik wii nipakishkaak gonaa maanda. miidash iidik, gichi mitig dash giiyeN iidik bedakizat, aapidji go (doo) michaakozi, gichi mitigosh. (doo) giishkanakazi dash giiyeN maaba mishiiwaatig gonaa, (doo) giishkanakazi owo. miidash giiyeN zhewe iidik naanetaa zhewe gii nipakishkaak iwi kina iwi wiigobiish maanpii. miidash owo nenibozhoo gii biindjinakoset zhewe

"I would not go there no way, no how,"

the ducks declared to each other.

This must have angered Nenibozhoo. Not one duck came to him when he tried to call for them.

"My younger siblings come to me,"

he tried to coax them to come to him as he walked all along the shore of the lake. So, then Nenibozhoo dove quietly into the lake. He was still wearing the basswood belt that was still full of basswood strips. Nenibozhoo dove into the water and swam underwater to where the ducks were floating about on the lake. Then as he got closer to the ducks, as he looked through the water, he saw an inordinate number of little duck legs, as these were the little legs of the ducks who were floating about on the lake. So Nenibozhoo went as close as he could to the ducks, and he took one basswood strip off of his belt, and he tied it gently and carefully to the leg of one duck, then he did it again, and again. He had tied so many duck legs with the basswood and he tied them securely. It is amazing that those ducks did not feel anything being tied to their legs. Finally, he ran out of basswood strips he had on his makeshift basswood belt. That is when he suddenly broke to the surface of the lake.

"Oh my goodness! It's Nenibozhoo, that is who it is,"

the ducks supposedly shouted in unison. They made such a racket, the noise was deafening, and they were scared crazy by Nenibozhoo's sudden appearance on the surface of the water. They could not fly away, some would be able to fly a little but they were attached to Nenibozhoo with the basswood strips. The ducks kept trying to fly, and they eventually were able to fly as they flapped their wings in unison, and they were able to lift Nenibozhoo out of the water. Oh, that Nenibozhoo must have looked so terrible as he was dangling beneath the ducks as they flew away, with him still hanging from the basswood strips.

The ducks flew inland, and they were oh so loud as they strained to stay airborne. They carried Nenibozhoo aloft, and they carried him away. They were so noisy those ducks. Then further inland, in the forest somewhere, the ducks did everything to break free of Nenibozhoo, and eventually the basswood strips gave way. And in the forest there happened to be an old tree standing there. Its top had broken off and it was now a drying out, dying old tree. Supposedly, the basswood strips all broke just as the ducks were flying over this old tree. So this is where Nenibozhoo fell, he

niyiing, giishkanakadooNing, gii biindjinakoset zhewe. besha dash giiyeN iidik miikan zhewe bemimok. miidash iwi, aaniish yaat,

"aaniish iidik ge zhichige yaaN.",

(doo) inendam giiyeN nenibozhoo, (doo) kidawidik gonaa.

"aaniish iidik ge zhichige yaaN zhinda ji wiyii kogaa yaaN."

miidash giiyeN maanda minik iidik owo mishiiwaatig gaa zhibagonezit, maanda gonaa, gii daashkanakoshkaa gonaa. gegoo gonaa (doo) daashkaak gonaa, mii iidik gii daashkanakoshkaat, miidash go wodi michiyiing, mii sa giiyeN zhewe gii yaat owo nenibozhoo. aapidji giiyeN go (doo) shkendam, mandj giiyeN waa zhichigegoweN. mii giiyeN go zhewe waa dapinet. mii giiyeN e zhinoondawaat yaawaan e danaandigidoonidjin. miidash iidik besha iwi miikan, jiigi miikan e bidakizat owo mishiiwaatig. ikwewon dash giiyeN newe, niswiwon giiyeN newe ikwewon. aapidji giiyeN go (doo) migichi baabaapiwon.

"aaniish iidik ge zhichige yaaN.",

(doo) inendam giiyeN. aapidji giiyeN go zhewe besha (doo) bimidanaandigidooniwon. aapidji giiyeN bezhik (doo) migichi baabaapiwon newe ikwewon. aapidji giiyeN go maawondaagikwen newe zhewe bebaa bimosendjin.

miidash zhewe zaabit, nibaneshkiizhik gonaa gii naabiwidik gonaa. mii sa giiyeN e kidat,

"n (doo) waabigaagoo. n (doo) waabigaagoo."
"yaa-aa, wenesh owo.",

(doo) kidawok sa giiyeN gewe ikwewok. miinawaa gonaa go,

"n (doo) waabigaagoo."

(doo) naaniibowiwok giiyeN gewe ikwewok (doo) nandotoowaawaat miinawaa newe.

"n (doo) waabigaagoo. n (doo) waabigaagoo. gidisagoowashik.
gidisagoowashik.",

fell into this old tree. There happened to be a trail close to where this old tree stood in the forest. So he was stuck in this old hollowed out tree.

"What will I do now?"

Nenibozhoo thought to himself, or he may have said it out loud.

"What will I do to get out of here?"

As it is with dying hollow trees, they usually have a crack somewhere on them, as this old tree had a small crack down its trunk. Nenibozhoo was wedged almost at the very bottom of the old hollow tree, and he could not move. He was starting to get worried, for he did not know what to do to get out of this predicament. He foresaw his impending doom, he would die alone right there in the old hollow tree. Suddenly, he hears voices of people talking to one another. And this old tree was near a trail in the forest. He heard women talking, three women who happened to be out on the trail that day. They were enjoying themselves as they were laughing gleefully.

"What shall I do?"

again Nenibozhoo wondered. Oh, the women who were talking to each other were so close to him. And one of the women just kept on laughing heartily. And these women who were walking on the trail were oh so good looking.

And Nenibozhoo was viewing this with one eye, through the crack of the trunk of the tree he was stuck in. Apparently he said this,

"I am the white porcupine. I am the white porcupine."
"Oh my goodness, who is that?"

those women supposedly asked one another. Again, Nenibozhoo uttered,

"I am the white porcupine."

The women now stood quietly as they tried to hear which direction the voice was coming from.

"I am the white porcupine. I am the white porcupine. Come and chop a hole for me. Chop a hole for me to get out of here."

(*doo*) kida sa giiyeN.

"na gosha nayiinawi*nt* e kidat, 'gidisagoowashik.'",

(*doo*) kida gosha nayiinawi*nd* giiyeN *o*wo, waabigaag g*o*sha nayiinawi*nt* iidik e yaat niyiing wiimanakodooNing.

"togo*wa* nga naadin waagaakodooN.",

(*doo*) kida sa giiyeN *o*wo bezhik yaawaa, ikwe.

gii maadjiibatoot, (*doo*) naadit waagaakod, jina *da*sh gonaa giiyeN gii ndendi, mii gii bip*a*skaabiit. mii*da*sh giiyeN go gaa piichinowetoot,

"n(*doo*) waabigaagoo. n(*doo*) waabigaagoo. gidisagoowashik.
gidisagoowashik."

aaniish, (*doo*) biidoot giiyeN waagaakod *o*wo ikwe, mii giiyeN go (*doo*) biwewiiptaat, (*doo*) giishkowaat newe yaawaan mishiiwaatigoon. (*doo*) bagonekozi dash giiyeN iidik *o*wo mishiiwaatigooN, (*doo*) bagonekowaat newe. aaniish, (*doo*) bagashkaninidik gonaa *o*wo mishiiwaatigooN, baabagiye gonaa do*o* nibagonewaan iidik, maanda minik (*doo*) nibagonewaat newe mishiiwaatigoon. mii*da*sh iidik e kidat miinawaa,

"gibanikowashik, gibanikowashik. g*do* midjigoodeNwaan
gibanikowagek.",

(*doo*) kida sa giiyeN nenibozhoo. mii sa giiyeN maaba yaawaa ikwe e kidat bezhik,

"niin, nga giiskaan ndo *a*gowaaN.",

(*doo*) kida sa giiyeN. gii naazhawebinang iwi d*o* agowaaN, gii gidiskaakobidoot, naazhawebinang iwi do *a*gowaaN, maanda gii zhiiginang. miidash maanda minik nibagonekowaat newe mitigooNon, mii zhewe iwi gii gibisidoot. aaniish, mii miinawaa wodi nowonch wii migaayaak iwi, gichi waabigaak giiyeN zhewe *o*wo e yaat, wii debishkinet dash *n*iyii wii zaagadoodebatoot. mii*da*sh iidik *da*sh go maaba nenibozhoo, niibana gonaa nibagon*e*kowin *o*wo mitig, mii iidik,

"mii sa nongg*om* da debishkine yaaN.",

(*doo*) inendam giiyeN. mii gii nowodjibidoot iwi *n*iyii iwi sa midjigoodeN zhewe,

he supposedly says.

> "Listen to what he is saying, 'Chop a hole for me to free me,'"

is what the voice was supposedly saying, there must be a white porcupine inside that old hollow tree.

> "I will go get an axe,"

said one of the women.

She ran to go get the axe and she was gone just for a short time and she came back with the axe. And all the time Nenibozhoo kept on uttering his lament,

> "I am the white porcupine. I am the white porcupine. Come and chop a hole for me. Chop a hole for me."

Well, the woman came back with the axe, and she quickly began to chop at the old tree. She was chopping a hole where there was the crack and about where she thought the voice was coming from. As this was an old dried out tree, slightly rotting, she was able to chop a sizable hole in the trunk of the old tree rather quickly and she made a hole this size. And the voice was heard again and now it was saying,

> "Cover the hole up, cover the hole for me up with your dresses,"

Nenibozhoo supposedly said. Then one of the women volunteered,

> "I will take my clothing off."

She unfastened her dress and she slipped out of it and she folded it. As she had made a sizable hole in the trunk of the tree, this is where she placed the dress to cover up the hole. Well, the hole still had to be bigger so that it would be big enough for the big white porcupine to be able to crawl out as he was stuck inside of the old hollow tree. But this really was Nenibozhoo who was disguised as the white porcupine, and after the hole was made larger after awhile, Nenibozhoo thought,

> "I should be able to fit through there now."

That is when he grabbed the dress that was covering up the hole and held it over

gaa gibisidoong, mii sa gii zhiiginang, maanpii gii toot, (doo) zaagadoodebatoot wiimanakodooNing.

"yaa-aa. nenibozhoo gosha nayiinawind maaba.",

(doo) kidawok sa giiyeN ikwewok, (doo) gidjibowewok.

"nenibozhoo gosha nayiinawind maaba, yaa-aa."

mii sa giiyeN owo nenibozhoo.

"biidoon togowa iwi ndo agowin."

(doo) waabimigoon giiyeN, (doo) miziizininggowaandaan iwi niyii agowaaN.

"biidoon togowa iwi ndo agowaaN."

aaniish, (doo) gidjibowe giiyeN gewiin nenibozhoo, (doo) ziizininggowaandaan giiyeN agowaaN. aapidji giiyeN go (doo) migichi baabaapi.

"wenen giiyeN ge miinik iwi gdo agowaaN.",

doo inaan giiyeN newe ikwewon, maawondaagikwen.

"gaawiin sa wiya gdaa miinigoosii iwi gdo agowaaN.",

doo inaan giiyeN.

aaniish, gii gidjibatoot, gweyek go e danendang iwi niyii, iwi sa gonaa maanda sa gonaa nibisi, mii giiyeN wodi e patoot, niyii gii bigomabatoot iidik. waasa go noopiming gii zhiwinigoon newe yaawaan, zhiishiibeNon. miidash wodi gimaapii gii nimadaabiit, wodi sa gaa njiwinind. miidash wodi aaniish, (doo) naabit miinawaa nibising, yaa-aa, giyegeti giiyeN (doo) baatiinawon giyaabi zhiishiibeNon. gwonda dash gaa mbiwinigodjin, dibi gonaa iidik gewiinawaa. aanind giiyeN gaye go saseweyaabiisenigoban niyiin sa gonaa wiigobiisheNan kaadewaang. dibi gonaa gewiinawaa gewe gaa pizowaagoweN.

mii sa giiyeN gii niwewiiptaat, waagaakodooNs gaye gii makamaan newe ikwewon gaa nakaazanit gii gidisagoowagot. gii nigidjibatoowaadaan waagaakodooNs, mii giiyeN gii giishkowaat yaawaan, mitigooNson, zhinggobiin. gii naakomotoot

and around him, he quickly crawled out of the old hollow tree through the hole the woman had chopped for him.

"Oh no! This is really Nenibozhoo,"

cried out the women as they were already running away from him.

"This is really Nenibozhoo. Oh my!"

It really was Nenibozhoo, the trickster.

"Bring back my dress."

Nenibozhoo is seen by the woman as he is carrying the dress tucked under his arm.

"Bring my dress back to me,"

But Nenibozhoo was running away from the women as he carried the dress under his arm. Apparently he was laughing out loud as he ran away.

"Who would give you your dress?"

he supposedly said to that gorgeous woman.

"Nobody would give a dress to you,"

he continued to say.

Well, he quickly ran away from the women and he ran toward where he thought the lake with the ducks was located, then he finally arrived there running. Those ducks had taken him far inland. Well he eventually reached the shore of the lake, that lake he was carried away from by the ducks. And when he looked out on the lake, oh there were still so many ducks out there swimming around. But the ones who had taken flight with him as a passenger, it is not known where these ducks went. When last seen, some still had the basswood strips dangling from their legs as they flew away. It is not known where these ducks flew.

So Nenibozhoo quickly began to cut down some trees and he was using the axe he stole from the women who had chopped him free from the tree he had been stuck in. He took the axe with him when he ran away from the women, and he was using this to cut down these saplings, small fir trees. He began to construct a shelter, niyii, wiigwaam, mandj gonaa gaa nigokwaanigoweN gonaa iwi wiigwaam gaa naakomotoot. zhinggobiin dash gii saat zhewe, zhinggobigaan gii zhitoot.

aapidji go giiyeN zhinda gonaadjiwon e njitaat, zhaawoshkokamik giiyeN maanda zhinda. mii wodi niyiing, biboonishiweying. mii sa miinawaa msan gii zhitoot. yaawaan dash giiyeN besha go zhewe niyiing, jiigibiik go (doo) migomowon zhiishiibeNon.

"aaniish dash e nakii yin.",

doo igoon giiyeN, (doo) ganoonigoon giiyeN,

" aaniish zhinda e nakii yin."
"gaawiin go gegoo. nwii niimiwe sa.",

doo inaan dash giiyeN.

"nwii niimiwe nonggom go giizhiitaa yaaN, mii iwi da niimiwe yaaN.",

doo inaan sa giiyeN newe yaawaan, zhiishiibeNon.

"togowa bibaa dibaadjimon wodi, ooshti wodi."

yaa-aa. aapidji giiyeN wodi (doo) baatiinawok zhiishiibeNik naawondj.

"togowa bibaa dibaadjimon, wodi gosha niyii niimidiigamik (doo) zhichigaade, wii niimiwe giiyeN owo nonggom (doo) giizhiitaat."

mii sa gwonda gii nakozhowewaat wodi zhiishiibeNsak, (doo) bibaa wiindamawaawaat wodi e bimigomowonidjin, wii niimiding zhewe.

"wii zhaa yek giiyeN. nwii zhaamint niinawind go. aapidji go (doo) gonaadjiwonini e zhitoot niimidiigamik."

mii gosha giiyeN go gwonda zhiishiibeNik e zhibinakozhowewaat zhewe besha jiigibiik.

mii dash giiyeN iwi niyii, ooN, gii biiskaan dash iwi agowaaN, gaa gidjibatoowaadang. mandj gaye gonaa gaa nigonigoweN owo nenibozhoo, gii biiskang iwi, ikwe dash

a house, and it is not known how big this house was that he built. The house he made was made out of fir trees.

The ground he was working on was very level and soft, as this was virgin soil. This was in the area around Ponshewaing. After he built the house, he cut firewood. As he was working, there were some ducks who swam by close to the shore.

"What are you doing?"

the ducks asked Nenibozhoo as they spoke to him.

"What are you doing here?"
"Oh, nothing really important. I am just going to host a dance,"

he supposedly replied to the ducks' queries.

"I am going to host a dance when I am finished with the building, that is when I will start the dance,"

he apparently further told the ducks.

"Why don't you go out there and tell everyone about it."

Oh my! There were so many ducks out on the middle of the lake.

"Why don't you go and spread the word about this dance hall being built, and say he will host a dance once he is finished building it."

So these ducks swam out to the middle of the lake to tell the rest of the ducks that a dance was going to take place at the dance hall, which will soon be finished.

"You are invited to the dance. We will be going. That is one fancy dance hall he is building over there."

Unbelievably, those ducks started to swim closer to the shore where the dance hall was located.

Oh by the way, Nenibozhoo had donned the dress he had taken from the woman who helped to free him from the old hollow tree. It is not known how big Nenibozhoo was in stature, but he was able to wear the dress as it fit him, probably snugly, and

gonaa maaba dibishkoo (*doo*) zhinaagozi midjigoodeNwit. gaawiin dash (*doo*) gikenimigoosiin newe nenibozhoowit, zhiishiibeNon, gii biiskamaaget iwi *a*gowaaN.

"*nah*aa*w*, maajaak nshiimeNwidik.",

d*oo* inaan sa giiyeN,

"maajaan nshiimeNwidik, nwii niimiwe."

giyegeti giiyeN zhiishiibeNik (*doo*) minowendamok. aapidji giiyeN go (*doo*) gichi baapitoowok, (*doo*) migibaskobiig*a*batoowok. (*doo*) mibaapitoowaat, (*doo*) mibiindigeyaawonidawaat. gii zhitoon *da*sh giiyeN wodi wii n*a*madabit. mitigoon gonaa maanda gii naakosidoonan, wii n*a*madabit zhewe. mandj go *n*iyiing ge gibapanggowish. shkwaandem gaye gii zhitoon, zhinggobigaan iwi gaa zhitoot. mii sa giiyeN *i*wi,

"*nah*aaw, biindigek nshiimeNwidik."

aapidji giiyeN doo aangoomaan.

"nshiimeNwidik, gga niimim nongg*o*m zhinda."

mii*da*sh giiyeN gonaa gegoo gonaa, mitigooNan gonaa, mii giiyeN newe e baapaagowanggin, maanda gii zhisidoot. aaniish, mii giiyeN go gwonda gii nizhigaabowiwaat zhiishiibeNik, maanda dash wii zhigiitaawigaawok zhewe zhinggobigaaning. maanda waa zhigiitaawigaawaat. mii gaa zhigaabowinit kina newe zhiishiibeNon,

"*nah*aa*w*, wiyii niimik."

maanda zhisidoot newe mitigooNan. mandj gonaa minik newe mitigooNan gonaa maanda e p*a*gidoot, mii giiyeN iwi madwe*w*echiget nenibozhoo. gwonda e biniimiwaat zhiishiibeNik, maanda *da*sh zhigaataawigaawok. namadabit zhewe nenibozhoo, mii*da*sh giiyeN e inaat,

"gga bizanggowaabim sa ji niimi yek.",

d*oo* inaan sa giiyeN. aaniish, mii giiyeN gwonda (*doo*) bizanggowaabiwaat zhiishiibeNik, miinawaa *d*ash giiyeN, mii*da*sh giiyeN miinawaa (*doo*) nigamot, he looked like a woman when he had this dress on. Thus, the ducks did not know it was really Nenibozhoo disguised as a woman when he had the dress on.

"Okay, my younger siblings, come here,"

he called to the ducks.

"Come here my younger siblings, I will host a dance."

Oh, the ducks were just gleeful. They were chuckling with glee as they splashed about in the water. They were chuckling with glee as they filed into the dance hall. Nenibozhoo had made a special place for himself to sit. He had placed some logs in the area he was going to sit. He had made an entranceway, a door to enter this structure made of fir trees. So then he said

"Okay, come in my younger siblings."

He was really trying to win them over, as he kept alluding to their being related.

"My younger siblings, you will now dance in here."

Then he used these things, they were sticks he would use to bang together and he had set these by where he was sitting. And these ducks obediently lined up, as they were going to dance in this direction around the inside of the lodge. They would dance around in a circular direction. When the ducks had all lined up to dance,

"Okay, now you all dance."

He held the sticks in his hands. He hit the sticks against each other, and this is how Nenibozhoo was making music. And these ducks who came to dance, they danced in a circle. And as Nenibozhoo sat in his special place, he supposedly told the ducks the following,

"While you are dancing, you will dance with your eyes closed."

Again, unbelievably, the ducks did as they were told, they danced with their eyes closed. Then Nenibozhoo sang again,

"baapaagonanggoshinok. baapaagonanggoshinok.
baapaagonanggoshinok.",

(doo) nawam sa giiyeN owo nenibozhoo. aaniish, mii gwonda zhiishiibeNik maanda dash (doo) paginaawaat ninggowiingganiwaan.

"baapaagonanggoshinok, baapaagonanggoshinok."

miidash giiyeN (e) migaanit zhewe newe zhiishiibeNon maanda dash (e) nabit, (doo) migaanit zhiishiibeNon (doo) nowodjibinaat, (doo) biimigowebinaat. wodi dash (doo) paginaat, miidash gwonda gii niyaa wodi (doo) baapaagonanggoshinok. miidash go gewiin e nawang,

"baapaagonanggoshinok, baapaagonanggoshinok."

mii go miinawaa bezhik (doo) nowodjibinaat, (doo) biimigowebinaat, wodi dash (doo) paginaat. gichi niibana giiyeN gii biimigowebinaan, wodi dash (e) paginaat, biindik go zhewe, miidash gwonda gii niyaawaat, miidash maanda (e) pagizowaat. miidash niyii gwonda naamidjik, mii go gewiinawaa e ndoodamowaat maanda (doo) baapaagonanggoshiniwaat.

miidash giiyeN bezhik iidik maaba zhiishiibeN, eshkam giiyeN go (doo) banggiisheNwigiziwok (doo) inendam. (doo) bizanggowaabiwok (doo) niimiwok.

"aaniish iidik e nakiit nenibozhoo.",

(doo) inendam sa giiyeN. nenibozhoo giiyeN go, (doo) inendam go newe. (doo) dooskaabit iidik, gaaNwaaN gosha giiyeN gonaa (doo) biiwegaabowiwok. (doo) nowodjibinin dash zhewe owo (doo) biimigowebinin, wodi dash (doo) paginin.

"yaa-aa, nenibozhoo gosha nayiinawint gdoo nisigoonaan.",

(doo) kida sa giiyeN owo. zhinggobeN dash owo.

"nenibozhoo gdoo nisigoonaan."

yaa-aa, miidash giiyeN zhewe wii zaagadjibatoot owo, banggii giiyeN go gii ninaawobinaa, maanpii sa giiyeN go aanowi gii midjigonaa, miidash giiyeN maanda gii zhiniizhonooganebinaat. miidash giiyeN owo yaawaa, zhinggobeN e oonji

"baapaagonanggoshinok. Baapaagonanggoshinok.
Baapaagonanggoshinok,"

is the song that Nenibozhoo sang. So the ducks would begin flapping their wings as they danced.

"baapaagonanggoshinok, baapaagonanggoshinok."

Then as the ducks danced by where he, Nenibozhoo, was situated, he would selectively grab one, and twist its neck. He would throw the duck behind him, and the dying duck would flop around in tune with the ducks flapping their wings. And that is what Nenibozhoo kept singing,

"baapaagonanggoshinok, baapaagonanggoshinok."

He would grab another duck and twist its neck and throw that duck in back of where he was sitting inside the lodge. He twisted the necks of so many of the ducks and these ducks would flop around as they died. And the ducks who were dancing were flapping their wings just like the ducks who were dying.

Then, apparently one of the ducks sensed that there seemed to be fewer of them from the lessening sound. They were dancing with their eyes closed.

"I wonder what Nenibozhoo is doing?"

this duck thought to himself. He suspected that their host was Nenibozhoo in disguise. This duck supposedly opened his eyes to peek, and he noticed that they were definitely fewer in number. He was immediately grabbed and apparently had his neck twisted, but not completely, and he was thrown into the pile behind Nenibozhoo.

"Oh no! This is really Nenibozhoo and he is killing us,"

this bird shouted out. It was the helldiver.

"Nenibozhoo is killing us."

Oh my goodness, this bird started to run toward the door, and Nenibozhoo grabbed at him and must have held the bird around the hip area for a moment, and Nenibozhoo separated this bird's hips slightly. And it is said that is why the bird called the helldiver

niizhonoogang nonggom, maanda e oonji zhinaagozit nooganaang. mii giiyeN owo nenibozhoo gaa pinaat newe, gii niizhonooganebinaat.

maajiibatooshiwaat minik gonaa gaa shkonandawaa. e zhishpishininit giiyeN yaawaan zhiishiibeNon, gii zaagadaawinaat, wodi gwodji go, wodi gii oopashkobinaat, gii pashkobidjiget. miinawaa zhewe zhinggobigaaning, gii nookamigaget zhewe. msan gaye giizhaa gii zhitoonan, gii nookamigaget zhewe, gii boodowet zhewe, aapidji go gii minokozhawe. mii ninda zhiishiibeNon kina gaa pashkobinaat, miinawaa gii biinaat. mii giiyeN maanda dash (doo) kowaadang negoweki gonaa maanda, aapidji giiyeN (doo) gizhaanggideni. mitigoon maanda gii naakosidoot, miidash zhinda gii ninigowaat ninda. nbaneN, bezhik dash giiyeN kaadeNs gii zaagaakosidoon, gii nigowaat miinawaa, (doo) gizhaanggideni iwi. aapidji go wii minowiisini, zhiishiibeN wiiyaas wii miijin. miidash giiyeN e kidat, aapidji giiyeN go (doo) yekozi.

mandj gonaa e zhinaagodigoweN iwi miskowaazigan, gaawiin geniin ngii gikendaziin e zhinaagodigoweN iwi miskowaazigan, mii sa giiyeN iwi gii yaat, gii zhagishing, miidash giiyeN zhewe boodowaaneNing e zhidiiyeshing owo sa, gii gozhowet nenibozhoo, miidash giiyeN iwi gaa toot zhewe wodi niyiing, ginimaa zhinda gonaa bokonaang gonaa ginimaa gwodji gii toonaadik. zhidiiyeshing, mii giiyeN iwi waa koowaabidjigemigak. ginimaa wiya gegoo bidoodawaat ninda gaa nigowanindjinid. mii giiyeN zhewe gii ninibaat nenibozhoo, aapidji giiyeN go (doo) yekozi go. mii go giiyeN iidik gii ninibaat.

miidash giiyeN iidik gewiin maaba anishinaabe gonaa bebaa giiwiset, aapidji giiyeN (doo) bibaa aanowewizi. noopiming e bibaa zhaat, e zhaagobaneN wodi niyiing nibising gonaa. geget sa giiyeN gonaa miigowaaNson (doo) baatiinawon, aapidji giiyeN go, maanda (doo) zhinowaanimodani, eta bemaashinit miigowaaNson. mii nenibozhoo gii pashkobidjiget, wodi gonaa nizhaat go wodi, eta ishpishinanik miigowanon. shkode gosha giiyeN go (doo) biidjimaandaan. gii teni giiyeN zhewe zhinggobigaan. (doo) nitapaabit iidik zhewe zhinggobigaaning, gii biidjidiiyeshinoon giiyeN zhewe nenibozhoon dash (doo) naabit zhewe. aapidji giiyeN (doo) minokozhaweni maanda shkode. zhiishiibeN kaadeNsan giiyeN zaagaakosininiwon zhewe. maanda dash pidoot iwi niyii kaadeNs, mii giiyeN go maanda (e) bizhibiimskokaak, aapidji giiyeN (doo) minoshkodjiideni iwi niyii kaadeNs. aapidji giiyeN go (doo) minodeni.

miidash giiyeN niyii mitigooN gii daapinang, maanda gii kowaadang iwi, aapidji giiyeN go (doo) minoshkodjiizawon zhiishiibeNon, aapidji giiyeN go iidik, (doo) aninandowaanggowaat. niyii dash giiyeN mashkimod e bibaa bimoondang owo, giishkashkimodeN, maaba sa anishinaabe. ginimaa gaye gegoo gonaa (doo) minitoot,

looks that way when he walks. That is the damage Nenibozhoo did to that bird when he held him for a moment.

So the rest of the ducks started to run every which way, those who were left alive that is. Oh, the ducks were really piled up high, and Nenibozhoo hauled them out of the lodge and he took them elsewhere and he proceeded to pluck them. After he had plucked them, he dug up the soft earth outside of the lodge. He had made firewood earlier, and he built a roaring fire over the ground he had dug up. These ducks he had plucked, he then proceeded to clean them. After the fire had burned down to coals, he raked the soil and the ground was very hot. He then set some sticks around the area, and he buried the ducks under the hot soil. And when he covered up the ducks with the hot soil, he left one leg from each duck sticking out of the hot ground. He was going to have a good feast as he would be eating duck meat soon. Apparently, he was very tired from all of the activity he had been through so far that day.

As I, the storyteller, do not know what this thing called a miskowaazigan looks like or what it is, anyway, Nenibozhoo was tired, and he laid down near the fire with his rear to the fire, he pulled his blanket over him, and he must have put this miskowaazigan somewhere on his backside. His rear was facing the fire, and this is who was to be the sentinel, the one who would watch over the cooking ducks while Nenibozhoo slept. Just in case someone came by and did something to the ducks. And Nenibozhoo fell asleep as he had been extremely tired. And he apparently fell asleep almost instantly.

It just so happened that there was this Anishinaabe man out hunting, and he was having no luck at all. He was going inland and he ended up going toward this particular lake where Nenibozhoo was near. Oh there were so many feathers that were floating about and the wind was swirling around and the feathers were just being blown about by the wind. Those are the feathers that Nenibozhoo had plucked from the ducks he had killed and as the Anishinaabe man went closer to where this occurred, he saw a big pile of duck feathers. And he could also smell the smoke from the fire Nenibozhoo had made earlier. So he quietly moved about, and he looked around, and he came across the lodge made from fir trees as he peered through the trees. And as he peered at the lodge, he saw Nenibozhoo with his back toward him. The coals of the fire were still quite hot. Then as he inspected the scene, he noticed that there were duck legs sticking out of the ground here and there. So he made his way quietly to the area where the ducks were, he grasped at one leg and it just twisted off and out of the ground, and the little duck drumstick was so tender from being cooked. It was well done.

So he quietly picked up the sticks laying nearby, he quietly dug up the ground, he found the ducks that were well done and ready to be eaten, and he dug the rest of them up. This Anishinaabe man had with him a bag, a cedar bark bag. In case he was

mii zhewe wii biindjiwebinang. mii gosha giiyeN *owo* yaawaa, miskowaazigan, gegoo gii *ma*dwe nowet, mii*da*sh giiyeN maanda gii ninimowaat, bekaa wii yaanit newe, miskowaaziganon, gii ninimowaat.

kina newe gaa migidaanggobinaat *owo* sa anishinaabe, newe dash giiyeN gaa aabskikaanigin, newe sa go kaadeNsan, mii go neyaap miinawaa gii ninegowaakosidoot. giishkashkimodeNing gii biindjiwebinang, kina go, mii gosha giiyeN ko wodi *ma*d*w*e mizitaagozit *owo* miskowaazigan, *n*iyii *da*sh ko maanda zhininimowaat, miidash giiyeN go (*doo*) bizaanabit zhewe. mii*da*sh kina gaa bimaat newe zhiishiibeNon, gaa*wiin* iidik gaye gonaa wii jaagizogobaneN, mii sa giiyeN gii akowodjiwinet *owo* anishinaabe, gii maadjii*w*oomaat newe zhiishiibeNon, menozandjin.

mii sa *n*iyii maaba nenibozhoo gimaapii oogoshkozit, mii go giyaabi e zhisininik kaadeNsan, (*doo*) zaagaakosininini. mii*da*sh giiyeN, bezhik sa giiyeN (*doo*) gowedjibidoon, maanda doo pidoon,

> "zhaazhigo, zhaazhigo (*doo*) minozawinggobaneN.",

(*doo*) kida sa giiyeN. aapidji giiyeN go (*doo*) gichi zhiyaa.

> "zhaazhigo, zhaazhigo, zhaazhigo (*doo*) minozawinggobaneN.",

kina go (*doo*) nigodjibinaat wodi. mitigooN (*doo*) oodaapinaan wii mookiwaat yaawaan zhiishiibeNon, *n*iyii, (*e*) minozanit. gaa*wiin* wiya. gaa*wiin* go ginigeN bezhik. mii go eta kaadeNsan.

> "aashiizhimaadjii, geget sa gonaa ko gewe ndaa ninigaawigook gewe nninggonisak.",

(*doo*) kida *da*sh giiyeN.

> "ndaa ninigaawigook nninggonisak, gii bigimoodimiwaat newe."

mii giiyeN anishinaaben gaa zhini*k*aanaat *owo* nenibozhoo, nninggonis, mii iwi gaa zhini*k*aanaat. *owo* anishinaabe gewii*n* gii giiwewone.

aapidji giiyeN go (*doo*) shkendam nenibozhoo. mii*da*sh giiyeN iwi maanda gii kowaadang, gii p*a*skanegowaadang iwi *n*iyii shkode, gii zhidiiyenit wodi, gaakaashkidiiyewidizat, (*doo*) gaakaashkizowaat newe diiyeNon. mii*da*sh giiyeN gaa giizhiitaat, gaa shkwaa gaakaashkizowaat newe diiyeNon, gii bimaajaat, maanpii dash gichigomiing dash gii bibaa zhaa nikeyaa, (*doo*) bizhaa. miidash iwi

successful hunting, he would carry his prey in this cedar bark bag. Just then, the sentry made a slight sound, and this man gave the sentry some meat so he would be quiet.

After the Anishinaabe man had dug up all of the cooked ducks, and the legs that he had twisted off, he placed these legs back into the ground the way they had been previously. He put all of the ducks into his cedar bark bag, and every so often, the sentry would make a noise, but Nenibozhoo did not awaken, and the man quickly would give the sentry something to eat, and the sentry would become quiet again. Then when the man had put all of the ducks in his bag, and it is a wonder that he did not get burned while he was handling all of those hot cooked ducks, anyway, he picked up his load of ducks and the man carried off the cooked ducks.

Then after quite a long time, Nenibozhoo woke up from his long nap, and he looked and he saw that the duck legs were still sticking out of the ground just as they were when he went to sleep. Then he walked over and tugged at one of the legs while saying,

> "They are already well cooked."

He was very proud of himself.

> "Already, they are already well cooked,"

he states as he tests the doneness of the legs. He picked up the raking sticks and he dug up his ducks that were cooking and they were now well done. There was nothing. There was not one duck to be found. All he had were the little drumsticks of the ducks.

> "Oh for crying out loud, gee those nephews of mine really put one over me this time,"

he apparently said.

> "My nephews really made a fool out of me, as they stole the ducks from me."

This is how Nenibozhoo referred to the Anishinaabe, as his nephews, that is how he referred to them. The Anishinaabe hunter had taken the bagful of ducks to his home.

Poor Nenibozhoo, he was feeling very badly for his loss. So that is when he raked the coals of the fire and he got the fire going and it soon was very hot, that is when he sat on the hot coals and burned his rear to a crisp. So when he had charred his rear, that is when he made his way toward the big lake. The one called the red willow, it

miskowaabiiminagooNs e daming, maanda e nishpiik, g*doo* waabidaanaadik ko miskowaabiiminagooNs, (*doo*) miskowaakowat go iwi mitigooNs, mii giiyeN zhewe gii minaazhidiiyeshing, *o*wo sa nenibozhoo, gii minaazhidiiyeshing zhewe.

"mbe, mii go gwonda gewe nninggonisak e doodawigowaa, enowek go maanda ji nimaadjii-akiiwang, da nimashkiiminaawaa maanda gewe. miskowaabiiminagooNs maanda da zhinikaade.",

gii kida sa giiyeN.

"mii maanda ge mashkiimiwaat gewe nninggonisak. miskowaabiiminagooNs, wiya (*doo*) aakozit, mandj go e naapanegoweN, mii maanda ge naandowigot.",

(*doo*) kida sa giiyeN. mii sa giiyeN gaa giizhiitaat, mashkiki gaa shkwaa zhitoot, baamaa giiyeN go miinawaa zhewe yaawaan bemibizonit bineshiiNon.

"yaa-aa, bineshiiN.",

(*doo*) kida sa giiyeN, (*doo*) ganoondizat,

"bineshiiN."

*n*iyii *da*sh giiyeN zhewe wiigwaason gonaa, aapidji giiyeN go (*doo*) gonaadjiwonigoba*n* iwi wiigwaas e daming, miidash iwi yaawaan gii bookobinaat, zhinggobiiNson, gii bookobinaat, miinawaa giiyeN go bimibizowon zhewe bineshiiNson, mii*da*sh giiyeN gii p*a*shazhewaat newe bineshiiNson, mii*da*sh gii shoodjiganaamaat *n*iyiing, wiigwaasing, wiigwaasikemizhiing. miidash iwi maanda e *oo*nji zhidjiikoweyaak iwi wiigwaas, miinawaa gewe zhinggobiiNs, zhinggobiiNs, mii go zhewe gii maziniset. miidash iwi maanda e yaanigokowaak, zhaagoweNsak *da*sh zhinikaazawok *da*sh gewe zhinggobiiNsak.

"mbe, mii maanda gewe nninggonisak ge zhichigewaat, da gichi nakaazanaawaa maanda wiigwaas."

ozaam dash daa gitimishkiwok miinawaa giiyeN wodi *n*iyiin, zhigowiganan doo niwaabidaanan, mii giiyeN miinawaa gii zhiishiigodang newe *n*iyii zhewe, mii iwi ziisibaakodowaaboo. mii sa iwi gii aansitoot iwi. (*doo*) ziiwaagomidenigoba*n* giiyeN

grows this high, you probably have seen it, it is red in color, and he would rub his charred and by now bloody rear end on the bushes to try to comfort himself, and he left these little bushes red with his blood, that is where he scraped off his blood, and this is the one we now call the red willow.

> "There, now my nephews will have this for their medicine when the earth begins to flourish. This will be called the red willow,"

he supposedly said.

> "This is what my nephews will use for medicine in the future. When someone becomes sick, whatever ailment befalls him, the red willow will cure him."

he apparently said. So when he had finished making this medicine, the red willow, suddenly there was this bird which flew by and this annoyed him.

> "Oh darn, a bird,"

he supposedly said to himself,

> "It's a bird."

The birch tree at that time had unblemished bark, it was so beautiful with its unblemished bark, so as this bird flew by Nenibozhoo, he broke off a small evergreen tree, and he swung the evergreen at the bird and smashed the bird against the birch tree, and it was the evergreen needles that marred the unblemished bark of the birch tree. So that is why the birch tree has markings on its bark, it is the evergreen that left its mark when Nenibozhoo was punishing the bird for annoying him. It is the one called zhaagoweNsak, and these evergreens grow low to the ground.

> "There, my nephews will make great use of this birch bark."

He knew his nephews would become too lazy when he saw the taps in the maple trees, and at that time, syrup came out of the trees so the people did not have to work to get maple sugar, so Nenibozhoo urinated into the maple trees and diluted the maple syrup and it is now maple sap. So he diluted the maple syrup. This had already been maple syrup, but he diluted it; a long time ago, what came out of

iwi, *niyii*, gichi zhaazhago iwi sa e njigaak zhewe kisinaamizhiing, ziiwaagomide go. miidash iwi nenibozhoo gaa aansitoot.

mii sa e koozit *owo* nenibozhoo. gaa gichi giibaadizit. aapidji go gii giibaadizi *owo* nenibozhoo. aapidji go niibana gii zhichige. giyaabi go ngii gikendaan gaa zhichiget, *ozaam* dash, *ozaam* dash.

nenibozhoo makwan gii n*i*saapan

nenibozhoo (*doo*) bibaa giiwiset, makwan gii nisaan. gaa shkwaa p*a*konaat, mii iwi gii minozawaat, iwi go wiisinit dash, mitigoon (*doo*) ziiboweshkaanit gii anashkwewigoon. wii p*a*kowemaat go m*a*kwan, wiyii go (*doo*) wiisinit, miinawaa go (*doo*) ziiboweshkaanit newe mitigoon. miidash gii bidagowiiziit, wii oogadiskaakonaat wodi (*doo*) aasoo-waakoshiniwaat gewe mitigook. miidash gaa zhin*a*soondjiishkoozat wodi. e piichi yaat dash wodi, yaa*w*aan, mayiingg*a*non gii noondawaan (*doo*) *b*imab*a*toonit. miinawaa (*doo*) noondaagozit nenibozhoo,

"gegowan go zhinda bizhaakegowan.",

(*doo*) inaat.

"wodi nikeyaa nipatook."

miidash mayiingganak gii inendamowaat,

"togo*wa* wodi zhaadaa nenibozhoo (*doo*) yaat, ginimaa gegoo d*oo* yaanaadik wodi waa miiji ying."

gii zhaawaat wodi, gii waabimaawaat zhewe makwan, zhaazhigo gaa minoz*a*-gaazanodjin, gii gidamowaa*w*aan newe.

miidash gaa maajaawaat, mii iwi nenibozhoo gii g*a*shkitoot iwi wii gidiskonang nindj wodi (*doo*) n*a*soodenik mitigoong. gii biniisaboozat. (*doo*) gwetaanigidaaza *o*wo, mitigoon aanowi naadimowaat, gii n*a*soondjiishkaagonid. mii mitigooNson gii b*oo*kowaak*o*binaat, gii gichi pash*a*zhewaan newe, wiigwaaskemizhiin. mii nonggo*m* e *oo*nji pasaaNzawaat wiigwaaskemizhiik.

the maple tree was already syrup. So this is what Nenibozhoo diluted, so that his nephews would not become lazy.

That is the length of my story of the one called Nenibozhoo. He was very foolish. He was extremely foolish. He did many things. I know of many more things about him, but it is too much for one sitting, it is just too much.

When Nenibozhoo Killed a Bear

Nenibozhoo was out hunting and he killed a bear. After he had skinned it and cleaned it, he began to cook the bear. When he was about to begin eating, he was disturbed by the squeaking of trees rubbing against each other, it annoyed him. Again, as he was about to take a bite of the bear meat, the trees made the irritating sound. So Nenibozhoo climbed up the tree to go and untangle them where they were rubbing against each other. As he was attempting to untangle the trees, he got his hand stuck between the trees. At that moment he heard some wolves running nearby. Nenibozhoo shouted to them,

> "Don't come here."

He said to them,

> "Keep on running in that direction."

Then the wolves thought,

> "Let's go to where Nenibozhoo is at, he may have something there for us to eat."

So they went there, and sure enough they saw the bear, which was already nicely cooked, and they proceeded to eat up all of the bear meat.

So when the wolves left, that is when Nenibozhoo was able to free his trapped hand from the trees. Nenibozhoo slid down from the tree. He was very angry at the tree for trapping his hand, for this was a tree he was trying to help. Nenibozhoo broke off a small shrub and he began whipping the birch tree that had trapped his hand, and he left welts on the bark of the tree. That is why the birch tree now has markings on its bark.

gaa biniisaboozat, gaa shkwaa pashazhewaat dash newe mitigoon, mii gii nandowaabidang gonaa nenibozhoo gonaa gewiin wiiyaas wii miijit. gaawiin dash go gegoo, mii go eta kanan zhewe e tenigin. miidash gii waabidang, nayii, makwan dip.

"nga miijin. zhewe, nga biindoode zhewe.",

(doo) inendang giiyeN.

gii kawenaanaagodowendang dash, mandj iidik waa zhichigegoweN wii debinang, zhewe gonaa, biindji gonaa, dibaang wii miijit. miidash ndaawaach ginebigooNsing gii zhiwidizat, gii biindoodet zhewe. gii gichi waawiisinit, ozaam dash niibana gii wiisini. gaa shkwaa wiisinit, gii aanowitoo wii zaagadoodet. miidash wodi dibaang gii baataasinanik giiyeN iwi makwan dip.

gii bimoset, mitigoong gii mipataakoshing, (doo) mipataakoshkowaat mitigoon. mii (doo) gagwedjimaat newe,

"wenesh giin."

"yaawaa sa niin, wiigobimish ndoo aaw."

mii gii gikendang ozaam waasa noopiming (doo) miyaat nenibozhoo. (doo) nimaajaat, gimaapii miinawaa mitigoong miinawaa (doo) nipataakoshing,

"wenesh kiin.",

dash (doo) inaat.

"zhinggwaak sa ndoo zhinikaanigoo.",

(doo) kidawon giiyeN newe mitigoon. miidash (doo) nigikendang nenibozhoo gichigomiing nikeyaa (doo) nizhaat.

gimaapii go (doo) niniisaakiiye, miinawaa mitigoong (doo) nipataakoshing. aaniish, (doo) gagwedjimaat newe,

"wenesh kiin."

"giizhik sa ndoo zhinikaaz."

"ooN.",

(doo) kida nenibozhoo. (doo) niminowendang.

"mii zhago besha nibiishing (doo) nidagoshinaaN."

So after he had slid down from the birch tree and after he had finished punishing the birch tree, he began to look for some bear meat to eat. But it was all gone, having been eaten up by the wolves, all that was left was a pile of bones. That is when he saw the bear's head.

"I will eat that. I will crawl in there,"

he supposedly thought.

He pondered over his predicament, as he did not know how he would get inside the bear's head to eat it. So, then he changed himself into a small snake, and he was now able to crawl inside of the head. He ate all he could, and he had eaten too much for he could not crawl back out of the head. So the bear's head was now stuck on his head [*as he returned to his normal shape.*]

He began to walk, and he was unable to see, so he bumped into a tree. He asked the tree,

"Who are you?"
"I am the basswood."

Then Nenibozhoo knew he was heading much too far inland. So he must have turned around and began walking again and, eventually, he bumps into another tree.

"Who are you?"

he asks this tree.

"I am called the pine,"

replied the tree. Then Nenibozhoo knew he was going toward the big lake.

Eventually, he could tell he was going downhill and that is when he bumped into another tree. He asked this tree,

"Who are you?"
"I am called the cedar."
"Oh!"

said Nenibozhoo. He was pleased.

"I will soon be arriving at the water's edge."

gimaapii go (*doo*) nimoozh*a*toon zidaang *n*iyii miizhashk, gimaapii nibiish, (*doo*) nibigomaadigaat. eshkam go naawondj (*doo*) nidagoshin, gimaapii ozaam (*doo*) gowiindimaani iwi nibiish wii bimaadigaat, miidash giiyeN (*doo*) maadigaat. anishinaaben dash gii debiwaabimigoon.

"na gosha wodi, makwa."

(*doo*) kidawok gewe.

"togo*wa* oonisaadaa.",

(*doo*) kid*a*wok.

mii gii naaskowaa*w*aat, gii nidaminewewaa*w*aat, mii gii gichi baanggidibewaa*w*aan newe nenibozhoon, gii daashkidibegonaamaawaan dash newe, iwi makwan dip.

nenibozhoo gii gowaadigaabatoot, pane mitigowaakiing gii nim*a*batoot.

mii iwi.

nenibozhoo miinawaa makwak

yaawaa sa nwii dibaadjimaa, nenibozhoo. aaniish, nenibozhoo gonaa (*doo*) dibaadjimigoozit, mii owo zhinda gaa oshki bimaadizit. iwi dash go, nwii dibaadjimaa, iwi gonaa gaa wiidjinakiimaadjin gonaa gewii*n*, yaawaan dash newe, wesiiNon, m*a*kwan, miinawaa waawaashkeshiwon, miinawaa gonaa ninda aanind wesiiNik gonaa, bebiizhiiNwidjik gonaa. ninda *d*ash m*a*kwan gii nisastaawigoon gonaa maanda (*doo*) nibwaach*aw*aat gonaa ji kida yinggoba*n*, (*doo*) ganoonaat. dibishkoo gonaa kiinawi*n* e zhiganoondi ying, mii gaa zhiganoonaat newe. mii*d*ash giiyeN ngoding (*e*) nibwaach*aw*aat ninda ngodigamik m*a*kwan, aapidji giiyeN go (*doo*) minowaabimigoon, aaniish, gii gos*a*godigenon *d*ash gaye gonaa. aa*n*iish gii madji*y*aawoshi gonaa maaba nenibozhoo.

mii*d*ash giiyeN iwi (*doo*) dibaadjimotaawigod newe ikwewon e ndaadjin zhewe. niizh*a*won giiyeN maaba ikwe niidjaaniseNon, naanedaa *d*ash ninda wiidigemaaganon gaa*w*ii*n* (*doo*) yaasiiwon maaba ikwe, maaba nenibozhoo zhewe (*e*) nidisaat newe. mii*d*ash giiyeN newe ikwewon (*doo*) dibaadjimonit.

He soon feels the grasses under his feet and then he steps into the water and he continues to wade into the water. He is getting further out into the lake, it is much too deep for him to keep wading, so he now begins to swim. That is when he is spotted by several native hunters who happened to be going by in a canoe.

"Look at that, it's a bear,"

they said.

"Let's go and kill it,"

they said further.

So they approached what they thought was a bear, and they caught up to him, and that is when one of them clobbered the bear's head with a paddle, and he hit it so hard that it split the bear's head, which Nenibozhoo had been wearing.

So then Nenibozhoo got out of the water and he was last seen running into the woods and he was gone.

That is it.

Nenibozhoo and the Bears

I will now talk about the trickster, Nenibozhoo. Well, one story about Nenibozhoo is that he was the first Anishinaabe to live on earth. But, I will talk about the time he lived among the animals, the bears, the deer, and even all of the small animals, as these are the ones he lived with and worked with so to speak. Back then, it could be said that he was understood by the animals, especially the bears when he spoke to them, and vice versa. They conversed with each other just like we do today. So this one time he was visiting this one family of bears, and these bears welcomed him into their home and they were pleased by his visit, although the bears may have had some reservations about Nenibozhoo, they even may have been afraid of him. Well, this Nenibozhoo was known as a person to be feared, as he could be evil and mean-spirited when it suited him. [*He was also kind and gentle as well.*]

Anyway, the female bear of the house spoke to Nenibozhoo. The female bear had two bear cubs with her, and the male bear, her mate, was not at home at that time when Nenibozhoo stopped by for a visit. And this woman, the female bear, began to tell Nenibozhoo about her dad.

"maaba gaye noos, akiweziiNwi gonaa maaba aapidji. aapidji *dash* go doo mbazhawenimaan ninda gwiiwizeNson gonaa nga kid, *ma*kooNsak dash gewe (*doo*) mbashkamigizinit gonaa. bekaa gonaa gewii*n* gonaa wii zhazhaanggishing gonaa, wii nanawebit, wii nibaat gaye gonaa, mii maaba akiweziiN e zhibagosendang. miidash gaa zhikida yaang ndaawaach, noopiming gonaa, waasa gonaa ji zhitoow *ya*anggidoba*n* gewii*n* njike gonaa ge daat. miinawaa gaye gonaa bekish gonaa ji naagodoowenima*a* *ya*anggit. mii*da*sh go maaba akiweziiN gaa zhiminowendang iwi. miidash gaa zhichige yaang iwi, gii gopii yaang, gii oozhitoowa*a* *ya*anggit iwi waa daat maaba akiweziiN. aaniish, mii*da*sh go gaa giizhtoowa*a* *ya*anggit, mii go gii gopiit, gii biindoodegozit zhewe g*a*ye gonaa gewii*n* waa daat. ngii naagodoowenimaanaa*n* *da*sh gonaa.",

(*doo*) kidawidigenon sa ninda ikwewon, maaba nenibozhoo (*doo*) dibaadjimotaawigot. aa*n*iish, nenibozhoo gewii*n*, (*doo*) madji*y*aawosh gewii*n*. mii gonaa gewii*n* gii gikenimaat wodi gaa dagoshininit newe akiweziiNon e ndaanit. miidash iidik gaa inendang iwi,

"geget sa gonaa maaba (*doo*) gonaadjiwi akiweziiN. aapidji g*a*ye go (*doo*) wiinna, aapidji go daa minopogozi.",

(*doo*) inendam sa. aa*n*iish, *ma*kwa akiweziiN maaba, miidash iidik gaa zhinendang iwi,

"giyegeti go nga oogiim*a*nanaa maaba m*a*kwa akiweziiN.",

(*doo*) inendam sa giiyeN. aa*n*iish, mii*da*sh go giyegeti gaa zhichiget. ngoding go iidik go, mii gii zhaat wodi e ndaanit newe. (*e*) nidagoshing, (*doo*) nakweshkaawigot giiyeN zhewe shkwaandemoninik gonaa e ndaanit.

"aanii*n*, mii na nenibozhoo (*doo*) binisi yin.",

d*oo* igoodigenon sa ninda akiweziiNon.

"anish*aa* gonaa n*doo* bibaamose.",

d*oo* inaan *da*sh giiyeN maaba nenibozhoo. mii go zhaazhigo go gii gikenimigoon zhewe (*e*) binjizhaat newe akiweziiNon. mii*da*sh go giyegeti maaba nenibozhoo gaa zhichiget, gii giim*a*nanaan ninda akiweziiNon. miinawaa iidik gii p*a*konaat gaa nisaat. miinawaa iidik gii giikiishkodang wiiyaas. miinawaa giiyeN gaye ninda nagazhiiyan gii biindjishkowaadaanan giiyeN ninda gaa biin*na*toot. e zhichigewaat

> "My dad is an old, very old bear. He was very annoyed with the antics of my boys, these bear cubs when they would fool around. My dad wanted to lay around and wanted peace and quiet as he rested and slept, this is what he wished for. So we said amongst ourselves that we would build a home for him further inland where he could stay by himself in peace and quiet. But we would also be able to check in on him occasionally. So my dad, the old bear, liked this idea. So that is what we did, we went inland and made a home for my dad. And when we finished his new home, he moved in right away. We still do take care of him as best we can,"

this female bear must have said to Nenibozhoo as she talked to him. Well, as we said earlier, Nenibozhoo was a bad character at times, and he had some spiritual powers. So he knew where the old man bear's house was located and Nenibozhoo could see him and that the old bear was at home. So Nenibozhoo thought,

> "Oh my, that old bear looks very nice and healthy. He is very fat and he would really taste good,"

this is what he thought. Well, this was an old man bear, he was old, so Nenibozhoo decided,

> "I am going to go and kill this old bear without anyone knowing about it,"

Nenibozhoo must have thought to himself. Well, I guess that is what he eventually did. One day he went to the old man bear's home. When he arrived there, he was met by the old man bear at the door of his home.

> "Well hello Nenibozhoo, are you coming to kill me?"

this old bear must have asked Nenibozhoo.

> "Oh, I am just out walking around the area,"

Nenibozhoo must have reassured this old bear. The old man bear already knew of Nenibozhoo's intentions for coming there even before he got to the old bear's home. So, this is what Nenibozhoo did, he killed the old bear. He then skinned the bear after he had killed him. He then cut up the meat into portions. He then cleaned the intestines and then he made sausage using the cleaned intestines as casings.

gonaa nonggo*m* gonaa baandjishkowedjik ko gonaa, n*doo* waabimaak naanigodinong gonaa. miidash iidik e inendang go *o*wo,

> "maanoo go zhinda nga yaa. baamaa*mpii* gonaa maaba gii gidamowak maaba m*a*kwa akiweziiN, mii ji m*a*daabii yaaN.",

gii inendam giiyeN.

> "nga ninibwaach*aw*aak gewe ninda debenimaadjik akiweziiNon.",

(*doo*) inendam sa iidik maaba nenibozhoo. aaniish, mii*da*sh baamaa*mpii* gaa gidaang kina iwi wiiyaas, mii gii m*a*daabiit.

> "nga nibiindigoowaak gewe.",

(*doo*) inendam *da*sh iidik. mii*da*sh go giyegeti maaba zhewe *o*wo ikwe e oosowit ninda m*a*kwa akiweziiNon, mii go zhewe gaa nji panggodjidagoshing. aa*n*iish, (*doo*) gichi minowaabimigoon sa giiyeN ninda zhewe e ndaanidjin, m*a*kwan. m*a*kwak gwonda, gaawii*n* go gwonda (*doo*) anishinaabesiiwon.

miidash maaba nenibozhoo e inaat ninda ikwewon,

> "gdaa niwiyii kawe gibiitoowinim gonaa, ginimaa gaye gonaa nis*w*agon, ginimaa gaye gonaa niiwigon, naanagon gaye gonaa. *a*ki gonaa n*doo* bibaa waabidaan. kina gonaa gegoo gonaa n*doo* bibaa waabidaan gonaa zhinda akiing e ndigowog. mii*da*sh zhinda ge zhiminowendamaambaa*n* ji njijiiwi yaaNmbaa*n*.",

d*oo* inaadigenon sa maaba nenibozhoo ninda ikwewon.

> "aaniish, gdaa daniz sa.",

d*oo* igoon dash giiyeN ninda ikwewon maaba nenibozhoo.

> "gaa*w*ii*n* *da*sh wiyii gonaa n*doo* minogesiimi*n*t gonaa, iwi *da*sh gonaa wii danizi yin zhinda, gwonda gwiiwizeNsak niizh e yawigik genii*n* gdaa wiipemaak.",

d*oo* igoodigenon sa ninda ikwewon. aaniish, niizhawon maaba niidjaanison ikwe, m*a*kooNsak.

People still make sausage this way today, as this is what I have seen being done by the people who still do that today. So Nenibozhoo decided,

> "I think I will stay right here for awhile at least. After I have eaten up the meat from this old bear, that is when I will go down toward the lake where the other bears live,"

Nenibozhoo thought.

> "I will go to visit the bears who are related to this old man bear,"

Nenibozhoo supposedly thought. So when he had eaten up most of the bear meat, that is when he made his way down to where the relatives of this old bear lived.

> "I will stop and drop in on them,"

he must have thought. So that is where Nenibozhoo went, he stopped by the home of the daughter of this old bear he had killed, that is where he went. Well, these bears looked favourably upon him and welcomed him into their home again. These are bears, they are not Anishinaabe people.

So, Nenibozhoo said to this female bear,

> "I would like to stay with you and your family for a few days, it could be for three days, or maybe four, or even for five days. I am going around looking at the land. I am going around and looking at everything that grows and lives on earth. I would really appreciate it if I could make your home my home base, so to speak,"

Nenibozhoo may have said to the female bear.

> "Well, I guess you could stay here,"

Nenibozhoo was told by the female bear.

> "However, our home is not the best there is, and if you stay here, you will have to sleep with my two boys,"

Nenibozhoo was supposedly told by the woman bear. Remember, the female bear had two cubs.

"nahaaw, mii go iwi.",

doo inaadigenon dash maaba nenibozhoo.

"mii go iwi. nga gichi minowendam go ji wiipemigoowaa gwonda makooNsak.",

(doo) kidawidik sa. aaniish, miidash go zhewe gii nigadang iwi mashkimot. aaniish, mii go biindenik newe zhewe nagazhiin wodi gaa biindjishkowaadanggin.

aaniish, mii sa gonaa, (doo) wiisinit gonaa (doo) wiidoopamaat e zhiwiisiniwaat gonaa gewiinawaa gwonda makwak. miidash giiyeN iwi, makwak gaa nibaawaadji gonaa, ginimaa gonaa shpiitaadibikak, mii maaba nenibozhoo gii aabazhewang maanda mashkimot. mii (doo) miijit iwi niyii, makwa wiiyaas, miinawaa ninda nagazhiin gaa biindjishkowaadanggin. aaniish giiyeN ninda makooNson (doo) mameskowaabimigoon.

"gegiinawaa na maanda gwii miijinaawaa.",

doo inaadigenon dash go ngoding go. geget sa gonaa giiyeN gwonda makooNsak wii miijinaawaa iwi nayii, makwa nagazh, baandjishkowaadek. aaniish, mii sa maaba nenibozhoo gii giishkodimowaat iwi, bemigii gonaa maanda nagazh.

"nahaaw, maanda gegiin.",

doo inaadigenon newe bezhik makooNson. miinawaa aanind miinawaa gii giishkodang aanind,

"maanda gegiin."

giimooch go. gaawiin dash, (doo) nibaawok gwonda e niidjaanisodjik ninda. geget sa gonaa gwiiwizeNsak (doo) minopidaanaawaa iwi makwa nagazh. miidash giiyeN gaa shkwaa gidaamonit kina iwi,

"wiingge gidaamok maanda.",

doo inaan tayii gonaa maaba nenibozhoo giiyeN ninda makooNson. miidash giiyeN gwonda makooNsak iidik gaa gidaamowaat iwi, mii iwi gii gagwedjimaat miinawaa nenibozhoo,

"That would be okay with me, that is fine,"

Nenibozhoo must have told the female bear.

"That is acceptable. I would be honored to sleep with the bear cubs,"

he must have said. Thus, that is where he left his bag when he made his forays into the world. This was the bag that contained the sausage he made from the old man bear, the father of the female bear who lived here.

So, when the bears ate, Nenibozhoo ate with them, he ate what they ate. And when the bears had gone to sleep, and sometime late at night, Nenibozhoo untied his bag. He then ate the bear meat sausage he had made. Of course, the bear cubs desirously looked at him as he ate.

"Do you two want to eat some of this?"

he must have said to them. Oh, those bear cubs were very willing to eat the sausage Nenibozhoo was offering to them. So Nenibozhoo sliced small portions of the sausage for the bear cubs to eat.

"Okay, here is some for you,"

he probably said to one bear cub. Then he cut another small piece of sausage.

"Here is some for you, also."

He said this quietly to the bear cubs. The adult bears were sound asleep. Those bear cubs really enjoyed eating the sausage, which was made from bear meat. Then when the bear cubs had finished eating,

"Make sure you eat it all,"

Nenibozhoo also had said to the bear cubs. So when the bear cubs had eaten all of their little portion of sausage, that is when Nenibozhoo asked the cubs, "aanii, kina na ggii gidaanaawaa iwi gaa shamininigok.",

d*oo* inaadigenon sa gonaa giimooch, wii bibowaa noondaawigot giiyeN newe niigikigoowaan gwonda makooNsak.

"eN*he*N, kina go ngii gidaanaa*n*.",

(*doo*) kidawon *da*sh giiyeN ninda m*a*kooNson. mii*da*sh giiyeN maaba nenibozhoo e inaat newe makooNson,

"g*doo* nis*a*dopowaawaa na gmishoomisowaa.",

d*oo* inaan giiyeN. aa*n*iish, gaawii*n* *da*sh wiyii gwonda m*a*kooNsak gewiinawaa gii nisastawaasiiwaan.

ngoding *da*sh gonaa maaba nenibozhoo (*e*) maajaat gonaa, aaniish pane ensa giizhigak (*doo*) bimose. baamaa*mpii* gonaa naakoshinik (*doo*) dagoshin. mii*da*sh giiyeN ngoding gaa maajaanit, gwonda makooNsak mii giiyeN newe gashiwaan e inaawaat,

"gegoo gosha *n*iyii gaye ko nd*oo* sh*a*migoonaa*n* owo nenibozhoo.",

d*oo* inaawaan giiyeN newe gashiwaan.

"aapidji go (*doo*) minopogod wiiyaas. *zhaa*zhowaach gaye go nagazhiing go (*doo*) zhinaagot iwi.",

(*doo*) kida sa giiyeN maaba bezhik m*a*kooNs. aa*n*iish,

"bekaa.",

(*doo*) kidawon sa giiyeN newe gashiwaan gwonda m*a*kooNsak,

"giishpmaa nongg*om* niibaadibik (*e*) shaminek iwi, gegowa kina gidaanggegowan. nga waabidaan. gegoo nayiinawi*nd* go maaba nenibozhoo nd*oo* inenimaa.",

(*doo*) kidawidik sa maaba ikwe, maaba e niidjaanisot ninda m*a*kooNson. aaniish, makwa go gaye maaba ikwe, anish*aa* gonaa nd*oo* kit gonaa iwi ikwewish (*e*) kid*a* yaaN.

"Well, did you eat it all, the meat that I fed you?"

He must have whispered to them, so that the parents of the bear cubs would not hear what he was saying to the cubs.

"Yes, we ate it all up,"

these bear cubs supposedly said to Nenibozhoo. So then, Nenibozhoo says to the bear cubs,

"Did you recognize the taste of your grandfather?"

he said to them. However, the bear cubs really did not understand what he meant by the question he posed to them.

Well, Nenibozhoo was venturing about the earth daily, as this is one of his tasks, he was supposed to go around and see everything. He would leave in the morning, and he would return in the evening. So, this one day when Nenibozhoo had left for one of his ventures, these bear cubs spoke to their mother.

"Nenibozhoo usually feeds us something at night,"

this is what the bear cubs said to their mother.

"The meat tastes very good. It sort of looks like intestines,"

this one bear cub must have said. Well,

"Wait."

the mother of the cubs must have said.

"If he feeds you some meat again during the night, do not eat it all. I want to see it. I have an eerie feeling about this man, Nenibozhoo,"

the female bear must have uttered, the mother of these bear cubs. Well, this is really a bear, it is not really a woman, I just use the term "woman" for the female bear on occasion.

"gegowa nonggo*m* kina gidaanggegowan iwi. giimooch gga g*a*kidoonaawaa wiiyaas ge shaminek.",

d*oo* igoowaadigenon sa gwonda m*a*kooNsak newe gashiwaan.

"nahaaw."

aa*n*iish, mii sa giiyeN miinawaa gimaapii nenibozhoo noondaadibik iwi, kina gaa nibaawaat gewe, mii giiyeN miinawaa (*doo*) aabazhewang iwi mashkimot. mii miinawaa (*doo*) miijit iwi wiiyaas, makwa wiiyaas miinawaa iwi nagazh gaa biindjishkowaadang. miinawaa gii pakowekodomowaat gwiiwizeNson iwi nagazh, maaminik gonaa. gaa*wiin dash* giiyeN gwonda gwiiwizeNsak gaye kina gii gidaaziinaawaa iwi. aaniish, gii igoowaan gashiwaan, gaawii*n* kina ji miijisigowaa iwi, wii waabidaan maaba ikwe iwi, wegodigowendik iidik iwi wiiyaas. gegoo go d*oo* inenimaan go ninda nenibozhoon maaba ikwe.

mii*da*sh giiyeN iwi gaa maajaanit newe nenibozhoon gizhep, mii maaba ikwe (*doo*) g*a*gwedjimaat newe makooNson,

"aaniis*h*, ggii shamigoowaa na miinawaa wiiyaas dibikoong *o*wo nenibozhoo.",

d*oo* inaadigenon sa.

"eN*he*N."
"kina go ggii gidaanaawaa."
"kaa*wiin*, ngii shkonaan genii*n*.",

(*doo*) kida sa giiyeN *o*wo bezhik m*a*kooNs.

"mii go genii*n*, giimooch genii*n* gwodji ngii g*a*kidoon banggii iwi.",

(*doo*) kidawidik sa maaba gewii*n* bezhik. miidash giiyeN gii inaat maaba ikwe newe e niidjaanisot newe,

"togo*wa dash* go naadik iwi gaa shkondami *y*ek.",

d*oo* inaadigenon sa.

"ganabach go maaba newe akiweziiNon nenibozhoo gii oonisaadigenon.",

"Do not eat up all of the meat this evening. Secretly hide some of the meat he will feed you tonight,"

the cubs must have been told by their mother.

"Okay."

Well, sometime during the night, after the adult bears were sound asleep, again Nenibozhoo untied his bag. He again ate some more bear meat and sausage he had made. He also cut off small pieces of the sausage for the bear cubs to eat. However, the bear cubs did not eat up all the sausage that Nenibozhoo had given to them. Because that is what their mother had told them to do, not to eat it all, but to save some of it for her to see what kind of meat it was. Also, this female bear suspected something was amiss concerning this man, Nenibozhoo.

So then, when Nenibozhoo left for one of his journeys to see the world the next morning, the mother of the cubs asked them,

"Well, did Nenibozhoo feed you some meat last night?"

she must have asked them.

"Yes."
"Did you eat all of it?"
"No, I saved some of it also,"

said this one bear cub.

"Me too, I secretly hid a little bit of it,"

the other bear cub must have uttered. So then the female bear, the mother of these two little cubs told them to,

"Go get that little bit that you saved, that you did not eat up."

she must have told her cubs.

"I suspect that this Nenibozhoo must have gone and killed the old man bear,"

(*doo*) kida sa iidik maaba ikwe. aaniish, mii maaba ikwe newe ooson. mii*da*sh giiyeN gwonda gwiiwizeNsak gii biidoowaat iwi *n*ayii makwa nagazh. gii waabidang maaba ikwe iwi.

"giyegeti, makwa wiiyaas sa maanda.",

(*doo*) kida *da*sh giiyeN. mii giiyeN go zhaazhago maaba ikwe gaa gichi mowit.

"mii go giyegeti maaba nenibozhoo newe akiweziiNon iidik gii oonisaat.",

(*doo*) kida giiyeN.
aaniish, gwonda *da*sh m*a*kwak (*doo*) gosaawaan ninda nenibozhoon.

"aaniish gonaa ge naapin*aa* yinggoba*n*.",

(*doo*) kidawok *da*sh iidik gonaa (*doo*) maawondjidiwaat gonaa gewiinawaa gonaa e nchiwaat. (*doo*) denchiwok go iidik gewiinawaa gwonda m*a*kwak.

"gaa*wiin* sa wiyii go maaba gdaa g*a*shkiyaasiinaa*n* gegoo ji doodawa*a* *yaa*ng nenibozhoo.",

(*doo*) kida *da*sh giiyeN maaba bezhik.

"gaa*wiin* go gegoo ge zhig*a*shki yinggoba*n* go, aapidji go madjiyaawosh maaba.",

(*doo*) kidawidik sa maaba gaa nitamigiigidat makwa. bezhik *da*sh giiyeN go miinawaa owo gii giigida makwa,

"ngii gikendaan iwi niyii ge zhichigaandiba*n* maaba ji aazhidowaa *y*ing.",

(*doo*) kidawidik sa.

"aaniish, gdaa dibaadjim sa.",

(*doo*) inaadik sa maaba e kidat iwi.

"aa*niish*, mikomiing sa oshkigibading, p*a*kowaakod gga wepidaana*an*."

this female bear supposedly said. Well, this female bear was the daughter of that old man bear. So then these young boys, the bear cubs, brought out the bear meat sausage. Then the woman bear saw it and recognized it.

> "This is definitely bear meat,"

was what she uttered. Then this female bear broke down sobbing uncontrollably.

> "Oh that Nenibozhoo, he definitely went and killed that old man bear, my dad,"

sobbed the female bear.

Well, these bears are all afraid of this trickster called Nenibozhoo, as he had some spiritual powers.

> "What harm could we cause on him, personally?"

they asked one another as they had gathered to meet among themselves to discuss this situation. There were a sufficient number of these bears in this area, they were a sizeable group.

> "There is nothing we can do to harm this one called Nenibozhoo,"

one of the bears volunteered.

> "There is no way to harm him as he is a powerful being,"

continued this first bear to speak. So then another bear got up to speak and he said,

> "I know what we can do to get back at Nenibozhoo for what he has done to us,"

is what this other bear uttered.

> "Well, speak your piece then and tell us how,"

this bear is probably told by the others.

> "Well, when the lake first freezes over, and the ice is nice and smooth, we will play by hitting a ball with sticks."

zhinda gonaa nonggom e zhooshkowaadedjik gonaa pakowaakod e bimiwepidanggik.

"nayiin dash gga nakaazanaanan, bogomaaganan.",

(*doo*) kidawidik sa maaba.

"oshkigibading go, e piichi gonaadjiwong go mikom, mii iwi pii ji digowok iwi, ji tawong owo nenibozhoo. gewiin gonaa e nchit, gegiinawin e nchi ying. aaniish, g*doo* denchimin go.",

(*doo*) kidawidik sa maaba gaagidat.

"miidash go maanda pii go besha go (*doo*) niyaa ying, mii njida go newe shiimeNon ji wepidawaa *ying*. aaniish, wii damino go gewiin aabidek owo.",

(*doo*) kida giiyeN.

mii owo jiibayaaboos e inint, mii owo nenibozhoo shiimeNon. gii nitaa (*doo*) nigamo giiyeN go maaba oshkinowe. aapidji giiyeN go (*doo*) gonaadjiwi. kina giiyeN gii bazindaawigoon bemaadizindjin (*doo*) nigamot. miidash iwi iidik gwonda makwak gaa inendamowaat,

"mii sa maaba ge nisaa *yinggit*."

aaniish, gaawiin maamdaa nenibozhoo, madjiyaawosh. miidash go gii giizhaakonaawaat iwi.

"mii iwi pii, iwi pakowaakod (*doo*) wepidam *ying* mikomiing, mii iwi pii ji nisaa *yinggit* maaba nenibozhoo shiimeNon.",

(*doo*) kidawok iidik.

"nahaaw."

aaniish, noomag dash go maanda go, gimaapii go iidik (*doo*) nikisinaak, mii gii gibading maanda gichigomi zhewe e ndaawaat. giyegeti go gii gonaadjiwon go iwi mikom iidik. miidash giiyeN wii daminowaat maanda pakowaakod, wii wepidamowaat mikomiing. mii gaye zhaazhigo gii giizhaakonigewok waa zhichigewaat. taahaa, giyegeti giiyeN maaba gewiin jiibayaaboos wii damino.

Just like today, those who skate and play hockey on the ice, similar to that.

"We will use curved sticks similar to wooden clubs we use daily."

This bear must have continued to say.

"When the ice first freezes, while it is smooth, that is when we will challenge Nenibozhoo to a game. His group against our group. We do have a sizeable group,"

this bear who had the floor must have said.

"Then while we are playing, as we get close to his younger brother, we will attack him. His younger brother of course, will want to play, too,"

this bear continued.

The one called Jiibayaaboos, that was Nenibozhoo's younger brother. This young man was an accomplished singer. He also was very handsome. When he sang, every living being stopped by to listen to him sing. So, these bears decided that he would be the one to pay for Nenibozhoo's action.

"This is the one we will kill."

Well, they could not bring harm to Nenibozhoo himself, as he was too powerful. So they finalized their plans, and their plan was to take it out on Jiibayaaboos.

"At that time, when we play ball hockey on the ice, that is when we will kill Nenibozhoo's younger brother,"

they supposedly uttered.

"Okay."

Well, the plan was agreed to while it was warm, and it was still a long time before it would get cold, and eventually it got colder and finally the ice formed on the lake near their home. Oh, the ice was so nice and it was very smooth. So then the day arrived when they would play hitting the ball on the ice. Remember, they had agreed to a plan on how they would repay Nenibozhoo for his act. Oh, just as they thought, Jiibayaaboos was chomping at the bit to play ball hockey.

"nahaaw, mii go iwi.",

(*doo*) inendamo*w*ok sa iidik gwonda m*a*kwak.

"mii go ji aashidoowaa ying nenibozhoo. mii go nonggo*m* *o*wo ge wepidawa*a* *y*ing iwi bogomaagan *o*wo jiibayaaboos.",

(*doo*) kidawidigenak sa.

mii giiyeN gaye maaba nenibozhoo gaa*wiin* gegoo bogomaagan. mandj iidik gaye gaa doodamagoweN *naa*nedaa iwi bogomaagan. mii giiyeN bidjiinak gii maadjiibatoot mitigowaakiing, (*doo*) bibaa *na*ndopakweyang iwi bogomaagan waa nakaazat gewii*n* wii wiidookaazat. aaniish, e inaadjimin dash go ko *o*wo nenibozhoo, bezhik go maanda bogomaagan gii nip*a*kweyang, mii giiyeN go gegaa go degiizhitoot, mii gii noonde-aanoowaabidang, gwodji miinawaa gii pagadang iwi. mii miinawaa bezhik (*doo*) ni*na*ndowaabidang gwodji gonaa iwi bogomaagan ji p*a*kweyanggoba*n*. wiikaa *d*ash giiyeN baamaa*mpii* gii m*a*kaan gonaa, iwi gonaa waa nakaazat iidik, gaa minowaabidang sa gonaa. mii gii wewiiptaat iidik, gii zhitoot iwi bogomaagan.

mii*d*ash gii nim*a*daabiit, zhaazhag*o* giiyeN gonaa shkwaakomigodinigoba*n* wodi degoshing mikomiing. gaa*wiin* giiyeN go wiya (*doo*) waabimaasiin go gwodji go. anish*aa* dash giiyeN gonaa wodi (*doo*) bibaa naaniibowit mikomiing, taaya, gii maaminanaamidaanan giiyeN wiindjisan (*doo*) mitatenik. mii iidik gii daapinang newe. taaya giiyeN, mii newe wiindjisan *o*wo jiibayaaboos gaa inin*d*, mii zhaazhago gwonda m*a*kwak newe gii nisaawaat. taaya, *geget* sa *g*onaa shkendam *o*wo nenibozhoo, wiikaaneNon gii nisint.

mii*d*ash giiyeN gii bibaa modemod, (*doo*) sadaawendang gonaa. e niniiwigonigadinik giiyeN gonaa, ngoding gonaa (*doo*) modemot gonaa (*doo*) *b*imoset, mii giiyeN gii biganoonigot newe jiibayaabooson.

"aaniish e *o*onji mowi yin, nsayeN.",

doo igoodigenon dash.

"giyaabi sa wiyii niin n*doo* bimaadiz.",

"Okay, this is it,"

the bears collectively must have thought.

"We will now repay Nenibozhoo for killing the old man bear. The one we will attack with these curved sticks, these clubs is Jiibayaaboos,"

they must have said to one another.

For whatever reason, Nenibozhoo did not have a stick to play ball hockey with. It is a mystery as to what he had done with his curved stick, everyone else had theirs. So he now realized that he did not have a stick to play with, thus he quickly ran into the woods to look for a stick that he could use to play ball hockey. And as the stories about Nenibozhoo go, he quickly found a suitable stick that he cut down, and as he was almost finished fashioning it into a useable stick to play ball hockey with, he did not like it for some reason and he threw this stick away, which he had almost finished. Then he began to look for another tree to fashion his stick out of. It took him a long time to finally find one he was happy with, one that he liked the looks of and the feel of so that he would use it to play ball hockey. It took him a long time. So he quickly whittled it down and shaved it down so that it would be useable in playing ball hockey.

Then he set out, back down toward the lake, and when he got to the ice where the game was to be, the game had finished, there was no one around. He did not see anyone around the area. So he was just walking around the ice where the game had taken place, looking around and [probably pretending he was playing], as he looked around, he noticed something, and he saw human hair in several different places on the ice. He picked up the strands of hair he had seen on the ice. Oh my, this was the hair of his younger sibling, the one called Jiibayaaboos, the bears had already killed him. And Nenibozhoo was overcome and shaken with grief because his younger brother had been killed.

So then, he went around crying uncontrollably, this was how he expressed his sadness for the loss of a loved one. He just went around crying uncontrollably. Then on the fourth day as he was walking around still crying, his younger brother Jiibayaaboos spoke to him.

"Why are you crying, my older brother?"

he must have been asked by his younger brother.

"I am still living,"

(*doo*) kidawon giiyeN.

"gaawii*n* giigii*n* g*doo* bimaadizisii.",

d*oo* inaan *da*sh giiyeN maaba nenibozhoo.

"ggii nisigoo sa nayiinawi*nd*, wodi p*a*kowaakod gaa danakamigak. mii wodi gaa t*a*pinigoo yin."
"n*doo* bimaadiz sa go.",

d*oo* igoon *da*sh giiyeN newe shiimeNon.

"gaawii*n* wiyii, gaawii*n* giinawi*nt* bimaadiziwin e yaam*aa* *y*ing giyaabi gdoo *y*aaziin.",

d*oo* inaan *da*sh iidik.

"p*a*kaan sa bimaadiziwin gd*oo* *y*aan. aanii gonaa ge gii zhiwebak iwi, gwonda ge ninibodjik, neyaap miinawaa ji bipskaabiiwaat zhinda akiing ji bibimaadiziwaat. gaa*wiin* sa go wiikaa daa zhiweb*a*sinoo *i*wi. gga maajaa sa.",

d*oo* inaadigenon *da*sh maaba nenibozhoo newe shiimeNon. gaawii*n* (*doo*) waabimaasiin. aaniish, gaawii*n* maanda bimaadiziwin giyaabi *o*wo d*oo* *y*aaziin, p*a*kaan bimaadiziwin.

"maanda sa nshiimeN, gga zhaa, epanggishimok. ge nizhaawaat baamaa*mpii* anishinaabek ge ninibodjik. miikan gga nizhitoon ge nizhaa yin, gga niwaabazhigaakowaak gewe mitigook. mii wodi ge tanamaazi yin gegii*n*. mii wodi kina anishinaabek baamaa*mpii* ge bizhaawaat. nahaaw, maajaan dash, gga ninigam bekish. gga bazindawin."

aaniish, mii sa jiibayaaboos (*doo*) maajaat. epanggishimok (*doo*) zhaa.
maanda dash mii gaa ninaw*a*ng e nimaajaat. nga goji nigam.

"maanoo niin na, niin nga maajaa.
maanoo niin na, niin nga maajaa.
*nin*ggaabiiwinooning, niin nga nizhaa."

his younger brother said to him.

"You are not alive,"

Nenibozhoo must have responded to his younger brother.

"You were killed while you were playing ball hockey. That is where you died."
"Oh, but I am still alive,"

Nenibozhoo is told by his younger brother.

"The type of life we have here on earth is not the life that you now have,"

he must have said to his younger brother.

"You have a different kind of life. How can it be that those who will die in the future come back to life and be living like we do here on earth. That would never happen. Okay, you will leave this place now,"

Nenibozhoo must have said to his younger brother. He does not see him. The reason is, Jiibayaaboos no longer has this life form, he has a different form of life.

"My younger brother, you will go toward the western doorway. This is the direction the spirits of the Anishinaabe people will go when they die. You will blaze a trail as you go, you will mark the trees along the way so that those who will follow will know the way. That is where you will sing your songs of beauty. That is where all of the Anishinaabe people will come to when they die. Okay, leave now, and sing your song as you go. I will listen to you sing as you go away."

Well, then Jiibayaaboos left. He was going toward the west.

This is the song he sang as he went. I will attempt to sing it.

"Maanoo niin na, niin nga maajaa.
Maanoo niin na, niin nga maajaa.
Ninggaabiiwinooning, niin nga nizhaa."

aaniish, mii sa jiibayaaboos gii maajaat. mii sa nenibozhoo gii boonishkendang. aaniish mii sa e kowaak maanda n*do* dibaadjimowin. gichi miigwech gaa bazindawa yek.

[*Another ending to this story follows.*]

mii sa jiibayaaboos gii maajaat. nenibozhoo giiyeN gii bazindawaan newe shiimeNon (*doo*) nidebitaawigozinit. jichkana giiyeN gii gichi bigomaanimodinik, dibishkoo *d*ash giiyeN gonaa wiya (*e*) shkendang gonaa, mii giiyeN gaa nowe*w*ek maanda mitigowaaki, bineshiiNik, wesiiNik. mii*d*ash giiyeN gaa boonaanimodinik maaba nenibozhoo, gaawii*n* giiyeN giyaabi gii noondawaasiin newe shiimeNon. miidash iwi gii boonendang, gaa*wiin* giiyeN giyaabi gii shkendazii. e zhiyaapa*n* gonaa gii zhiyaa. miinawaa iwi wodi gewe jiib*a*yag e ninaagidowaat maanda miikan, *n*ayii giiyeN temigat zhewe, *oo*demin. mii gwonda giiyeN anishinaabek e ninibodjik e nimiijiwaat ji bibowaa nidagoshiniwaat zhewe.

aaniish, mii sa nenibozhoo gii boonendang. gaa*wiin* giiyeN giyaabi gii shkendazii. aaniish, mii sa e kowaak maanda n*do* dibaadjimowin. gichi miigwech gaa bazindaw*a* yek.

So then, Jiibayaaboos has left this world. Now, Nenibozhoo has stopped grieving for his brother. Well that is the length of my story. Thank you very much for listening to me.

[Another ending to the story follows.]

And so Jiibayaaboos has left this world. Nenibozhoo listened to his younger brother singing as he went away. Suddenly there was a gust of wind that came up, and the sound it made, reminded Nenibozhoo of the troubles one goes through when one is grieving, it was a mixture of noises, birds, animals, the forest, and other such noises. Then when this wind died down, that is when Nenibozhoo no longer heard his brother singing off in the distance. That is when he no longer grieved, he felt better. He was back to his normal self. And this road the spirits follow, there is a big strawberry somewhere along the way. This is what the spirits eat on their journey to the western door, to the west.

And so, Nenibozhoo quit grieving. He no longer grieved. Well, that is the end of my story. Thank you very much for listening to me.

· PART 2 ·

LEGENDS AND CULTURAL STORIES

bizhiw gaa zhiwebazipa*n* gii aandoodegozit

aaniish, mii sa giiyeN gii daat *o*wo, yaawaa bizhiw, gwodji gonaa megowe mitigowaaki. miidash wodi gimaapii giiyeN gaa zhi-aandoodegozit. pakoweyan giiyeN newe gaa yaawaadjin, gaa wiigwaamidjin, pakowe gaa inin*t*. miidash wodi gii bimoset, *n*iyiing, megowe mitigowaaki, *o*wo sa bizhiw, mii*da*sh maaba, yaawaa, gaa zhikowaat newe, waaboozooN.

"yaa-aa, bizhiw iidik yaandoodegozit.",

gii inendam *da*sh giiyeN. mii*da*sh wodi niigaan wodi gii nipatoot *o*wo, aagowidaaki, miidash giiyeN wodi gii niniimit.

"bizhiw, nindaa naagaanaa,
bizhiw, nindaa naagaanaa,
bizhiw, nindaa naagaanaa."

(*doo*) kida *da*sh giiyeN, *o*wo sa yaawaa, waaboozooN. aapidji giiyeN go gichi niimi.

mii*da*sh giiyeN maaba, yaawaa, bizhiw gii yaat, (*doo*) noondawaat newe (*doo*) naaminidjin, (*doo*) nigamonit. miidash wodi gii nizaagewet, waaboozooNon giiyeN gii gichi naaniimiwon, miidash iwi (*doo*) gichi nigamonit.

"bizhiw, nindaa naagaanaa,
bizhiw, nindaa naagaanaa,
bizhiw, nindaa naagaanaa.",

(*doo*) kida dash giiyeN *o*wo yaawaa waaboozooN. mii iidik *o*wo yaawaa, bizhiw gii nimaajaat. ziibiiweN *da*sh giiyeN iwi midjiwoni zhewe, gichi ziibiiweN go. mitig dash giiyeN (*doo*) takamaakoshin, miidash giiyeN zhinda gii nibimoset *o*wo bizhiw, (*doo*) nibimoset. miidash (*doo*) naabit wodi nibiing, midjiwonik ziibiiweN, mii*da*sh (*doo*) naabit wodi, geget sa giiyeN gonaa (*doo*) mowiniinggowe, aapidji giiyeN go (*doo*) mowiniinggowe.

"niin na gonaa *o*wo, niin na gonaa *o*wo waaboozooN nd*oo* ik iwi e zhinaagozi yaaN.",

gii kida dash giiyeN. aapidji giiyeN (*doo*) mowiniinggowe *o*wo bizhiw.

This Is What Happened to the Lynx When He Moved

Well, the one called the lynx supposedly resided somewhere in the forest. So this is about the time he moved to another location. He used bulrushes to make his home. So while he was walking through the forest, the hare came across his trail.

"Oh my! I take it that the lynx is moving,"

the hare supposedly thought to himself. So he ran on ahead and as he got over the next hill, he began to dance.

"Bizhiw, nindaa naagaanaa,
Bizhiw, nindaa naagaanaa,
Bizhiw, nindaa naagaanaa,"

supposedly sang the hare. Apparently he was dancing very fast as well.

Then the lynx heard the hare singing and dancing. Then as he appeared over the hill, he saw the hare dancing and also the hare was singing very loud.

"Bizhiw, nindaa naagaanaa,
Bizhiw, nindaa naagaanaa,
Bizhiw, nindaa naagaanaa,"

the hare supposedly sang. However, the lynx kept on going as he paid no attention to the hare. It just so happened that there was a rather large stream flowing through the area they were near, and there was this log that had fallen across this stream, so the lynx walked across the stream on this log. He happened to look down at the water below as he walked across the stream on the log, and he saw a reflection of his face and he saw that he had very, very watery eyes.

"That hare was talking about the way I look,"

the lynx apparently said to himself. The lynx's eyes were very watery and his face was wet.

mii iidik miinawaa wodi gwodji (doo) nizhaat owo, miinawaa wodi gii niwaabidang ziibiiweNs. miidash owo yaawaa, owo sa waaboozooN miinawaa wodi (doo) madwe nigamot, niyiing, aazhoodaaki. gii nakweshkawaan sa go newe yaawaan, miidash giiyeN e inaat owo bizhiw,

"aanipiish gdoo iizhaa.",

doo inaan sa giiyeN.

"mowiniinggowe oodenaang ndoo zhaa.",

(doo) kida sa giiyeN owo yaawaa, waaboozooN. mii go miinawaa wodi gwodji gii nipatoot, miinawaa wodi (doo) madwe nigamot owo waaboozooN.

"bizhiw, nindaa naagaanaa,
bizhiw, nindaa naagaanaa.",

(doo) kida dash giiyeN, (doo) nayam, (doo) nigamo owo, niimi dash. maanda dash e pagizat, (doo) niimit, waaboozooN. miidash maaba gwodji miinawaa gii nipatoot, owo yaawaa waaboozooN.

miidash wodi miinawaa ziibi gii niwaabidang owo bizhiw (doo) bimoomaat, yaawaan, pakoweyan. (doo) aandoodegozi. midjiwonik ziibiiweN, mitig takamaakoshin zhewe, miidash wodi e naabit nibiishing naamiyiing e niyaat, mii giiyeN, maanda dash (doo) naabit wodi nibiishing, (doo) ganawaabidang iwi midjiwonik ziibiiNs, aapidji giiyeN go (doo) mowiniinggowe. mandj gonaa gaa zhinaagozigoweN gii mowiniinggowet, owo sa yaawaa bizhiw. miidash iwi gii nishkaadizit.

"niin na gonaa owo ndoo bapogozomik waaboozooN, waaboozooNish.",

(doo) kida giiyeN.

"niin na gonaa ndoo bapogozomik waaboozooNish. giyegeti go nonggom nga nisaa.",

gii kida dash giiyeN. miidash iwi gii bigidjiwebinaat newe do pakoweyan gaa takamiit zhewe, gii bigidjiwebinaat do pakoweyan. gii gidjibowet owo waaboozooN, aapidji giiyeN gii gwetaanibowe waaboozooN, (doo) bimabatoot megowe mitigowaaki. miidash maaba, yaawaa, maaba sa bizhiw, (doo) minaashkowaat newe, wii nisaan newe waaboozooNon, wii nisaan go, (doo) minaashkowaat. miidash maaba, (doo) zegazi dash maaba waaboozooN, ggii gikenimaan wii nisigot newe, yaawaan, bizhiwon.

Then the lynx must have gone elsewhere, and he came across the stream again. Then again, the hare could be heard singing over the next hill. That is when they met each other, and the lynx supposedly asked the hare,

"Where are you going?"

he asked him.

"I am going to mowiniinggowe town,"

the hare apparently replied. So the hare again runs further ahead, and he begins singing again.

"Bizhiw, nindaa naagaanaa,
Bizhiw nindaa naagaanaa,"

is what the hare was singing as he was dancing. He would move like this while he danced, that rabbit. And the hare ran away again to somewhere further ahead.

Then the lynx saw the stream again as he was carrying the bulrushes on his back. Well, he was changing his residence, he was moving elsewhere. The stream was flowing by, and there was this log that lay across the stream. He started to go across again, and he looked down at the water below, and he saw himself again, and his face was all wet from his leaky watery eyes. I, myself, do not know how a lynx with a wet face would look like. So that is when the lynx became angry.

"That hare, that darn hare is making fun of me,"

the lynx apparently said.

"That darn hare is making fun of me. Boy, I definitely will kill him now,"

the lynx supposedly said. So right then and there, the lynx dropped his load of bulrushes as he crossed the stream. The hare took off, he ran as fast as he could go, as he ran away through the forest. So the lynx began to chase the hare as he was going to kill the hare. The hare was now very frightened as the hare knew he would be killed by the lynx.

miidash wodi, (doo) bimabatoot, maanda gaye (doo) ninanakamigaani iwi, miidash go maanda e nipatoot, (doo) nigidaakiiyepatoot waaboozooN, aapidji go gwetaanibizo. mii giiyeN wodi ngoding maanda (e) nizhibimabatoot, mii gii waabidang, niyii, pashkowaanik, dibishkoo gonaa gichigomi gonaa, nibis, nibis iwi gaa waabidang. miidash wodi gii nibigomabatoot wodi besha, niyii dash giiyeN maanda, waabshkoki, miinawaa maanda niyii nibis. miidash giiyeN gaa kidat,

"geget go zhinda niyii, oodena zhinda da te.",

owo sa waaboozooN.

"oodena da te zhinda. niyiin, adaawegamigoon da baatiinadoon miinawaa gichi gowaanaasawin gaye zhinda da digowo, miinawaa niyii shkodejiimaan da bibigomibide.",

(doo) kida sa giiyeN owo waaboozooN.

miidash giiyeN giyegeti zhewe shkodejiimaan gii bibigomibidek gowaanaasawining. gichi gowaanaasawin giiyeN maanda, gii bibigomibide zhewe iwi shkodejiimaan. miidash iwi, (doo) gowaashkondjitaasawok dash giiyeN bemiwidoot gonaa yaawaa, shkodejiimaan. (doo) gowaashkondjitaasawok. aapidji giiyeN go baatiinad.

adaawegamigoon gaye maanda (doo) nizhisinoon wodi. ziiganigegamigoon, miinawaa nayiin adaawegamigoon, wiisiniigamigoon gaye. miidash giiyeN owo, yaawaa, owo gewiin owo yaawaa waaboozooN wodi gii nizhaat, nayiing, gowaanaasawining. (doo) niganawaabimaat newe e nakiindjin. aapidji giiyeN (doo) gichi gowaashkondjitaasiwok e nakiijik. aapidji go (doo) baatiinawok, miinawaa zhewe gaa biyaadjik, niyiing, (doo) gowaashkoniwok shkodejiimaaning.

miidash giiyeN e inendang,

"geget sa gonaa owo nga binisik owo yaawaa bizhiw bidagoshing.",

(doo) inendam giiyeN. miidash zhewe gii aandjinaagozit, owo sa yaawaa waaboozooN. gii aandjinaagowidizat, yaawaa dash giiyeN gaa zhinaagozit, mizhoweN, mizhoweN owo waaboozooN, mii gii aandjinaagozit zhewe sa. aaniish, mii sa giiyeN (doo) minaanaaniibowit gewiin owo waaboozooN, (doo) bibaa waabimaat yaawaan, (e) gowaashkondjitaasawindjin. miidash owo gewiin (doo) nibigomabatoot owo bizhiw iidik, wiikaa gonaa maanda, gii waabimaat yaawaan, (doo) ganawaabimaat yaawaan, (e) gowaashkondjitaasawindjin, zhewe niyiing, jiimaaning. aapidji giiyeN go baatiinawok bemaadizidjik. aaniish, (doo) minaaniibowit gewiin, yaawaa, owo sa yaawaa, mizhoweN. mii zhaazhigo gii mizhoweNwit, owo sa waaboozooN, gii gowekonaagozi.

As the hare ran along, the ground was uneven, as it looked like this, the hare ran up the hill through the forest and he ran as fast as he could go. Then as he ran by this one area, he saw that it was clear of trees, it looked like it was a big lake, or a lake, it was a lake he saw. Then when he got closer to it, he saw it was a marsh and there was a lake there as well. So he apparently said this,

> "There is going to be a town located right here, right now."

It was the hare who said this, and he continued,

> "A town will be here. There will be many stores and there will be a big pier here as well, where the steamboat will arrive."

This is what the hare supposedly said.

Then, it happened, a steamship arrived at the dock located there. This was a very big dock where the steamship landed. There were workers there who were unloading this big steamship. They worked hard at unloading this boat. There were so many things that were being unloaded.

There were stores all in a row. There were bars and stores and also restaurants. Then the hare went to the dock. He was watching the workers unloading the steamship. The workers were busy unloading the steamship. And there were many people who had arrived on the steamship as well, and they were departing the ship.

Then the hare supposedly thought,

> "Oh my goodness, I will be killed by the lynx when he arrives here."

This is what he supposedly thought to himself. So, right then and there, he changed his shape and his looks. He now looked like a rabbit, he changed himself into a rabbit. Now he was standing among the people, as if he was one of them, he stood among them as he watched the workers unloading the steamship. That is about the time the lynx came running onto the scene, of course this was much later, and the lynx saw these people unloading the boat. Apparently there were so many people there. Also there was this rabbit standing around there as well, among the people and it was the new persona of the hare, as he had already changed his appearance.

miidash iwi gii ganawaabimaat, yaawaan, bizhiwon (doo) minandowaabiwon giiyeN zhewe, owo sa yaawaa, waaboozooN, mizhoweN, zhaazhigo gii mizhoweNwi, miidash iwi giiyeN zhago niyaanik, ninaakoshinik owo sa.

"geget sa gonaa ndaa gii bibaa oodetoo."

(doo) inendam giiyeN. gii bibaa zhaat giiyeN wodi niyiing, adaawegamigoon e nizhisininik.

nayiing gii biindiget, ziiganigegamigoong.

"giyegeti, ziiganigegamik na gonaa zhinda e ndigowok.",

(doo) inendam. gii minakwet. miidash maaba gewiin, yaawaa bizhiw (doo) miyaat gowaanaasawining, mii go zhago wii dibikak. miidash maanda gii gagwedowet, bezhik gonaa gii gagwedjimaat, gii gagwedjimaadigenon, endigoweN zhewe owo waaboozooN ji gii dagoshing.

"gaawiin zhinda (doo) nji dagoshisii owo.",

(doo) inaa sa giiyeN owo yaawaa, bizhiw. gaawiin giiyeN wiikaa (doo) waabidaziin zhewe iwi oodena ji digowoninik, miinawaa gowaanaasawin. miidash gii nizhaat wodi, aapidji giiyeN go pakade bizhiw. gii nizhaat wodi, gii nibiindiget niyiing, ziiganigegamigoong. miidash maaba waaboozooN waabimaat newe, aaniish, waabimaan wiyii, wiin dash gaawiin nisadowanaagoosiin. waabimaan newe bizhiwon, aapidji giiyeN (doo) gichi baabaapi, yaawaa waaboozooN. bizhiw bemizhiyaat gewiin, gii biindiget ziiganigegamigoong. gii nandodang iwi niyii, shkodewaaboo ji minakwet. aaniish, mii gaye yaawaa ziiganigenini gii ninimawaat, naagaaNsing. gii minakwet bizhiw.

mii go maanda zhago nidibikak. geget sa gonaa (doo) maamkaadendam. miinawaa wodi gii nizaakowong, zhewe niyiing, ziiganigegamigoong. miidash wodi gii nizhaat miinawaa wodi bezhik niyii, adaawegamik, gaye wodi gii waabidaan. gii mininaabit yaawaa bizhiw, aapidji giiyeN (doo) gonaadjiwonini iwi adaawegamik. miidash miinawaa gii nizaakowong. miidash iwi shanggegamik, aapidji giiyeN go pakade, shanggegamik gii nibiindiget. miidash iwi miinawaa gii nandodang wii wiisinit. gii shamin miinawaa zhewe. aapidji giiyeN go (doo) gonaadjiwiwok ikwewizeNsak zhewe bemiiwizadjik niyiing, shanggegamigoong. aapidji giiyeN go (doo) gonaadjiwiwok ikwewizeNsak. miidash iwi gii wiisinit zhewe, gii shamin.

aapidji giiyeN (doo) minodoodawaa owo bizhiw. mii maanda zhaazhigo gii dibikak.

The hare in his new shape watched the lynx as he moved about looking around for someone or something. The hare had already changed his shape into that of a rabbit. It was also getting to be late, it would soon be evening there.

"I think I should go downtown,"

thought the hare who is now the rabbit. So he went to where the stores were located.
The hare, now the rabbit, went into a saloon.

"Oh wow! There is a saloon here,"

he supposedly thought. He had a drink. And at the same time, the lynx was down at the dock, and it was getting to be very dark, it was on into the night. So the lynx must have asked someone if a hare had shown up there.

"No one of that description has arrived here,"

the lynx was apparently told. The lynx did not recall ever seeing this town with the great big pier around here before. The lynx then went toward town and he apparently was very hungry. So he went to the saloon. Of course the hare in his new form was in there and he sees the lynx, and the lynx does not know it is the hare in his new shape. So the hare, now the rabbit, was enjoying himself and he was laughing heartily. So the lynx was by this saloon and then he enters it. The lynx ordered a shot of whiskey for himself to drink. So the bartender gave him some whiskey in a small shot glass. The lynx drank.

It was now already dark. The lynx was still puzzled. The lynx then left the saloon. Then when he got outside, he saw this store. The lynx was looking around this store, and this store was very fancy. He then exited this fancy store. As he was very hungry, because he had not eaten all day, he went into the restaurant. Then he placed his order. His meal was served to him shortly. Oh, the waitresses who were working in the restaurant were very pretty young women. These young women were so beautiful. The lynx ate his meal that had been served to him by the waitress.

The lynx was treated royally. It was now night time.

"aanipiish gonaa iidik ji nibaa yaaN.",

(doo) inendam giiyeN.

"kaawiin na zhinda gibeshiigamik (doo) digowosanoo.",

(doo) kida sa giiyeN.

"eN, (doo) digowomigat go. mii go zhinda bezhik maanda wiigwaam, mii go zhewe e ndigowok."

mii go gii biindiget zhewe, niyiing, zhewe sa wiigwaaming, iwi bezhik wiigwaam. gii biindiget zhewe, yaawaa bizhiw. miidash iwi, aapidji giiyeN (doo) baatiinawon ikwewon zhewe e yaanidjin, aapidji giiyeN go. (doo) madwewechigewon gaye.

"geget sa gonaa zhinda (doo) minowaanigoziwok e yaadjik.",

(doo) inendam giiyeN. miidash giiyeN gii gagwedowet,

"gaawiin na wiyii, zhinda, niyii wiya zhinda gdaa daapinaasiiwaa ji gibeshid, ji nibaat.",

(doo) kida sa giiyeN bizhiw.

"eN, daa nibaa go wiya."

miidash giiyeN newe ikwewizeNson,

"ndoo yaan go niyii aachkinigan ji nibaa yimban.",

doo igoon giiyeN. aaniish, miidash giiyeN gii niwiidjiiwaat.

"mii sa zhinda."

eta giiyeN go (doo) gonaadjiwon aachkinigan, nibaagan gaye, aapidji go (doo) gonaadjiwon.

"mii sa zhinda ji nibaa yin."

"Where will I sleep tonight?"

the lynx thought to himself.

"Is there an inn nearby?"

he apparently asked.

"Oh, yes. There is an inn here. The inn is just next door."

So the lynx enters the building next door. The lynx entered the building. He notices that there are so many women inside the inn, so very many people. There was also loud music being played by the people in the inn.

"Boy, these people here know how to have fun,"

he thought. Then he asked,

"Would you have room for another person to stay for one night, just a room for sleeping?"

the lynx supposedly asked.

"Sure, we have a place where someone could sleep."

Then it was a young woman who said this to the lynx,

"I have a room where you can sleep."

So the lynx went with the young woman to the room.

"Here it is."

Oh, the room was so nicely decorated and the bed was very pretty and looked so comfortable.

"You will sleep here."

miidash giiyeN, aaniish mii go mandj gonaa e zhiwogoweN owo bizhiw, mii go waa zhiwiishimot zhewe gonaadjiwoninik nibaagan, miidash gii,

> "gga giiskoniye sa.",

doo igoon giiyeN.

> "gaawiin maamdaa.",

doo inaan giiyeN.

> "mii go gonaa ge zhinibaa yaaN."
> "aanipiish giin, ji nibaa yin.",

doo igoon sa giiyeN miinawaa newe ikwewizeNson.

> "mii sa go zhinda geniin ji nibaa yaaN."

miidash go giiyeN gii wiishimot owo bizhiw, aapidji giiyeN go (doo) yekozi, gii nibaat zhewe. mii go iidik maaba ikwewizeNs zhewe gii wiishimot, (doo) nibaat, (doo) wiipemaat newe bizhiwon.

aaniish, mii iidik (doo) gichi nibaat maaba bizhiw. miidash giiyeN gii yaat, gimaapii giiyeN (doo) goshkozi, owo sa bizhiw, aapidji giiyeN go (doo) biinggedji. aapidji giiyeN go (doo) kisinaani. miidash iidik maaba, niyiing, gii wiishimot megowe waabshkoki. miidash giiyeN go newe niyiin miishkoon maanda gaa zadjiinanggin iidik, mii giiyeN owo ikwewizeNs, miishkoon maanda gii zadjiinang.

> "geget sa gonaa ndoo gwetaaninigaawik owo madji waaboozooNish.",

(doo) kida dash giiyeN.

> "aapidji ndoo nigaawik. gegaa zhinda agowodji yaaN, gegaa nibow yaaN, agowodji yaaN."

gii bizagowiit owo bizhiw, gaawiin gegoo oodena. aanowi (doo) mininaabit, mii go waabang, aanowi go (doo) mininaabit, gaawiin gegoo oodena. gaawiin go gegoo. mii go eta waabshkoki yaabidang. mii sa giiyeN gii maajaat, gii maajaat owo bizhiw. dibi gaye giiyeN iidik gii webinaagoweN, yaawaan, pakoweyan, (doo) aandoodegozit.

aapidji giiyeN go (doo) shkendam bizhiw,

So then, the lynx was just going to get right into the bed, and it is not known how he was dressed, but he was just going to jump right into the nice clean bed.

"Take off your clothes,"

the young woman said to the lynx.

"I cannot,"

the lynx supposedly replies to the young woman.

"I will just sleep the way I am dressed."
"Where will you be sleeping?"

the young woman asks the lynx again.

"Well, I will sleep here also."

So the lynx laid down, as he was very tired from running all day, he fell asleep quickly. Apparently this young woman laid down in the bed and she slept with the lynx.

And so, the lynx was sound asleep. Then, when he finally awakened, he was shivering from being cold. It was very, very cold where he was sleeping. Apparently this lynx had laid down in the marsh. As for what he thought was the young woman, all he was holding onto was a handful of grasses and weeds.

"Oh, that darn hare sure made a fool of me,"

the lynx supposedly said.

"He really mistreated me. I almost froze to death here."

The lynx arose, and there was no town. He looked around and it was now getting to be morning, and he tried to look for the town, but there was no town to be seen. Nothing. All he could see was the marsh around him. Then, the lynx started off. He did not know where he had dropped the bulrushes he was carrying as he was in the process of moving his home to a new location.

The lynx was feeling very sorry for himself.

"geget sa gonaa ndoo nigaawik madji waaboozooNish, nechiiwonaagozit.",

(*doo*) kida sa giiyeN owo bizhiw. mii sa gii maajaat. dibi gonaa e zhaagoweN gonaa. mii iwi, mii sa e koozid ndo aansookaan.

binoodjiiNon gii gimoodipan owo makwa

aaniish, mii sa giiyeN, yaawaak, anishinaabek gonaa, odaawaak gonaa, maanpii go maanda yaawaak go gwonda odaawaak maanda gaa zhiwebazidjik, zhinda gaa danakiidjik gichi zhaazhago. miidash iwi gii yaawaat gwonda binoodjiiNik, e gaachiiwidjik go, bemi-oshkidaminodjik gonaa gwodjiing. mii gwonda, (*doo*) bibaa daminowaat iidik, gwodji gonaa (*e*) daawaat gewe anishinaabek. miidash iwi, maaba makwa iidik gewiin (*doo*) bibaa yaat gonaa megowe mitigowaaki, gaa zhiwaabimaat binoodjiiNon (*doo*) bibaa daminonit. gegoo gonaa maanda (*doo*) bibaa bimiikodaanaawaa, ginimaa gaye waaskoneNsan, gewe sa binoodjiiNik. miidash giiyeN maaba makwa gaa zhizhaat wodi.

binoodjiiNik, (*doo*) gaachiiwiwok gonaa gwonda, gaaNwaaN gonaa bebaa bimosedjik gonaa (*doo*) aawok gwonda binoodjiiNik. gii zhaat wodi dash (*doo*) yaanit newe. dibishkoo gonaa wiin gonaa niidjaaniseNwit mii gaa zhiwaabimaat. gaawiin gaye gosagosiin. mii go e zhiminowaabimigod gewiin. mandj gaye gonaa e nowegoweN owo makwa, (*doo*) danaandigidoong gewiin owo makwa (*e*) binjibaat. yaawaak, zhewe gewiin niidjaaniseNon (*doo*) yaawon niizh. miidash giiyeN gii maadjiinaat newe. maanda go gii nininaat go newe sa yaawaan anishinaabeNson, maanda go gii nininaat. miidash giiyeN iidik gimaapii gii dagoshiniwaat e ndaawaat gewe makwak. gichi mitigoong, (*doo*) wiimbanakozi giiyeN owo mitig. miidash wodi gii biindiganaat wodi. mii giiyeN gewe binoodjiiNik, makooNsak gewe, mii wodi dash (*doo*) yaawaat, (*doo*) biinaanit newe, oosowaan newe baanaadjin binoodjiiNon, miinawaa ikwe, yaawaa owo makwa, (*doo*) yaa giiyeN go gewiin zhewe. aapidji giiyeN go (*doo*) minoyaawon go newe, newe sa (*doo*) gimoodit owo, owo sa yaabe makwa, newe yaawaan binoodjiiNon, anishinaabeNson.

aaniish, wiiba sa gonaa iidik gonaa, aapidji gonaa gaa nigadiziwaat gewe sa anishinaabeNsak, odaawaaNsak. bezhik giiyeN ikwewizeNs miinawaa bezhik gwiiwizeNs. miidash gii wiidookawaawaat ko newe. mii giiyeN go gewiinawaa, besha go, (*doo*) migaawaa giiyeN owo mitig, gegopii giiyeN go gewiinawaa gewe yaawaak anishinaabeNsak, (*doo*) gashkitoowok maanda wii doodamoowaat, wii bidagowiiziiwaat zhewe. (*doo*) zaagadjipatoowaat giiyeN ko gewe makooNsak, (*doo*) wiidookawaawaat newe sa, yaawaan anishinaabe binoodjiiNon, (*doo*) wiidookawaawaat.

"Oh that darn ugly hare really made a fool of me,"

the lynx supposedly uttered. So he left. The lynx had no idea where he was going to go.

That is the end of my story.

When the Bear Stole the Children

Well, there were these Anishinaabe people, these Ottawa people that this happened to, and they have lived and worked the land in this area for many, many years. There were these two children who were very young and small and they were just beginning to play around outside. These children were playing about near their home. Then there was this bear who happened to be in the area, but in the forest, and he saw these children playing around outside of the home. The children were just exploring, looking at the flowers and plants that grew in the area. So this bear approached the children.

These were young children, they were barely able to walk. So this bear approaches them. He must have looked upon them as if they were his own cubs. And these children were not afraid of the bear. The children looked upon the bear as if he was one of their parents. It is not known what language the bear speaks when talking to other bears. He had two bear cubs back in his den already. So he picked up the children and carried them away. Then they arrived at the bear's home, the den. The den was in a big hollow tree. The bear took the children into the den. And the bear cubs along with their mother, the female bear, were already in the den when the male bear brought the Anishinaabe children into the den. The children fit right in with the bear family, as if they were with their own, even though the male bear had stolen the children.

Well, it took the Anishinaabe children very little time to get used to the way the bears live. One of the children was a girl and the other one was a boy. The children and the bear cubs played with each other. The entrance to the hollow tree was rather large, and the Anishinaabe children soon were able to climb up the tree, just like the bears. The bear cubs and the children would run outside of the den and they would play with each other outside of the den.

gichi gonesh dash gonaa maanda zhewe gii yaadigenak. mii*dash* *n*iyii gwonda gii w*o*naachaawaat gwonda sa e niidjaanisodjik newe, newe sa niidjaaniseNwaan gewe sa *o*daawaaNsak, (*doo*) *w*onaachaawaat, aanowi (*doo*) nandonewe*w*aat. gaa*wiin* sa giiyeN gwodji (*doo*) makawaasiiwaan. gimaapii iidik, aaniish, gii baatiin*a*wok gewe, gegoo e w*o*naadizidjik nendogikenimaadjik gegoo wiya e zhiwebazidjik, gii nookiiwaat wii nandogikenimind.

"(*doo*) yaawok sa go gewe gniidjaaniseNwaak,"

gii igoowaan dash, yaawaa dash maaba jaas*a*kiit, maaba sa anishinaabe gonaa gaa noonind.

"(*doo*) yaawok, aapidji go (*doo*) minoyaawok gewe gniidjaaniseNwaak. mii sa *o*wo gaa gimoodimin *y*ek, makwa."

mii iwi, niidjaaniseNwaan. mii*dash* giiyeN ngoding, mandj gonaa minik gaa yaawaagoweN sa go gewe binoodjiiNik, mbe sa giiyeN gonaa *dash* (*doo*) yaakoow*o*ziwok gewe binoodjiiNik.

"ngoding gonaa gga waabimaawaak gewe gniidjaaniseNwaak.",

gii inaawok dash gewe e niidjaanisodjik newe.

"ngoding gonaa gga waabimaawaak."

miidash iidik *o*wo wodi *dash* (*doo*) yaawaat gonaa zhewe gewe, (*doo*) maamaajaawok *d*ash giiyeN gwonda yaawaak, gwonda sa, (*doo*) *b*ibaa *n*andoziwaat gonaa, (*doo*) *b*ibaa nandogimoodiwaat gonaa gitigaaning, gewe sa yaawaak m*a*kwak, gichi m*a*kwak. mii*dash* giiyeN ngoding gii aapidendit *o*wo yaawaa, ikwe yaawaa, *o*wo makwa, (*doo*) aapidendi. mii*dash* giiyeN e zhigowiinonenimaawaat gwonda binoodjiiNik newe sa gashiwaan.

"aanipiish wiyii ngashinaan."
"(*doo*) *b*ibaa nibwaachawe.",

(*doo*) kida sa giiyeN *o*wo yaawaa, yaabe m*a*kwa.

"(*doo*) *b*ibaa nibwaachawe. niiwonigak da, wodi sa go da dagoshin, da p*a*skaabii."

This went on for a long time, as the young children were no longer toddlers. All that time, the Anishinaabe people who had their children stolen from them by the bear kept on looking for their children. They looked everywhere, and they could not find them. So the Anishinaabe parents finally went to a person who had some powers to see things, a seer, and they asked this person to try to find their lost children.

> "Your children are still alive,"

they were told by this person, this was an owner of the shaking tent ritual who they gave tobacco to, to help them to find their children.

> "Your children are living quite comfortably. It was the bear who took your children away from you."

Those were their children. Then later on, it was not known how long the children lived with the bears, but they were now getting taller.

> "You will get to see your children sometime in the future,"

the seer said to them.

> "You will get to see them again."

And where the bears lived, the adult bears would leave the den from time to time to go get food for the young ones to eat, and they would go to the gardens to steal some food. Then this one time the female bear did not return from one of her forays outside of the den. Then the younger ones began to miss their mother, the female bear.

> "Where is our mother?"
> "She is gone visiting,"

the big male bear told the young ones.

> "She is gone visiting. She will come back in four days."

mii iidik maaba sa yaawaa, maaba sa ikwe makwa gii minisind wodi (doo) gimoodit kitigaaning. mandaaminon (doo) gimoodit. gii nisind wodi, anishinaaben gii nisigot. miidash iwi gaa zhiwebaziwaat gewe anishinaabek, giishpin (doo) nisaawaat newe yaawaan makwan, kina go gegoo (doo) minozawaawaat, wii oshkiwiisiniwaat, wii oshkimowaawaat newe makwan. kina go gegoo (doo) miijinaawaa, (doo) dagozaanaawaa, (doo) miijinaawaa. kina go gegoo baashkominisagan, kina go gegoo wendjishing go. anishinaabe gewiin gaa bizhiwiisinit gichi zhaazhago. kina giiyeN gegoo gii dagondaanaawaa, owo zhewe dash (doo) mowaawaat sa newe makwan gaa nisaawaadjin.

miidash niyii giiyeN naawonigak, mii giiyeN gii bibiindiget owo sa, newe sa gashiwaan. aaniindi giiyeN gonaa minik gegoo baadoot. nowonch go gegoo wendjishing miijim. aapidji giiyeN go niibana gegoo (doo) biidoon, baashkominisagan ensa zhinaagok. mii iwi wodi gii mowan, gii minozawind, wodi dash gii mowan, mii iwi gii yaat, iwi gaa dagondamowaawaat gwonda anishinaabek, iwi sa gii mowaawaat newe makwan gaa nisaawaat, miidash maaba, naawonigadinik dash mii maaba nimaajaat, nipaskaabiit, mii giiyeN (doo) shkwaa nibwaachawet, (doo) nipaskaabiit, miidash iwi, kina go gaa dagondamonit gaa mowagodjin, mii kina (doo) maadjiidoon iwi. aaniindi giiyeN gonaa minik gegoo baadoonit newe sa gashiwaan, (doo) dagoshininit gewe binoodjiiNik, gichi aawaak gonaa zhewe. miidash giiyeN iwi ngoding,

"mii maanda gaa naadi yaaN.",

(doo) kida giiyeN owo mindimooyeN makwa.

"mii maanda gaa naadi yaaN."

eta giiyeN makooNsak (doo) gichi wiisiniwok. baashkominisagan, nowonch go gegoo. iwi gaye anishinaabe makooNsak, aapidji giiyeN gonaa, zhago gonaa (doo) aawiwok, (doo) gichi aawiwok gonaa gewe.

miidash iidik iwi ngoding gonaa zhewe dash yaawaat gonaa, kina giiyeN (doo) maajaawok gewe. miinawaa (doo) bibaa nandogimoodiwaat kitigaaning gewe sa yaawaak, makwak, owo mindimooyeN miinawaa owo nini.

miidash giiyeN gwonda gaawiin gii wonendaziinaawaa iwi, gii gimooding go wii [. . .] gwonda sa yaawaak, mii iidik pane go maaba anishinaabe gii nandonewaat go newe, newe sa gii wiindamowind dash yaanit go niyiing, mitigoong (doo) daanit newe makwan gaa gimoodimigoodjin niidjaaniseNwaan. pane go iidik go (doo) nandomaabit go, yaawaa go baashkozigan ginimaa gaye mitigowaabiin, gaawiin sa go wiikaa go anishaa go (doo) bimosesii gwodji, mii go pane go zhiwiid go. mii iidik wodi (doo) nizhaat gonaa, dibi gonaa iidik gonaa, megowe mitigowaaki, waasa giiyeN go, miidash wodi gii waabimaat newe gichi mitigoon. aapidji giiyeN go (doo) miskowanagekobidjigaazawon go. gichi mitig go, (doo) mishiiwi, mishiiwaatig dash owo.

Apparently, this female bear was killed by the Anishinaabe as she was foraging for food in one of the gardens of the Anishinaabe people. She was stealing corn. She was killed by the Anishinaabe. And it was the custom of the Anishinaabe of that time, when they killed a bear, they had a big celebration and a big feast so they cooked many things to eat along with the bear meat. They ate all kinds of food and they cooked many different things, they ate jams and many other good things. All the things the Anishinaabe people ate a long time ago. This is how they feasted when they killed a bear, they made everything that they ate along with the bear meat.

Then on the fourth day, the female bear returns to the den. She brought with her so many food items. She had all kinds of good food with her. She brought all kinds of food with her, jams of different kinds. So this bear apparently brought all the food that the Anishinaabe ate when they celebrated the killing of the bear, this female bear brought all this food back with her after four days. Oh wow, their mother brought home so many good food items, and the children were now quite grown up. Then,

"This is what I went to get,"

said the old female bear.

"This is what I went to get."

Goodness gracious, the bear cubs ate ravenously. They ate all kinds of food and jams. Also the Anishinaabe children who were by now quite older and bigger.

Then this one time, the adult bears left the den again. They were gone to steal food from the gardens of the Anishinaabe people again.

The Anishinaabe parents never forgot that they had their children stolen [...] from them, and this man always was looking for a big tree that might have a bear den in it, as this is what the seer had told them, the children were living in a bear's den that was located in a big tree. He always had his bow and arrow with him when he went anywhere, and he did not just go for a walk, he went looking for his children and he was always prepared in case he found them. He would go far into the woods, and he would keep looking, then this one time, he saw this great big tree. This tree had many claw marks on its trunk, its bark, and it was reddish in color from the claw marks. This was a great big tree and it was starting to get dry as it was also hollow.

mii gosha giiyeN wodi dash naabit, gii yaawon dash giiyeN yaawaan, binoodjiiNon. gichi aawaaNsak gonaa zhago, gii nisadowinawaan dash giiyeN niidjaaniseNwaan gaa wonaachaadjin. mii iidik gii naaskowaat, miidash giiyeN iwi niyaat gonaa, mii giiyeN gaa zhimiigaanigot newe sa niidjaaniseNon owo anishinaabe.

> "gegowa, niin nayiinawind gii niidjaaniseNnim. ngii gimoodimigoo nayiinawin gwiiyaw."

mii iidik maaba gimaapii gii aangowadjaat newe neniizh go. ninda dash yaawaan, giyegeti gonaa makooNsak neyaap giiyeN zhewe gii biindoodepatoowon niyiing, wodi sa e ndaawaat gewe, bagonezit owo gichi mitig, neyaap zhewe gii biindigeyoodepatoowok.

mii sa giiyeN,

> "biwiidjiiwishik. gga maadjiininim e ndaa ying."

giyegeti gosha giiyeN gegoo (doo) zhiyaawok gewe anishinaabe makooNsak. aapidji giiyeN go (doo) nandogaanoowaakogazhiiwok, mii iwi maanda (doo) bidagowiiziibatoowaat zhewe mitigoong. miidash giiyeN gii maadjiinaat, (doo) bimosewaat iidik. aaniish, (doo) baashkozigane, mii go iwi zhewe e aabidak yaawaan, makwan minaashkaagoowaat, mii go wii baashkoziwaat go. mii sa gii webinaat newe sa. miidash giiyeN go bemibigomiwinaat newe niidjaaniseNon. mii gii oomakawaat, gichi waasa gonaa wodi megowe mitigowaaki.

aaniish, mii sa iidik e kowaak ndo dibaadjimowin.

shagi gii pakinaagepan

"yaawaak sa nwii dibaadjimaak, bineshiiNik.", (doo) kidawok gosha ko gonaa debaadjimodjik gonaa. naanigodinong gonaa (doo) gagwedowewok, wegowendik iidik bineshiiN e maamawi gizhiibizogoweN gaa bimaadizit. miidash iwi waa oonji dibaadjimagowaa gwonda bineshiiNik. yaawaa dash giiyeN ogimaa bineshiiN, daanison giiyeN maaba (doo) yaawon bezhik, wii wiidigemaagoninit dash giiyeN doo inenimaan. miidash giiyeN ninda gaa zhinandomaat bineshiiNon. aaniish, mii sa iidik gii wiindamawaat iwi e oonji nandomaat. kina gonaa zhewe gaa bigiiwitaabinit dash yaat, miidash giiyeN e inaat.

Then when the man looked at the entrance of the den, he saw two children. They were now quite big, and he recognized them as his own children who had been lost for some time now. So he approached them, and as he got close to them, the young children tried to fight him.

"Don't, you are my children. You were stolen from me."

Eventually, he was able to win them over and the children quit trying to fight him. And these bear cubs, who were now older as well, they just ran back into the den, through the hole of the tree, they ran into their home.

So then,

"Come with me. I will take you to our home,"

he said to them. Oh, those young children were acting strangely. They had such long nails on their hands and their feet, as they used these to climb up and down the tree. So they left, and they started walking to their home. The man had his weapons with him as he always carried them with him just in case he came across some game that he would shoot at and kill, especially if a bear began to chase after him. So they left the bear cubs back in the den. So he brought his children back home with him. He was able to find his children deep in the forest.

Well, I think that is the end of my story.

The Time When the Blue Heron Won

"I am going to talk about birds," is how the storyteller would usually begin his story. Sometimes, people would ask who was the fastest bird ever to live on the earth. So now I will talk about these birds. There was this chief of the birds who wanted to have his only daughter be married. So he called all the birds to gather around him. He told them why he had called them together. Then when they had all settled and sat around him, he told the birds the following.

> "maanda sa ziitaagani gichigomiing, naawondj (*doo*) gowiinde niyii, minis, bagaanan dash zhewe (*doo*) digowonoon. wegowen *dash* go ge naadigoweN iwi bezhik bagaaneNs ji biidoowit, ge nitami dagoshing, mii owo ge wiidigemaat ninda ndaanison."

mii sa iidik e kidat maaba ogimaa bineshiiN.

aa*n*iish, mii sa giiyeN gwonda bineshiiNik gii gizikewaat. aa*niish*, gewii*n* giiyeN shagi (*doo*) dagoshin.

"maanoo go genii*n* nga wiidjiiwe.",

(*doo*) kida sa giiyeN gewii*n*.

"aa*n*iish, gdaa wiidjiiwe sa.",

doo inaadigenon *da*sh maaba ogimaa bineshiiN newe. mii*da*sh giiyeN gewii*n* gii giziket maaba shagi. aa*niish*, gii nidesigoodjin giiyeN shkweyaang. zhaazhigo giiyeN gii nibinaabiminaagoziwok gewe aanind bineshiiNik. aaniish, (*doo*) gizhiibizowok gewe.

aaniish, mii*dash* giiyeN gwonda nidibikadinik bineshiiNik, mii iwi (*doo*) nibaawaat, mii*da*sh wiyii go maaba yaawaa, shagi e zhi-aabijibizot. naanigodinong gonaa (*doo*) booniit, jina gonaa gwodji (*doo*) kawewiisini. mii go miinawaa iwi gaa waabananik iwi baamaa*mpii* gwonda bineshiiNik (*doo*) gizikewaat. mii*da*sh wiyii go maaba shagi mii go pane e zhi-aabijibizot. wiin *da*sh go iidik maaba wodi shagi gaa nitami dagoshing, wodi minising e pizowaat naadiwaat iwi bagaaneNs.

wewiip miinawaa maaba shagi iwi bagaaneNs gonaa gaa biindoomat, ji kida yinggoba*n* gonaa, mii gii bipskaabiit. gaa*wiin* go gwodji go, mii go eta go (*doo*) bibooniit waa wiisinidji, jina gonaa (*doo*) boonii. mii go miinawaa (*doo*) bigiziket, (*doo*) bimaajaat. miidash giiyeN go maaba shagi gaa nitami dagoshing. ngogiizhigat giiyeN gii niigaanii miinawaa niibaadibik, mii giiyeN baamaa*mpii* gwonda gewii*n* bineshiiNik kina gii bibigomibizowaat. zhaazhig*o* wiyii gonaa maaba shagi zhewe gaa dagoshing.

aaniish, mii*da*sh go maaba shagi newe gaa miinin newe ogimaa bineshiiN daanison. anish*aa* gonaa maanda gonaa wii baaping gonaa, mii maanda dibaadjimowin e oonji dibaadidamaaN.

"Somewhere out on this ocean there is an island, and on that island there are these nuts which are plentiful there. Whoever will be the first one to get a nut from that island and bring it to me, that bird will get to marry my daughter."

This is what the chief of the birds supposedly said.

So with that, all the birds who were there flew away in search of the island with the kind of nuts the chief bird wanted. Just then the heron arrived.

"I too will go,"

said the heron.

"Well, go along then,"

the chief bird supposedly told the heron. Then the heron started to fly after the other birds. The heron looked like he was hanging awkwardly in the sky, that is the way he looks when he flies, he is not a graceful flying creature. The other birds had a head start and already some of them were so far ahead that they could no longer be seen anywhere on the horizon. Of course, some of the birds were very fast flying creatures.

However, when it got dark, most of these birds would stop and they would go to sleep. But this heron, he just continues flying. He would stop only to eat and rest for a little while. Whereas the rest of the birds would wait until morning before they would again resume their flight. But, the heron just kept on going, only stopping for short breaks. So, this heron was the first one to get to the island the birds were flying to, the island with the nuts, the type of nut the chief requested.

The heron then quickly stored and secured a nut on his body somewhere, and he quickly made his way back. He did not stop anywhere for extended periods, he would just stop to rest and eat, he would stop for just a short time. He would then quickly take flight again, and leave again. And, lo and behold, it was the heron who was the first one to make it back with the nut. He beat the other birds back by a whole day and a night, and the rest of the birds made it back a day later. The heron had already been back a whole day before them.

So the heron was given the chief's daughter in marriage. This is just a humorous tale, maybe you will laugh at it, that is why I am telling this story to you now.

oodjiigaawesi miinawaa enigooNs

yaawaa sa nwii dibaadjimaa, oodjiigaawesi miinawaa yaawaa, enigooNs. gwonda enigooNsak (*doo*) nitaanakiiwok. (*doo*) zagakanigewok gwonda niibing, (*doo*) gichi nakiiwok go. maaba dash oodjiigaawesi, gaawii*n* maaba (*doo*) kitigesii. gaawii*n* go gegoo, mii go eta (*doo*) nigamot.

miidash maanda gaa bibooninik, mii iwi (*doo*) gidimaagozit, gaa*wiin* gegoo waa miijit. miidash iidik maaba oodjiigaawesi e inendang iwi,

"aa*n*iish naa, ndaa gii oon*a*ndodimowaa maaba enigooNs gonaa maanda gegoo gonaa, ge miiji yaaNmbaa*n*. ndaa oodaaw*a*maa.",

(*doo*) inendam sa gonaa iidik. mii*da*sh maaba iidik wodi oodjiigaawesi gaa zhaat ninda enigooNson e ndaanit.

"wegone*sh* dash.",

doo igoodigenon sa.

"aa*niish*, gegoo sa gonaa g*doo* bidaaw*a*min gonaa ge miiji yaaNmbaa*n* gonaa. n*doo* bakade.",

(*doo*) kidawidik sa maaba oodjiigaawesi.

mii*da*sh giiyeN maaba enigooNs e inaat newe,

"aanii*sh* dash gaa nan*a*kii yin gonaa gegii*n* gii niibing."

"aa*niish*, ngii nigam sa.",

(*doo*) kidawidik sa maaba oodjiigaawesi.

"aaniish naa, gdaa nigam sa miinawaa.",

doo inaadigenon *da*sh maaba enigooNs. aapidji giiyeN (*doo*) nichiiwot gonaa gwodjiing gonaa ji kida yinggoba*n*. aa*niish*, (*doo*) biboon. anish*aa* dash giiyeN gonaa maaba (*doo*) zhawenimaat enigooNs ninda oodjiigaawesiwon, ndaawaach giiyeN gonaa waa miijinit gonaa gii miinaan. mii*da*sh giiyeN maaba enigooNs ninda oodjiigaawesiwon gaa maajaanit, mii giiyeN e kidat iwi,

The Cricket and the Ant

Well, I am now going to talk about the cricket and the ant. The ants, they are very hard workers. They work very hard and they store many food items during the summer. But, this cricket, he does not plant or do anything to put food away. He does nothing of the sort, he only sings.

So when the winter came, he was now very poor as he had nothing to eat. So this cricket thought the following.

> "Well now, I should go ask the ant if I could get something to eat from him. I will borrow some food from him,"

he must have thought. So this cricket went to see the ant at his home.

> "What is it?"

the cricket is asked by the ant.

> "Well, I am, er, I have come to borrow some food that I could have to eat. I am hungry,"

the cricket said.

So the ant says the following to the cricket.

> "Well, what did you do this past summer."
> "Well, I just sang,"

the cricket must have responded.

> "Well, you should sing some more then,"

said the ant to the cricket sarcastically. Oh, the winter storm was very strong outside. Of course, it was wintertime, and that is normal for winter. So this ant felt sorry for the cricket and he gave the cricket some food to eat. And when the cricket left with the food, the ant was heard saying this:

> "mii zhaazhigo gii biwezhamit owo memaakadewaakogaadet.",

(*doo*) kida giiyeN maaba enigooNs.

goon e naadjimigaazat

yaawaa sa nwii dibaadjimaa, anishinaabe. iwi *dash* gonaa waa *oonji* dibaadjimak, yaawaa gonaa gete anishinaabe gonaa gii ganamaagewok maanda biboong wii bibowaa zhibaapanidow*aa y*ing maaba goon benggishing. miidash maaba anishinaabe iwi waa dibaadjimak iwi gaa zhiwebazit. gi*n*imaa gonaa, gaa*wiin* gonaa ginimaa gii minowendaziinaadik gonaa gibeying (*doo*) biboonik. mii*da*sh giiyeN maanda gaa minookaminik, giyaabi gonaa (*doo*) babiiwe*y*aanggizo maaba goon, mii giiyeN ninda gii mip*a*shazhewaat goonon, miinawaa giiyeN gii madji waawiinaadigenon gonaa.

miidash giiyeN maanda iwi gaa bigiiwet gonaa maanda gii bibaa giiwiset, mii giiyeN iwi gii aapowet. aapidji giiyeN go (*doo*) waabshkiiyewon niniwon gaa binibwaachawigoodjin. mii*da*sh giiyeN e kidanit iwi,

> "*a*nish*aa* gonaa g*doo* binibwaachawin, iwi gonaa eta g*doo* biwiindamawin, gaa*wiin* gonaa n*doo* minowendaziin nonggo*m* wodi iwi gii bibaa giiwise yin, iwi gii p*a*shazhewi yin. miinawaa ggii tanggishkaw, gaa*wiin* gonaa iwi nishizinoo iwi gaa zhichige yin. gaa*wiin da*sh wiyii gonaa gegoo, baamaa*mpii da*sh miinawaa nga bidagoshin.",

doo igoodigenon sa ninda.

> "baamaa*mpii* midaaswi shi niizhagiizisagak, mii miinawaa ji bidagoshinaaN. gga binibwaachawin dash."

mii*da*sh giiyeN ninda gii nimaajaanit niniwon.

mii*da*sh giiyeN iwi gaa waabananik gonaa gii goshkozit, mii iidik maanda (*doo*) maam*a*nanendang gaa naamidang zhewe gii binibwaachawigot newe ge gichi gonaadjiwondjin niniwon. mii*da*sh giiyeN iwi gaa minookaminik wewena, mii giiyeN (*doo*) zhiitaat. aaniish, gii gikendaan gaa igot,

> "midaaswi niizhagiizisagak, mii ji binibwaach*a*winaa*n* miinawaa.",

"Oh, that black-legged creature has come by and tricked me,"

said the ant.

A Story about Snow

I am going to talk about an Anishinaabe man. The reason I am going to talk about this man, is in the olden days, the elders cautioned people against mistreating nature, and in the wintertime, not to get angry with the snow that falls to the ground. And this is what happened to this one man I am going to talk about. He must have become angered by the long winter. And when spring finally came, there was still snow on the ground in some areas, and this man must have kicked at the snow, and made some derogatory remarks about the snow.

So then, when he came home after he had been out hunting, he had a dream. He dreamt that a man with very white skin came to visit him. And this visitor said to him,

"I am just paying you a visit just to tell you that I did not appreciate what you did to me when you were out hunting, you mistreated me. You even kicked at me, and that is not a good thing you did. But, it is nothing really, however, I will visit you again later."

The man is told by his visitor.

"I will come back again in twelve months. I will visit you again."

Then this visitor left, the man in his dream left.

So, the next morning as soon as he awoke, he remembered his dream about the big handsome pale stranger who visited him. So when spring finally arrived, he prepared for the coming winter. He remembered that the visitor told him he would be back to visit him again.

"I will come and visit you again in twelve months,"

gii igoon newe pii waa nimaajaanit. aaniish, mii sa giiyeN gii wewiiptaat gii maniset, (doo) giishkang gonaa msan. aaniish, (doo) kosidoot go zhewe gaawitaawigamik e ndaat, waa zhiminobidoot go. gibe niibin giiyeN go gii manise.

aaniish, gimaapii sa giiyeN giyegeti miinawaa (doo) digwaagidini, gimaapii giiyeN go (doo) kisinaani go. gimaapii miinawaa, mii zhago (doo) baabiiweponinik,

"taaya, mii sa giyegeti zhago iidik wii biboong.",

(doo) inendam dash iidik maaba anishinaabe. aaniish, gii gikendaan wii binibwaachawigoon newe niniwon ge gichi waabshkiiyendjin gaa bowaanaadjin. giyegeti sa giiyeN gimaapii mii zhago (doo) webinichiiwidininik. aapidji giiyeN go (doo) nichiiwidini, (doo) zookponini miinawaa (doo) noodinini, ensa giizhigak go, (doo) nichiiwidini. geget sa gonaa giiyeN gonaa gimaapii e nishpishininit newe goonon.

aaniish, mii sa giiyeN go eta (doo) bigidiniset wii bibowaa aatenik iwi shkode gonaa gewiin e ndaat. taaya, giyegeti giiyeN ngoding (doo) nichiiwidinini niibaadibik, aapidji go. gichi jichkana giiyeN mii gegoo wodi shkwaandeming gii bibanggisininik, gichi goonon, (doo) wiikodjitoowon wii bibiindigenit e ndaat.

aaniish, (doo) gizhide biindik aanowi, (doo) boodowet gonaa, mii dash giiyeN maaba goon (e) ninigizanit. aaniish, (doo) nibiishiwi gonaa maaba nenigizadji goon, mii dash giiyeN maanda nibiish wii aatewaabaawinigot, doo aatewaabaawinigoon sa gonaa. aaniish, mii sa go gaye e zhi-aabijitaat iwi (doo) boodowet. aaniish, gimaapiich giiyeN go gaawiin go (doo) nibaasii go. gaaNwaaN go gonaa ginimaa gonaa de wiisinidik gonaa. maanda gaye shkode mii go (doo) aatewaabaawek, maaba (doo) nigizat goon zhewe shkwaandeming waa biindiget.

zhago dash go giiyeN go wii aanoowitoot, mii giiyeN gonaa gii gidagininik. aaniish, mii sa giiyeN gonaa iwi gaaNwaaN giiyeN gonaa gii nji bimaadizi. mii dash ko gwonda gete anishinaabek gonaa gaa kidawaat,

"gegowa baapanidawaakegon maaba goon.",

gii kida. mii gonaa gaa zhigiikonggewaat gonaa iwi. aaniish, mii dash gonaa minik dibaadjimowin e yaamaaN. gichi miigwech gonaa gaa bazindawa yek.

is what this visitor in his dream had said to him. So he quickly began to prepare for the coming winter, he cut firewood all spring, summer, and into the fall. He piled the firewood all around his home, so that he would not have to go far to get it when he needed it during the winter. He cut firewood all summer.

Then eventually, summer gave way to fall, and it was starting to get colder and colder. Then it started to snow, albeit just snow flurries at first.

"Oh no, it will soon be winter,"

the man must have thought. Well, he knew that he would be visited by the big handsome and very pale man whom he had dreamt about. Then shortly, the snow came down heavily, furiously, and blanketed the area. The snow storm came daily, it snowed and the winds lashed the snow at anything standing, oh, the storms were strong. The snow started to pile up higher and higher around his home.

All he did was put wood in the fire to keep his fire going and to heat his home. Oh my, then one night the storm was very, very strong. Then suddenly, he heard something land against the door of his home, and it was a big drift of snow and it was trying to come into his home.

However, it was warm inside the house, as he had kept the fire going so the house was heated, and the snow melted. And when snow melts, it turns into water, and the water from the melting snow was starting to drown out the man's fire, it was putting out his fire. And the man just kept on putting wood on the fire to keep it going. He did not go to sleep as he had to keep the fire going. He would have just enough time to grab a bite to eat occasionally. The fire would be doused by the water made by the melting snow that was coming in through the door.

He was almost giving up because he was tired from lack of sleep, when the thaw came to the area. So the man barely survived the winter. And this is why the elders used to say,

"Do not make unkind remarks about the snow."

they said. That is how they used to counsel people on how to act toward nature. Well, that is the end of this story that I have. Thank you very much for listening to me.

anishinaabe *ikwewize*Ns miinawaa do animookaadjiiNmon

yaawaak sa nwii dibaadjimaak, anishinaabek. giigaanggooNs gonaa maaba ji kida yinggoban gonaa. aaniish, miidash gonaa anishinaabek zhaazhigo gaa zhichigewaat iwi, owo gonaa maaba giigaang (doo) ninitaawigit, midaaswigon giiyeN ko wodi gwodji gonaa bogodakamik gii zhigoowaan wii daanit. mandj gonaa owo anishinaabe gonaa gaa oonji zhichigegoweN iwi, miidash dash go iwi gaa zhichigewaat iwi. miidash iidik maaba ikwewizeNs e ninitaawigit, mii iidik gaa igot niikigoon iwi ji zhichigenit. wodi gonaa bogodaakowaa gonaa e ko biinnakamigaak ji daat midaaswigon. baamaampii dash wii bigiiwe miinawaa gii shkwaa midaaswigonigadinik. aaniish, gii debwetawaan dash go ninda niikigoon.

yaawaan dash giiyeN maaba giigaang (doo) biminaan, animookaadjiiNon, wiin gonaa (doo) dibenimaan. gichi animookaadjiiNwidik gonaa owo. miidash wodi gaa gikendang wii oodaat midaaswigon bogodaakowaa, mii ninda iidik gii kidat ji maadjiinaat dayon. aaniish, miidash go gii maadjiinaat, gii ooyaat go wodi midaaswigon, bogodaakowaa.

aaniish, mii sa iwi gaa naakonigewaat gewe anishinaabek zhaazhago, miidash gaa shkwaa midaaswigonigadinik, mii gii bigiiwet. miidash iidik maaba ikwewizeNs gaa inendang iwi, giigaang, wii maajaat zhewe, iwi gonaa gewiinawaa gonaa e ndaawaat. giimooch giiyeN gonaa maanda e nakaazang gonaa iidik gaa gakidoot gonaa gwodji gwodjiing. miinawaa gonaa gimaapiich gonaa gegoo gonaa maanda nakaazawin gii zaagadjitoon, (doo) gakidoot gwodji. aaniish wii maajaa. gimaapii dash go iidik gaa debisenik gonaa gegoo minik waa nakaazat, wii bibowaa aapidji gaye gonaa mesanaming gegoo biindik. ngoding dash giiyeN gonaa, mii maaba gii nonaadizit ikwewizeNs, giigaang. gaawiin gii gikenimigoosiin dibi gonaa iidik gaa zhaagoweN.

miidash ko gwonda zhaazhago iwi anishinaabek maanda ko mashkodeng naadowesiwon gii bibaa nandowaabimaawaan, miidash gonaa ginimaa gwonda gaa bibaa nanakiiwaagoweN odaawaak iwi, miidash giiyeN (e) bigiiwewaat, mii ninda minisan naawondj e gowiindegin, gichi manidoo minis gowiindek nonggom, mii giiyeN zhewe gii bigibaawaat, mandj gonaa iidik gaa minchiwaagoweN. gii midenchiwidigenak go gwonda odaawaak. miidash iidik iwi (doo) bibaa ninaabiwaat zhewe minising, mii giiyeN gii ninaaskomawaat iwi wodi wiigwaam dash tenik. aaniish, mii sa iidik gaa zhaawaat wodi, (doo) nandogikendaanaawaa wegowendik e ndaagoweN zhewe. miidash giiyeN wodi gii makawaawaat ninda giigaanggon gaa nonaadizipaniin zhinda. mii giiyeN zhewe iwi e ndaat owo, miinawaa gaye newe dayon, giyaabi giiyeN go maaba (doo) bimaadizi animookaadjiiN. aaniish, gii gikaadik dash gonaa maaba animookaadjiiN. mii iidik maaba ninda giigaang newe

The Story of the Young Anishinaabe Woman and Her Dog

I am going to tell a story about the Anishinaabe people. This is about a teenage girl. And it was the custom of the Anishinaabe people of long ago, when a young person came of age, he or she was expected go out into the wilderness alone for ten days. I do not know why the Anishinaabe did this, but that is what they did. So when this young girl came of age, she was told by her parents to go out and seek her vision. She was to go to the sacred area and fast for ten days. She was not to come home until the ten days had passed. She believed what her parents told her.

This young girl had a pet dog she had been raising. This dog was big. Then when she was told she had to go out and seek her vision, she said that she wanted to take her dog with her. So, she took the dog with her when she went out into the wilderness for ten days.

As this is what the Anishinaabe of long ago customarily did, when the ten days were up, the girl returned home. Apparently, this teenage girl had decided that she would leave their home, and go somewhere else. Secretly, she would hide a household item or a tool somewhere outside of their home. Later on, she would take another item and hide it outside somewhere, and she did this over several weeks or so. She made up her mind to leave. Then after some time, she had taken enough items she could use for her home, and she did this over a length of time so that the items would not be missed by her parents, and she finally had enough items for her home. Then one day, the teenage girl was gone, she was no longer in the community. No one knew where she had gone, or what happened to her.

The Anishinaabe people back then used to travel to the plains and the prairies looking for the Lakota, and some of these Anishinaabe people were making their way back home, made landfall at the Spirit Islands, the islands that are in Lake Michigan, and it is not known how many Ottawa were in this group, but they stopped at one of those islands. It is not known as to their size in number. Then, they went looking around the island, probably for food, that is when they came across a house situated there. So they approached the house, to find out who was living there. This is where they found the teenage girl who had been lost many years ago, she was now a woman. She was the one who lived in this house, and she still had the dog. This dog had to be very old by now. This is who the teenage girl had taken as her spouse. This teenage

gaa wiidigemaadjin. niizhawon *da*sh giiyeN maaba giigaang newe niidjaanison. aa*n*iish, (*doo*) ikwewi gonaa nonggo*m*, (*doo*) gichi ikwewi gonaa. (*doo*) anishinaabe denggowewok giiyeN gaye gwonda animookaadjiiNik. gegaa *da*sh giiyeN go nes*a*statawaawaat gwonda (*e*) giigidanit iwi, wii giigidawok sa iidik go (*doo*) inendamok. mii*da*sh giiyeN go eta iwi e zhig*a*shkitoonit,

> "anishinaabe.",

(*doo*) kidawok giiyeN gwonda animookaadjiiNik. mii giiyeN gonaa e zhinisastawaawaat iwi.

aaniish, gaawii*n* gwonda gaa bim*a*kawaadjik newe (*doo*) dibenimaasiiwaan newe ikwewon. (*doo*) giigaanggooNsowiba*n* gonaa zhinda piich *o*wo e nonaadizit *o*wo. miidash iidik gii bigiiwewaat, zhinda gonaa gaa ninji maajaawaat gewe. miidash giiyeN gii dibaadjimowaat, gii wiindamawaawaat wiidji anishinaabewaan zhinda.

> "ngii bim*a*kawaanaa*n* gaye *o*wo giigaanggooNs gaa nonaadizipa*n*.
> maanda nayiinawi*n*t minising *o*wo daa *o*wo, gichi naawondj. mii go newe
> iidik waadigemaadjin newe gichi animookaadjiiNon ko zhinda gaa
> bimiwinaadjin.",

(*doo*) kidawidik sa maaba debaadjimot.

> "miinawaa niidjaanison (*doo*) niizh*a*won maaba ikwe. gegaa go
> gewiinawaa go e *a*nishinaabemowaat gewe, ji kida yinggoba*n* gonaa. (*doo*)
> nisastaawigoziwok go gegaa go wii giigidawaat.",

(*doo*) kida sa iidik maaba debaadjimot.

miidash giiyeN maaba ikwe newe wiidjishaanon iidik (*doo*) yaawon, ginimaa sayeNon gonaa, mii iidik maaba wodi gaa zhimaawondjiwaat gonaa waa wiidjiiwigoodjin wii zhaawaat wodi minising. aaniish, mii sa iidik gii maajaawaat, gii oon*a*ndowaabimaawaat ninda, maaba nini dawemaan. aaniish, gaa*wiin* gonaa (*doo*) minowendazii*n* gaa zhinoondang iwi, animookaadjiiNon wodi (*doo*) wiidigemaan *o*wo giiyeN. gimaapii *da*sh giiyeN go giyegeti gii m*a*kawaawaan. mii*da*sh giiyeN go giyegeti, animookaadjiiNon giiyeN iidik maaba waadigemaat zhewe, miinawaa giiyeN (*doo*) niizhawon niidjaanison, animookaadjiiNik (*doo*) niizhawok. gegaa go, *zhaa*zhawaadj giiyeN go (*doo*) zhi-anishinaabedenggowewok go gewe animooNsak.

mii*da*sh giiyeN iwi maaba nini ninda e dawemaawit, e piichi gowaanisagendang iidik iwi, mii giiyeN gii kidat ji nisaat newe wiin, newe dawemaan, miinawaa go newe gichi animookaadjiiNon, miinawaa go newe animooNson.

girl now had two children. Well, she was now a woman, an older woman. These dog children had human faces. The Anishinaabe warriors could almost understand these dog children as they tried to speak, at least they thought they were speaking. And all these dog children could say, as they could barely speak, all they said was,

> "Anishinaabe."

the dog children must have attempted to say. At least, that is what the Ottawa men understood them as saying.

Well, these men who found this woman who had vanished from their community when she was a teenage girl, none of them were closely related to her. This woman was a teenager when she left the community. So these men left the island and came home. So they told the people of the community about their journey and also that they came across this woman who was the teenage girl who had vanished years ago.

> "We found that teenage girl who vanished years ago. She is living on one of the islands out there on this great lake. She has as her spouse that dog she had raised when she was young,"

said the one who was telling about their journey.

> "This woman also has two children. They can almost speak our language. They are almost understood when they try to speak,"

continued the one who was talking.

Apparently this young woman had a sibling, he may have been her older brother, and he gathered up a group of men who would go with him to this island to go see his sister. So this group set out for the island, and they were going to look for this man's sister. Of course, what he heard about his sister being married to a dog did not sit well with him. Eventually, they found the house and the man's sister who was living there. And it was true what they had heard, she had taken the dog to be her spouse, and there were two offspring from this union. The dog children had human-like faces.

So this older brother of the woman, because of being greatly troubled and very disturbed by their discovery of the life his sister was living, said that he, and he alone, would kill his sister and the dog as well as the offspring of this union.

miidash giiyeN gwonda anishinaabek iwi pii gii naakonigewaat iwi, gaawiin giiyeN owo anishinaabe ji wiidigemaasik yaawaa, wesiiNon. miidash iwi ninda nonggom minisan wodi, mii iwi pii anishinaabe gii zhinikaadang iwi, animoowaaning dash (doo) kidawaat. miidash wiyii maaba gichimookamaan, Fox Islands doo idaanan newe. anishinaabe dash wiin iwi animoowaaning, mii gonaa iwi gaa zhinikaadang. mii iwi oonji owo ikwe zhewe animookaadjiiNon gii nji wiidigemaat.

miidash gonaa maanda e kowaak iwi gonaa ndo dibaadjimowin. gichi miigwech gonaa gaa bazindawa yek.

anishinaabe binesiwon gaa maadjiinigodjin

mii sa giiyeN owo yaawaa anishinaabe mikomiing dash (e) yaat, (doo) okwawaa giiyeN owo anishinaabe. niyii giiyeN e nakaazat, pashkowegani biiskawaagan miinawaa pashkowegani wiikwaan, wewena go zhinda (doo) shkaakogaadeni. miidash giiyeN niyiing mikomiing dash (e) yaat, gii gakaget maanda gii nigokowaanigawang iwi niyii, okwawaagan. niyii eshkanaak dash zhewe gii bidagisidoot, niyii gaye zhinda waagaakodooNs miinawaa go mookamaan maanpii (doo) teni, niyiing biindji agowining. mii sa giiyeN, (doo) wiikoweshin dash giiyeN maaba, wodi gonaa giigooNon wii waabimaat wodi (doo) mikozhawenit, wii badjibowaat dash. baamaa sa giiyeN go zhewe (doo) zhagishing mikomiing, (e) wiikoweshing, baamaa sa giiyeN go gegoo (doo) noondaan (doo) biyaanik, (doo) bimadwewenik. mii giiyeN zhinda gii binowodinigot dibaang, wegowendigenon go. maanda dash (doo) pagizat, mii iwi gii kowebinang iwi niyii, iwi sa waakoweshing, wegodigowendik gonaa, ginimaa gaye gonaa pashkowegaaNon. mii, aapidji giiyeN go (doo) mandidowon, aapidji giiyeN go gichi ninggowiingganan. mii gii nowodjibinigot, aanowi gidiskiiyaat, gaawiin gii gashkitoosiin. mii gosha giiyeN e zhimbishkaat. miidash iwi eshkanaak zhewe gii bidagisidoot, mii giiyeN iwi zhago maanda (doo) nimbiwinigot newe, mii gii debibidoot iwi, maanda gii doodang, mii go gii nimidjigonang iwi eshkanaak.

gii mbiwinigot newe gichi binesiwon, ishpiming, aapidji go (doo) mandidowon. mandj go waa zhiwebazigoweN, gaawiin gii gikendaziin. wegowendigoweNnon gaye newe e wiidinigodjin, gaawiin sa go gii gikendaziin. mii gii maadjiinigot, aanowi, maanda giiyeN aanowi (doo) pagiza wii gidiskiiyaat iwi zhewe waa niyaat, gaawiin dash gii gashkitoosiin. gii maadjiinigot, ishpiming, dibi go iidik go. (doo) bimiwinigot, gichi waasa ishpiming. gimaapii giiyeN mii maanda aki zhinda gii binaabidang. maanda dash giiyeN (doo) ayaanigokoweyaani (e) ganawaabidang go iwi, maanda gonaa dash (doo) ninanakwenit. gii maadjiinigot.

So, from that time on, the Anishinaabe people made a law that forbade any union of human and beast. And these islands out there, the Anishinaabe people call them Animoowaaning. The white people, the Americans, call the islands Fox Islands. Whereas the Anishinaabe always referred to them as Animoowaaning, that is what they called them. The reason they called the islands that is to acknowledge the teenage girl who had lived with her dog there.

That is the length or the end of my story. Thank you very much for listening to me.

The Man Who Was Taken Away by the Great Eagle

There was this native man who was ice fishing out on the frozen bay. This man was wearing a leather coat and a leather hat, and the coat and hat were fastened snugly to keep him warm. When he got to the ice, he chopped a hole in the ice about this big, this is his ice fishing hole. He had with him an ice chisel that he stood beside him, and he also had a small axe and a knife that were inside his coat. This man sat on the ice over the fishing hole and he was covered with some kind of skin, and he did this so he could watch for the fish to swim by the fishing hole, and he would spear them as they swam by. Then while he was doing this, suddenly he heard some kind of sound approaching him. Just then something grabbed at the area of his head, it was something unknown. So he was startled by this, he threw off the skin that was covering him. He saw something very big, the wings were so huge. The talons of the great bird grasped him, he tried to break free, but he could not. He was starting to be lifted upward into the sky. So when he knew he was unable to get free, he grabbed his ice chisel, which was sticking up on the ice near him, and he held onto it as he was being carried away.

He was lifted up into the sky by this great big bird, this bird was huge. The man had no idea what was to happen to him. He had no idea who it was that was lifting him into the sky. He just did not know who this was. He was being taken away, although he tried to get free, he just could not shake himself loose from the grasp of the great bird. He was taken far up into the heavens, and he had not a clue as to where he was being taken. He was carried further and further upward. He was so far up that he eventually lost sight of the earth. It looked so small as he watched the earth as he moved his head about, trying to keep sight of the earth. Thus he was taken away.

gichi gonesh gii bimiwinigoon, ishpiming (doo) bimiwinigot newe binesiwon. miidash giiyeN gimaapii wodi gegoo (e) waabidang (doo) yaanik, gichi aazhibik dash giiyeN wodi e ndigowok ishpiming. aazhibikoon wodi (doo) digowonoon ishpiming. miidash wodi iidik e zhiwinigot. miidash giiyeN aani wii nisigot. niyiing giiyeN maanda giiyeN ko doo paginigoon niyiing wii pagiteyaakoshimigoon aazhibikoong, wii nisigot, wii biigodjiishimigot gonaa. miidash giiyeN ko iwi eshkanaak, gaa nowodjibidoot, (doo) mindjigonaan giiyeN go iwi, mii giiyeN ko gaa nigaakiiget, wii bibowaa pataakoshing, niyiing, aazhibikoong. mii giiyeN ko (doo) nigaakiiget iwi. mii giiyeN go miinawaa. gonesh go giiyeN gii nidjiikaagoon newe sa, yaawaa, gichi binesiwon. miidash giiyeN gimaapii iidik maaba binesi gii gikenimaat bibowaanawiwaat wii nisaat newe anishinaaben, miidash ndaawaach go gii maadjiinaat, gii maadjiinaat wodi dash iidik ishpiming wodi nowonch.

aapidji giiyeN wodi (doo) gonaadjiwon ishpiming iwi aazhibik. dibishkoo gonaa zhinda gonaa, (doo) zhinaagot wodi iwi aazhibik. miidash giiyeN wodi gaa zhiwinaat ninda anishinaaben, miidash giiyeN wodi gii oobigidinaat wodi ishpiming, yaawaak giiyeN, yaawaak sa gonaa, migiziwaasheNsak, maanda gonaa (doo) ishpigaabowiwok. niiwin giiyeN (doo) yaawok zhewe banadjaaneNik zhewe sa niyiing, mii newe waa, wii mowagot newe banadjaaneNon, mii newe aani wii oonji nisigot newe, newe yaawaan, newe sa binesiwon. aani oonji (doo) pakiteyaakoshimigot niyiing. miidash giiyeN wodi gii oobigidinigot. miidash giiyeN gewe binesiwok, yaawaa gichi binesiwok, maanda giiyeN gii aanigokominigiziwok gewe binesiwok, (doo) ganawaabimigot owo anishinaabe. (doo) ganawaabimigot newe, mii giiyeN go maanda, maanda giiyeN e pidenik ninda shkiizhigoowaan, shkodeNsan giiyeN zhinda maanda (doo) pideniwon, mii maanda e pidenik. gii oobigidinin wodi.

aaniish, mii giiyeN iidik pane (doo) mi-aaptawat iwi, niyii gaye zhinda waagaakodooNs (doo) teni, miinawaa zhinda mookamaan (doo) teni. mii gii oobigidinigot wodi, mii go giiyeN gewiin newe e ndoodamonit newe binesiwon, (doo) ganawaabimigot, gaa bigidinigot. mii giiyeN go niyiing maanpii shkiizhigooning shkodeNsan maanda e pidenik, (doo) ganawaabimigot. (doo) bazanggowaabinit, mii go shkodeNsan maanda (doo) zhisenik, newe binesiwon. aaniish, mii sa giiyeN zhewe gii yaat. aapidji giiyeN go (doo) baatiinadoon kanan zhewe bemaanggodegin. mii newe (e) zhaanggodamowaadjin gewe. miidash iidik maaba binesi (doo) bibaa giiwiset gonaa gewiin, waawaashkeshiwon, ginimaa gaye go maanishtaanishon gwodji bemiwindjin, (doo) migimoodit, miidash (doo) maadjiinaat wodi ishpiming, niidjaaniseNon (doo) maadjiidowaat wii wiisininit, maaba sa yaawaa gichi binesi. miidash iwi giiyeN e inendang owo anishinaabe,

> "geget sa gonaa ndaa gii naadimawaak gwonda, banadjaaneNsak na gonaa gwonda. ndaa gii naadimawaak.",

He was flown away up high from the earth by this great bird for such a long time. Then after a while he noticed something and he saw a big cliff looming out somewhere way up there, there was a very tall cliff, there were rock cliffs located up there. So this is where this great bird was taking him. Then this great bird tried to kill the man. The great bird tried to smash the man on the side of the cliff, that is how he tried to kill the man. But the man had grabbed his ice chisel just as the great bird had begun to lift the man upward, this is what the man used to brace himself and stop himself from smashing into the face of the cliff. He would brace himself with the ice chisel every time the great bird would try to smash the man into the cliff. Again and again he would do this. The great bird tried again and again to kill the man. Eventually, the great bird realized he was not able to kill the man, then the great bird took the man farther up the great cliff.

Oh, the cliff looked so beautiful and peaceful way up there, wherever it was. The cliffs looked similar to the cliffs that are on earth. Then the great bird took the man further up, and he let the man go in the aerie where there were young birds who stood this high, as big as the man. There were four of these young hatchlings, and apparently he was to be a meal for these hatchlings, that is why this great eagle tried to kill him. That is why the great eagle tried to smash him into the face of the cliff. So that is where the great eagle placed the man, in the nest. And those great birds looked at the man. And as they looked at the man, the man noticed that there were sparks shooting out from the eyes of these birds. The man was put there by the great eagle.

Well, he had his tools fastened to his midriff, he had his axe, and he had his knife still on him. He still had these when the great big bird placed him in the nest, and the great eagle just watched him and the man saw the sparks coming out of the eyes of the great eagle as well. When the great bird blinked its eyes, sparks just flew all over the place. So the man stayed there in the nest. As he surveyed the nest, he saw that there were so many bones laying around in the nest. These were all that was left when these birds had eaten whatever. So this great bird when he hunted would get a deer from the forest or a sheep he stole that was being raised somewhere, and he would bring these to his offspring for them to eat. Then the man had this thought:

> "Gosh, I should help these young birds, these are just young hatchlings. I should help them somehow,"

(*doo*) inendam.

waawaashkeshiwon giiyeN ngoding (*doo*) bibigidjiwebinaan newe zhewe, newe binesiwon, (*doo*) bigidjiwebinaan ninda waawaashkeshiwon. mii go maaba gii yaat, gii bizagowiit anishinaabe, gii pakonaat ninda yaawaan, gii pashiibinaat waawaashkeshiwon miinawaa gii biigodowaat. aaniish, waagaakodooNs doo *y*aan, gii biigodowaat waawaashkeshiwon. maanda gii aanigokodowaat gonaa maanda, wii minomowaawaat gonaa gwonda banadjaaneNik, newe. mii*da*sh waawaashkeshiwon, mii*da*sh giiyeN (*doo*) waawiisiniwaat gwonda yaawaak, gwonda sa banadjaaneNsak, (*doo*) waawiisiniwaat. mii giiyeN gewii*n* maaba gichi binesi, mii giiyeN gewii*n* e zhiwiidoopamaat newe, newe sa niidjaaniseNon, doo mowaan gewii*n* waawaashkeshiwon maaba sa gichi binesi. mii giiyeN gimaapii miinawaa (*doo*) maajaat maaba binesi, dibi gonaa e zhaagoweN. mii gaye naanigodinong maanishtaanishon maanda (*e*) biwebaabiisaadjin, (*doo*) paginaat zhewe. mii go maaba gaye anishinaabe, mii go g*ay*e wiyii gewii*n* go newe (*doo*) pakonaat newe yaawaan, maanishtaanishon. ginimaa gaye bizhikiiNs e gaachiiwit, maanda gonaa e ishpigaabowit. oshkibizhikiiNs naanigodinong gaye, mii newe baanaadjin. gonesh zhewe gii yaa owo anishinaabe, gonesh go.

(*doo*) dagoshiniwok giiyeN gewe aanind yaawaak, binesiwok zhewe, dibishkoo gonaa e niginad newe gaa maadjiinigodjin, (*doo*) biniginawok zhewe biganawaabimigot. aaniish doo yaa *da*sh wiyii giiyeN go, doo zhiindawaan giiyeN gegoo wii doodaawigot, gaa*wiin da*sh giiyeN gegoo wii doodaawigoosiin. mii giiyeN go eta iwi e zhiwaabimaat maanda shkodeNsan maanda zhinda shkiizhigooning maanda (*doo*) pideniwon. mii giiyeN go gaye wii biwiisininit zhewe newe sa bekaana*z*indjin gonaa binesiwon.

aapidji *da*sh giiyeN go maanda (*doo*) gonaadjiwon wodi ishpiming, maanda sa *n*iyii, aazhibik. aazhibik, dibishkoo gonaa gegiinawi*n* zhinda e naabidam*a y*ing maanda, mii go e zhinaagodinik wodi ishpiming. dibi gonaa iidik, gaawii*n* gii gikendaziin. miidash ngoding gonaa *da*sh (*doo*) yaat zhewe, (*doo*) nibaa sa giiyeN ko, aaniish, doo komowaan gegoo wii bibowaa doodaawigot. (*doo*) nibaa giiyeN ko gewii*n* owo gichi binesi. maanpii giiyeN doo toon maanda dip, maanpii naami ninggowiinggan, aapidji go (*doo*) michaanoon ninggowiingganan, maanpii doo toon, (*doo*) nibaat owo binesi. mii giiyeN go gewii*n* gewe banadjaaneNik, mii giiyeN go maanda e ndoodamowaat gewiinawaa (*doo*) nibaawaat, maanpii naami ninggowiinggan (*doo*) nji nibaawok. gewii*n* gaye gonaa (*doo*) nibaa owo yaawaa, owo sa anishinaabe. mii*da*sh giiyeN gonaa gewii*n* iwi maajit, iwi sa *n*iyii, wiiyaas, mii go gewii*n* go iwi maajit go iwi *n*iyii, oshki wiiyaas. gaawii*n* benaa*da*dinik (*doo*) miijisiinaawaa, gewe.

m*a*nidoo binesiwok gonaa gwonda debaadjimagik, yaawaak ginimaa gaye gonaa (*doo*) animikiidigenak gewe. animikiik giinawi*n* e nigok, mii naa gonaa ginimaa e yaawiwaagoweN gewe.

he thought.

Later on, the great bird returned with a deer he had killed and dropped it into the nest. So the man got up and he began to skin the deer, and proceeded to chop the meat into smaller pieces. Well, he still had his axe with him, so that is what he used to chop up the meat. He cut the meat into sizes so that the hatchlings would be able to eat it comfortably. The great bird too, would eat the deer meat along with the hatchlings. Soon, the great bird would leave again, the man did not know where the great bird would go. Sometimes the great bird would have a sheep swaying in its grasp when it returned and the great eagle would drop the animal into the nest. The man would then proceed to skin the dead sheep. Sometimes, the great eagle would bring back a small calf who stood this tall. The man was there for a very long time.

Other great eagles would arrive to look at the man, and these were just as big as the one that took the man there. But the man, as he stayed there, was wary of the big eagles, for he thought that they would do something to him, but they never did anything to him. All he ever noticed about these great eagles, was that they all had these sparks flying from their eyes. Those other great eagles also would come to the aerie and eat there as well.

Oh, it was so beautiful and peaceful up there, high on this great cliff. The cliff was similar to the way the cliffs look here on earth, and that is how they were up there. This man did not know where he was. And while he was there, he would sleep when he felt safe, as he was watching out for himself so that the great birds would not harm him in any way. The great bird would sleep also. When this bird slept, he would put his head under his great wing. The hatchlings too, that is how they slept, they would put their heads under their wings. So when he knew the birds were sleeping, the man would go to sleep as well. He would eat what they ate, and the great birds ate raw meat, so that is what the man ate. The great birds did not eat meat that was rotting.

These are spirit birds who I am talking about, as they may have been the thunderbirds. They may have been the ones we Anishinaabe people call the thunders.

mii gosha giiyeN gii ganoonigot, (*doo*) nibaat, anishinaaben giiyeN zhewe (*doo*) binaaniibowiwon, (*doo*) nibaa giiyeN gonaa ko gewii*n*. (*doo*) n*a*madabidik gonaa (*doo*) nibaat. (*doo*) binaaniibowiwon zhewe anishinaaben, yaawaan giiyeN, maanpii miigowanon (*doo*) *zh*ibiwon dibaaning. mii*d*ash (*doo*) biganoonigot,

> "aaniish, mii sa ji maajaa yin.",

doo igoon giiyeN,

> "gga giiwe, gga maajiinin wodi gaa *oo*ndininaaN, mii wodi ge zhiwininaaN.",

doo igoon giiyeN.

> "giyegeti gdoo minodoodam, g*doo* minodoodaw, *n*niidjaaniseNik g*doo* gichi zhawenimaak. wewena (*doo*) wiisiniwok *n*niidjaaniseNik maanda e zhichige yin, maanda *d*ash (*doo*) ayaanigokodiman iwi wiiyaas wewena wii wiisiniwaat *n*niidjaanisak.",

doo igoon giiyeN.

> "miidash ji maadjiininaa.",

doo igoon giiyeN.

> "aaniish, gga miinin dash *n*iyii iwi sa *n*iyii e zhichige yin, maanda gii bowaan*a*winaaN wii nisinaaN. gdaa niwiyii nisin sa go giyegeti.",

doo igoon giiyeN.

> "ggii bowaanawin dash. aaniish, gga nowemin dash.",

doo igoon giiyeN newe.

> "gga nowemin, gga nowemin.",

doo igoon.

So this one time when he was asleep, and he did sleep occasionally, a man came and spoke to him. This Anishinaabe man usually went to sleep while he was sitting. So as he was sleeping, this man with a feather on his head came and stood before him. This stranger spoke to this Anishinaabe man.

> "Well, it is time for you to leave,"

the Anishinaabe man is told by this visitor.

> "You will go home. I will take you back to where I took you from, I will take you back there,"

the man is further told by his visitor.

> "You have truly done a great kind deed for me, as you greatly helped my offspring. My offspring have eaten very well and it is because of what you did, when you cut up the meat so that they could eat well,"

added the visitor.

> "Therefore, I will take you back,"

the Anishinaabe man is told by the visitor.

> "Thus, I will give something for your good deed, and also because I was unable to kill you. I really did try to kill you,"

the man is told by this visitor as he is sleeping.

> "I was not able to do it. So therefore, I will be related to you,"

the man is told by his visitor.

> "I will be your relative. I will be related to you,"

the visitor continued.

> "maanda dash gwii inint, gga miinin niyiin, noozawinan, anishinaabe noozawinan. bemosayaa gga zhinikaazam wodi gegiinawaa e danakii yek, bemosayaa. gga waawiizam dash, gga waawiindaasam, bemosayaa, aanowigoo."

nowonch go ninda noozawinan go. giizhigoo binesi, mii iwi giizhigoong gii minowinigot newe anishinaaben ishpiming. mii iwi giizhigoo binesi. kina go ninda noozawinan go, gii nimiinigot.

> "mii iwi ge zhichige yek. mii iwi ge noozawi yekgowan newe.",

gii igot newe sa binesiwon, manidoo binesiwon ninda. gaawiin go gwonda gonaa nigika go ge naagoziwaat gonaa, ginimaa (doo) animikiidigenon newe gaa nowodinigoodjin. animikiik gii nowemigoon.

> "mii sa, miidash iwi ge zhichige yin. mii go zhinda ji yaa yaaN. maanda go nga zhinibagashin, miidash zhewe ji namadabi yin. maanda dash zhinda ndo kweganaang maanda mii ge doodaman, ji mindjigoni yin."

doo igoon sa giiyeN newe binesiwon.

> "maanda ge doodaman ji mindjigoni yin. kina gaye go gdo nakaazawinan (doo) maadjiidoon."

aaniish, mii iidik gaye gaa igot go, kina go gaa igot go, gichi niibana gii wiindamaagoon noozawinan, anishinaabe noozawinan, aapidji go niibana. gaa igot go, mii go gaa zhichiget. mii wii waabaninik.

> "mii iwi pii, mii iwi pii ge maadjiininaaN."

mii sa, gii biyaawon giiyeN zhewe dash yaat newe binesiwon, maanda go dibishkoo (doo) zhagishing, mii iwi giiyeN (e) bizhishininit. mii sa gii bidagowiiziit zhewe newe gichi binesiwon dash (doo) yaanit. maanda dash gii ninaat, maanda eshkanaak bekish zhinda doo toon, maanda gii ninaat newe binesiwon. nenggaach giiyeN maaba binesi gii yaat miinawaa gii nibizagowiit, mii go nenggaach go maanda ninggowiingganan maanda gii ninang. gii niisabizowaat, nenggaach go maanda go gii zhichigewaat go, gii zhichiget owo manidoo binesi, maanda go gii zhichiget. gichi ishpiming, dibi gonaa iidik, gaawiin gaye daa gikendaziin wiya. gichi gonesh giiyeN gii bimibizowok.

> "I am going to say this to you, I will give you these names, Anishinaabe names. You will now be called 'Bemosayaa' in the place you are now settled. You will be given names, and you will continue to give names to your people, names like Bemosayaa, and Aanowigoo."

The Anishinaabe man was given all kinds of names. It was the sky eagle who gave these names to the man up in the heavens to repay the man for his kindness. It was the sky eagle. The Anishinaabe man was given all of these names.

> "This is what your people will do from now on. These are the names you will have,"

the Anishinaabe man is told by this great eagle, this was a spirit eagle. These great birds rarely appear to people, it may have been the thunderbird who had taken the man away to that aerie far, far away. The thunderbirds became his relatives.

> "And thus, this is what you shall do. I will stay here. I will crouch down so that you can sit on my back. Then you will hold on to my neck once you are sitting on my back,"

the man was told by this visitor, it really was the great big bird.

> "You will hold me around my neck. You will also take all of your tools with you."

Well, he was also told all these many, a great many, names, Anishinaabe names, there were so many names. So as he was told, that is what he did. Then it was now close to morning.

> "That is when I will take you back."

So, that morning, when he awoke, the great eagle approached him, the bird got as low as he could, as if he was trying to lay down, that is the way this bird approached the man. So the man climbed up onto the back of the great eagle. He held on to the neck of the great eagle as he was told when he was sleeping, and he also held his ice chisel the way he was shown in his sleep. And this great eagle slowly stood up, and he slowly spread out his wings. The great bird slowly descended, and he slowly flapped his wings as he soared. This is from somewhere way up high, the man had no idea where he was. Oh, they flew for such a long time.

gii niisabizot maaba yaawaa binesi, gaa niisabizot zhewe gonaa ishpiming, gimaapii giiyeN gegoo doo naabidaan wodi maanda pizonit ninda maadjiinigodjin. gegoo giiyeN go (doo) bagoneyaani, mii maanda (e) waabidang maanda zhinda gegiinawin e danakii ying. miidash wodi gaa niisabizot gonaa gimaapii, miidash gii bimibizonit dash, gweyek dash wodi gaa ndinigot, mii wodi gaa pizonit. miidash go wodi gii oobigidinigot. mandj naa pii gonaa gaa aawinigoweN, e piichaanigobaneN gonaa. gonesh wodi gii yaa ishpiming gii naadimawaat newe banadjaaneNon wii wiisininit. miyaaw wodi gii oobigidinigot wodi, mii go miinawaa gaa doodang owo binesi, nenggaach maanda gii zhizhagashtaat. gichi mandido owo, gaawiin go (doo) yaasii, (doo) gaachiiwisii, gii nizhagashtaat. aaniish, mii sa maaba anishinaabe gii niisaandowet, bekish gonaa doo niskakiiwigon iwi eshkanaak, maanpii gaa toot. maanda gii doodam maanda gii aagokwenaat newe binesiwon. mii sa miinawaa maaba binesi gii bizagowiit, gii maajaat. aapidji wewena gii ganoonigoon waa zhichiget, miidash go gaa doodang maaba anishinaabe.

> "newe gaye noozawinan, gegowa wiikaa wonendagegowan ninda noozawinan maananaaNnan, noozawinan waa zhinikaaza yek.",

gii igot.

aaniish, mii sa gii maajaat maaba anishinaabe, gaa binjibaat gonaa gii zhaa. aaniindi giiyeN gonaa gaa zhimaamkaadendamonit wodi, newe sa gonaa, wodi gonaa gewiin e ndaat gonaa, gaa zhimaamkaadendamonit gaa dagoshing miinawaa. mii go bizhinaagozit, gaawiin gegoo, gaawiin gaye gegoo giigooNon (doo) biinaasiin. (doo) okwawaaban owo debaadjimak. gii dagoshing wodi, gii dibaadjimot, mii iwi gaa zhiwebazit, gii dibaadjimot, kina go gii dibaadidang. maanda gaa nidoodaawigot gaye newe binesiwon, aanowi (doo) nisigot, (doo) pakiteyaakoshimigot gichi aazhibikoong. miidash iwi eshkanaak gaa nakaazat gii nigaakiiget. miidash gimaapii gii gikenimaat maaba binesi gaawiin wii nisaasik newe anishinaaben. miidash ndaawaach go gweyek gii maadjiinaat niidjaaniseNon dash (doo) yaanit, gii oosaat wodi. miidash gaa naabimaat owo anishinaabe newe, shkodeNsan zhinda maanda (doo) pipideniwon (doo) bazanggowaabinit, mii gewe animikiiNsak. mii sa iwi kina go (doo) dibaadjimot gaa zhiwebazit maaba anishinaabe. gii naadimawaat gaye newe banadjaaneNon miidash gii gichi minowendang owo gichi binesi, gii zhawendamowaat newe niidjaaniseNon. gii pakonimawaat miinawaa maanda gii aanigokodang wiiyaas, wii wiisiniwaat gewe. aaniish, gaawiin jiibaakowesiiwok gewe, oogii oshki wiisiniwok gewe. kina gii dibaadidang. miidash iwi gaye, miidash iwi gwonda nonggom anishinaabek, odaawaak, mii gwonda e yaadjik giyaabi e nakaazawaat newe niyiin, noozawinan. kina go noozawinan jiinggadamowaat. kina go gii wiindamaawigoon waa zhichigewaat pii (doo) daapinamawaat, iwi niyii iwi sa noozawin. kina go gii wiindamaaget go,

This great eagle swooped downward, and after a length of time, the man noticed something off in the distance as they were flying along. There was something that looked like a hole to this man as he looked around, and it was the earth he saw off in the distance, a small dot. Then as the great bird had swooped down far enough, he started to fly, and he flew to the place where he originally got the man, that is where the great bird flew. The great eagle placed the man at the very spot he had taken him from. It is not known at what time of day it was when this man was returned to earth. This man was away for a long, long time, when he was up there helping the hatchlings to eat. This great bird took the man to the exact spot he had gotten him from, and again the great eagle crouched down so the man could get off of his back safely. This was a great big bird, he was not small, as he crouched down. Well, this man then climbed down from the back of the great eagle, and he used his ice chisel to balance and brace himself as he climbed down. The man then hugged the great eagle around its neck. Then this great eagle arose, and he flew away. This man had been given careful instructions on what he was supposed to do, so that is what this man did.

> "And those names, never, ever forget these names which I am giving to you. These are the names you will be known by,"

was what the man was told by the great spirit eagle.

Well, this man then went back home. Oh, the people of his community were awestruck or probably dumbfounded by his arrival as he had been gone for such a long time. He still looked the same and he did not have any fish with him. This man had supposedly gone ice fishing. So when he arrived at his home, he told what had happened, he told the people everything that happened to him. He told them about how the great eagle tried to kill him by smashing him into the face of this great cliff. He told them how he used his ice chisel to save himself. He told them that this great eagle finally realized that he was unable to kill this man. He told them that the great eagle finally took him to the aerie to be with the hatchlings. He told about the sparks coming out of the eyes of these great birds. These hatchlings were the little thunders. This man told everything in detail. He told about how he helped the hatchlings. That is why the great eagle was pleased with the man, because he showed mercy for the great eagle's offspring. For he skinned the animals the great bird brought back, and the man also cut the meat into manageable chunks for the young birds to eat. Well, the great birds do not cook, they eat only fresh meat. The man told every detail about his disappearance. So this is where the practice of the naming ceremony comes from that the Ottawa still do today, the giving of the names. All these names, and they also chant and sing for those names. He was told by the great eagle everything they are supposed to do when they have a naming ceremony.

bemosayaa, aanowigooN, kina go. niibana go noozawinan, gaa*wiin* gonaa ngii gikendaziinan. gichi niibana gii miinigoon noozawinan. miidash gwonda anishinaabek nonggo*m* e noozawaadjin newe waawiindaasawaat.

aanind gonaa (*doo*) minodaapinaanaawaan, aanin*d dash* g*a*ye go kaa*wiin*. (*doo*) zhiinggendaanaawaa aanind. mii sa gaa zhiwebazit *o*wo anishinaabe, *o*wo sa debaadjimak nonggo*m*. mii gaa zhiwebazit *i*wi, binesiwon gii maadjiinigot, gichi waasa ishpiming, gichi aazhibikoong gii zhiwinigot.

mii sa *i*wi minik debaadjimigozit *o*wo anishinaabe gaa dibaadjimak.

anishinaabe *i*kwewizeNs gaa maadjiinin

aaniish, nga dibaadjim sa gaa zhiwebadagobaneN zhinda *n*iyiing zhaabowiganing, anishinaabek e danakiiwaat. bazhishig go anishinaabek zhewe gii danakiiwok gichi zhaazhago, ayaanikaach gii bidanakiiwok anishinaabek zhewe. mii*d*a*s*h giiyeN gii oodetoowok gaye go, miidash *o*wo yaawaa, *o*wo sa *i*kwewizeNs, giigaanggooNs go, giigaanggooNs gonaa e inint, mii dinoowo *o*wo, (*doo*) bibaa waawaaskoneNsike giiyeN. wodi dash *i*wi niyiing, wodi zhaabowiganing nibising nikeyaa niyaa, (*doo*) nizhiziinggaa *i*wi niyii aki gonaa, mitigowaaki gonaa *i*wi. mii iidik maaba *i*kwewizeNs wodi gaa nizhaat, waawaaskoneNsan giiyeN do*o* nip*a*kibidoonan. (*e*) oshki minookamik gonaa maanda, (*e*) baashkaabagoniik sa gonaa waawaaskoneNsan. mii*d*a*s*h maaba *i*kwewizeNs wodi (*doo*) nidadaminot bekish, besha go niyiing, nibising go, (*doo*) dadaminot *i*kwewizeNs wodi, (*doo*) niwaawaaskoneNsiket wodi. gegopii go waasa go wodi (*doo*) nizhaa, waasa go (*doo*) zhiziinggaabii *i*wi aki wodi. mii*d*a*s*h giiyeN zhewe (*doo*) nidadaminot, bekish (*doo*) nipakibidoot waawaaskoneNsan. besha gonaa niyii gonaa nibis gonaa, mii giiyeN zhewe (*doo*) niyaat (*doo*) nitan*a*kamigizit zhewe, baamaa sa giiyeN go niniwon zhewe baadaasimosenit. aapidji giiyeN go (*doo*) maawondaagoniniwon, *o*shkinowen, *o*shkinoweNson.

"aaniish e nakii yin.",

d*oo* igoon giiyeN.

"niyiin sa n*doo* bibaa miikodaanan, waawaaskoneNsan."

He told about the names "Bemosayaa" and "Aanowigoo," he told everything. There are so many names, I do not know them all myself. This man was given so many names. And these are the names that the Anishinaabe people give today when they have their naming ceremony.

Some of the Anishinaabe people look at the traditional practices favorably, while others do not. Some of the Anishinaabe people now hate anything that is traditional. Anyway, this is what happened to this man I am talking about. This man was taken far away by this great eagle, way up high someplace where there are these great cliffs.

That is the end of this story about this man I was talking about.

The Story of the Anishinaabe Girl Who Was Taken Away

Well, I will tell you a story of what happened here a long time ago to these Anishinaabe people who resided in the area of Zhaabowiganing. There were just Anishinaabe people who lived here long ago and there were successive generations of Anishinaabe people who lived in this area for many, many years. They had settlements all around the area. There was this young girl, a teenager who was out picking flowers, which grew all over. And she was getting toward the point of the land that juts out into the lake near Zhaabowiganing, and this path she was going along, it was wooded. And this girl just went along the shoreline as she continued to pick flowers. This was during the spring, that is when many flowers first bloom. This teenage girl was wandering about and playing and taking her time as she picked the flowers as she went along the shore of the lake out toward this point of land. Eventually she was far out on the point of land. She just went along playing and picking flowers as she went and she was not paying attention to how far she had gone. As she was wandering along the shore of the lake picking flowers, suddenly there was this man who was walking toward her. He was a very handsome young man, a very young man.

"What are you doing?"

she was asked by the young man.

"I am tending to the flowers, I am picking them."

aaniish mii iidik zhewe (*doo*) yaawaat, (*doo*) naaniibowiwaat gonaa zhewe, (*doo*) ganoonigot newe *o*shkinowen, mii*da*sh giiyeN,

"togowa kawe*sh* wiidjiiwishin. gga oowaabidaan e ndaa yaaN.",

d*oo* igoon sa giiyeN.

"e ndaa yaang.",

d*oo* igoon giiyeN.

"gga wiidjiiw. mii go zhewe ji bitakokii yaaN go, ji dash t*a*kokii yaaN, mii go gegii*n* ji nitakokii yin go."

nibiishing dash, mii*da*sh giiyeN gonaa zhewe gii niyaat go zhewe (*doo*) takokiinit go, gaa*wiin* giiyeN gegoo nibiish.

dibishkoo gonaa maanda e naabidaming zhinda, mii e zhinaagok wodi e nizhaawaat. mii gii niniigaaniit dash maaba *o*shkinowe, (*doo*) maajaawaat, (*doo*) wiidjiiwaat newe *o*shkinowen. mii*da*sh giiyeN gimaapii wodi gii nidagoshiniwaat. aapidji giiyeN go (*doo*) gonaadjiwonini wodi, dibishkoo gonaa zhinda e naabidaming maanda e danakii ying, mii go e zhinaagodinik. wiigwaam giiyeN zhewe gii teni, gii nisaakonigenit zhewe. aapidji giiyeN go gichi wiigwaam iwi. aapidji giiyeN go (*doo*) gonaadjiwon biindjiyiing iwi sa wiigwaam. gii biidaas*a*mabiwon giiyeN wodi yaawaan, akiweziiNon, mi*n*dimooweNon gaye.

"aanipiish gaa zhaa yin.",

(*doo*) inaa sa giiyeN *o*wo, owo sa *o*shkinowe.

"ooN, maanda sa gonaa ngii bibaa *b*imose."
"aanii dash maaba gaa *o*onji biinat.",

(*doo*) inaa sa giiyeN *o*wo *o*shkinowe.

"pane g*doo* ganamoowin wii bibowaa *b*ibaamendamod*o*waa gwonda anishinaabek wodi gewiinawaa e danakiiwaat. gegowa bibaamenimaake*n* gd*oo* inint pane. aaniish dash gaa *o*onji biinat. (*doo*) manidoowok nayiinawi*nt* gewe anishinaabek, (*doo*) manidoowok gewe. kina, (*doo*) *w*onaachaawaat ninda, kina go gga binisigoomi*nd*. yaawaak gga binisigoonaanik, dibashish bem*o*sek, mii newe wiikaanisiwaan gewe anishinaabek, dibashish bem*o*sek e nigiwog. gga binisigoonaanik gewe."

And they stood there, and the young man spoke to her.

> "Why don't you go with me for a little while? You will come to see where
> I live, my place,"

the young man supposedly said to her.

> "Where we live,"

he corrected himself.

> "You will come with me. Where I step is where you will step."

So he walked out into the water, and where he stepped that is where she stepped, and it was as if there was no water there at all.

It looked like the land we see here, that is what it looked like. This young man led the way, and she followed him as she left with him willingly. Then after some time they arrived where this young man apparently lived. The place looked so beautiful to this teenage girl and it looked just as nice as it does here, it was a pretty area. There was a house located there and the young man opened the door to the house. The house was very big. The inside of the house was decorated nicely and it was well maintained. She noticed an old man and an old woman sitting inside, they sat facing her as she went into the house.

> "Where did you go?"

the young man was asked.

> "Oh! I just went for a walk around here."
> "Why did you bring her here?"

the young man was asked.

> "I have always cautioned you not to bother the Anishinaabe people where
> they live. I have always told not to bother them. So why did you bring her
> here? The Anishinaabe people are strong spiritually, they are spiritual.
> When they realize she is gone, we will all be killed by them. The ones who
> will come to kill us are the ones who live below, they are relatives to the
> Anishinaabe people, the ones we call 'Dibashish Bemosek.' Those are the
> ones who will come to kill us,"

"gaa*wiin* gosha wiyii gonaa ginimaa daa zhiweb*a*sinoo *i*wi.",

(*doo*) kida sa giiyeN *o*wo *o*shkinowe.

naamiyiing *da*sh giiyeN *i*wi wiigwaam, naamiyiing *da*sh go (*e*) nendaagok *i*wi wiigwaam, aapidji giiyeN go (*doo*) gonaadjiwi giiyeN *o*wo wesiiNwegan, zhizhash*a*wegoshin zhewe. mii*da*sh giiyeN *o*wo *i*kwewizeNs zhewe gii oon*a*madabigot newe, gaa*wiin* gegoo pabiwin, mii go e zhin*a*madabit go zhewe (*doo*) namadabigot. pane go bezhigonong gii namadabiwaat gewe sa yaawaak, *o*wo mi*n*dimooyeN miinawaa *o*wo akiweziiN. mii gosha giiyeN ko (*e*) bibiindigeshkaanit gwodji giiyeN wodi wiigwaam, maanda (*doo*) binikaani shkwaandem, gaa*wiin* giiyeN wiya (*doo*) bimiwinaasiin, mii go e zhibimibizot *o*wo *a*kik. wodi *da*sh *o*wo akiweziiN, mi*n*dimooyeN gaye (*doo*) namadabit, mii wodi gii oonookshkaat.

"mbe, gdaa ni-ininaaba*n*.",

(*doo*) inaa sa giiyeN *o*wo yaawaa, *o*wo sa *o*shkinowe.

"(*doo*) manidoowok nayiinawi*nd* gewe anishinaabek. gaawii*n* ginigeN gdaa wonenimigoosii gii oogimoodi yin maaba giigaang.",

(*doo*) inaa sa giiyeN *o*wo *o*shkinowe. miidash gwonda gii nookiiwaat, mii *i*wi gaa miigowewaat newe jaaskiindjin, gii *n*andowaabimaanit, dibi go *da*sh (*e*) yaagoweN *o*wo giigaang, wegowendik gaye gaa gimoodigoweN, miidash iwi gaa miigowewaat, mii go wodi gii nikaak, gii bigomishkaak wodi sa niyiing dash (*doo*) yaat *o*wo ikwewizeNs, gii oobiindigemigak wodi. mii*da*sh giiyeN, geget sa giiyeN g*o*naa (*doo*) maamkaadendam *o*wo *i*kwewizeNs.

"(*e*) *n*andonewigoo yaaN iidik.",

(*doo*) inendam giiyeN. mii*da*sh giiyeN, gonesh sa giiyeN go zhewe gii tanizi *o*wo *i*kwewizeNs. mii*da*sh giiyeN ngoding, ngoding e *i*nint *o*wo sa *o*shkinowe,

"maadjii*w*ish maaba, gaa oondinat go maaba gga zhiwinaa. gegowa gaye gegoo nidoodawaake*n*. bekaa go wodi gga maajiinaa go.",

(*doo*) inaa sa giiyeN *o*wo.

"gegaa go zhago miinawaa, nowonch dash meshkowaak maaba da bibiindigeshkaa maaba *a*kik, nowonch da mashkow*a*zi ge bibiindigeshkaat."

"I doubt that would happen."

the young man supposedly replied.

Apparently, the lower part of the house was even more beautiful and there was this beautiful animal skin spread out on the floor. Then the girl was taken to go sit on the floor, there was no chair to sit on, the young man made her sit on the floor, and she sat there quietly. The old man and the old woman also sat on the floor and they sat in that one spot. And suddenly, the door would move on its own, and a pot would come into the house on its own, no one was carrying it, it just came inside the house on its own power, it seemed. This pot would stop right in front of where the old man and the old woman were sitting.

"There, I tried to tell you about this,"

the young man was told.

> "The Anishinaabe people are a spiritual people. They will not forget about you for stealing this teenage girl,"

this young man was further told. It was her people who had asked the seer, the owner of the shaking tent ritual, they asked this person to find out what happened to their kin, and it was the offerings they gave to this seer, that is what was in the pot that came to the house where she was taken to by the young man, this offering came to find the girl. The girl was awestruck by what she saw.

"I guess someone is looking for me,"

the girl supposedly thought. This girl was there for some time, as she lived there with these people. Then one day, the young man was told,

> "Take her back, take her to where you got her. Do not do anything untoward to her, either. You will just take her back to where you found her."

the young man was instructed by the old people.

> "It is almost that time for another attempt to try to find her, and this time the medicine inside the pot that will come, it will be much stronger and more dangerous."

aaniish mii sa giiyeN,

"nahaaw, mbe maajaadaa.",

doo igoon giiyeN newe. (doo) zaginikenigot miinawaa, (doo) nizaginikenigot, wodi dash gaa binji biindigewaat, mii wodi iwi shkwaandem, mii wodi e zhiwinigot. niyaawaat, miidash giiyeN e igot,

"mii go ji nitakokii yaaN, gegiin ji nitakokii yin."

mii giiyeN (doo) ninaasaabowinaat go zhewe (doo) nitakokiiwaat. mii giiyeN go zhewe iwi nibiish, (doo) maadjiinigot giiyeN. mii go wodi go gaa zhiwinigot wodi sa gaa oondinigot. miidash giiyeN zhewe gii yaat, gii naaniibowinit giiyeN zhewe,

"aaniish, mii sa ji maajaa yaaN. gegaa go zhago, wiiba go gga bidisagoo zhinda. aapidji go gdoo gichi nandonewigoo.",

doo igoon giiyeN newe oshkinowen.

"aapidji go gdoo gichi nandonewigoo. gegaa go da bimazitaagoziwok gewe neyaadimaagowaadjin wii makaagoo yin.",

doo igoon giiyeN. miidash gewe yaawaak, animikiik. miidash maaba gii nipakobiit miinawaa, maaba sa oshkinowe. pane wodi naamibiing gii nizakowenit, gii gidjibowet. giyegeti giiyeN, mii zhago gegoo (doo) bijiinggowewenik owo ikwewizeNs zhewe naaniibowit.

"aaniish naa iidik e zhiwebazi yaaN.",

(doo) inendam sa giiyeN.

"mii go zhinda ji yaa yin. gegowa gwodji zhaaken.",

gii igoon giiyeN newe, newe sa gaa maadjiinigodjin. mii giiyeN zhewe, (doo) maamiginaanan giiyeN waawaaskoneNsan zhewe bemaanggodenigin. (doo) bibaa wowiiniwidoodam giiyeN. baamaa sa giiyeN go wiya zhewe (doo) bigagiigidanit.

"yaa-aa. maaba gosha nayiinawin e yaat.",

So then,

"Okay, let's leave from here,"

the girl was told by the young man. He takes her hand, and he led her from the room, and they walked toward the door where they had entered many days before. And as they were walking along, he said to her,

"Where I step, that is where you will step."

So she followed his directions, where he stepped, that is where she stepped. They were going right through the water, and he was taking her back. As instructed by the old people, the young man took her back where he had found her. And he stood before her, at the point, on the shore.

"Well, I must leave you now. Soon, someone will find you here. Many of your people are out searching for you, as they have been since you left,"

she is told by the young man.

"They are trying to find you in every way they can. Soon, those who are assisting them in their search for you, they will come rumbling,"

the young man continued. And he was referring to the thunders. That is when this young man turned around and returned to the water. When last seen he was submerging in the water, as he was getting away before the people came to find him. And so it was, there was a gentle rumble that approached the girl where she stood.

"What is happening to me?"

she supposedly thought to herself.

"You will stay right here. Do not go anywhere else."

she had been told by this young man who had taken her away. So, she began to pick flowers that were growing around where she was standing. She was fidgeting as she was not sure of what to do. Suddenly, someone spoke to her and said,

"Oh my goodness! She is right here,"

(doo) bikidawon giiyeN.

"maaba sa nayiinawin."

eta giiyeN go (doo) biidjibowediwon wodi, nendonewigodjin. aapidji go (doo) gichi nandonewigaaza, (doo) baatiinawok nendonewaadjik. mii sa giiyeN gii makawin maaba ikwewizeNs.

"aanipiish binjibaa yin.",

(doo) inaa sa giiyeN.

"gichi niibananching zhinda ndoo bimosemin (doo) nandonewigoo yin."

miinawaa go gwonda, gii nigiiwenind maaba. mii wodi niyiing, zhaabowiganing maanda gii nji zhiwebat. giyegeti go maanda gii zhiwebat gii gimooding owo ikwewizeNs. yaawaak dash gewe naamibiing manidook e yaadjik, mii gewe gaa gimoodit owo oshkinowe newe yaawaan, giigaanggon.

mii sa giiyeN wodi (e) nibigomaawonididawaat gewe, gii makawaawaat newe. geget sa giiyeN gonaa, mii giiyeN go wodi gii bimadwemazitaagoziwaat gewe yaawaak animikiik, wodi epanggishimok ko (e) bimazitaagozidjik. aapidji giiyeN go gii zegazi owo akiweziiN wodi naamibiing wii nisindawaa.

miidash giiyeN,

"aaniish, mii sa gonaa gii makaawigoo yin.",

(doo) inaa sa giiyeN owo ikwewizeNs. gii gagwedjimin gaa zhiwebazit. aaniish, gii dibaadjimo sa wodi e zhinaagodinik wodi gii ooyaat.

"aapidji (doo) gonaadjiwon wiigwaam wodi gii yaa yaaN. aapidji go (doo) gwetaani gonaadjiwon. miinawaa iwi gaa miigowe yek iidik iwi nandogikenimigoo yaaN zhewe, mii go wodi gii oobigomishkaak iwi nakaadjigan, wodi (doo) namadabit owo akiweziiN miinawaa mindimooyeN. mii go wodi gii bigomishkaak, niyiing, (doo) namadabiwaat gewe. aapidji dash go gii zegazi owo akiweziiN. 'gga nisigoomin bibowaa maadjiinat maaba.', gii inaa owo gaa maadjiiwizhit. 'gegowa wiikaa miinawaa doodangge, gga doodazii iwi gwodji anishinaabe, anishinaabek ji gimoodi yin, anishinaabe ikwe waabimat ji gimoodi yin.'", that is what that person said as he approached her.

"Here she is!"

There were many people who ran toward her, these were the ones who had been out searching for her. All these people were out looking for her, this was a massive search party. So this girl was now found.

"Where did you come from?"

she was asked by the people.

"We have walked by here many times searching for you."

And then they took her home. Remember this happened at the place called Zhaabowiganing. This really happened a long time ago, that this girl was kidnapped and taken someplace. It was the spirits who live under the water, that was who came and took the girl away for a little while.

Anyway, the people arrived at their town with the girl they finally found. And at that moment, the thunder could be heard coming from the west. And the old man spirit who lived under the water was fearful that those thunder beings will come to kill them at their underwater home.

So then,

"Well, at least you were found alive and well,"

the teenage girl was told. So she was asked what really happened to her. So, she told as best she could the details of what the place looked like that she was at.

> "The house I was at, it was very nice. In fact, it was very beautiful. And the gifts you had given to the seer, those came right into the house, and it came right to where the old man and the old woman were sitting. That offering stopped right there, in front of them. Oh, that old man was really frightened. 'We will all be killed if you do not take her back,' is what the young man was told by the old man. 'Never do this again, that is you will never kidnap an Anishinaabe woman when you see one again.'"

gii inaa giiyeN owo sa oshkinowe.

aaniish mii sa giiyeN gii dibaadjimowaat gwonda anishinaabek, gii makawin owo ikwewizeNs. gii dibaadjimot gewiin e zhinaagodinik wodi gii yaat. aapidji go gii minoyaa wodi gii ooyaat. aapidji gaye go gii gonaadjiwon gii namadabit, mii go zhewe pane go gii namadabit go.

miidash, mii iwi zhaabowiganing gii nji zhiwebadaban, gichi zhaazhago. mandj gonaa iwi pii. anishinaabek wodi gii danakiiwaat, gii bidanakiiwaat ayaanikaach, mii maanda gaa zhiwebazidjik. gaawiin dash wiyii, wiya gonaa nonggom wodi anishinaabe, gii makamaawok iwi. anishinaabe iwi dibendaanaaban iwi, wodi iwi aki, gii makamaawok dash iwi, miinawaa gii zakawamawaawok niyiin, wiigwaamewaan. yaabshkiiyedjik dash nonggom zhewe (doo) yaawok.

mii sa iwi e kowaak iwi ndo dibaadjimowin.

anishinaabek gaa madekodaagaazadjik

aaniish mii sa giiyeN gewe anishinaabek gonaa gewiinawaa (doo) bimaadiziwaat gonaa, daawaat gonaa, miidash giiyeN, miidash giiyeN e kidawaat,

> "geget sa gonaa gdaa gii oobiboonishimin e dizhiiniwaat wesiiNik.",

(doo) kidawok giiyeN gewe anishinaabek. miidash giiyeN go gii maajaawaat, niyiing gonaa megowe mitigowaaki, dibi gonaa iidik gonaa, (doo) maajaawaat. miidash go wodi gii yaawaat, gii zhigewaat, niyii gonaa, wiigwaam gonaa. niyii gonaa takiigaanek, gii takiigedigenak giiyeN gonaa, mandj gonaa gaa zhinaagodigowen takiigaan. anishinaabe wiigwaam, mii iwi gaa zhitoowaat. aapidji giiyeN gonaa (doo) yaani, (doo) wesiiNkaani iidik wodi sa gii dagoshiniwaat. wesiiNik, waawaashkeshiwok, nowonch go e zhinaagozidjik go wesiiNsak gaye.

miidash giiyeN, aanind dash gewiin gwodji wodi nikeyaa (doo) zhigoziwok gonaa wiichikesiwaan gonaa newe. wiinawaa dash gonaa eta, gewiinawaa gonaa, (doo) miyaawok gonaa wiidigemaaganon owo nini miinawaa binoodjiiN, maanda piitizi ikwewizeNs, miinawaa dash gonaa bezhik gonaa yaawaa, oshkiniigaaNon doo yaawaan. giyegeti giiyeN wesiiNkaani zhewe, aapidji go.

This is what that young man was told by that old man.

So the Anishinaabe people spread the word to the other communities, that the girl had been found. And she told her story of where she went and what it was like there, she told this to the people. She told about how she sat in that one spot and how nice it looked in that house. She was treated very well while she was there.

And this is what supposedly happened a very long time ago at the place we know as Zhaabowiganing. I do not know when this took place. The Anishinaabe have always lived in this area, and they have continued to live in this area for many generations since that happened, and this happened many generations ago. Today, there are no longer any Anishinaabe people living in that area, as the land was stolen from them. The Anishinaabe owned that land but it was stolen from them and their homes were torched, burned down to get them to move away from there. Only the white people live there now.

That is the end of my story.

The Anishinaabe People Who Were Wished Ill Luck

There were these Anishinaabe people who lived in this particular area and decided to move elsewhere, and they supposedly said to one another,

"We should spend this winter where the animals are plentiful."

So they packed up and they left their home, and they went into the woods and they did not really know where they were going. So, eventually they built themselves a home out in the wilderness. The structure they built was a takiigaan, and I do not know what this structure looked like, but that is where they lived. It was a typical Anishinaabe home at that time. The place they decided to settle at for the winter was bountiful with animals of all kinds. There were many animals such as deer and many kinds of smaller animals.

Some of their friends and relatives moved to a different location. In this area where the animals were plentiful, it was just this one family, the man and his wife and their teenage son and a little girl who may have been around one or two. And this area where they settled for the winter was well populated with animals of all kinds, big and small.

(doo) giiwise giiyeN gewiin oshkiniigish. miidash giiyeN geget sa giiyeN gonaa niyii, wiiyaas aabiindjitoonaawaa. mii gii naakomotoot giiyeN owo nini, niyii gonaa, mitigoon gii naakoshimaat, miidash (doo) nibaakodjigoodoot zhewe iwi wiiyaas. mii giiyeN gonaa e zhigichi zagakanamowaat wiiyaas. maaba gaye ikwe, maanpii dash (doo) goodoot iwi, miinawaa maanda mitigoon gii naakosidoot, miidash (doo) baakodogoodoot, (doo) baasang wiiyaas maaba ikwe. miidash giiyeN zhewe dash (doo) yaawaat gonaa, gichi waasa giiyeN (doo) yaawon newe wiichikesiwaan, gaawiin go maamdaa go ji nandonewaawaapan gaye ji wiindimawaawaapan zhewe ji wiyii bizhaanit. miidash iidik,

> "geget sa gonaa gdoo waandjiinitoonaan wiiyaas.",

(doo) kida sa giiyeN owo nini. (doo) baatiinad wiiyaas. mii go eta wiiyaas e goodenik. eta wiiyaas maajiwaat, oshki wiiyaas. nowonch go gegoo.

> "gaawiin gaye gonaa wiya (doo) yaasii gonaa zhinda besha ge shamaa yinggoban gonaa maanda aanind gewiin.",

(doo) kida sa giiyeN.

mii giiyeN go pane go ensa giizhigak (doo) giiwiset. miidash gaa minisaadjin wodi wesiiNon, mii sa go (doo) biinaat go zhewe (doo) yaat. (doo) bizagakanaat, (doo) baakodogoodoot wiiyaas. bibooni. gaawiin (doo) banaadasinooni, (doo) mashkowaakodininiban gonaa.

mii go owo ikwe (doo) gichi jiibaakowet, iwi go pii waa dagoshinindjin wiidigemaaganon miinawaa do oshkiniigiimowaan, mii (doo) gichi jiibaakowet. gaa bidagoshinindjin iwi yaat, (doo) waagomowaat wiiyaas, nowonch sa giiyeN go. gii bitapaabiwon giiyeN zhewe anishinaaben, aapidji giiyeN go (doo) maanaadiziwon, maanda giiyeN go, aapidji giiyeN (doo) ganoowaakodjaaneNwon, maanda dash giiyeN (doo) zhiwaagodjaaneNwon newe sa, akiweziiNon dash giiyeN newe (e) bitapaabinindjin.

> "nahaaw, bibiindigen.",

doo inaan dash giiyeN owo nini.

> "nahaaw, bibiindigen. bibiindigowishinaang."

mii sa giiyeN gii bibiindigenit. miidash gaa shkwaa wiisiniwaat,

The young boy also hunted successfully. Oh, they had all kinds of meat that they brought back from their hunt each day. The man erected a drying rack so they could hang the meat from the poles so the meat would cure. And supposedly, they were storing up a lot of meat. And the woman was busy helping to hang the meat up to dry so it could be stored. And this place they were spending the winter was such a long way from where their relatives and friends had moved, so they could not go to get them and have them share in their largesse.

"Oh, we really have so much, so much meat,"

the man supposedly said out loud one day. And they had so much meat, there was meat stored and there was meat hanging on the drying racks. They were eating meat every day and it was fresh. They had all kinds of meat.

"Isn't there anyone around near here that we could feed some of this meat to?"

the man apparently said.

The man hunted every day. And any animal he happened to kill, he brought the meat home. He would put the meat away, and he would hang some of the fresh meat up to dry. This happened during the winter months. The meat did not spoil or rot, as it would freeze as it hung on the drying racks.

The woman cooked meat every day, and she would prepare the meat so that it would be ready by the time the man and the young boy would get home from their hunt. Then when they arrived back at their winter home, they would just come in and help themselves to the cooked meat. Then one evening, a man came and looked in their home while they were eating, and this man was ugly looking as he had a very long nose and it was bent as well. This man who peeked into their home was an old man.

"Come in,"

the man of the house said to this old man.

"Come on in. Enter our humble abode."

So this old man entered their home. Then when these people had finished eating,

"gaa*wiin* na wiyii go gdaa wiisinisii.",

d*oo* inaan sa giiyeN.

"eN*he*N, ndaa wiisin go.",

(*doo*) kidawon sa giiyeN.

"n*doo* bakade go genii*n*."

(*doo*) kidawon giiyeN.

"mii nayii gonaa e *oo*nji bibaa *b*imose yaaN gonaa, gwodji gonaa gegoo miwaabidamaaN gonaa ge miiji yaaN.",

d*oo* igoon sa giiyeN.

giyegeti giiyeN (*doo*) gichi waawiisini akiweziiN. aapidji giiyeN go (*doo*) nichiinaagozi. aapidji giiyeN go (*doo*) ganoowaakodjaaneN. mii sa giiyeN gaa shkwaa wiisinit,

"*na*haa*w*, gichi miigwech gaa shami yek. gichi miigwech."

miinawaa giiyeN bekaa gii nibizagowiinit, (*doo*) baakodenigenit, pane. gaa*wiin* go (*doo*) bibaamenimaasiidik go gaa nizhaanigoweN.

mii go miinawaa e naakoshik, maaba gaye ikwe (*doo*) jiibaakowet, d*oo* taagonikowaat newe e ninaakoshinik, mii go miinawaa gaa zhiwebazit, mii go miinawaa e piichi wiisiniwaat, (*doo*) bibaakodenigenit newe akiweziiNon (*e*) m*a*yaanaadizindjin.

"*na*haa*w* *b*ibiindigen.",

d*oo* inaan giiyeN *o*wo nini.

"*b*ibiindigen. gaa*wiin* wiikaa wiya n*doo* biindigaakosiinaa*n*.",

d*oo* inaan giiyeN. (*doo*) naam*a*dabinit zhewe. gaa shkwaa wiisiniwaat,

"gaawii*n* na go gdaa wiisinisii."

"eN(*he*N), ndaa wiisin go. mii na wiyii gonaa e bibaa *oo*nji yaa yaaN, wii wiisini yaaN gonaa *gi*nimaa gonaa gegoo miwaabidamaaN gonaa ji miiji yaaN.",

"Would you like to have something to eat?"

the man asked this old man.

"Why yes, I would like to eat,"

the old man apparently replied.

"I, too, am hungry,"

the old man said.

"That is why I walk around the area in case I happen to see something to eat,"

the man was told by the old man.

Golly, that old man could eat. This old man looked really ugly. He had this long, long nose. And after he had eaten his fill,

"Okay, thank you for feeding me. Thank you very much."

With that, the old man got up and opened the door flap and he was gone. The people of the house really did not pay any attention to where the old man had gone.

So the next evening, this woman again had prepared a nice meal for her family, and again while they ate, the ugly old man came by and opened the door flap of their home.

"Okay, come on in,"

the man says to the old man again.

"Come in. We never have anybody come by,"

the man supposedly told the old man. So the old man sat and waited. When this family had finished eating,

"Would you like to have something to eat?"
"Yes, I would like to eat. That is the reason why I go around, so that I come across something that I can eat,"

doo igoon sa giiyeN. mii iwi niizhing.

aaniish, miinawaa yaabananik, miinawaa (doo) maajaawaat, (doo) giiwisewaat, (doo) bibaa giiwisewaat. miinawaa maaba ikwe (doo) jiibaakowet. aapidji giiyeN (doo) waandjiinitoonaawaa wiiyaas. miinawaa e piichi wiisiniwaat, mii gosha giiyeN miinawaa (doo) bibaakodenigenit newe (e) mayaanaadizindjin. (doo) baakodenigenit.

"nahaaw, bibiindigen.",

doo inaan giiyeN. aaniish, (doo) bibiindiget akiweziiN, (doo) naamadabit.

"gaawiin na wiyii go gdaa wiisinisii.",

doo inaan giiyeN. mii maanda niswing, niswagon.

"eNheN, ndaa wiisin go. ndoo bakade go geniin."

mii go naasaap e igot.

"mii na wiyii gonaa e bibaa oonji mose yaaN gonaa geniin iwi."

miidash giiyeN gegoo dash inendang owo sa nini. gaawiin sa giiyeN wiya waabimaasiin, yaawaan wesiiNon, gii waabimaasiin giizhigadinik, mii iwi e ko niswing. gaawiin giiyeN go ginigeN wiya bineshiiN. aaniindi gonaa. wesiiN, gaawiin go wiya, mii gaye owo oshkiniigish, gaawiin go wiya.

miidash maanda miinawaa gizhep, (doo) maajaawaat, (doo) bibaa giiwisewaat. miidash maanda, mii iwi e ko niiwing. gaa naakoshik, mayegenimaan giiyeN gaye maaba ikwe newe sa giiwisenit. gaawiin gegoo (doo) biidoosiinaawaa. eshkam dash giiyeN gonaa maanda (doo) yaani gonaa, wiiyaasimiwaa, mii pane gonaa gichi (doo) jiibaakowet gonaa, (doo) mesowaabidaan gonaa. aaniish, (doo) jiibaakowet miinawaa doo taagonikowaat newe gaawisendjin. mii sa miinawaa e piichi wiisiniwaat, mii zhago miinawaa maaba nechiinaagozit (doo) bibaakodeniget, maanda bininang iwi niyii gibidekaan, (doo) bibaakodeniget.

"nahaaw, bibiindigen.",

doo inaan giiyeN owo nini.

"bibiindigen."

the man was told by this old man. This was the second time this happened.

Well, the next day, the man and the boy left to go hunting. The woman also began to cook. They had so much meat that they dried and stored. So that evening while they were eating, the ugly old man came by and opened the door flap and looked in on them as they were eating. The old man just opened the door flap and looked in.

"Come in."

the man supposedly said to the old man. So the old man entered, then he sat down.

"Would you like a bite to eat?"

the man offered to the old man. This is the third time this happened in three days.

"Yes, I would like to eat. I, too, am hungry."

The man is given the same response he had been given by the old man the previous two days.

"That is the reason why I walk around."

That is when the man started to sense something was amiss. This was the third day he had not seen any animals while he was out hunting during the day. He had not even seen any birds at all anywhere. What was going on? This was strange, both [the man and the boy] had not seen any animals in three days of hunting, not one.

So the next morning, they set out into the forest to go hunting as they normally did. This was the fourth day. So the evening of the fourth day, the woman was becoming suspicious of the man and the boy. They did not bring anything back with them from their hunting trip. Then she realized that although she cooked a lot of meat, it was always replenished, but now she noticed that the amount of meat was dwindling. Well, she cooked for her family again as she normally did, she fed the hunters. Then while they were eating, the ugly old man came by and opened the door flap and peered into the lodge.

"Come on in,"

the man supposedly told the old man.

"Come in."

(doo) bibiindiget akiweziiN, (doo) namadabit. aapidji giiyeN (doo) maamiishidaase owo akiweziiN. aapidji giiyeN (doo) nichiinaagozi.

miidash giiyeN gaa shkwaa wiisiniwaat,

"gaawiin na wiyii go gdaa wiisinisii.",

doo inaan giiyeN.

"eN(heN), ndaa wiisin go. ndoo bakade go geniin.",

(doo) kida sa giiyeN akiweziiN.

aaniish, mii gii shamaawaat. (doo) gichi waawiisinit akiweziiN, (doo) naamadabit, (doo) waawiisinit. aapidji giiyeN go niibana wiiyaas miijin, akiweziiN. miidash iidik iwi, miidash giiyeN maaba gaawiin (doo) minowendazik maaba sa nini. gegoo dash inendang.

"mii sa ganabach maaba e bibowaa oonji nisak owo wesiiN.",

(doo) inendam giiyeN. gaa shkwaa wiisininit newe, mii giiyeN go zhewe kina go, (doo) baatiinadani gonaa iwi wiiyaas, eta go gaa minodenik, mii gosha giiyeN kina e zhigidaamonit iwi. (doo) bizagowiinit, (doo) nizaakowominid. mii giiyeN go gewiin shkweyaang. (doo) nikoowaabimaat, dibi go waa nizhaanigoweN, mii giiyeN go zhewe gaa nizaakowominit, mii giiyeN go zhewe gookookoon e ninji gizikenit. mii go owo gookookoo, owo sa go zhewe gaa gichi waawiisinit, mii go owo gookookoo. miidash go zhewe (doo) niyaat gwodjiing shkwaandeming, mii go (doo) giziket, (doo) maadjiibizot. miidash iidik newe medwekodaagowaadjin, e bibowaa oonji nisaawaat wesiiNon, newe sa gookookoon.

"mii na gonaa iwi e zhiwigoo yaaN. mii iidik gii noondawit owo gookookoo, 'geget sa gonaa gaawiin go wiya ge shamaa yinggoban maanda wiiyaas. aapidji go baatiinad.', gii noondawit iidik owo gookookoo.",

(doo) kida sa giiyeN, miidash giiyeN e kidat. mandj dash gonaa maanda gaa zhichigegoweN. gegoo sa go gii zhichige, newe gookookoon wii zhiyaanit, niyii dibishkoo gonaa e zhichigeng gonaa gegoo, wii aamawin owo gookookoo gonaa, mashkiki gonaa e zhinakaazang. miidash giiyeN, miinawaa aanowi giiwisewaat, newe do oshkiniigiimon, gaawiin go wiya (doo) waabimaasiiwaan wesiiNon. dibi iidik gwonda gaa zhaawaagoweN wesiiNik. miidash giiyeN e kidat owo sa nini,

Of course the old man came in and sat down. This old man had fuzzy dishevelled leggings. Oh, he looked so unattractive, he was ugly.

So when the family had finished their evening meal,

> "Would you like something to eat?"

the man supposedly said to the old man.

> "Oh, yes, I would like to eat. I, too, am hungry,"

the old man apparently responded.

So, they fed the old man. The old man sat down and he ate, and he ate. That old man ate all the meat that had been cooked. And the man of the house suspected something was amiss, and he did not have a good feeling about this old man. He suspected something was not right.

> "I think this old man is the reason why I have not killed any animals lately,"

he thought to himself. This old man had finished eating, and he had eaten all of the meat up that had been cooked, and so much had been cooked, he still ate every last bit of the cooked meat. The old man got up and went outside. The man followed right behind the old man as he went outside. He wanted to keep an eye on the old man, to see which way he went, and just as the old man got outside of the lodge, the man saw this owl flying away. Just as he got outside the door, the old man changed into an owl and he flew away. So this was why they had not seen or killed any animals in the last four days, it was this owl that had placed a curse on them.

> "So that is what was done to me. I guess that owl heard me when I said, 'Isn't there anyone who is around nearby whom we could feed some of this meat to. It is so plentiful.' I guess that owl heard me,"

the man supposedly uttered. It is not known what he did next. Anyway, he might have done something to try to reverse the bad spell that had been cast upon them by the owl, and he might have made up some medicine and that is what he probably did. So they tried to go hunting in their area again, him and his son, and they still did not see any animals. They had no idea where these animals had gone as they were so plentiful previously. So the man apparently said this, "ndaawaach sa gonaa ndaa maajaamin, maanda gonaa waasa gonaa ndaa zhaamin. e ko biinanaagok gonaa maanda, gookookoo bibowaa yaat.",

(doo) kida sa giiyeN.

"ndaa oogiiwisemin wodi.",

(doo) kida sa giiyeN.

miidash iwi besha giiyeN nibis zhewe (doo) digowoni, gaawiin go gichi waasa, (doo) nipashkowaani giiyeN go wodi iwi, miidash giiyeN gii maajaawaat. aaniish, miidash giiyeN gwonda njike do daaniseNon, maanda piitiziwon dash (doo) yaawaat zhewe. mii giiyeN gaa kidanit pii waa bipaskaabiinit, gaawiin giiyeN dagoshinisiiwon. miidash giiyeN go maanda e zhijaakosekowet gonaa maaba, (doo) mesonaan giiyeN go iwi wiiyaasim, gwodjiing maanda e zhibaakodjigoodek. mii iidik maaba gookookoo (doo) binaadit iwi, niibaadibik wiiyaas (doo) maadjiidoot. dibi gonaa e zhiwidoogoweN, mii owo madwekodaagedisiiN, (doo) maadjiidoot iidik iwi wiiyaas.

miidash maaba ikwe wii pakadet, wii pakadewon newe daaniseNon. miidash giiyeN ngoding, gaawiin giiyeN go gegoo waa minozang. (doo) pakade giiyeN go zhewe. miidash giiyeN e kidanit newe daaniseNon,

"towogan, towogan.",

(doo) kidawon sa giiyeN. gaawiin giiyeN (doo) nitaa giigidasii owo ikwewizeNs.

"towogan, towogan.",

(doo) kidawon sa giiyeN, wodi (doo) zhinoogewon niyiing nibising. miidash giiyeN maaba yaawaa, wodi (doo) bibaamoset gonaa, moozoon, mandj gonaa e zhinaagozigoweN owo mooz, gaawiin geniin wiikaa ndoo waabimaasii, wesiiN gonaa maaba mooz e zhinikaazat, gichi wesiiN, mendidot go, wodi (doo) bimoset mikomiing, mii gaa zhitakishing, gii takishing. maanda gonaa gaa ninanikowenit, miidash giiyeN maanda, aapidji giiyeN (doo) maanggitowoge owo mooz, mii giiyeN eta towoganan bedakisigin, miidash maaba ikwewizeNs gaa waabidanggin.

"geget sa gonaa nga gidimaagozimin, ji gowinaandamaang iidik.",

> "I think we should leave this place, we should go far away from here.
> We should go someplace that has not been spoiled by the owl's curse,
> someplace clean."

The man said.

> "We could go hunting there."

He probably said.

Apparently there was this lake that was close, and there were some clearings in the woods around this lake, and the man and his son left their area. Thus the woman was alone with their daughter who was very young. She had been told by her man that they, the man and their son, would be back in a few days, and they did not return as they had promised. And the meat supply was dwindling as she had been cooking it for their meals, and she now could tell that more meat was missing from the previous days' supply as it hung over the drying racks outside. It must have been this owl who would come by at night and steal some of the meat from the drying racks. She did not have any inkling where the owl took the meat to, as this was the one who was causing them their hardship, but the owl was the one who took the meat.

So now, this woman and her little girl would soon be hungry as their meat supply was running low. Then that day came, there was no more meat for her to cook. They were now hungry staying in that area. That day, her daughter said,

> "An ear, an ear."

And she was a small child.

> "An ear, an ear,"

her daughter said and she pointed toward the lake that was nearby. Apparently, there happened to be a moose that was walking on the ice of the lake, and I do not know what a moose looks like as I have never seen one, and the animal called the moose is a very big animal, anyway, I guess this moose was walking on the ice and it fell through the ice. And as the moose would move its head from side to side, and the moose has very big ears, and that is all that could be seen sticking out of the ice was its ears, and this is what this little girl had seen.

> "Oh my, we are so poor, we are out of food and I guess we will perish here
> from starving to death,"

(doo) inendam giiyeN owo ikwe.

> "gga maajaamin gonaa, gga nandonewaanaanik gewe, gewe sa gaa maajaapaniik. gaawiin gaye (doo) dagoshisiiwok, (doo) nisagowaadigenon newe gookookoon.",

(doo) kida sa giiyeN (doo) ganoonadizat owo ikwe. aaniish, miidash giiyeN gii zhiitaat. gii maajaawaat, gii naagonaawaat newe, ishpaagoonigaa gaye. gii naaganaat newe.

aaniish, (doo) bimoomaagoban newe niidjaaniseNon. aaniish, gimaapii sa giiyeN gonaa gii nikowaawaan oshkiikowenit wiya iidik (e) bibaa giiwisenit. miidash gwonda gii nizhigewaagobaneN gwonda, mii sa e ndaawaat. wiiyaas dash giiyeN, wiiyaas giiyeN gwonda, (doo) nitaagewon go giiyeN. gaawiin dash go (doo) bibaamenimikosiiwaan gonaa ji zhaanipan newe gookookoon, gaa nji shamaawaat.

> "aaniin, mii na dagoshini yek."
> "gdaa nizhigadjibiiwinim sa nayiinawind wii dagoshin yin wodi, nga bizhaa gii kida yin."
> "gaawiin sa go ginigeN ndaa zhiyaasii wodi doo zhaa yaaNmbaan. mii sa go miinawaa zhinda giishpin wodi ootakokaadimaaN iwi binjibaa yek, mii go waa zhiyaa yaaN miinawaa zhinda. mii go miinawaa owo gookookoo waa bizhaat zhinda wii bigidaang maanda niyii wiiyaas geshkitoo yaaN gonaa giiwise yaaN.",

(doo) kida sa giiyeN owo anishinaabe.

> "gaawiin dash ngii gashkitoosiin wodi wii zhaa yaaN. gii gichi minozhichigem dash gii bimaajaa yek, zhinda gii bizhaa yek. mii sa go miinawaa gaawiin gegoo zhinda ndaa gii nitoosiin zhinda yaa yaaNmbaan.",

(doo) kida sa giiyeN owo anishinaabe. aapidji giiyeN (doo) waandjiinatoon wiiyaas. mii giiyeN maaba ikwe gii niwewiiptaat gii nijiibaakowet wii wiisinit gonaa gewiin, (doo) saakowaget gaye, aapidji giiyeN maaba (doo) minozekowe, owo sa ikwe.

miidash giiyeN maanda niminookaminik, mii gii zhiitaawaat, zhewibiiyaak gonaa maanda nibis, (doo) nigizat maaba yaawaa mikom. gii zhiitaawaat, gii maadjiiwonewaat miinawaa gii aawadjinet owo anishinaabe, miidash gii maajaawaat. miidash giiyeN wodi gii waabimaawaat mibigomogowiindjininit newe gichi moozoon. mii owo ikwewizeNs gaa waabidanggin gichi towoganan. mii go gii nibot zhewe niyiing mikomiing owo gichi mooz. mooz na gonaa, mandj gonaa e zhinaagozigoweN owo mooz.

the woman must have thought to herself.

> "We will leave this place, we will go to look for them, the ones who left us here. They have not come back, maybe the owl has killed them,"

the woman supposedly said to herself. So she prepared to leave. Then they left, they followed the trail through the snow, as the snow in the area had been very deep, so the trail could still be seen. She followed the trail the men had left in the deep snow.

She had to carry her child on her back for the child would not have been able to walk through the deep snow. So eventually they came across fresh tracks in the snow, obviously made by someone out hunting. The man and the boy had built a lodge in this new hunting area they had moved to, and the woman came upon this lodge. There was meat as the men were killing animals in this new territory. Also, the owl did not bother them over here as the owl did not come in this area.

> "Hello. You have arrived, finally."
> "I got tired of waiting for you to come back as you said you would come back soon."
> "I just did not feel right that I should go back there. If I had set foot back there where we were, I know that the same thing that happened there would happen here. That old owl would have come here and eaten up our meat that I am able to get by hunting,"

the man supposedly responded.

> "Thus, I was not able to go back there for that reason. It is very good that you came over this way on your own. I would not have been able to kill any animals here if I had gone back there,"

the man supposedly uttered. And they had so much meat here. So this woman quickly began to cook the meat, so she could eat as she was hungry, and she cooked the meat by leaning it on a stick near the hot coals, and she fixed a good meal.

Then when spring finally came to the land, they prepared to leave when the ice began to melt on the lake, they prepared to return to their summer home. The man carried bundles of their meat and other items on his back. So when they went by this one lake, they saw a moose floating in the water. This was the moose, the ears of the moose the little girl had seen earlier in the winter. The moose perished right there in the lake after it had fallen through the ice. Again, as I said earlier, I do not know what a moose looks like.

mii sa gii aawadjiw*o*newaat, wii giiwewok dash, gaa binjibaawaat degwaagininik, mii wodi waa zhaawaat. mii sa iwi gaa zhiweb*a*ziwaagobaneN gewe anishinaabek, anishinaabek go gwonda gaawisedjik.

*i*kwewok ko ooshame gii mashkow*a*ziwaat

dibaadjimowin zhinda ndoo *y*aan waa wiindamawinigok. aaniish gga bazindawim dash. anishinaabek gonaa zhaazhag*o* nwii dibaadjimaak, gonaa gaa bizhiweb*a*ziwaat gonaa, gaa bibimaadizidjik. gwonda *d*ash go waa dibaadjimagik anishinaabek, gii gidjibowewaagoba*n* zhinda. ginimaa gonaa aakoziwin gonaa gaa digowog. dibi gonaa nikeyaa gaa zhaawaagoweN, ginimaa zhaawonong gonaa nikeyaa. gibeying go gwonda gii mibowewok. gii zegaziwok gonaa maanda aakoziwin gonaa wii t*a*konigoowaat. miidash iwi gaa *oo*nji maajaawaat zhinda. maaba gonaa nini, gonaa wiidigemaaganon miinawaa daanison bezhik, miinawaa aapidji giiyeN go gaachiiwi binoodjiiNs, gwiiwizeNs. mii iwi gaye maaba gaa nchit, anishinaabe waa dibaadjimak.

miidash gonaa maanda niibana gonaa nisagon (*e*) mibowewaat, gimaapii gaye gonaa, gii gonaadjiwonini gonaa e waabidam*a*waat *a*ki. wewena gonaa ziibi gonaa gii digowoniwidik zhewe, miinawaa gonaa gii giigooNkaani gonaa iwi ziibi. miinawaa gonaa wesiiNik gonaa (*doo*) yaawok gonaa. mii*d*ash iidik gaa zhimisowinamowaat zhewe ji danakiiwaapa*n*.

"mii gonaa zhinda ji zhige yaaNmbaa*n*.",

gii kida dash giiyeN maaba nini, maaba anishinaabe.

> "gaa*wiin* gonaa gwodji miinawaa ge zhaa yinggoba*n*, mii gonaa zhinda gonaa. gaa*wiin* gonaa gdaa yaaziinaa iwi aakoziwin.",

gii inendamok iidik.

> "iwi gichi aakoziwin."

miidash giiyeN zhewe gii zhiget maaba anishinaabe. mii gonaa zhewe gii kitigeNsawit gaye gonaa, niibing gonaa. gibeying go gwonda zhewe gii yaawok anishinaabek.

So they carried and hauled their belongings with them as they made their way back to their summer home, the place they had left the previous fall. This is a story of what had happened to Anishinaabe people a long time ago. This happened to these Anishinaabe hunters, a long time ago.

The Time When Women Were Stronger

I have this story to tell you. Now, listen to me. I will talk about Anishinaabe people of long ago, and how they lived and some of the things that happened to them as they lived their lives. These particular Anishinaabe people of whom I will tell you, they had been on the run, that is they were running away from something. It may have been some kind of illness that had overcome their community, but they were going away from their home. It is not known which way they went, probably they went toward the south somewhere. They were on the run for a long time. They were afraid that this illness would overcome them as it did their fellow Anishinaabe. So that is why they left their homeland. There was this man, his wife, one daughter, and small baby boy. This was the size of this man's family that I will be talking about.

After many, many days of running away from their former home, as they moved into the woods they came across land that looked like a good place to settle. There was a nice river that flowed through this land and the river had plenty of fish. There were many animals in the woods nearby. So they liked the looks of this land and they wanted to settle here.

"I might as well build the house here,"

the man supposedly said.

"I do not think we should go any further, we will stay at this is the place. I do not think we have that illness among us,"

they must have surmised.

"That great sickness."

So then, the man built their house on that land with the river going through it. In the summer, they put in a garden. These people lived there for a long time.

gimaapii dash giiyeN maaba nini gii nibo, mii go ganabach maaba gaa nitami nibowigoweN giiyeN niyiing, aaniish, mii sa gaawiin wiya giyaabi. miidash go maaba giigaang gaa zhigiiwiset, dibishkoo gonaa nini. wesiiNon go (doo) nandowaabimaat go. maaba gaye go ikwe, mii go gaye maaba gaa zhigiiwiset. aaniish gaachiiwi oshkiniigish, memeshkod gwonda (doo) giiwisewok.

gimaapii giiyeN gaye maaba, maaba gonaa mindimooyeN iidik gewiin, mii go gonaa gewiin gii nibot. aaniish, miidash go eta niizhawaat giyaabi gwonda, gichi ikwe gonaa maaba, giigaang gaa zhi-aawit zhewe degoshiniwaat, maaba gaye oshkiniigish, gichi oshkiniigish gonaa zhago maaba. kina gonaa gegoo doo kinoomawaawaan gonaa gwonda, miidash iwi, wiin go maaba gimaapii oshkiniigish gii nitaawigit gewiin. aaniish, miidash go aanowi niizhawaat, miseNon miinawaa wiin. wiin dash maaba oshkiniigish gonaa nipiitizit gii giiwise ndaawaach, wiin dash maaba, newe miseNon, mii maaba wiigwaam gaa ganawendang. miidash giiyeN iwi maaba oshkinowe, maaba nitaawigit sa gonaa maaba oshkiniigish, mii giiyeN iwi gii mayegenimaat newe miseNon. gaawiin giiyeN wewena gonaa waabisiiwon gonaa doo inenimaan.

miidash iidik giiyeN ngoding gii gagwedjimaat,

> "gegoo na gdo shkiizhigoon (doo) zhiyaanoon.",

doo inaadigenon sa newe miseNon.

> "eN (heN), gaawiin gosha nayiinawint wewena gonaa ndoo waabisii gonaa. gegoo go ninda ndo shkiizhigoon (doo) zhiyaanoon.",

(doo) kidawon giiyeN.

> "iwi sa gonaa e oonji gagwedjiminaaN,"

doo inaadigenon dash maaba oshkinowe newe miseNon,

> "ndaa gii nandowaabimaa gaye gonaa wiya zhinda ge naadimaak."

wii wiidigemaagani gonaa iidik e inendang. miidash giiyeN ninda miseNon e inaat,

> "gaawiin na gdoo gikenimaasiik gwodji anishinaabek ji yaawaapan. gichi gibeying dash go zhinda e ko yaa ying, gaawiin wiikaa anishinaabek gdoo waabimaasiinaanik."
>
> "aaniish, ndaa nandogikenimaak sa, endigoweN anishinaabek ji yaawaat.",

Eventually, after many years, the man of this family died, and he was the first to die of this small family and so he was no longer around. So it was this teenage girl who did the hunting, just as the man did. She hunted the game just like her father had done while he was living. The mother also assisted in the hunting. The boy was still too young to hunt, so the mother and the daughter took turns hunting.

And, as life happens, after some years, the mother, now an old woman, also departed to the spirit world. So, there were just the two of them left, the girl, now a young woman, and the boy, who was now into his late teens. As it always was, the young were instructed on how to do things, and the young boy eventually became a grown man. Well, there was just the two of them. The young teenage man did the hunting as he was now of age and the older sister took care of the house and the gardening and the work around the house. After a while, the young man began to notice that not all was right with his older sister. He noticed that she seemed to have a hard time seeing properly.

So the young man asked his older sister,

> "Is there something wrong with your sight?"

he supposedly said to her.

> "Why, yes, I have a hard time seeing things. There is something wrong with my eyes,"

the older sister apparently said to the young man.

> "The reason I am asking you is,"

the young man must have said to his older sister,

> "I could go seek someone who could help you with the chores."

He must have been thinking about getting a woman for himself, to marry. And he tells his sister this:

> "Do you have any idea where there may be some Anishinaabe people living near where we live? We have lived here many years, and we never have had any visitors drop by and we have never seen any other Anishinaabe people."
> "Well, I will try to find out if there are any Anishinaabe people near here,"

(*doo*) kidawon *da*sh giiyeN ninda miseNon.

mii*da*sh giiyeN gii *ma*zinibakosidjigenit. niyii gonaa wiinsiibigoon gonaa newe gaa niibiishaabookaadanggin iidik maaba, mii*da*sh giiyeN gii *ma*zinibakosidjigenit.

ngii waabimaak ko genii*n* mi*n*dimooweNik gonaa zhaazhigo (*e*) *ma*zinibakosidjigewaat. gaa*wiin* niin gonaa, niin wiyii go gaa*wiin* niin gonaa nisadowinaziin gonaa maanda gaa zhichigeng, iwi gonaa *ma*zinibakosidjigeng gonaa, aanowi ngii waabimaak gaa zhichigewaat. miidash iidik maaba *o*shkinowe newe miseNon iwi gaa zhichigenit, mii*da*sh iwi giiyeN e kidanit iwi gaa shkwaa *ma*zinibakosidjigenit.

> "gichi waasa anishinaabek (*doo*) yaawok ginimaa gaye go midaasagon, ginimaa gaye go, ginimaa gaye go ooshame go, ginimaa gaye go niizhtana nisagon gdaa bimose ji dagoshini *y*imba*n* wodi.",

d*oo* igoodigenon sa iidik maaba *o*shkinowe miseNon.

> "gichi waasa."
> "aaniish, ndaa zhaa sa wodi.",

d*oo* inaadigenon dash newe miseNon.

> "ndaa *n*andowaabimaa gonaa ge naadimaak. gaa*wiin* gonaa n*doo* minowendaziin, ndoo shkendam gonaa maanda (*doo*) gikeniminaaN iidik (*doo*) waabisiwon wewena.",

d*oo* inaadigenon sa maaba *o*shkinowe newe miseNon.

> "nahaaw, gga zhiitaawin ge wiyii maadjiidoo yin gonaa."

aaniish, mii sa giiyeN newe miseNon gii zhiitaawigot wewena. wewena giiyeN zhiwo *o*wo, aaniish *o*shkinowe, (*doo*) daawok gaye wewena, miinawaa gaye (*doo*) minobimaadizi. mii*da*sh giiyeN waa maajaat zhewe e ndaawaat, mii giiyeN e igot newe miseNon,

> "gaawii*n* kina ggii wiindamawisinoo zhewe gaa *ma*zinibak*o*sidoowi yaaN. bekaa, gga wiindamawin. ngii zhibiiyaan go maanpii niyiing wiigwaasing, maanda waa naagadoo yin wodi wii dagoshinan gewe anishinaabek e danakiiwaat. ensa naakoshik gaye go wii gibeshi yin, gaye go ngii zhibiiyaan *i*wi.",

the older sister supposedly said.

Then she proceeded to make tea and she read the tea leaves. She made the tea out of the plant called winter green, and she used this method to divine or conjure up an answer to his question.

I saw this practice done when I was growing up, the elder women used to read tea leaves to see the future or to look for something. I never could understand how they did this although I did watch them do it, but I just never picked it up. Anyway, that is what this young man's older sister did, she read these tea leaves and then she says the following.

> "There are Anishinaabe people who live maybe about ten days away or maybe even up to twenty days' walk for you to get there. Far, far away,"

he was apparently told by his older sister.

> "Far from here."
> "Well, I should go there then,"

he must have said to his older sister.

> "I will go look for someone who could help you here. I am not happy, in fact I am saddened because I know that you have failing eyesight,"

the young man apparently told his older sister.

> "Okay, I will prepare things for you that you will need and that you will take along for your journey."

So, his older sister prepared enough provisions for him to take on his journey. He was also well attired for the trip as he had been a good hunter and they had lived a good life. And as he was ready to leave their home and begin his search for other Anishinaabe people, his older sister said that she had omitted to tell him something that she saw when she read the tea leaves.

> "I did not tell you everything I saw when I read the tea leaves. Wait, so I can tell you everything. I also wrote down on this birch bark the direction you will go to get to the area where these Anishinaabe people live. I also indicated the areas where you should be each evening where you will make your camp for the night,"

doo igoodigenon sa newe.

> "iwi dash go pii ginimaa niswagon wii dagoshinan anishinaabek e danakiiwaat, gegoo zhewe digowomigat, gga waannoshkaan maanda zhewe. gaawiin zhewe gga noogshkaasii zhewe. niwaannosen, debwetawishin nonggom e ininaa, giishpmaa wii bimaadizi yin."
> "nahaaw, nmiseN,"

doo inaadigenon dash,

> "gaawiin zhewe, gga debwetawin go, mii go e izhi yin, mii go ge zhichige yaaN.",

doo inaadigenon sa maaba oshkinowe newe miseNon.

aaniish, mii sa giiyeN maaba oshkinowe gii maajaat. (doo) naagadoon maanda gaa zhibiiyang maaba ikwe, waa naagadooshkang, (doo) takamoset maaba oshkinowe. naakoshinik, mii (doo) ninandowaabidang gonaa wii gibeshid. miinawaa gizhep, mii miinawaa (e) maajaat. mii go miinawaa gibe giizhik go (doo) bimoset. gimaapii giiyeN, mii zhago (doo) jitisenik wodi iwi waa waannoshkang.

> "mii sa zhago zhinda (doo) dagoshinaaN.",

(doo) inendam sa iidik. mandj iidik e zhinaagodigoweN zhewe gaa ganamawin, wii waannoshkang, wii bibowaa nigaashkaat sa gonaa zhewe.

miidash giiyeN (doo) bimoset gonaa gii zaagaakowang gonaa, niyii gonaa kitigaaning go, kitigaan gonaa e zhinaagok, mii giiyeN e zhinaagodinik iwi zhewe. wiigwaam giiyeN go (doo) teni, zhaazhigo gonaa anishinaabek gonaa wiigwaam gonaa gaa zhinaagodinik.

> "aaniish iidik gaye maanda.",

(doo) inendam dash iidik.

> "mii maanda iwi nmiseN gaa ganamawit."

noomak dash giiyeN zhewe gii naaniibowi, (doo) ganawaabidang wiigwaam. aapidji giiyeN go (doo) gonaadjiwonini zhewe.

> "aaniish, nga zhaa go ndaawaach.",

his older sister said to him.

> "When you are about three days from the area where these Anishinaabe people live, there is something in this area that is evil, and you should bypass this area. Do not stop there. Walk around this area, do not stop there, if you value your life, please, trust me on this and believe what I am saying to you,"
> "Okay, sister,"

he replied to her.

> "I will not go there as I believe what you are saying to me, and I will do as you are advising me to do, I will do your bidding,"

this young man apparently assured his older sister.

So, the young man left on his quest to find other Anishinaabe people. He followed the birch bark map his sister had drawn for him, and he made his way across the land. In the evening he would look for a suitable area to make camp. When morning came, he broke camp and set off on his journey. He would walk all day. Then the day arrived as he neared the area he was to bypass.

> "I am almost to that place I am to avoid,"

he supposedly thought to himself. I do not know what the area he was told to avoid looked like.

So as he walked toward this area, he came to a clearing, and it was a field and it seemed that there was also a garden there. He also saw a house located there, the way the houses of the Anishinaabe people looked long ago.

> "What is this here?"

he supposedly thought to himself.

> "This must be what my sister forewarned me about."

Apparently, the young man stood there for a length of time looking at this house that stood before him. The area before him looked very nice and well taken care of.

> "Well, I just have go to check this out,"

(*doo*) inendam *dash* iidik, doo aagonetawaan miseNon. nenggaach iidik wodi wiigwaaming gii nigiikiigigaabowit. (*doo*) nisaakosin *dash* giiyeN waasechigan, yaawaan dash giiyeN zhewe yaabimaadjin, ikwewon owo. aapidji giiyeN go maandaagikwen zhewe (*doo*) *animakobiwon* giiyeN zhewe biindik. gegoo gonaa maaba gonaa doo zhitoonaadik maaba ikwe. gaawii*n* (*doo*) waabimigoosiin ninda ikwewon.

"gaawiin n*doo* waabimigoosii.",

(*doo*) inendam.

gimaapii dash gaye go (*doo*) madwe giigidawon ninda ikwewon.

"aaniish *dash* wiyii (*e*) binji gikweshigaabowi yin. mininaak *dash* gonaa (*doo*) bibiindigesiwon.",

doo igoodigenon sa.

"aa*niish*, gaa waabimit iidik.",

(*doo*) inendam *dash* iidik. aaniish, mii*dash* giiyeN gii nizhaat wodi wiigwaaming.

"bibiindigen.",

doo igoon giiyeN.

"bibiindigen."

aaniish mii sa go gii nibiindiget.

"bibiindigen.",

doo igoon sa.

"ggii gikenimin go wii dagoshinan.",

doo igoon *dash* giiyeN ninda maandaagikwen. aapidji giiyeN go (*doo*) gonaadjiwi owo ikwe.

"e ko niizhagonigak go g*doo* gikenimin zhinda wii bimose yin.", he supposedly thought, as he now had doubts about what his older sister had told him about the area. So, he slowly approached the house. There was an open window and inside the house he saw this woman sitting inside. From what he could see of her as she sat with her back to him, she was very beautiful. This woman must have been working on something as she did not seem to sense his presence. The woman did not see him.

"She does not see me,"

he supposedly thought.

After some time, the woman spoke to the young man.

"Why are you sneaking up on me? Why don't you just come in,"

the young man was told by this woman.

"Oh my, I guess she saw me,"

the young man thought. Then he walked toward the house.

"Come in,"

he was told.

"Come in."

So he entered the house.

"Come in,"

she had said to him.

"I knew you would be coming."

he was told by this beautiful woman. Oh, this woman was very beautiful.

"I knew two days ago that you would be coming by,"

doo igoodigenon sa.

"gichi waasa gdoo binjibaa.",

doo igoon giiyeN.

"gichi zhaazhago zhinda e ko daa yaaN.",

doo igoodigenon dash ninda ikwewon.

"zhaazhigo gonaa geniin gii nibowiban nwiidigemaagan.",

doo igoodigenon sa.

"nshike go dash zhinda ndoo yaa. aaniish, gga zhitoomowin ge miiji yin.",

doo igoon sa giiyeN.

"nga jiibaakoweNsiw gonaa banggii, ji wiyii shaminaaN."

aaniish, mii sa giiyeN gii jiibaakowenit. gii bitaagot zhewe wii wiisinit.

"gdoo bakademidik. waasa gdoo bizhibimose.",

doo igoon giiyeN.

miidash giiyeN gaa shkwaa wiisinit, miinawaa giiyeN semaan gii biidaawigoon, doo pwaagani gaye maaba anishinaabe gewiin. aaniish, mii sa gii nashkinewaat do pwaaganon. miinawaa giiyeN gewiin iwi shkodekaanon giiyeN maaba ikwe, newe shkode zhitoot e nakaazanggin, mii maaba shkodekaan e inind. mii go anishinaabe gaa nakaazat giiyeN iwi asin, shkode gonaa wii zhitoot. ngoding, gii paskaneganaandang iwi asin, mii go gii zakawaat maaba anishinaabe ninda do pwaaganemon.

aaniish, mii sa (doo) dibaadjimotaawigot.

"gii shkwaa biindaakowe yin gonaa, gga waabidawin e ndaa yaaN.",

doo igoodigenon sa ninda ikwewon. gichi wiigwaam giiyeN go zhewe e ndaanit go. aaniish, mii sa giiyeN gaa shkwaa baabiindaakowet, mii iwi,

he must have been told by her.

> "You have come from far away,"

she supposedly said to him.

> "I have lived here for many years,"

he was told by this woman.

> "My husband died many years ago,"

he was further told by her.

> "So, I am living all alone here. Well, I will fix you something for you to eat,"

she said to him.

> "I will cook up a little something so that I can feed you."

So, she began to cook. In no time, she brought him his meal to eat.

> "You must be hungry. You have been walking a long time."

she supposedly said to him.

When he finished eating, she brought him some tobacco, as he had a pipe with him that he smoked occasionally. So, with the tobacco she had given him, he loaded up his pipe. The woman also had flint, the stone that is used to start a fire. This is what the Anishinaabe people used to make fire, the flint. So this man struck the flint once and he lit his pipe immediately.

Then the young man was spoken to by this woman.

> "After you have finished smoking your pipe, I will show you around my home,"

the young man was told by this woman. This was a huge house this woman lived in. So when he had finished smoking his pipe,

"nahaaw, wiyii maajaan, gga waabidaan e ndaa yaaN.",

doo igoon sa giiyeN. aazhoowisak giiyeN wodi gii zhiwinigoon. aapidji giiyeN go (doo) gonaadjiwonini zhewe iidik biindik. nowonch giiyeN go gegoo (doo) temigat biindik. anishinaabek gonaa, netaa mazinikodjigedjik gonaa gaa zhitoowaat, netaa mookodaasadjik gonaa. nowonch giiyeN gonaa maanda (doo) zhinaagot zhewe e temigak biindik. aasamoogabak giiyeN go aanind go (doo) goodemigat go maanda anishinaabe gaa zhitoogobaneN. miinawaa dash gaye ninda ikwewon doo igoon,

"gichi zhaazhigo (doo) nibowiban nwiidigemaagan."

ninda dash gewiin gaa zhichigaadek zhewe, e goodek aasamoogabak, (doo) bebakaaniziwok iidik gwonda gaa zhitoodjik. (doo) nisadowinaan gonaa maaba oshkinowe iwi. gaawiin eta (doo) bezhigosii mookodaasonini sa gonaa ji kida yinggoban gaa zhitoot iwi.

dewewiganon giiyeN gaye, ensa zhinaagoziwaat giiyeN, bwaanakikoog gaye, kina go (doo) bebakaaniziwok anishinaabek ninda gaa zhiwaadjik. mii go zhaazhago maaba oshkinowe newe gii nisadowinawaat. miinawaa dash giiyeN iwi doo igoon,

"maanpii dash mii ge daa yin.",

doo igoon giiyeN.

"gga waabidawin gaye iwi."

aapidji (doo) gonaadjiwonini giiyeN iwi zhewe aachikinigaadenik.

"mii zhinda ji daa yin. gdaa kawe naweb gonaa zhinda, gichi waasa giyaabi waa zhaa yin.",

doo igoodigenon sa.

"gdaa daniz gonaa zhinda, miinawaa gaye gonaa gdaa giiwise gonaa. giishpmaa dash gaye bibowaa giiwise yin, gdaa giigooNke.",

doo igoodigenon sa. aaniish, mii sa go gii nakowetawaat.

"nahaaw, gwodjiing miinawaa gga bibaa zhaamin.",

doo igoon dash giiyeN.

"Okay now, come with me, as I will show you my home,"

he was apparently told by the woman. He was led into the next room by this woman. The inside of the house was very nice. There were many things in the house. The carvings were made by artisans, excellent carvers. The items were all different shapes and sizes. The walls were covered with these carvings, which apparently were made by men. The woman then says to him,

"My husband died many years ago."

But, the things that decorated this house, the carvings and woodwork, all had been made by different people. This much the young man could tell, just by looking at the items. It could be said that these were not done by one person.

There were drums of all kinds and also waterdrums that had obviously been made by different people all around the house. This young man could tell that they were made by different artists and craftsmen. The woman went on to say to him,

"So this is where you will live,"

She supposedly said to him,

"I will show you where you will stay."

Apparently, the room was very nice.

"This is where you will live. You should rest here for a while for you still have a long trip ahead of you,"

the young man was apparently told by this woman.

"You should live here, and you could hunt around here as well. If you do not want to hunt, then you could fish,"

he was told by her. So, he apparently responded to her.

"Good, now let us go outside,"

he was supposedly told by her.

miidash giiyeN wodi iwi gitigaanini gii bibaa waabidawigot. aapidji giiyeN go (*doo*) maandaagonaagodoon asiniin e tegin gitigaaning. gaawii*n* gonaa giinawin gonaa newe gdaa g*a*shkitoosiinaanan ji zhitoo ying, giiyeN e zhizhinaagok ninda asiniin. nowonch gonaa gegoo (*e*) mazinaabikigaadek gonaa zhewe asiniing. gimaapii *da*sh giiyeN go wodi, mii giiyeN gewe giizhikeNsak (*doo*) bidakozowaat naawokitigaan, (*doo*) giiwitaakoziwok giiyeN giizhikeNsak. mii*da*sh giiyeN e igot iwi,

> "gaawiin wodi gd*oo* inen*a*misanoo ji waabimadowaaba*n* giizhikeNsak.
> gegowa wiikaa zhaake*n* wodi.",

d*oo* igoon sa iidik.

> "nahaaw, gaa*w*ii*n* gonaa ndaa zhaasii.",

d*oo* inaadigenon dash.

miid*a*sh giiyeN iwi e waabang, mii iwi iidik e zhinendang wii giiwiset.

> "nga kawe yaa gonaa zhinda jina.",

(*doo*) inendam sa iidik. miidash giiyeN iidik gii inaat iwi,

> "nga giiwise waabang.",

gii inaan giiyeN. aapidji dash giiyeN go gizhep gii g*o*shkozi. zhaazhago giiyeN newe ikwewon wodi gii g*o*shkozinigoba*n* gewii*n*. wodi gonaa e nizhaat gonaa iwi jiibaakowegamigooninik iwi wiigwaam, giyegeti go giiyeN (*doo*) danakamiig*o*ziwon zhewe *da*sh (*doo*) nakiinit biindik gonaa. mii*da*sh iidik e inaat iwi,

> "nwii giiwise."

aaniish mii sa giiyeN gii shamigot.

miid*a*sh giiyeN waa maajaat wii giiwiset, e igot,

> "giishpin maaba waawaashkeshi (*doo*) nisat, gegowa biinaake*n*, niin, nga naanaa. kina nayiinawi*nd* maanda ngii gikendaan zhinda aki."
> "gichi zhaazhigo sa zhinda e ko yaa yin.",

d*oo* inaan sa giiyeN.

So then, he was taken to see her garden. As he looked around, he saw that there were these strange looking rocks around the garden. We would not be able to make the designs that were etched on those rocks. Then as he looked around, he noticed that there was this cedar grove further toward the middle of this field, and these cedar trees were growing in a circular pattern. That is when she spoke to him.

"I do not want you to go looking around that cedar grove. Do not ever go there,"

he was told by this woman.

"Okay, I will not go there, ever,"

he must have assured her.

So the next morning, he decided that he would go hunting.

"I will stay here for a little while,"

he must have decided. So he said to her,

"I will go hunting tomorrow."

he told this woman. So he awoke very early in the morning. The woman was already awake before he was. She was in the kitchen of the house and she was busy fixing breakfast. So he says to her,

"I will go hunting."

So she then fed him breakfast.

As he was leaving, she said to him,

"If you happen to kill a deer, do not bring it out with you, I will go get it. I know every inch of the land around here."

"That is understandable, because you have lived here a long time,"

he supposedly replied to her.

> "mii go eta ji biinanat waawaashkeshi (doo) nisat, miinawaa gga goonaa. mii go ji bigiiwe yin. niin dash nga naanaa.",

doo igoon sa giiyeN.

> "nahaaw.",

doo inaadigenon sa. wiin wiyii gonaa gaye waawaashkeshiwon gonaa gii nisaat gonaa e ndaawaat gii giiwiset, wiin giiyeN gonaa ko gonaa gii bigobimoomaan. zhinda dash ninda ikwewon,

> "gegowa biinaaken, niin nga naanaa.",

doo igoon. aaniish, mii sa go iwi gaa zhichiget. mii go (doo) nisaat waawaashkeshiwon mii go biinanaat, mii go zhewe zhigoonaat gonaa, gwodji mitigooNsing. (doo) nigiiwet, miinawaa giiyeN degoshing zhewe e danizit, giizhaa, giiyeN go (doo) teni waa miijit miinawaa giiyeN gaye wii giziibiigiit doo igoon. giizhaa giiyeN nibiish (doo) te*migad* e gizhaagomidek wii giziibiigiit maaba nini.

> "gdoo yekosimidik gibe giizhik (doo) oobimose yin.",

doo igoon giiyeN.

> "da gichi nishin da giziibiigii yin. gii shkwaa wiisini yin miinawaa gaye gga nibaa, noomak go gga nibaa, mii iwi ji nawebi yin.",
> "nahaaw."

aaniish mii sa giiyeN go gaa zhichiget iwi. naakoshik e nidagoshing, mii go gaa shkwaa wiisinidji, mii go (doo) giziibiiget. miidash go waawaashkeshiwon (e) nisaat, mii go wodi (doo) ooniganaat wodi go, dibi go iidik e tapinaagoweN. ji bibowaa shkwaa wiisinit giiyeN go iwi, mii iwi, mii (doo) dagoshininit ninda ikwewon, mii biinaanit ninda waawaashkeshiwon. giyegeti giiyeN iidik maaba ikwe gezhiikaat, gaa*wiin dash* wiyii maaba nini gii gikenimaasiin, miidash bidjiinak gii maaminanenimaat.

> "giyegeti go owo nga kawe dibenimaa maaba.",

(doo) inendam dash iidik.

"All you will do after you kill the deer is clean it and then hang it up in a tree somewhere. Then you will come straight home. I will then go get the deer,"

he was apparently told by this woman.

"Okay,"

he must have said to her. Whenever he hunted before, he usually always carried his kill back home with him. And here, this woman was telling him,

"Do not bring it back with you, as I will go get it."

he is apparently told by this woman. So that is what he did. As soon as he killed a deer, he cleaned it and hung it up in a tree. He would then go home, and when he got back to the house, there was a meal waiting for him and she would tell him to wash up. The water was already heated and ready for the man's use.

"You must be tired from walking around all day,"

the young man was told by this woman.

"It will do you good to freshen up. After you have eaten, you should take a nap, take a long nap so that you will be well rested,"
"Okay."

So, that is what he did. When he got home in the evening, he would eat, then he would bathe. And when he killed a deer, he would leave it wherever he had slain it. Then, he noticed that this woman would always return with the slain deer before he had finished eating. Oh, this woman must be very fast, for he did not really know her and he was now beginning to realize the traits of this woman.

"Okay, I will try to get the best of this woman,"

he decided.

"aapidji go waasa nga zhaa. giishpmaa waawaashkeshi (*doo*) nisag wodi mii go zhewe ji goonak. nga kawe dibenimaa maaba ikwe, mandj iidik ge piiskaagoweN."

mii*da*sh giiyeN gaa zhichiget iwi, *naa*nedaa giiyeN waawaashkeshiwon gii nisaan, waasa gonaa zhewe gonaa e danizit, gichi waasa gonaa gwodji. mii*da*sh giiyeN go zhewe gii goonaat, gii nigiiwet.

mii*da*sh giiyeN gaa nidagoshing wodi,

"ggii nisaa waawaashkeshi.",

d*oo* igoon giiyeN. mii giiyeN go zhewe shkwaandeming nakweshkaawigot.

"*na*haa*w*, mii go ji wiisini yin, ji zhiitaa *y*imba*n* ji wiisini yin.",

d*oo* ig*oo*digenon sa. aa*n*iish, mii sa giiyeN gii wenabit gonaa *o*wo, gaa migiizhiitaat gonaa giziinggowewit gonaa. mii*da*sh iidik iwi gii nimaajaanit, gii naanaanit newe waawaashkeshiwon. zhaazhigo gii wiindamawaan gaa t*a*pinaat newe, mii giiyeN go gaaNwaaN go gii de shkwaa wiisinit, mii iwi (*doo*) bidagoshininit, waawaashkeshiwon (*doo*) biidoomaani. mii newe gaa nisaandjin. mandj iidik maaba ikwe e piichibizogoweN. mandj gaye iidik e piichiiwigoweN, aapidji iidik m*a*shkowazi. mii*da*sh giiyeN e igot iwi gaa shkwaa wiisinit gonaa,

"giziibiigiin. gga naweb."

aaniish, mii sa giiyeN gii giziibiigiit. giikiimigoshi gaa shkwaa giziibiigiit, mii giiyeN go iidik gii oonibaat. noomag gonaa ginimaa gii nibaadik maaba, mandj gonaa iidik minik. ginimaa gaye gonaa ngodibagiiswaan giinawi*n* gonaa ji kida yinggoba*n* gonaa. mii gii g*o*shkozit miinawaa. mii*da*sh giiyeN (*doo*) gagwedjimigot iwi,

"ggii gikendaan na gonaa gegoo gonaa ji madwewechige *y*imban gonaa."
"eN, n*doo* gikendaan sa gonaa."

iwi gonaa gewii*n* anishinaabe gonaa gii madwewechiget, bibig*o*wan gonaa gaa nakaazat, miinawaa bwaanikikoon, miinawaa *o*wo yaawaa, zhiishiigwan e inint iwi.

mii*da*sh giiyeN gaa nan*a*kaanigot newe. ensa naakoshik giiyeN, mii giiyeN ji bibowaa nibaanit, mii iwi kawe dewe*w*igamowaat miinawaa (*doo*) m*a*dwewechige gaye. bibigowan, miinawaa zhinggowebanaan iwi zhiishiigwan e daming. mii sa giiyeN iwi gaa zhichiget ensa naakoshik.

"I will go as far away as I can. And if I kill the deer, I will hang it up right there. I want to see how fast this woman really is."

So then, that is what he did, it was by chance that he killed a deer when he had gone the furthest away he ever had from this woman's home, it was very far off. So he hung up his kill and he went back home.

So when he arrived back home,

"Did you kill a deer?"

he was queried by the woman. The woman met him right at the door as he got back to the house.

"Okay, you will eat right away, you should get ready to eat,"

he was told by her. So he sat down to eat after he had finished washing up. That is when the woman left to go get the deer. He had told her roughly where he had slain the deer, and he was just finishing up his meal when the woman returned carrying the deer on her back. It definitely was the deer he had slain. It was astounding as to how fast this woman could travel. And he did not know how strong she was, but she had to be very strong. So, when he finished his meal, she spoke to him saying,

"Wash up. Then rest."

So, he washed up. He felt drowsy after and so he went to sleep. He must have slept for some time, but it is not known how long he rested. He may have rested for only an hour in our modern terms. The young man awoke. That is when she asked him this.

"Do you know how to play music?"
"Yes, I know a little."

The way the Anishinaabe people of old made music was with flutes, and drums and rattles or shakers, that is what he knew.

So, this is how she spent the evenings with him. Every evening, he would drum for her and make music for her. He played the flute and shook the rattle as he made music. This is what he did every evening before they retired for the night.

miidash giiyeN ngoding e inendang.

"aaniish iidik gaa oonji ganamawit maaba newe wii bibowaa zhaa yaaN gewe zhinggobiiNsak (doo) bidakozowaat. nonggom naakoshik dagoshinaaN nga oogiimaab wodi, e piitendit waawaashkeshiwon (doo) naanaat. giishpmaa gegoo nitoo yaaN.",

(doo) inendam sa iidik.

miidash giiyeN e giizhigadinik gii giiwiset. mii giiyeN naanedaa gaa zhinisaat waawaashkeshiwon. mii iidik wewiip gii bigiiwet, gii giizhendang go wii oonaabit wodi giizhikeNsak (doo) bidakozowaat. wegodigowendik iidik owo ikwe zhewe e zaagitoogoweN. aaniish, gaawiin dash wiyii go gii wiindamawaasiin.

"nwii oozaagiinggowen wodi gii nimaajaa yin.",

ji gii inaat gaye. mii giiyeN go zhewe gii gikenimigot iidik gii nisaat waawaashkeshiwon.

"ggii nisaa waawaashkeshi."
"eN, gichi waasa ngii tapinaa owo.",

doo inaan sa giiyeN.

"waasa gonaa noopiming."
"nga naanaa."

mii giiyeN go eta gii wiindamawaat gonaa zhaazhowaach gonaa wodi e zhinaagodinik wodi gaa tapinaat newe. mii giiyeN gii nimaajaanit. gaa nijekaakowiinit giiyeN mitigowaakiing, mii giiyeN go wodi wewiip gii patoot wodi newe giizhikeNson (doo) mazawekozinit, gii oozaagiinggowenit wodi.

aaniish sa giiyeN wiyii gonaa, (doo) maamkaadendam. aapidji giiyeN go zhewe kanigaandibewan (doo) baatiinadoon. kaneNan gaye gonaa, anishinaabe gonaa iidik gonaa, anishinaabe kaneNan sa gonaa. geget sa gonaa (doo) maamkaadendam.

"mii na gonaa maaba iwi gaa oonji izhid ikwe wii bibowaa binjizhaa yaaN zhinda.",

(doo) inendam sa iidik. taaya, mii giiyeN (doo) makowendang newe miseNon giiyeN gaye gaa igot.

Then this thought came to him one day.

"I wonder why she does not want me to go see what is in the cedar grove.
This evening I will go take a quick peek in there, while she is gone to get
the deer. Well, that is if I kill one when I hunt,"

he supposedly thought.

Then, the next day he went hunting again. He was fortunate to kill a deer that day quite far from home. He quickly came home, as he had made up his mind to go look in the cedar grove that evening. He wanted to find out what she was protective about. Of course, he did not tell her about his plans.

"I will go and peek in the cedar grove once you have left,"

he definitely did not tell her that. As soon as he got home, she seemed to instinctively know that he had killed a deer.

"You killed a deer?"
"Yes, I killed one far, far away from here,"

the young man supposedly told the woman.

"Far inland, deep in the woods."
"I will go get the deer."

So, he gave a general description of what the area looked like where he had killed the deer. The woman left right away. As the woman entered the woods, the young man quickly ran to the cedar grove and took a look.

Oh, he was bewildered and shocked at what he saw. There were many human skulls strewn about on the ground. There were also all kinds of bones, and these were human bones. Oh, he was stunned and also shocked by what he saw before him.

"Now I know why she told me not to come looking around in here,"

he thought. And at that moment, he remembered what his older sister had cautioned him about this area he was now at.

"niwaannoshkan maanda zhinda gaa zhibiimaaN. gegowa zhinda ninigaashkaak*en*.",

gii igoon giiyeN. aa*niish*, gii makowenimaan giiyeN giyegeti.

"mii na gonaa nmiseN gaa *oo*nji kidat iwi, gaa *oo*nji izhid wii bibowaa nigaashkaa yaaN zhinda. gaawii*n*, nga maajaa sa zhinda.",

(*doo*) inendam sa iidik.

"gaawii*n* zhinda ndaa yaasii."

miidash giiyeN iwi niibaadibik, iwi gaa shkwaa nigamotawaat, miinawaa gaa shkwaa madwewe*t*oomawaat iwi e naakoshinik, mii iidik gii oonibaat. mii*da*sh giiyeN maanda noondaadibik, mii giiyeN e zhi-aapowet. aapidji giiyeN (*doo*) gichi dewe*w*ige. mii giiyeN wodi (*doo*) namadabit newe, megowe, newe sa gonaa kaneNan gaa waabidanggin kosininik. mii giiyeN naawoyiing (*doo*) namadabit, (*doo*) dewewige giiyeN. (*doo*) naapowe gonaa maanda. taaya, mii*da*sh giiyeN maanda e piichi dewe*w*iget, taaya, mii gosha giiyeN zhewe megowe kaneNan anishinaaben e nji bazigowiind*o*senit, *o*shkinowek.

aapidji giiyeN go gwonda, *o*shkinowek (*doo*) minowendamo*w*ok (*doo*) bibimaadiziwaat. (*doo*) zaasaakowewon giiyeN gaye, (*doo*) niimiwon giiyeN gaye, (*doo*) baapiwon. aapidji giiyeN go (*doo*) minoyaawon go. mii*da*sh giiyeN gii goshkoset, jichkana gonaa gii bigoshkose gonaa iwi gonaa (*doo*) zegaamidang gonaa. taaya, ge*get* sa gonaa giiyeN (*doo*) maamkaadendam.

"mii go ji maajaa yaaN.",

(*doo*) inendam *da*sh iidik.

"nongg*om* go gii waabang, nga maajaa."

taaya go, aanii giiyeN gonaa gibeying wii waabaninik gonaa. *zha*zhaanggishing iidik zhewe (*doo*) naanaagodowendang, iwi gaye gonaa e ndaawaat, gaa binjibaat gonaa (*doo*) makowendaan, miseNon gaye. aa*n*iish gii waabanini sa giiyeN go aanowi gimaapii. gaawii*n* giiyeN gegoo d*oo* inaasiin. gaawii*n* gegoo gii zhiwiindamawaasiin iwi gii oogiim*oo*zaabidang newe kaneNan wodi giizhikeNsak bidak*o*zowaat.

"mii go nongg*om* ji maajaa yaaN.",

"Bypass this area I have marked out on this map. Do not stop in this area,"

he had been told by his sister. Now he was seriously thinking about what she had said.

"Is this why my sister told me not stop here? Well then, I will leave this place,"

he must have thought.

"I will not stay here."

So then, that night after he had sung some songs and played music for the woman, he went to sleep. But during the night, he had a dream. He dreamt that he was drumming very hard and very fast. And he dreamt that he was sitting among the human skulls and bones that he had seen piled up in the cedar grove, and all the while, he was drumming. He was dreaming this. Oh my goodness, while he was drumming, there were men, young men who arose up standing erect around him, they arose from those piles of human bones.

These young men seemed so pleased that they had come to life again. They were yelling, shouting, whooping as they danced around and these young men were also laughing as an expression of their happiness. Oh, these young men were having a very good time. Then he suddenly awakened from this frightful dream he was having, and he was dumbfounded by this dream.

"I am going to leave this place,"

he supposedly thought to himself.

"When morning comes, that is when I will leave."

It was an extremely long time for the dawn to arrive, for it seemed that he laid awake forever. He lay there thinking about his home and his sister. Well, as usual, morning eventually came. He did not say anything about his dream. Least of all, he did not mention to her that he had sneaked to the cedar grove and seen the pile of human skulls and bones in the cedar grove.

"Today is the day that I leave from here,"

(doo) inendam dash iidik. aaniish, mii sa go iwi gaa shkwaa wiisinit gizhep, mii go baapizh go, mii go gii maajaat. gaawiin gegoo gii inaasiin ninda ikwewon.

miidash giiyeN go pii waa jekaakowiit zhewe jiigaakowaa, mii gii aabinaabit, (doo) waabidang wiigwaam, giyaabi giiyeN zhewe shkwaandeming (doo) naaniibowiwon, (doo) ganawaabimigoon giiyeN. taaya, mii giiyeN go gaa nijekaakowiit zhewe mitigowaakiing, mii go gaa nji webiit, e piichibizot go. mii gaye bidjiinak giiyeN (doo) gikendang (doo) zegazit, (doo) zegazi go. (doo) gosaan ninda ikwewon. gibe giizhig giiyeN go gii bimabatoo. aapidji gonaa jina gonaa gii bimosedik. mii gaye iidik e inendang owo, mii go eta nandowaabimaat gwodji wii bizaagewebazonit newe ikwewon. aapidji giiyeN go (doo) zegazi go. gaawiin go gii gikendaziin go e zhiyaat gonaa. gimaapii dash giiyeN maanda naakoshini. miidash giiyeN gaa zhiwaabidang iwi zaagaapatenik shkode gonaa gwodji gonaa pakokomigaak gonaa. niigaan gonaa zhewe gonaa bemipatoot, (doo) zaagaapateni giiyeN wodi gimaapiich.

"yaa-aa, wiya iidik e yaat.",

(doo) inendam dash giiyeN. miidash giiyeN wodi gaa zhaat wodi zaagaapatenik. (doo) nigaagiimoozaabit wodi. yaawaan dash giiyeN zhewe e yaanidjin, aapidji giiyeN (doo) mandido owo anishinaabe zhewe. megowaa giiyeN gaye go wodi doo midizhi minozang zhewe, (doo) nisaakowaan gonaa iwi wiiyaas gonaa. gimaapiich dash giiyeN gaye gii waabimigoon.

"maajaan, nshiimeN.",

(doo) madwe kidawon sa giiyeN. (doo) madwe naanoondaagoziwon giiyeN go newe. gaawiin giiyeN gaye wiikaa gii gikenimaasiin wiya gaye gonaa sayeNon, shiimeNon gaye ji gii yaanit.

"aaniish niyii gaye gonaa maaba nshiimeN e oonji zhinikaazhid.",

(doo) inendam dash iidik. aaniish, miidash go gii zhaat newe anishinaaben e nji jiibaakowenit, gii nidagoshing wodi.

"geget sa gonaa ndoo minowendam zhinda bizhaa yin, nshiimeN.",

doo igoon giiyeN. aapidji giiyeN go (doo) gichi zaginindjiinigoon newe.

"niin go zhinda zhi-inendamaaN binjizhaa yin.",

he supposedly thought. Well, as he planned, after he had his breakfast, he quickly left. He did not say anything to the woman.

When he got to the edge of the forest, he looked back toward the house, and he saw that she was standing at the door watching him. So, as he went into the forest, out of sight, he took off, and he ran as fast as he could. This was when he also realized that he was scared, he was very frightened. He was afraid of this woman. He ran all day. He would only slow down to catch his breath and he walked just for a little while, but mostly, he ran. And he was always watching out for her, thinking that she could show up in front of him at any moment. He was very frightened. He was so scared that he did not really know what he was doing. Eventually it was getting to be late afternoon, and it soon would be evening. Then he noticed that there was smoke from a fire somewhere ahead of him over the next knoll. As he was running, he noticed the smoke ahead of him.

"Oh my, somebody must be near here,"

he thought. So, he made his way toward where the smoke was rising into the sky. He went slowly toward the smoke as he was not sure who would be there. And he saw a very big man standing by the fire. This giant of a man was cooking some meat, he had it on a stick that was stuck into the ground and slanted toward the fire so that the meat would cook. After a while, the big man noticed that he had a visitor.

"Come here, my little brother,"

this big man apparently uttered to him. The big man was actually shouting this to him. And this young man had never known to ever have had an older brother or even a younger sibling.

"I wonder why this man is calling me his younger brother,"

the young man supposedly thought. Anyway, he went to where the big man was cooking meat by the fire.

"I am very pleased that you arrived here, my little brother,"

the young man was told by the big man. The big man shook the young man's hand very long and hard.

"It is because of me, I willed you to come here, that is why you are here," doo igoodigenon dash.

"ngii gikendaan go gaa danizi yin.",

doo igoon sa iidik.

"owo ikwe wodi gaa gibiitoowot, aapidji nayiinawin owo (doo) minowendam owo anishinaabe wiiyaas (doo) miijit.",

doo igoon giiyeN.

"mii nonggom ji gii nisigoban owo paskaabii yimban wodi.",

doo igoon giiyeN.

"gichi niibana nayiinawin zhaazhigo niniwon (doo) gidamowaan owo.",

(doo) kidawidigenon sa ninda gichi anishinaaben.

"miidash nonggom ji gii nisigoban nipaskaabii yimban owo. mii go zhago maanda minodek wiiyaas nesaakowamaaN.",

doo igoon sa iidik.

"gga shamin geniin. gdoo bakademidik, gibe giizhik gdoo bimibowe.",

doo igoon sa.
mii sa giiyeN go maanda e nenimigot newe. miinawaa giiyeN (doo) kidawon iwi,

"ggii waabidaanaadigenan go newe kaneNan zhewe naawogitigaan e kosinggin. mii newe maaba ikwe gedamowaadjin niniwon.",

doo igoon sa iidik.

"ngii waabidaanan sa go newe. aapidji go ngii ganamaak wii bibowaa zhaa yaaN wodi. ngoding dash gonaa (e) naadjiwonet gonaa, mii wodi giimooch gii zhaa yaaN.", the younger man was told by the big man.

"I know where you lived,"

the younger man was told by this big man.

"That woman you stayed with, she has a great fondness for human flesh,"

this young man was told by the big man.

"Today would have been the day that she would have killed you if you had gone back there,"

he was told by the giant of a man.

"She has eaten the flesh of many, many men already,"

this big man must have said.

"If you had gone back there today, she surely would have killed you. Oh, this meat I am cooking here on the stick will soon be done,"

the young man was supposedly told by the big man.

"I will feed you also. You must be hungry as you have been on the run all day."

The young man is told.

The big man thinks of him as one would think about one's own close and dear relative. The big man went on to say this.

"You must have seen those pile of bones piled up in the middle of the field. Those are the bones of the men this woman has eaten."

the young man is told.

"Yes, I did see those bones. She strictly forbade me from going to that area. Then out of curiosity, I went there to look while she was out to get the deer I had killed deep in the woods,"

gii inaadigenon dash ninda gichi anishinaaben.

> "nahaaw, wewiip maanda miijin wiiyaas. gga kinoomawin e ndaa yaaN. gga giiwenin. anish*aa* gonaa (*doo*) zhaweniminaaN, mii zhinda (*e*) binjizhaa yaaN genii*n*. mii go nongg*om* ji gii nisigoba*n* maaba ikwe, bemowe-ikwe.",

d*oo* zhinikaanaani sa giiyeN newe.

> "noodinong nayiinawi*n* maaba (*doo*) piichibizo. gaawii*n* gdaa niganaasii giigii*n*. na, gaye go nongg*om* gga goji yin go. gga waabamin e piichibatoo yin.",

d*oo* ig*oo*digenon sa giiyeN ninda gichi niniwon.

> "gga gidaakiiyemi*n* zhinda."

aaniish, mii sa giiyeN gii gidaakiiyewaat zhewe, gaa gondang g*o*naa *i*wi wiiyaas g*o*naa maaba maajipa*n*. mii*da*sh giiyeN gimaapiich wodi ziingg*a*kamigaak,

> "gd*oo* waabidaan na wodi ziinggakamigaak.",

d*oo* ig*oo*digenon sa ninda niniwon.

> "eN(*he*N), nd*oo* waabidaan sa go."
> "gd*oo* gizhiikaapatoo na go (*e*) *b*imap*a*too yin.",

d*oo* igoon sa giiyeN.

> "eN(*he*N), nd*oo* gizhiikaa sa go."
> "togowa dash wodi patoon miinawaa gga bip*a*skaabii. gga baabiiwon go zhinda. mii ji gikendamaaN e piiskaa yin.",

d*oo* ig*oo*digenon sa ninda gichi anishinaaben.

aaniish, mii sa maaba *o*shkinowe, mii iwi gii maadjiibatoot, (*doo*) patoot wodi iwi ziingg*a*kamigaanik. waasa go ginimaa ngodibagan, ginimaa gaye go ooshame. aaniish, jina sa giiyeN gonaa wodi gii bibigom*o*set miinawaa gii bip*a*skaabatoot. giyaabi giiyeN go zhewe (*doo*) yaawon newe gichi anishinaaben.

the younger man told the bigger man.

"Okay, eat up this meat quickly. I will show you where I live. I will take you to my home. It is because I am showing you mercy, that is why I am here. Today was the day that she would have killed you, the one called Bemowe-ikwe."

That is what the big man called her.

"She is as fast as the wind. You would not be able to outrun her yourself. Okay, I will test you. I want to see how fast you can run,"

he is told by this big man.

"We will go up this hill here."

So they went up this one hill after he had quickly swallowed the meat he was eating. Then far out in the distance they could see an outcropping of some land.

"Do you see that outcropping of land way over there?"

the young man was asked by the big man.

"Yes, I see it.
"Do you fancy yourself to be a fast runner?"

the young man was asked by the big man.

"Why sure, I am a fast runner."
"Okay then, why don't you run to that outcropping of land and run back. I will wait for you right here. Then I will know how fast you can run,"

the young man was told by the big man.

And so this young man began running toward that outcropping of land far off in the distance. It may have been at least a mile or even farther. It did not seem that long, and the young man was back where he started running from. The big man was still there waiting for him.

"aa sa naa, nshiimeN, gdoo nigaas.",

doo igoon sa giiyeN.

"gaawiin go ginigeN gdaa niganaasii maaba ikwe. (doo) gwetaanibizo nayiinawin maaba mitigowaakiing (doo) bimabatoot, dibishkoo go noodin go.",

doo igoon sa giiyeN.

"na, gga kinoomawin, nowonch wodi ishpakamigaak, mii wodi ge zhaa ying, gga waabidaan e ndaa yaaN. gichi waasa geniin ndoo binjibaa.",

doo igoon giiyeN. miidash giiyeN gii niwiidjiiwaat, gii gidaakiiyewaat wodi nowonch ishpakamigaanik.

waasa dash giiyeN go wodi dash (e) naabiwaat go, gomaa giiyeN go (doo) nipiidikamigaa. zhaawoshkowaabiminaagot gonaa, zhaawoshkokamigaa gonaa gwodji gonaa waasa aki (e) waabidami ying. miidash giiyeN e zhinaagodinik wodi maaba oshkinowe gii naabit.

"mii sa zhewe e ndaa yaaN, zhewe piidikamigaak.",

doo igoodigenon sa ninda gichi anishinaaben. aapidji giiyeN go maaba (doo) mandido anishinaabe.

"aaniish, gaawiin sa nayiinawin gdaa niganaasii maaba ikwe.",

doo igoodigenon dash miinawaa.

"gga bimoomin sa."

niyii dash giiyeN iwi, niibiik, niibiin ko gonaa gii nakaazanaawaan makakooNan (doo) zhitoowaat, mii giiyeN maaba owo gichi nini bemoondang iwi.

"gga bimoomin. mii zhinda ji boozi yin, niibii makakoong. aaniish, gaawiin gdoo depiiskaasii owo ji niganadiban owo bemowe-ikwe.",

(doo) kidawon sa giiyeN.

> "Oh my, my younger brother, you are very pitiful,"

he was told by the big man.

> "There is no way you can outrun this woman. She runs through the forest, very fast as if she were the wind,"

the younger man was told by the big man.

> "Look, I will show you where I live, see, way over there, the higher hill is where we will go and I will show you where I live. I come from a long ways from here,"

the young man was further told by the big man. So he went with the big man and they made their way to the higher ground.

And as they looked into the distance, they could see the contours of the land. They could see the greenish-bluish hue of the land, as it looks when we look at land that is far away from us. And this is how the land looked to the young man as he looked off into the distance.

> "See, that is where I live, there in that high area,"

the young man was told by the big man. And, remember this man is a giant of a man.

> "Well, there is no way you could outrun this woman,"

the young man again was reminded by the big man.

> "I will carry you on my back."

They used to use the elm tree to make crates to carry stuff in, and this was the kind of box this big man had with him.

> "I will carry you on my back. You will get in the elm wood box. The reason being is that you are not fast enough to outrun that Bemowe-ikwe,"

the big man supposedly uttered.

"aaniish, ndaa booz sa zhinda.",

doo inaan sa giiyeN.

"nahaaw. wewiip. mii zhago (doo) banggishimok.",

doo igoon giiyeN.

"mii go (doo) banggishimok, mii go ji gikeniminang, mii go ji gikenimik gegiin, gaawiin gwii bipaskaabiisii. mii go ji binaanik, wewiip dash gga maajaamin. mii ji de dagoshinaaN wodi e ndaa yaaN ji bibowaa daminewit. aapidji wiyii go gizhiikaa, gaa ininaaN go.",

doo igoon sa giiyeN.

aaniish, mii sa giiyeN gii bimoomigot, aapidji giiyeN go (doo) naanggowebinigoon, dibishkoo gonaa binoodjiiN gonaa.

"nahaaw, minjigonomaakowiin.",

doo igoon sa giiyeN. mii sa giiyeN (doo) maadjiibatoonit, giyegeti giiyeN go (doo) mabatoowon, aapidji go. megowe mitigowaaki gaye go miinawaa go nibooskakamigaanik (doo) nigidaakiiyebatoonit. gaawiin giiyeN go gegoo (doo) pasikaziin maaba gichi nini. aaniish, mii sa giiyeN go eta (doo) minjigonomaakowiit. gimaapii giiyeN mii iwi gii ganoonigot.

"aaniish naa nshiimeN, e zhiyaa yin."
"gaawiin go gegoo.",

doo inaadigenon sa.

"ndoo minoyaa go."
"nahaaw, mashkowanamaakowiin.",

doo igoon sa iidik. mii giiyeN go nowonch go (doo) gizhiikaapatoonit.

"mii go gegaa (doo) banggishimok.",

"Well, I guess I should get in this crate,"

the young man said to the big man.

"Okay. Hurry. The sun will soon set,"

the young man was told by the giant of a man.

"The sun is beginning to set. She will sense where we are at. She will know that you will not be returning to her. She will set out quickly to try to find you and she will come to get you, so we will leave right now. I will just make it to my home in time before she can catch up to me. She is very fast, just like I told you earlier,"

the younger man apparently was told by the big man.

Well, the big man hoisted the elm wood crate with the young man in it onto his back, and the big man lifted him up very easily as if he were a small child.

"Okay, now hang on,"

the young man was told by the big man. That is when the big man began to run, and he definitely was running fast. The man ran through the forest and down into the valley and then up the other side. The man did not run into anything as he ran fast. Well, all the young man could do was hang on as best he could. After some time, the big man spoke to the younger man.

"Well, my young brother, how are you doing?"
"Nothing is wrong,"

the young man replied.

"I am doing fine."
"Okay then, hang on tighter,"

the young man was told by the big man. That is when the big man ran even faster than before.

"It is almost sundown,"

(*doo*) kidawon giiyeN. giyegeti giiyeN (*doo*) gizhiikaawon, aapidji go. gichi waasa waa zhaawaat wii de dagoshing naa wodi ji bibowaa daminegot newe yaawaan, bemowe-ikwen. noomak *dash* giiyeN go gii bimab*a*toowon, aapidji giiyeN go (*doo*) gwetaanibizowok. mii*dash* giiyeN e igot iwi,

"aaniish naa e zhiyaa yin."
"gaa*wiin* go gegoo."
"*nahaaw*, mashkow*a*namaakowiin. mii zhago wii gizhiikaa yaaN. nowonch nonggo*m* nwii gizhiikaapatoo.",

d*oo* igoon giiyeN. giyegeti giiyeN go (*doo*) gizhiikaawon. aapidji giiyeN go (*doo*) gizhiikaapatoo maaba gichi nini. gimaapii giiyeN miinawaa mii gii ganoonigot.

"zhaazhigo aapta ngii baashizikaan. mii zhaazhigo wii banggishimok.",

d*oo* igoon giiyeN.

"zhaazhigo gii bimaajaa maaba ikwe. g*doo* biminaashkaagonaa*n*. g*doo* gikenimigonaa*n* gaye go *dash* (*doo*) yaa ying.",

d*oo* igoon sa giiyeN. miidash giiyeN nowonch giyetin da mab*a*toonit.

"nga de dagoshin.",

d*oo* igoon giiyeN.

"gaawiin ndaa daminewigosii."

taaya, eta giiyeN (*doo*) gwetaanibizowon, aapidji go.

"aa*niish*, mii go zhago besha.",

(*doo*) kidawon *dash* giiyeN miinawaa.

"mii zhago ji debitawat. gegaa go zhago da bimbiigazi go aapidji."

the big man must have uttered. And this giant of a man was really moving fast. They had a long way to go before they got to the big man's home and before that strong woman caught up to them. The big man had been running for a long time and running very fast with the young man in the box that the big man carried on his back. Then, the big man said to the young man,

> "How are you feeling?"
> "Nothing is wrong."
> "Okay, hang on tighter. I am about to begin running really fast this time. I will be running very, very fast. Faster than before,"

the young man was told by this big man. And, he definitely was traveling much faster. This big man could really run very fast. Eventually, the big man again spoke to the young man.

> "I have already passed the halfway point. The sun has already set,"

he was told by the big man.

> "This woman has already left her home. She is chasing after us. She also knows approximately where we are at right now,"

the young man was told by the big man. That is when he felt the big man start to run even faster.

> "I will be able to make it to my home,"

the young man was told by the big man.

> "She will not be able to catch up to me."

Oh my, now the big man was moving faster than before.

> "Well, we are getting closer,"

the big man supposedly said.

> "You will soon hear her off in the distance. She will make a terrible chilling sound that you will soon hear."

miidash giiyeN gimaapii gewiin maanda (doo) bazindjitoot gonaa, aaniish gonaa, (doo) gwetaanibizo gaye, (doo) bimoomigoon ninda gichi niniwon. mii giiyeN zhago (doo) noondawaat newe ikwewon. gaawiin dash wiyii giiyeN go, megowaa dash giiyeN go maanda (doo) mabatoonit, (doo) naagazatawaat ninda ikwewon, maaba oshkinowe, dibishkoo gonaa gwodji gonaa (doo) biindigebizong gonaa bagoneyaak, mii iidik gaa zhigikendang. mii go eta go (doo) madwewek go iwi, dibi gonaa iidik gonaa (doo) biindigebizogoweN, mii gaye go iidik gii wonendamaat.

ngoding dash giiyeN gonaa gimaapii giiyeN gonaa (doo) goshkozi maaba oshkinowe. biindik giiyeN zhewe michisag (doo) zhagishin, e ndaanit ninda gaa maadjiinigodjin. miidash giiyeN iwi,

"taaya, gdoo bimaadiz na gonaa go nshiimeN.",

doo igoodigenon sa ninda gichi anishinaaben. (doo) yaawon giiyeN go zhewe newe, wiidigemaaganon giiyeN maaba nini. daanison giiyeN go (doo) yaawon maaba nini, giigaanggooNs gonaa. giyaabi giiyeN wodi gwodjiing newe ikwewon (doo) noondawaan. aapidji giiyeN (doo) madwe nishkaadizi maaba ikwe, wii biindige. aaniish, gaawiin dash maamdaa wii biindiget, (doo) aadaakowagaade sa iwi shkwaandem. miidash giiyeN e kidanit ninda gichi niniwon,

"geget sa gonaa maaba ikwe ndoo zhiinggitawaa. togowa ndaanis.",

doo inaan dash giiyeN newe daaniseNon maaba gichi nini.

"togowa ndaanis, animookaadjiiN zaagadjiwebin. ginimaa go owo da oomowaan ninda e gwaanisagimbiigozindjin ikwewon.",

(doo) kidawidik sa maaba gichi nini. miidash giiyeN maaba giigaanggooNs gii bizagowiit, kodaazhegaaN gonaa iwi iidik iwi, mitigooNwidik gonaa iwi gaa nakaazat, niyii dash giiyeN naawosak e tek gichi mitigonaagan, (doo) bagoneyaa dash giiyeN maanda mitigonaagan naawoyiing, (doo) nimakosin maanda mitigonaagan. miidash giiyeN maaba giigaanggooNs zhewe gaa bizhaat maanda gii bizhi-aatowaawebinang iwi gichi mitigonaagan. taaya, gichi animookaadjiiNon giiyeN zhewe (e) bibizagowiinit. miidash giiyeN maaba gichi nini e inaat newe,

"nahaaw ndayi, naa wodi owo ikwe oomowan. aapidji ndoo zhiinggitawaa owo. nahaaw ndaanis, jichkana nisaakowebinan iwi niyii, shkwaandem."

So the young man tried to listen for this woman as he was being carried in this box on the back of this big man who was running very fast through the woods. Then he heard this woman making an awful sound. Then while this big man ran, the young man listened for where the sound the woman was making was coming from. Apparently all he heard was the roaring sound made by the wind when going fast into a narrow area, that is what the noise sounded like that young man heard. That was the sound he heard and he did not know where he was going, as he could not see being inside the box, and that is when he lost consciousness.

After a length of time, the young man began to stir and awakened from his state of unconsciousness. He found himself laying on the floor of the big man's home.

"Wow, my younger brother, you are alive,"

the young man was supposedly teased by the big man. This big man's wife was also present inside the house. The man's teenage daughter was also there. And, he could still hear the woman outside of the house. Oh, he could tell that this woman was very angry, as she wanted to come inside. But, she could not come in, as the door was locked securely. That is when the big man spoke up and said,

"Oh, I am really getting annoyed by this woman making all that noise.
Okay, my daughter,"

the big man said to his daughter.

"My daughter, put the dog outside. Maybe he could go eat that woman
who is making that really awful noise,"

the big man must have further added. So this young teenage girl got up and she picked up this big stick, it looked similar to a poker used to stoke a fire, and she moved toward a big wooden bowl that had a small hole in it and it was upside down in the middle of the floor. So this teenage girl used this big stick to lift up this big wooden bowl. Lo and behold, there was a great big dog who got up from under this big wooden bowl. And this big man instructed his dog and his daughter the following.

"Okay my pet, go kill and eat that woman. I am sick and tired of her
screeching and yelling. Okay, my daughter, open the door quickly."

miidash maaba gewiin giigaanggooNs gii nizhaat wodi shkwaandeming, jichkana gii nisaakowebinang iwi, pane animookaadjiiN. mii sa giiyeN eta maaba bemowe-ikwe gii madwe ziiziinggiit, animookaadjiiNon iidik gaa takomigot, (doo) nisigot sa gonaa. pane giiyeN. mii sa gii bizaan zhabit.

miidash giiyeN iwi maaba gichi nini e kidat,

> "mbe, mii sa iwi. aanii giiyeN gonaa da gii zhi-anishinaabekaaning ikwewok ji gichi mashkowaziwaat. gaawiin go wiikaa miinawaa daa zhiwebasinoo iwi, owo ikwe iidik ji gichi mashkowazit, ooshame go ji mashkowazit, nini dash. gichi noondaach ikwewok da piichiiwiwok ge nibimaadizidjik.",

gii kidawon dash giiyeN maaba oshkinowe newe.

aaniish, miidash gonaa gaye gaa bizhiwindawaawaagoweN gewe gaa dibaadjimagik. gichi miigwech gonaa gaa bazindawa yek.

anishinaabe waabshkibinesiwon gaa debinaadjin

miidash go owo dash go waa dibaadjimak, oshkiniigish maaba, gii nowiigiizi gonaa iwi oshkiniigit. yaawaa sa maaba anishinaabeNs, aapidji gonaa (doo) gaachiiwiban, ginimaa gaye gonaa ngodwaaswi (doo) sabiboonigizigoban, ginimaa gaye gonaa niizhwaaswi (doo) sabiboonigizigoban, mii ninda niikigoon maaba oshkiniigish gii nibowonit. bezhik dash giiyeN gonaa zhewe mindimooweN gonaa, geget gonaa ji kida yinggoban, mii iidik maaba gaa daapinaat newe, gaa inendang sa gonaa ji koginaapan ninda gwiiwizeNson. (doo) nowiigiizi maaba. aaniish, miidash go gii miinind ninda gwiiwizeNson wii ganawenimaat. aaniish, (doo) nowiigiizi sa maaba gwiiwizeNs, aaniish, mii sa go iwi gii ganawenimaat. miinawaa gaye maaba oshkiniigish (doo) wiidookowaat gonaa wiidji gwiiwizeNson, mii gonaa gewiin gegoo gaa oonji gikendang. miinawaa gaye gonaa (doo) miinaa gaye gonaa mitigowaabiin gaye go bikwakooNsan gaye, (doo) wiikodjitoot gonaa gewiin wii bimodaakowet. anishinaabeNsak gonaa, mii gonaa gaa zhikinoomawindowaa iwi, wii gwenaakowewaat gonaa ninda mitigowaabiin wii nakaazawaat. miidash go maaba oshkiniigish iwi gaa zhiyaat go. miinawaa gaye gii nitaa bagizo gaye. miinawaa gonaa (doo) googiit gaye, mii go e zhinonaadizit go, niyii dash ko ndoo zhiwaabidaan iwi ziibiing niyiin, mitigooNson gonaa, memdige go naasaap go naanigodinong jiigi ziibi, miidash ko iidik zhewe naamiyiing gii mookiset. aapidji dash giiyeN go gibeying ko gii nonaadizi. miidash gwonda gaa inendamawaat gwonda aanind begizodjik.

So the girl went to the door and quickly opened it and the dog ran outside and was gone. And this woman just made frightful sounds as the dog attacked her and killed her. And that was the end of her. And she now lays still.

So this big man said,

> "Okay, that settles it. How can it be that a woman can be that strong among the Anishinaabe people. That will never happen, ever again, that a woman will be that strong, and stronger than a man. The women from now on will not be as strong as that of a man."

This is what the big man said in the presence of this younger man.

Well, this is what must have befell these people I am talking about, that is, the big man's words came to pass. Thank you very much for listening to me.

The Man Who Caught the White Eagle

This young man I am going to talk about now, he was orphaned as a child. This young man was very small, maybe he was six or seven years old when his parents died. So there was an older woman in the community who decided to raise this young child as her own. This child was an orphan. So this older woman was given the child to raise as her own. And so she raised this orphaned child. And as this child grew up, he played with the other children, and this is how he learned to do things that were expected of him. Someone gave him a small bow and some arrows so he could learn how to shoot an arrow and hit a target. This is what the young boys of the time were taught, they had to know how to shoot an arrow using a bow. And this young boy learned to use a bow and an arrow. And this boy learned quickly and easily. Also, this boy learned to swim very well, he was an excellent swimmer. Also, when he went into the water, it seemed he could go under for a long, long time. I used to see the reeds and shrubs along the river, and this young boy apparently would swim to and hide among those reeds and bushes that grow along the river. And he would be gone for long periods of time when he went under. And the other people who would be swimming there as well, they were awed by this feat.

> "geget sa gonaa maaba oshkiniigish gibeying naamibiing (*doo*) yaa.",

gii inendamok go *da*sh ko iidik.

aaniish, mii*da*sh go gaa nizhiyaat go iwi. miinawaa gaye gizhiikaapatoo gaye (*doo*) mab*a*toot, miinawaa gaye waasa (*doo*) patoo, waasa. miidash iwi pii gonaa (*doo*) nigichi aawit gonaa, (*doo*) nitaagit sa gonaa, oshkinowewidik gonaa, mii giiyeN ninda ngoding do ogimaamowaan e igoowaat gwonda anishinaabek,

> "ndaanis ndaa na wiyii inendam wii wiidigemaagonit.",

doo igoowaadigenon sa ninda do ogimaamowaan. miidash giiyeN iwi maaba ogimaa gaa kidat,

> "gwonda gonaa e nitaagidjik gonaa oshkinowek, gaa*wiin* gonaa ooshame gonaa nis*w*imdana e nisabiboonigizit, gaa*wiin* gonaa owo. mii gonaa owo e de ninggoni yaaNmbaa.",

gii kidawidik sa.

> "maanda dash nd*oo* inendam, gwonda oshkinowek ji zhichigewaapa*n*. yaawaan, waabshkibinesiwon, wegoweN go ge biidoowigoweN oshkinowe, mii owo ndaanison ge miinak ji wiidigemaat."

mii iidik gaa kidat maaba ogimaa zhewe.

aaniish mii sa gwonda oshkinowek iidik, aaniish gii baatiina zhaazhago anishinaabe e oshkibimaadizidjik gaye, mii iidik gaye gii maawondjidiwaat go iidik waa giiwisedjik. aaniish, (*doo*) baatiinawok go. miidash maaba zhinda debaadjimak, maaba gaa bigidimaagozit oshkiniigish, aaniish, (*doo*) nitaagi gosha go gewii*n*. mii iwi gashiwon iidik e igot ngoding,

> "gichi ogimaa giiyeN (*doo*) nandowenimaan wiya ji biidaagopa*n* waabshkibinesiwon. yaawaan dash giiyeN meshkodj da miinaan, daanison. mii giiyeN maaba ge wiidigemaat wegoweN waabshkibinesiwon ge biinaagoweN."

mii*da*sh giiyeN maaba oshkinowe gaa inaat newe, wiikaa gonaa baamaa*mpii* gii ganoonaan maaba oshkinowe newe gashiwon gonaa ndaa kid gonaa, aaniish, mii newe gaa nitaaginigodjin.

> "Gee, he really can stay under the water for a very, very long time,"

is what the people used to think about him.

Well, that was the way he was, he excelled at many thing. And he could run very fast, and he could run far, very far. Then when he became of age, as he got older, that is when the chief of their community told the people the following.

> "I would like my daughter to become married,"

the chief must have said to the people. And this is what the chief further said to the people:

> "I am talking about young men, none older than thirty years of age, not anyone older than thirty. I would like a young man of that age for a son-in-law,"

the chief supposedly said to the people.

> "This is what I have in mind for these young men to do. Whomever of the young men, the one that brings to me a white eagle, that is the one who will have my daughter's hand in marriage."

Apparently, this is what the chief had told the people.

So all of the young men gathered and there were many young men in the community who were of the age range set by the chief as ideal, and the young men gathered to get ready to hunt. There were many young men who qualified for the age range. And this young man who I began talking about, this one who was poor and who was an orphan, he too was now of age. That is when his mother, the old woman who raised him said to him,

> "The chief would like someone to bring him a white eagle. He would give the lucky person to do so his daughter's hand in marriage. The young man who will marry his daughter is the one who brings him the white eagle."

So this young man replied to this old woman, who we can call his mother, he replied to her after a long silence, as this is the woman who raised him.

"gaawiin sa wiyii niiniin owo ogimaakweNs ginigeN ndaa ganawaabimigoosii. gaawiin niyii gonaa e zhidiniwaat gonaa gwonda oshkinowek e niikozidjik, gaawiin niiniin iwi ndoo zhiyaasii. pane gonaa maanda bigikendamaaN gonaa ndoo bigidimaagiz. aaniish, aanowi go ggii nitaawigish. aaniish, nonggom dash mii gonaa bidjiinak gowekotaa yaaN gonaa ji zhitoo yaaNmbaan gonaa geniin ge nakaaza yaaN, niin gonaa geniin."

wiikaa dash giiyeN go maaba mindimooyeN miinawaa gii ganoonaan newe gwisison.

"bekaa, gga wiindamowin, giishpmaa sa maamiikozhiwebazi yin, (doo) nisat owo waabshkibinesi, miidash go giyegeti ji wiidigemat maaba ogimaakweNs. miinawaa gwonda anishinaabek zhinda waadji danakiim yinggok, gga zhitaawigowok ge daa yin. miinawaa go gga miinagoo kina go gegoo ge nakaaza yek, gga miinagoom."

aaniish, mii sa iwi gii shkwaa danaandigidoong gewiin maaba sa mindimooweN.

aaniish, noomak go dash maaba oshkinowe go bekaa go gii yaa. gaawiin go wewiip go gii ganoonaasiin. gimaapii dash giiyeN go miinawaa gii nakwetawaan maaba newe gashiwon, maaba oshkinowe.

"gaawiin sa gonaa aapidji gonaa gegoo ndoo yaaziin gonaa ge nakaaza yaaNmbaan gonaa ji giiwise yaaN, ji nandowaabimak maaba waabshkibinesi.",

(doo) kidawidik sa maaba oshkinowe.

"nahaaw, bekaa.",

(doo) kida sa giiyeN mindimooweN miinawaa.

"yaawaa sa zhinda (doo) yaa gdo oodenawinaaning e wiichkisimak.",

doo inaadigenon.

"gegoo gonaa maaba ndoo zhinaadimaak gonaa e oowaandamaza. miidash owo ge zhaamak. mii owo ge oowaandamawak."

> "Oh, that daughter of the chief would not even look favorably upon me. I am not well off as the young men who have parents. For as long as I can remember, I have always been poor. However, you did raise me well. And now I am getting old enough so I can begin to take care of myself and make the things for myself that I will need for living."

Again, there was a long silence between them, then the old woman spoke to her son.

> "Wait a minute, I will tell you this, if you get to be so lucky as to kill the white eagle, then you will definitely get to marry the chief's daughter. And the people of the village, they will build a house for you and your wife. Also, the two of you will be given everything that you will ever need."

Well, the old woman had her say and she finished talking about it.

Again, the young man remained silent for some time. He did not respond to her right away. Eventually, after a long silence, this young man responded to what his mother had said.

> "I really do not have much and I do not have the tools needed to go hunting for this white eagle,"

the young man must have said.

> "Okay, wait,"

the old woman supposedly said.

> "I have someone in this village who is my friend,"

she must have said to him.

> "This friend usually helps me when I am in need of something. I will go to him. I will go to talk to him about our situation."

noomak dash go iidik maaba oshkinowe bekaa gii yaa. gaawiin go gegoo gii zhinakwetawaasiin newe gashiwon. gimaapii dash giiyeN, mii iwi e inaat newe gashiwon.

"nahaaw, oowaabam maaba e wiichkisiwi yin. giishpmaa gegoo wii zhigashkitoot ji naadimaak. aaniish, mii sa go ge zhiminowendamaaN geniin iwi. nga gwedji nandowaabimaa geniin maaba yaawaa, waabshkibinesi."

miidash giiyeN iwi maaba mindimooyeN wodi gii zhaat, maaba sa iidik e maawondaawizhichiget dash yaat. dibishkoo gonaa gwonda gaa jiisakiidjik gonaa gaa zhimamaawondaawizhichigewaat, mii iidik maaba dinoowo owo. miidash giiyeN maaba mindimooyeN wodi gaa zhaat gii ooganoonaat newe. (doo) minoyaa dash go maaba iidik anishinaabe. aaniish, (doo) maawondaawizhichige gonaa, nowonch gaye anishinaabek gonaa (doo) binoonigoon gonaa gegoo gonaa wii maawondjiinat gonaa, ji kida yinggoban gonaa. miidash giiyeN iwi gaa shkwaa wiindamawaat maaba mindimooweN newe e maawondaawizhichigendjin, mii iidik iwi e binji nibwaachawaat, mii iidik maaba gaye e maawondaawizhichiget, nowonch go iidik wii nandozhawenimaan go mindimooyeNon. aaniish, gii gikenimaan gaye ninda do oshkinowemon maaba mindimooweN. gaawiin gonaa maaba gegoo gonaa doo yaaziin, gaawiin gonaa mishi gonaa waa gashkitoot gonaa (doo) piitizisii.

"nahaaw, nga naadimawaa owo ggwisis.",

doo inaadigenon dash maaba memaawondaawizhichiget.

yaawaan dash giiyeN maaba memaawondaawizhichiget (doo) bimiwinaan, ginebigoon, maaba medawewet ginebik e inind. niyiing dash giiyeN newe doo nji ganawenimaan maaba memaawondaawizhichige nini, niyiin ko zhaazhigo gii yaanaawaan, gichi moodayin, danaasang gonaa (doo) nakaazam iwi. gaawiin gaye gonaa moodaang gonaa (doo) zhinaagosinoo iwi. banggii dash gonaa gegoo gibagan, gii gibanakaadenoon gaye gonaa iwi, (doo) bagoneyaa dash giiyeN maanda naawoyiiwong iwi gibagan. naanigodinong dash ko maaba memaawondaawizhi- chigeN iidik, mii giiyeN ko iwi iidik (doo) niboodewizit, mii giiyeN ko (doo) madwewechiget. miidash giiyeN ko maanda iwi bibigon madwewenik, mii giiyeN maaba ginebik zhewe (doo) bigidakizat niyiing gichi moodaang, (doo) bibazindang maanda boodaadjigan. miidash giiyeN gaa zhichiget maaba iwi memaawondaawizhichiget, iwi bibigon, mii giiyeN iwi gaa boodaadang. aaniish, mii sa giiyeN zhago maaba ginebik (doo) bigidakiza iidik (doo) bibazindang iwi, madwewechigenit ninda beminigodjin ji kida yinggoban gonaa. miidash go maaba iidik memaawondaawizhichigeN ninda (doo) bigidakizanit, mii giiyeN jichkana gii noodinaat kweganaaning. miidash giiyeN miinawaa gii

Again, the young man was quiet for a long time. He made no attempt to respond to his mother for a long time. After a long wait, he finally said the following to his mother.

> "Okay, go to see your friend to see if he would be able to help you in any way. That would please me if he could help us. I too will go look for the white eagle."

So then the old woman went to see her friend, the one who could do magical things. He was like the ones who perform the shaking tent ritual, he did awe-inspiring things also. So this is who the old woman went to see and talk to. This man lived a good life and was well-off. He was always asked by the people to perform his acts of magic, which the people paid him to do, thus he lived a good life. So the old woman told him why she came to see him, and this man really wanted to help this old woman and her son. Well, he knew of the young man and how this old woman had raised him. He knew this young man was poor, as he was not really of age to be on his own yet.

> "Okay, I will help your son,"

this magician must have said to the old woman.

This magician had this rattlesnake that he kept. He kept this snake in a large bottle-like container, as the people used to have these kinds of containers years ago, and they used these to store things in them. Those containers did not really look like bottles that we see today. This container also had a cover over it, and this cover had a hole in the middle of it. And this entertainer or magician would usually play the flute when he got bored or lonely. Then when the snake heard the flute music, the snake would stick its head out of the hole in the middle of the cover of the container. So this man began playing the flute. So in a few moments, the snake was sticking its head out of the bottle-like container listening to the music played by its keeper, so to speak. So this magical person suddenly grabbed the snake's neck when it stuck its head out of the container. And the magical person then stretched

zhiibiigatagobinaat, giyetin go, maanda iidik koowaabiigazi maaba ginebik. miidash giiyeN zhewe iwi gii boodowet, mii gonaa zhewe e nji maawondjiinat, mii giiyeN gii jijiinggonigaabowit maaba memaawondaawizhichiget. doo dakonaan go ninda ginebigoon, (doo) zhiibiigatagobinaan go, miidash giiyeN iwi gii binigamot. aaniish, kina gwonda nigamowinan gii yaanaawaan, gwonda gonaa nowonch gonaa gaa zhichigedjik gonaa anishinaabek, gaa zhiyaadjik sa gonaa. aaniish, gii nibwaakaawok gewiinawaa gwonda, gii makadekewok sa gonaa gegoo gonaa wii gikendamowaat giiyeN iidik.

miidash giiyeN maaba iwi zhinda jiigishkode maaba gonaa memaawondaawizhichigeN gii jijiinggonigaabowit, mii giiyeN go gii webinigamot go. nenggaach dash giiyeN go ninda ginebigoon ishpiming nikeyaa doo zhigowiidinaan, bekish (doo) nigamo. gaawiin dash ngii gikendaziin iwi gaa nawang. aaniish, ozaam gonaa ngii gaachiiw gonaa geniin iwi pii gii noondamaaN maanda sa dibaadjimowin. miidash giiyeN go maanda iwi e nipiichi nigamot go, mii gaye bekish go (doo) nibizagowiit go, miidash go maanda (e) shkwaa namaazat gonaa ji kida yinggoban, mii giiyeN iwi gii naaniibowit gonaa, gii miyaawigaabowit. miidash giiyeN maaba mindimooweN ganawaabimaat iidik newe maawondjiininit, gaawiin giiyeN giyaabi newe ginebigoon zhewe gii takonaasiin, niyii giiyeN iwi dekonang, bikwak. aapidji giiyeN go maanda (doo) gonaadjiwon iwi bikwak, wewena giiyeN go niswiwaade iwi, miinawaa giiyeN (doo) giinaakowon, asin. gegaa giiyeN go (doo) zhaabowaabiminaagot. giyegeti giiyeN go (doo) gonaadjiwonini iwi bikwak zhewe gaa giizhitoot, mii owo ginebik. miidash giiyeN gii miinaat maaba sa yaawaa, memaawondaawizhichige nini mindimooweNon maanda bikwak.

"mii sa iwi.",

gii inaan newe.

"mii maanda gii giizhitoo yaaN."

miidash giiyeN iwi gii inaat ninda.

"wegodigowendik go maaba ge bimodamogoweN gdo oshkiniigim,
gaawiin go ginigeN daa pashkondaziin iwi."

pii gonaa gewiin gonaa e pidek bikwak e zhidaming, gaawiin go gichi waasa gwodji go pidesanoo, gaawiin go. miidash giiyeN maaba mindimooyeN gii daapinang iwi, gii nigiiwedoot iwi e gichi gonaadjiwoninik bikwak.

miidash giiyeN e inaat newe do oshkiniigiimon,

the snake to its full length and he held it in the stretched out position. So where he had his fire going, that is where he usually performed, he knelt down by the fire. He still held this snake stretched out in his hands, and he began to sing. Back then, all the Anishinaabe people had their own songs, at least the ones who had some kind of power, spiritual power, these people knew many songs. Of course the Anishinaabe people back then fasted so that they would know something that would benefit the people, so most of them had wisdom and knowledge.

Then as this man knelt by the fire, he began to sing a song. As he sang, he would slowly raise the snake toward the heavens. This man sang while he performed his ritual. I do not know what the song was that he sang. Of course, I was very young when I heard this story told. And while this magician was singing, the man began to stand up, and just as he finished singing his song, he was standing erect. As this old woman was watching him perform, she saw that he no longer had a snake in his hands, he now held an arrow in his hands. This was the finest arrow she had ever seen, and the three feathers at the end of the arrow were in perfect alignment, and the arrowhead was very sharp and shiny. And it seemed almost transparent as one could almost see through the arrowhead. This was an arrow of excellent quality that this magician had made, and it was made from that snake. The man gave this newly made arrow to the old woman.

> "This is it,"

he said to her.

> "I have finished it."

And he further told her the following.

> "Whatever your son shoots with this arrow, he will never miss the intended target."

When we see an arrow being shot, it does not really travel that far, it just does not go far. So this old woman took this beautiful arrow and took it home with her.

When she got home, she said this to her son.

> “maanda ngii ik owo memaawondaawizhichiget. wegodigowendik giiyeN go ge bimodamoneN, gaawiin go giiyeN go ginigeN gdaa pashkondaziin.”

aaniish, maaba oshkinowe (*doo*) gichi inendam. miidash iidik gaa inendang maaba oshkinowe,

> “nga gojitoon maanda bikwak nitam. endigoweN go ji debwet giyegeti owo memaawondaawizhichiget.”,

gii inendamodik sa maaba oshkinowe, gii kidawidik sa gonaa. miidash giiyeN maanda jiigaakowaa (*e*) nidagoshing, yaawaan giiyeN zhewe gii migizikewon, boonisen. mii sa giiyeN wewiip gii bimod iwi, mii sa giiyeN wodi gaa binjibizonit, gii zhaabowaakodjiiwaat gonaa ji kidayinggoban. aapidji go (*doo*) gichi inendam. miinawaa go iidik wodi gwodji go gii nizhaat. aabidek go wii gikendaan go endigoweN go maanda bikwakigan ji zhiwebadinik gaa kidanit newe memaawondaawichigendjin. miidash giiyeN wodi e niyaat, mii giiyeN miinawaa zhewe bezhik newe gii nisaakowaat newe boonisen. nowonch dash giiyeN gii zanagadini nonggom zhewe e nipizonit newe. aaniish, mii sa go gii bimod, gii naasaanowaan gonaa newe. aaniish, mii sa gaa zhinjibizonit.

> “(*doo*) debwe sa go giyegeti owo gaa kidat iwi gaa zhitoot maanda bikwak.”,

(*doo*) inendam sa iidik maaba oshkinowe. miidash giiyeN gii nigiiwet.

miidash wodi gaa dagoshing e ndaawaat, mii giiyeN e inaat newe gashiwon gonaa nga kid,

> “giyegeti go (*doo*) debwe gaa kidat owo gaa zhitoot maanda bikwak. aapidji nayiinawint go maanda wenkaamigat.”,

(*doo*) kida sa iidik.

aaniish, miidash iidik maaba oshkinowe e inaat newe gashiwon.

> “aaniish, maanoo sa geniin ndaa godjitoon endigoweN ji wiyii debinaagobaneN owo waabshkibinesi.”

aaniish, miidash giiyeN maaba mindimooyeN gii zhiitaawaat newe gwisison, iwi gonaa wii giiwisenit. mii gonaa giizhiitaat, mii maaba oshkinowe gii maajaat, mitigowaakiing, bibaamoset go mitigowaakiing. naanagon dash giiyeN gii giiwise, gaawiin giiyeN wiya migiziwaashon gii waabimaasiin. miidash gonaa iidik gii aanishiitang.

> "That magician told me this about this arrow. Whatever you shoot at, you will never miss your target."

Oh, this young man was elated at what he heard. So this young man thought to himself,

> "First, I will test this arrow out. Just to find out if what that magician said is true,"

this young man thought to himself, or he may have said it out loud. And he went out toward the forest, and as he got near the woods he saw a hawk taking flight. He quickly shot at this bird and while the bird was in flight, the arrow went into the bird. Oh, the young man was very happy. The young man retrieved the arrow and continued farther into the woods. He wanted to be absolutely sure that the words of the magician were definitely true, that this arrow would always hit its target. Then as he was walking along, he startled another hawk into flight. And this bird flew into a very thickly wooded area, where it would be much more difficult for an arrow to go through. So, he shot at the bird in the direction it was flying, and the arrow nicked the bird, but it was enough to knock the bird down and kill it.

> "That man who made this arrow was telling the truth when he said this arrow would never miss its target,"

this young man must have thought to himself, satisfied. So, he returned to his home.

When this young man arrived at his home, he spoke to his mother and he said,

> "What that man who made this arrow said is true. This arrow is very accurate,"

he must have said.

Well, this young man supposedly told his mother the following.

> "Well, I guess I should give it a try, to see whether I can get the white eagle."

So, this old woman quickly prepared the things her son would need while he was out hunting. Then when she got the backpack ready, her son left and went into the woods, walking around, hunting. He was gone for five days, and he did not see a single eagle of any kind. So he gave up the hunt for the white eagle.

"ndaa giiwe gonaa. gaawiin ganabach wiya waabshkibinesi.",

(doo) inendam sa iidik.

mii giiyeN iwi gii dagoshing gimaapii e ndaawaat, miidash giiyeN e inaat newe gashiwon,

"gaawiin ginigeN migiziwaashk ngii waabimaasii gwodji. gaawiin ganabach wiya waabshkibinesi e zhinikaazat.",

doo inaadigenon sa newe gashiwon.

"bekaa.",

(doo) madwe kidawon dash giiyeN gashiwon maaba oshkinowe.

"(doo) yaa sa go owo waabshkibinesi. maanda sa nikeyaa gichi ajiwing (doo) yaawok gewe.",

(doo) kidawidik sa maaba yaawaa, mindimooyeN.

"mii wodi zhaa yin, mii wodi ji waabimadiban owo waabshkibinesi."

noomak dash go giiyeN go maaba oshkinowe go bekaa gii yaa. gaawiin go wewiip go gii nakwetawaasiin newe gashiwon. gimaapii dash giiyeN go mii iidik gii inendang maaba oshkinowe, ndaawaach gonaa miinawaa wodi ajiwing, gichi ajiwing ji zhaapan, ji nandowaabimaapan dash newe waabshkibinesiwon. miidash iidik gaa inaat newe gashiwon,

"aaniish, ndaa zhaa sa wodi gichi ajiwing. gdaa zhiitaaw, miidash pii giizhiitaa yin, mii ji maajaa yaaN."

aaniish, mii sa iidik gaa giizhiitaat maaba mindimooweN (doo) zhiitaawaat newe gwisison, mii gii maajaat maaba yaawaa, oshkinowe, gii zhaat wodi gichi ajiwing.

mii sa iidik wodi gwodji gonaa gii bidagowiiziiwet gonaa. miidash iidik, shpashkodinaadik nanggaye wodi, shpashkodinaa sa gonaa, (doo) maanaadat iidik. aaniish, gii waabimaan sa giiyeN go migiziwaashon, gaawiin dash wiyii giiyeN waabshkibinesiwon gii waabimaasiin. baamaa giiyeN go zhaangswigon (e) giiwiset, gaawiin giiyeN wiya waabshkibinesi.

"I think I should go home. I do not think there is such a thing as a white eagle,"

he must have thought to himself.

When he got home, he said this to his mother.

"I did not see an eagle of any kind, anywhere. I do not think there is such a bird as a white eagle,"

he must have said to his mother.

"Wait,"

he heard his mother say.

"There is too such a bird as the white eagle. These birds are in the big mountains,"

this old woman supposedly said.

"When you go there, that is where you might see the white eagle."

The young man sat silent for a long time. He did not respond to his mother right away. So this young man was pondering the suggestion from his mother, he decided that he would go to the mountains, the big mountains, and try to look for the white eagle there. So he finally spoke to his mother and said the following.

"Well, I could go to the mountains. Prepare me for my trip and when you have packed my backpack, that is when I will leave."

So the old woman again prepared her son for his trip, this time to the mountains, and when she had finished packing for his trip, the young man left home and he went to the mountains.

So, somewhere in the mountains he began his climb. Oh, the terrain was difficult to traverse, as the mountain was high, and steep, and it was very difficult climbing. On occasion he saw an eagle, but it was not the white eagle he was after. He realized he had been out hunting for nine days, but still no white eagle to be seen.

"maanoo giyaabi ngogiizhigat.",

(*doo*) inendam *da*sh iidik maaba oshkinowe. mii iwi midaas*w*igonigak. gii bidagowiiziiwet giiyeN gwodji gonaa aasamayiing zhewe gichi *a*jiw.

(*doo*) naam*a*dabit giiyeN gonaa wodi gwodji gonaa gaa m*a*kang gonaa wii naam*a*dabit, gaa*wiin* waawaadj. ishpiming gaye (*doo*) naabit, kina go gwodji go (*doo*) naabi go. gichi ishpiming go maaba (*doo*) yaa iidik. waasa giiyeN gonaa iwi mitigowaaki michiyiing (*doo*) baabiidinakosinini. mii*da*sh giiyeN go e naakoshinik, mii gonaa maanda zhinda (*doo*) ninaabit ishpiming gonaa, mii giiyeN e zhiwaabimaat newe waabshkibinesiwon (*doo*) biidjibizonit, maanda gonaa (*doo*) zhiwaakaa*wo*bizonit gonaa.

"taaya, mii sa maaba nendowaabimak.",

(*doo*) inendam sa iidik maaba oshkinowe. ozaam dash giiyeN waasa ishpiming wii noondebimodawaat.

aaniish, mii sa iidik (*doo*) bidagowiiziit, (*doo*) wewiiptaa, (*doo*) wewiiptaa go. aaniish, gaa*wiin* go maamdaa ozaam go gibeying gwodji wii yaat, gwodji gewii*n* maaba wii nipizo waabshkibinesi. gimaapii *da*sh giiyeN go e niyaat, mii iidik wodi,

"mii go ginimaa ji depidegoba*n* maanda nbikwak.",

(*doo*) inendam sa iidik. mii giiyeN gii boonaandowet. (*doo*) koowaabimaat giiyeN maanda wii bizhibiimskobizonit, wewena iidik gii *zh*inoowaat. (*doo*) maagowaagobinaat newe mitigowaabiin, mii go gii bimodawaat, (*doo*) waabidaan iidik iwi bikwak, taaya, gichi ishpiming, taahaa, giyegeti giiyeN newe migiziwaashon gegoo giiyeN go banggii go (*doo*) pizowon iidik iwi maanda bikwak ginimaa gonaa kaak*a*naaning gaye gonaa gaa bimodawaagoweN newe.

nenggaach giiyeN go maaba gichi migiziwaashk (*doo*) niisabizo, (*doo*) naagadoo-waabimaat go. aa*niish*, gichi waasa giiyeN michiyiing gii banggishiniwon. aaniish, (*doo*) baabiidanakoziwok gwonda mitigook, gichi waasa michiying, pii e yaat ishpiming. mandj gonaa gaa zhichigegoweN zhewe wewiip wii niisaandowet zhewe aasamayiing *a*jiwing, ginimaa gaye gonaa gaa tibidjiisegoweN, mandj sa gonaa gaa zhichigegoweN, aapidji sa giiyeN go wewiip go gii niisaandowe zhewe. miinawaa gaye gonaa gii naagadoowaabimaan gonaa pii gonaa wodi michiyiing newe gaa nin*a*kewebizonit newe. mii*da*sh giiyeN go gii m*a*kawaat. mii go gii bimaajaat gaa m*a*kawaat.

"I will stay for one more day,"

the young man must have thought to himself. That would be ten days out in the wilderness hunting alone. So he climbed farther up this big mountain.

He sat somewhere up on that mountain, and he could see a long way, but there was no white eagle anywhere in sight. He looked up, farther up the mountain, and he looked all around for the white eagle. This young man was way up high on this big mountain. When he looked down from his vantage point, he saw the trees below and they seemed to be pointing toward him, way down below from where he was waiting. So he stayed there and kept looking, then toward evening, he happened to be looking up at the mountain, he saw a white eagle flying, soaring in a circle in the area where he was sitting.

"Oh wow, this is the one I am looking for,"

he thought to himself. But the white eagle was way too high for him to shoot with his bow and arrow.

So he got up and quickly climbed higher, as fast as he could because of the rough terrain. He could not stay there for too long, as this white eagle too would soon fly elsewhere. So as he went a little higher up the mountain, he thought he should try to get the white eagle.

"I think my arrow might be able to reach him now,"

he must have surmised. So he stopped climbing up the mountain. He watched the white eagle make its circle as it soared in the sky, and waited for the white eagle to get closer to him as it made its circle, and he aimed at the eagle carefully. He slowly drew the drawstring of the bow back, and he let the arrow fly through the air, and he watched the flight of his arrow go up and up, right into the white eagle and this great bird shuddered as the arrow found its mark, it may have hit him on the chest area.

The great white eagle slowly descended and the young man watched its slow spiraling descent to the forest below. Well, the bird fell into the forest way down below from where he was on the mountain. The trees below looked as if they were pointing at him, and they were so small, that is how high up he was on the mountain. I do not know how he quickly came down the mountain, maybe he tumbled down the mountainside, or he ran, but he got down very quickly. He had also carefully watched the area the white eagle fell into as it landed in the forest. So he went and found the white eagle. He then came home after he found this white eagle he had killed.

miinawaa gonaa gimaapii gonaa gii bidagoshin zhewe e ndaawaat iidik, gashiwon gii biwaabidawaat newe waabshkibinesiwon.

"maadjiidaw owo gichi ogimaa ninda.",

doo igoodigenon dash maaba oshkinowe newe gashiwon. aaniish, mii sa maaba oshkinowe gii maadjiidowaat do ogimaamowaan ninda waabshkibinesiwon.

aaniish, gii kida maaba gichi ogimaa iwi,

"wegowen ge biidoowigoweN oshkinowe waabshkibinesiwon, mii ninda ndaanison ge wiidigemaat."

aaniish mii sa go giyegeti gaa zhichiget. mii go ninda oshkinowen gii inaat ji wiidigemaanit newe daanison. aaniish, mii*da*sh giiyeN ninda anishinaaben maaba oshkinowe gii zhitaawigot waa daat gonaa, waa daawaat sa gonaa. miinawaa giiyeN kina gonaa gegoo gii miinaawok gonaa waa nakaazawaat. mii*da*sh gonaa iwi, mii gonaa e zhiwebak gonaa bimaadizi ying gonaa, (*doo*) danaandigigidooniwok gonaa bemaadizidjik, (*doo*) dazhindiwaat gonaa.

miidash giiyeN ngoding maaba oshkinowe (*doo*) bigiiwet gonaa (*doo*) shkwaa giiwiset, mii giiyeN iwi gegoo gii inaadjimotaagot ninda yaawaan gonaa e nan*a*kiindjin gonaa wiidji anishinaaben gonaa.

"gaa*wiin* maaba gwiidigemaagan wewena (*doo*) zhichigesii iwi (*e*) bibaa giiwise yin.",

doo igoodigenon sa.

"niniwon maaba giimoodj (*doo*) wiisookowaan.",

(*doo*) inaadik sa maaba oshkinowe, oshkinini. gaa*wiin da*sh giiyeN gonaa gii debwetaziin iwi. aaniish, (*doo*) *t*anaandigidooniwok go ko gonaa bemaadizidjik, gaa*wiin* gonaa aanind wii debazindawindawaa gonaa (*doo*) zhiyaasiiwok. mii*da*sh gonaa iidik gaa inendang iwi,

"gaa*wiin* gonaa ndaa bazindawaasii."

mii go ngoding go (*e*) giiwiset, mii go miinawaa naasaap go iwi gaa inaadjimotawin miinawaa, wiidigemaaganon (*doo*) yaawon waasookowaandjin gaa maajaandji.

So when he finally got home, he showed the white eagle to his mother.

"Take this to the chief,"

the young man was told by her, his mother. And so, this young man took this white eagle to the chief of their community.

Well, this great chief had said,

"Whoever the young man is, whoever brings me the white eagle, this is who shall marry my daughter."

And that is what the chief did. He told this young man that he would be married to his daughter. And when they were married, the people of the community built a home for them. And the newlyweds were also given many items that they would use in their new home. And as it so often happens in life, people talk about other people, they gossip about other people.

So one day when this young man returned home from a day of hunting, one of this fellow villagers told him something about his wife.

"Your wife does not do right by you while you are out hunting,"

this young man was told by his fellow Anishinaabe.

"She is secretly seeing another man,"

the young man must have been told by this person. However, he did not believe this person for whatever reason, he dismissed it as idle gossip. Of course there are those who gossip, and these are people who should not be listened to, so he may have thought this of the person who told him about his wife's supposed indiscretion. So he must have then thought,

"I will not pay no heed to what he said."

Again, when he returned from another hunting trip, he was told the same thing again, that his wife was seeing another man while he was out hunting.

"togow*a* d*a*sh go nonggo*m* nga n*a*ndogikenimaa.",

inendam d*a*sh go iidik go, (d*oo*) naanaagadowendam sa go iidik zhago go. miid*a*sh giiyeN e inaat newe wiidigemaaganon,

"nwii giiwise miinawaa. nowonch go nonggo*m* gibeying nwii ndend iwi d*a*sh wiyii go ko minik e ndendi yaaN.",

d*oo* inaadigenon sa.

aaniish, mii sa giiyeN gii zhiitaawigot waa bibaa maadjiidoot gonaa maanda wii bibaa giiwiset. miid*a*sh giiyeN gaa giizhiitaanit iwi, mii giiyeN gii maajaat. maanda d*a*sh gonaa iwi gonaa e danakiit gonaa, aaniish, gii mitigowaakaani, mii gonaa zhewe jekaakowiit gonaa mitigowaakiing, gaaw*iin* gonaa miinawaa waabimigoosiinidik gonaa gaa nizhaagoweN. aaniish, mii sa,

"(d*oo*) bibaa giiwise.",

(d*oo*) inendamawin newe wiidigemaaganon. miid*a*sh iidik gaye maaba oshkinini eta gii waakaawoset zhewe, *gimaapii dash* go iidik gii m*a*daabii zhewe. waa ko minowaabidang go iwi, iwi gonaa zhewe oodetoowaat gonaa gewiinawaa. baamaampii gonaa, nowonch gaye gonaa ginimaa besha gonaa wii zhaadik gonaa gaa inendamagoweN.

miid*a*sh giiyeN maanda e ninaakoshininik zhewe gaa tanizit, miinawaa gaye go gii wiinggezi wiya gonaa wii bibowaa waabimigot. gii g*a*kizowidik gonaa. miid*a*sh giiyeN maanda e ninaakoshinik dash (d*oo*) naabit wodi nikeyaa, oodetoowaat, gii waabimaan giiyeN wiya (d*oo*) biidaasamishkaanit. eshkam giiyeN go besha go (d*oo*) biyaawon. gii debitawaan giiyeN (d*oo*) binigamonit. miidash iidik iwi (d*oo*) ganawaabimaat go, gimaapii giiyeN go gii nisadowinawaan, mii giiyeN giyegeti newe wiidigemaaganon. (d*oo*) p*a*kaanaziwon giiyeN maaba ikwe (*e*) biwiidjiiwaadjin. aaniish, maaba iidik ikwe (d*oo*) inendam,

"(d*oo*) giiwise maaba genii*n* ndo niniim. aaniish, gaawii*n* (d*oo*) yaasii. gaawii*n* (d*oo*) yaasii.",

(d*oo*) inendam.

mii go iidik zhewe go dibishkoo go (d*oo*) bimishkaawon go. aapidji giiyeN go (d*oo*) minoyaawon, (d*oo*) baapiwon, bekish gaye (d*oo*) minigamowon. aaniish, gaaw*iin* d*a*sh go wiya daa minowendazii*n*. (d*oo*) sadaawendang iidik maaba nini. aaniish, gii m*a*kawendaan giiyeN maanda bikwak, aaniish gwekaa maanda bikwak, gii daapinang iwi miinawaa mitigowaabiin.

> "I will check into this to see if it is true,"

the young man must have thought, as he now had some doubt about his wife's fidelity. So this one day he told his wife the following.

> "I will leave for a hunting trip again. However, this time I will be gone for a longer time, longer than usual,"

the young man supposedly told his wife.

Then his wife prepared his backpack for him with the items he would need for his hunting trip. So when his hunting pack was prepared, he left his home to go hunting, or so it seemed. And the community where they lived, there was a forest nearby, and no one could see where he went as soon as he went into the woods. So then,

> "He is out hunting,"

his spouse must have thought to herself. However, this young man just walked in a circle through the forest around their community, and he eventually went down toward the community. He found a spot where he could watch what was going on in the village. Later on, he must have thought of going closer, to get a better look at things.

And later that day, as he stayed hidden from view, he was very careful to avoid being seen by anyone. Well, he was hiding, that is what he was doing. And that evening, he saw someone coming directly toward where he was hiding, he saw this canoe coming toward him. The canoe came closer toward where he was. He could hear someone singing as they came toward him. And he watched them coming, and he finally could make out who it was, and he recognized that one of the people sitting in the canoe was his wife. She definitely was with another man. Well, this woman must have thought the following.

> "My husband is gone hunting for a long time. Well, he is not here, he is not here for me,"

is what she thought.

The two people in the canoe were practically right in front of where the young man was waiting. Oh, these two people in the canoe were enjoying themselves, they were laughing and they were singing, they were having a great time. Well, anyone who has had this happen to them, they do not feel good about it, so too, this young man was not happy at what he saw. This young man had a heavy heart, as he was saddened by what he saw. Then he remembered the power of his arrow, as it always went straight to its target, and he then picked up his bow.

"gaawiin wiikaa gegoo ndoo bashkonaziin gwodji bimodamaaN.",

(doo) inendang sa iidik. mii iidik gii zhinoowaat newe wiidigemaaganon zhewe (doo) bimishkaanit dibishkoo dash yaat, gaawiin gaye (doo) waabimigoosiin, gii maagowaagobinaat newe mitigowaabiin, gii bimod. aaniish, mii sa go iwi, mii go gii nisaat. ginimaa gaye wiiyawing gaa banggisinigoweN iwi bikwak maaba nini, ginimaa gaye dibaang. miidash go zhewe gii nisaat. miidash giiyeN gii madaabiiset gii inaat newe niniwon ji bigibaanit. aaniish sa giiyeN maaba nini (doo) zegazi.

"ginimaa gaye niin nga bimok maaba."

gaawiin dash wiyii go ninda niniwon gegoo gii doodawaasiin. miidash giiyeN newe wiidigemaaganon zhewe gaa bizhewoshkosenik maanda do jiimaaniwaa gwonda, mii giiyeN newe wiidigemaaganon gii daapinaat. zhewe dash gonaa akiing gonaa tibewe gii paginaat. aaniish, (doo) nibow maaba. gaawiin giyaabi (doo) bimaadizisii. mii giiyeN miinawaa gii daapinaat, gii bimboomaat, miidash gii giiwenaat. dibi gonaa gewiin gonaa zhewe gonaa gaa nji nitaaginin maaba ikwe, mii zhewe gaa zhiwinaat, ooson e ndaanit. aaniish, ogimaa maaba. miidash gii wiindamawaat iidik gaa oonji nisaat. wiya iidik bekaanizindjin maaba ikwe (e) wiisookowaat zhewe bibowaa yaat maaba yaawaa, nini.

miidash giiyeN maaba gichi ogimaa ninda e inaat oshkininiwon,

"ggii gikendaan e piitendaagok gwiidji bimaadiz ji nisadiban.",

doo igoodigenon sa ninda ogimaan sa maaba oshkinowe.

"eNheN, ndoo gikendaan sa go."

miidash giiyeN maaba gichi ogimaa gii nandomaat iidik do oshkiniigiimon, baatiinawok go niniwok. miidash giiyeN gaa inaat maaba gichi ogimaa, ji godagiyaawaanit ninda yaawaan, oshkinowen, ninggonon gonaa ji kida yinggoban.

"baamaampii go gii nisaa yek, mii ji boonigodagiyaa yek."

"I have never missed anything that I have shot at with this arrow,"

he must have thought to himself. As his wife and her companion were directly in front of him and of course they did not see the young man as he was hidden, the young man drew his bow string back and let his arrow fly. As always, the arrow found its mark, and killed the woman. The arrow may have struck the woman in the chest or the head. She was dead, he had killed his wife. Then he walked down to the shore of the lake, and told the man in the canoe to land on the shore. Oh, this man was terrified and probably in shock at what happened and he thought,

"Maybe he will shoot me next with the arrow."

However, this young man did not do anything to this man. Then, as the canoe landed on the shore, the young man picked up the body of his dead wife. He then threw her body down on the ground of the shore. This chief's daughter was now dead. She was no longer living. Then the young man picked up his wife's body and he carried her back home with her body draped over his shoulder. And he took her to her dad's home, the home she was raised in. Well, this man was the chief of the community. The young man told the chief the reason why he had killed his own wife, the chief's daughter. And that reason was, when the young man was away, his wife, the chief's daughter, was seeing another man.

Then the chief said to this young man the following.

"You know the penalty for killing your fellow human,"

the young man is told by the chief.

"Yes, of course I know."

Then the chief summoned his boys and they were many of these men who came to the chief's assistance. Then the chief told these men that they were to do harm to this young man, we might as well call the young man the chief's son-in-law.

"Do not stop mistreating him, not until you have killed him."

anishinaabe *ikwe* wiinimoon gaa wiidigemaadjin

yaawaak sa nwii dibaadjimaak, anishinaabek. kiinawi*n* gonaa zhinda nonggo*m* e d*a*nakii ying, zhaazhago gonaa gwonda *o*daawaak zhinda gii danakiiwaat wiikowedoowing, mii gonaa gaa bizhiwebaziwaat gonaa gewiinawaa njike gii yaawaat. gwonda d*a*sh go waa dibaadjimagik niizh, niizh*a*wok gwonda *i*kwewok e zhiwiidigikooNdiwaat gonaa, iwi d*a*sh go maanda gii zhiwebaziwok, yaawaa gonaa gii misowinawaawaan gonaa newe *o*shkinowen gonaa bezhik. wewena gonaa maaba nini gonaa e zhiyaat gii zhi-aawidik.

aaniish gii wiichkisimaadigenon d*a*sh go maaba *o*shkinini ninda niizh *i*kwewon e zhiwiidigikooNwinit. baamaa*mpii* d*a*sh gonaa naagach ninda e gaachiiwinindjin gii wiidigemaadigenon maaba yaawaa, maaba sa *o*shkinini. maaba dash midjiigikwewis e inin*d*, aaniish, giyaabi go ninda go giimooch go gii wiichkisimaan ninda yaawaan wiinimoon. miidash gonaa gwonda gaa nan*a*kiiwaat zhaazhago anishinaabek, gii ziisibaakodokewaat ko, mii*d*ash iidik gwonda e *o*shkiwiidigemaagonidjik, mii iidik gwonda gaa zhizhitoowaat gonaa gewiinawaa ziisibaakodokewaat maanpii wiikowedoowing noopiming. dibi gonaa iidik gwodji gonaa maanda, ginimaa gaye gonaa niizhodibagan, ginimaa gaye gonaa niswidibagan gii piichaadik pii gii oozhigewaat wodi ziisibaakod waa nji zhitoowaat. aaniish, pane gonaa iwi ziisibaakod gonaa (*doo*) binakaazang, maanda gonaa (*doo*) wiisining gonaa (*doo*) dagowondjigaade maanda ziisibaakod.

maanda d*a*sh gii zhiwebazi maaba *i*kwe ninda niniwon gaa wiidigemaat, gegoo gonaa aakoziwin gii t*a*konigon. gaa*wiin* dash gii minoyaasii, jina gonaa ginimaa gii bimaadizidik iwi gonaa gaa wiidigemaaganit. aaniish, miidash maaba gaa nibot *o*shkikwe, mii iidik maaba midjiigikwewis gaa inendang iwi,

"niin nga wiidigemaa *o*wo *n*niinim.",

gii inendam iidik. gii mashkowendam go maaba. newe dash niikigoon maaba ikwe, gaa*wiin* gonaa aapidji gonaa gii wiidookaag*oo*siin ji kida yaaNmbaa*n* gonaa. miid*a*sh giiyeN ko gaa igot ninda niikigoon,

> "gaa*wiin* gonaa (*doo*) nishizinoo iwi e zhichige yin. gichi baab*a*giye gonaa maaba gniinim miinawaa wii miwiidigemat, bidjiinak gaye gonaa maaba *naa*namiyi gii nibob*a*n gwiidigikooN. gaa*wiin* d*a*sh gonaa (*doo*) gonaadjiwisanoo maanda e zhinakii yin.",

The Anishinaabe Woman Who Married Her Brother-in-Law

I am going to tell a story about the Anishinaabe people. Those of us who are living here now, the Ottawa, have always lived here for ages, and this is something that happened to them many years ago, before the coming of the white man to this land. I am going to talk about these two women who were sisters and they both were interested in this one young man in the community. This young man was a proper young man of his day.

This young man was friends with both of these women who were sisters. The young man married the younger sister a few years later. The older sister still secretly desired the young man for herself. The Anishinaabe people used to make sugar long ago and these recently wedded people had a sugaring bush just inland from the community of wiikowedoowing. It is not known how far this sugar bush was and this is where they built their sugar bush camp, maybe two or three miles from the community. The Anishinaabe always have used sugar, as it was used when the people ate.

Something happened to this woman who was married to this young man, she came down with some kind of illness. She was not well, and she did not live long after she was married. So when she had died, the older sister supposedly thought the following.

"I will marry my brother-in-law,"

she supposedly thought. She had her mind set on it. However the parents of this woman did not encourage her to pursue her wishes, they discouraged her from getting married to her brother-in-law. Her parents told her this.

> "That which you intend to do is not right. You are wanting to marry your brother-in-law much too soon, your sister just died a short time ago. What you are doing does not look good at all,"

gii inaawaan sa ko iidik gwonda gekaaNik. aaniish, gaa*wiin dash* go maaba midjiigikwewis go gii bazindawaasiin ninda niikigoon. aabidek go wii wiidigemaan ninda yaa*w*aan, wiinimoon.

aaniish, gii g*a*shkitoon *da*sh go maanda gaa zhinakiit, giyegeti go gimaapii gii wiidigemaan maaba nini newe wiinimoon. miidash maanda pii miinawaa nijitisek wii ziisibaakodokewaat, mii gwonda gii maajaawaat, wodi gii zhaawaat, ziisibaakot gwonda waa nji zhitoowaapa*n* aanin*d*. mii g*o*naa gaa zhigedjik zhewe, gewe nitam wodi, maaba *o*shkinini nitam newe *o*shkikwen gii wiidigemaat. aaniish, gii nibo dash maaba, miidash maaba wiin midjiigikwewis zhewe gii miik*o*set. miidash iidik wodi gii zhaawaat noopiming *i*wi pii ziisibaakot wii webizhitoowaat. aaniish, gii nakiiwok *da*sh go wodi, ziisibaakodokaaniwaang. (*doo*) gichi nakiiwok gwonda ziisibaakot gaa bizhitoodjik. miinawaa gaye gaa giizhiitaawaat, mii miinawaa maanda ziisibaakodowaaboo njigaak, mii miinawaa (*doo*) aawazibiiwaat, (*doo*) aawa*d*oowaat *i*wi ziisibaakodowaaboo.

gaa giizhiitaat *da*sh go maaba nini iwi wii mbizigewaat, mii giiyeN gii biganoonigot wiya, newe gonaa anishinaaben. gegoo gonaa maanda gii *o*onji n*a*ndomaa, gwodji go, gaawii*n* go zhewe ziisibaakodookaaning. aaniish, gegoo *da*sh gonaa ginimaa gonaa iwi gii *o*onji n*a*ndomaadik, wegodigowendik gonaa iidik. aabidek *da*sh go wii zhaa. aaniish, mii sa ninda wiidigemaaganon zhewe gii niganaat. aaniish, gaa*wiin* go aanowi go bidjiinak maaba gewii*n* ikwe wii skagamiz*a*ziin maanda ziisibaakodowaaboo. mii*da*sh go kina gaa giizhiitaat gonaa *i*wi, e zhiitaawaat ko gonaa waa skagamizagedjik, mii maaba nini gii bimaajaat. gii bim*a*daabiit. gaawii*n* go wii p*a*skaabiisii iwi go giizhigak, baamaa*mpii* waabang miinawaa mii wodi wii dagoshing, mii iwi minik waa ndendit.

aa*n*iish, njike go iidik maaba wodi midjiigikwewis iwi (*doo*) ganawendang ziisibaakodookaan. aa*n*iish, gaa*wiin* wiya wiidigemaaganon, baamaa*mpii* waabang wii dagoshinoon. gimaapii sa go iidik gaa naakoshinik, gimaapii go gii dibikat go. aaniish, niibaadibik ko gii skagamizagewok. mii*da*sh giiyeN maanda g*i*nimaa gonaa e nipiitaadibikadinik gonaa, aa*n*iish, nakiit gonaa njike zhewe, (*doo*) zaazaakowong gonaa zhewe ziisibaakodookaaning, ngoding giiyeN go (*e*) bibiindiget, mii giiyeN gii waabimaat ikwewon wodi niyiing waakwaandesing waasa wodi (*e*) biidaasimabanit. gaa*wiin* gaye gii waabimaasiin iidik gii bibiindigenit. waawaasa gonaa ginimaa ninda ziisibaakodokaanan gii tedigenan iwi pii, gaawii*n* go besha. miidash iwi iidik (*doo*) ganawaabimaat ninda ikwewon, wegowendigenon iidik. gaa*wiin* gaye gii waabimaasiin gii bibiindigenit. mii*da*sh giiyeN go, (*doo*) gichi ganawaabimigoon. gaa*wiin* gaye go ginigeN go (*doo*) zhoobiinggowenisiiwon gonaa ji biganawaabimigot. wewena *da*sh go iidik go gaa ganawaabimaat go ngoding go maanda (*doo*) danakamig*a*zit gonaa zhewe giiwitaashkodeng, mii*da*sh giiyeN gaa zhinisadowinawaat.

the parents must have told their older daughter. But, the older daughter did not heed the concerns of her parents. She had made up her mind that she had to marry her brother-in-law.

So as it turned out, she got her way, and the young man married the older sister, his sister-in-law. And it was now time again for them to make sugar, so this young man now married to the older sister went to the sugaring bush that was his and his first spouse, the younger sister of his new wife. He had built the sugar bush camp with his first wife. But his first wife had died due to some illness, and now the older sister had taken the place of her younger sister. So then they went to the sugar bush camp and began making maple sugar. They worked hard at their sugar bush camp. The Anishinaabe people who made sugar worked very hard. And when they finished one part of the process, the dripping of the maple sap into the containers continued and the sap had to be continuously gathered, so they would gather the sap.

Then one day when the man had finished setting up the process for the boiling to begin, someone came to tell him that he was needed back in the community. The business could not be done there, he had to go back into the community. It must have been something urgent, why he was asked to return to the community, and it is not known why. But he had to go back into the community. So he left his wife there alone to take care of the sugar making. This was not the first time that this woman had to boil down the sap, she had done it before so she knew how to do it. So after the man had prepared everything, he left for the village. He came back down to the village. He would not return that day, he would return the next day, that is how long he would be away.

So this older sister was left alone to take care of the sugar bush camp. Her husband had gone into the village and would not return till the next day. It soon became evening and it was soon nighttime, and it was dark. The Anishinaabe people used to boil down the sap well into the night, so this was nothing new to her. So as the night wore on, she was working at boiling the sap down, she would go out of the cabin occasionally, and then one time when she came back inside, she noticed someone there, a woman was sitting down at the other end of the cabin, the woman was facing her. She had not noticed anyone entering the cabin. These sugar bush camps were situated quite a distance from each other, as they were not near each other back then. So she glanced at this woman as she wondered who she was. She had not seen this woman enter the cabin. And this strange woman was really watching her every move carefully. Also, this strange woman did not show any signs of friendliness toward her, she did not smile or anything, but just glared at her. Then when she was stoking the fire and adding wood to it, she carefully watched this strange woman, and then she thought she recognized her.

taaya, mii giiyeN newe yaa*w*aan, wiidigikooNbaniin. mii gonaa gaa zhiwon*a*nit gonaa, mii *i*wi gaa *oo*nji nisadowinawaat, *i*wi gonaa pii begidenimin maaba *i*wi gonaa *a*gowinan gonaa gaa biiskoonadjin, mii *i*wi gaa *oo*nji gikenimaat. mii*da*sh go iidik baaba*g*iye go *i*wi gaa gichi zegazit maaba *i*kwe.

"aaniish gonaa iidik maaba nwiidigikooN zhinda binaadit, gii nibob*an* gaye.",

(*doo*) inendam *da*sh iidik. mii*da*sh giiyeN go bezhigonong go e naabimigot go, maanda gonaa (*doo*) danakamig*a*zit gonaa zhewe shkode (*doo*) ganawendang, miinawaa ziisibaakodowaaboo gaye (*doo*) ndemigak. mii*da*sh iidik gaa inendang *i*wi, eshkam go iidik (*doo*) zegazi go, (*doo*) gichi ganawaabimigot newe. gaa*w*i*in* gaye (*doo*) ganoonigoosiin.

"nga gidjibaa.",

(*doo*) inendam *da*sh iidik.

"nga zhisidoon maanda shkode ji wiyii bibowaa gonaa p*a*kinedek gaye gonaa gegoo. wenibik *da*sh go nizaakomaaN, mii ji maadjiibatoo yaaN.",

(*doo*) inendam *da*sh iidik.

aaniish, mii sa iidik *i*wi gii zhitoot *i*wi shkode. wewena iidik gii zhisidoot, wii bibowaa p*a*kinedek gonaa gegoo. mii*da*sh go wenibik go maanda zaako*w*ong mii go iidik gii bimaadjiibatoot. aaniish, miikaaNs gonaa go eta e ninimok wodi ziisibaakodookaaning, (*doo*) gichi niisaakiiyeminoni *da*sh giiyeN go zhewe *i*wi banggii go *i*wi miikaaNs (*e*) binaagadoot, miinawaa (*doo*) bigidaakiiyeminoni. mii*da*sh iidik zhewe gaa bipatoot. (*doo*) niisaakiiyep*a*toot miinawaa (*doo*) gidaakiiyep*a*toot, booskak*a*migaanik. zhewe *da*sh go (*e*) bigiizhidaakiiyep*a*toot, mii iidik gii noondaagot, gii bazindjitoot, aaniish megowe mitigowaaki go maanda, megowaa gonaa maanda bizhisigosin. taaya, gii debitawaan giiyeN wodi gaamidaaki (*doo*) biniisaakiiyep*a*toonit, mii go newe. mii*da*sh iidik *i*wi giyetin miinawaa gii gwekobagazat, miidash *i*wi (*doo*) giiwep*a*toot. e zhigishkitoot gonaa, e piichibizot sa gonaa. aaniish, (*doo*) gizhiikaa go gewii*n*.

zhaazhago go gewii*n* gwonda giigaanggok gii gichi gizhiikaap*a*toowok, nonggo*m* wiyii go gaawii*n* giigaanggok map*a*toosiiwok, ji gagwedjikandiwaap*an* gaye gonaa, zhaazhago gonaa anishinaabek gaa zhibimaadiziwaat. mii iidik (*doo*) *b*imap*a*toot, (*doo*) bigiiwep*a*toot maaba *i*kwe, ngoding *da*sh giiyeN go maanda (*doo*) bimap*a*toot, mii giiyeN gii nookoset jichkana, (*doo*) bazindjitoot. taaya, nowonch giiyeN besha newe (*doo*) noondawaan (*doo*) biidoowep*a*toonit. aaniish, (*doo*) p*a*shigiizhibikad maanda niibaadibik. taaya, mii iidik nowonch giyetin.

Oh my goodness, this was her dearly departed younger sister. The reason she knew who it was was that she recognized the clothing she was wearing as the clothing they had buried her younger sister in when they laid her younger sister to rest. Then at that instant, this woman, the older sister, was overcome with fear.

"What is my younger sister doing here, and she is dead,"

the older sister must have thought. And all this younger sister did was watch her as the older sister took care of the fire and the boiling sap. So the older sister decided that she should leave, as she was becoming increasingly frightened, as this strange woman just stared at her. Also, this apparition did not attempt to speak to her.

"I will run away from her,"

she decided.

> "First, I will carefully fuel the fire so that it does not scorch the maple sugar. Then when I go outside temporarily to get something, then I will run away,"

she may have thought to herself.

So she prepared the fire as she had planned. She carefully added wood to the fire so that it would not scorch the maple syrup. So when she made what seemed to be a regular trip outside of the cabin, that is when she started running from the sugar camp. There was only a small trail that led to the sugar camp, and the path came down the valley from the camp and up the valley on the other side. So she ran on this trail. She ran down the hill into the valley and then back up the hill on the other side of the valley. As she was getting to the top of the hill on the other side, that must have been when her younger sister realized she was gone, and the older sister stopped to listen for her younger sister and this was all woods back then. That is when she heard her younger sister come running down the hill on the other side of the valley. Then the older sister turned around and began running toward home. She ran as fast as she could. Well, she was still a fast runner, like she was in her younger days.

A long time ago, the teenage girls were fast runners as they were fond of running, now the teenage girls do not even run, like the Anishinaabe people of old. As this woman was running toward her home, she suddenly stopped and she listened for her sister. Oh no, her younger sister was gaining on her. And at night in the woods, it is pitch black sometimes, so you cannot see much. So, she again began to run, only now she was running faster.

"gaa*wiin* go ginigeN ndaa debinigo*o*sii.",

(*doo*) inendam *da*sh iidik. mii nowonch giyetin gii gaandjibatoot.

"nga de dagoshin go e ndaa yaang.",

(*doo*) inendam iidik. noomak *da*sh go iidik gaa bimaba*t*oot, miinawaa naa gii nookoset gonaa wii de n*a*sonaamot gonaa ji kida *y*inggoba*n*. mii*da*sh giiyeN iwi (*doo*) nookoset, (*doo*) noogigaabowit, (*doo*) bazindjitoot, taaya, nowonch giiyeN go besha (*doo*) biyaawon. taaya, giyegeti giiyeN, mii*da*sh go iwi e piichibizot go. gaawii*n* giyaabi ooshame daa gizhiikaapatoosii.

zhago *da*sh giiyeN go zhewe wii zaagaakong iidik e ndaawaat, gii pashkowaanigidik banggii zhewe gaa daawaat gonaa mitigogamik dash tek, mii giiyeN zhewe gii nookoset. (*doo*) mde naagodini *da*sh giiyeN go e ndaawaat go. aapidji *da*sh giiyeN gonaa besha shkweyaang (*doo*) noondawaan (*doo*) biidoowepatoonit. miidash iwi gii gaan*d*jizakamiit.

"mii go ji de dagoshinaaN.",

(*doo*) inendam *da*sh iidik,

"e ndaa yaang. gaa*wiin* go ginigeN ndaa debinigo*o*sii.",

(*doo*) inendam. (*doo*) waaskoneni giiyeN go giyaabi iwi e ndaawaat.

"taaya, giyegeti *da*sh go besha aanowi e ndaa yaaN."

mii gaye go zhago maaba besha, (*doo*) moozhaan gosha nayiinawi*nt* giiyeN go zhewe bokonaaning wii binowodinigot newe beminaashkaagoodjin.

mii go newe yaawaan dawemaan, yaawaan wiidigikooNbaniin, iwi gaye gonaa gii gagwedjikandiwaat gonaa gii bigiigaanggooNswiwaat gonaa, gii nisastawaan giiyeN go e nowenit (*doo*) nesenit (*doo*) p*a*kanaam*a*batoonit gaye. aanowi go besha e ndaawaat, eshkam gosha nayiinawi*nd* go besha go, (*doo*) moozhaan gosha giiyeN go (*doo*) inendam go zhewe wii bizagigowenigot.

"She will not catch me, she definitely will not,"

this woman thought to herself. Then she began to run really fast, faster than before.

"I will make it to my home before she catches me,"

she thought. She had run for some time again, then she stopped just long enough to catch her breath. Then when she had stopped, and as she listened for her pursuer, she realized that her pursuer was now getting much closer. Oh my, she was really close, and then this woman began to run like she had never run before. She was running as fast as she could, and she could not go any faster.

And as she was about to come to the clearing where their house was located, she again stopped at the edge of this clearing. Her home was visible as she looked across this clearing. And she heard her pursuer was practically on her heels. She then began to sprint toward home.

"I will be able to make home in time,"

she must have thought.

"There is my home, she will definitely not catch me,"

she thought. There was a visible light coming from her home.

"Oh my, I am so close to my home."

And the one who was chasing her was so close, she sensed her younger sister almost touching her back as it seemed that her younger sister was reaching out to grab her.

She knew it was her dearly departed younger sister, as she knew the sounds she made when she was out of breath when they used to race when they were teenage girls in their younger years. She was so close to her home, and as she ran she could feel her pursuer gaining on her and she could sense her pursuer reaching to grab her by the neck.

mii zhago shkwaandem go aanowi (*doo*) bigomoset. aaniish, mandj dash gonaa gaa zhinaagodinigoweN do shkwaandemiwaan gwonda mitigogamigoong gaa daadjik zhaazhago. ginimaa gaye gonaa p*a*shkwegan gaye gaa gibigoodjinigoweN zhewe. mii*da*sh giiyeN shkwaandeming gaa bigomoset, mii go gii bimookobizot zhewe shkwaandeming, mii giiyeN zhewe gii debinigot. gii bijigeshin dash zhewe shkwaandeming, mii go zhewe debinigot newe beminaashkaagoodjin. gwonda dash zhaazhago anishinaabek gii gichi boodowewok, miidash giiyeN go zhewe iwi shkodeng gaa panggishing maaba ikwe.

aaniish, gaa*wiin* sa wiyii go wewiip go gwonda zhewe e yaadjik gonaa daa bizagowiindisesiiwok ji gidjidaabaanaawaapa*n* zhewe shkodeng, (*doo*) goshkowigoowaan gaye. aaniish, aanowi go gii bizagowiindisewok, mii*da*sh (*doo*) nisadowinawaawaat zhewe shkodeng zhewe (*e*) banggishininit, aaniish, mii sa gonaa ginimaa aanowi gonaa wewiip gwodji aanowi gii oozhidaabaanaawaagoweN gonaa. *o*zaam dash wiikaa, *o*zaam gonaa maaba ikwe gii gichi jaagizo zhewe shkodeng.

iwi dash go nonggo*m* gaa inaadjimotawanigok, mii iwi gaa inaadjimotaawigoowaat ninda ikwewon, iwi gonaa minik gaa bimaadizindji. jina gonaa gii bimaadizi maaba zhewe shkodeng gaa panggishing, aaniish, gii gichi jaagizo. mii*da*sh ko gwonda anishinaabek gaa kidawaat iwi,

> "gaawii*n* (*doo*) nishizinoo iwi ji zhichigepa*n* wiya maaba sa ikwe gaa zhichiget. *o*zaam gonaa wewiip ninda wiinimoon gii miwiidigemaan."

mii*da*sh gonaa iwi minik gonaa maanda gekendamaaN dibaadjimowin. giyegeti giiyeN go maanda gii zhiwebat zhinda wiikowedoowing megowaa gonaa anishinaabek gonaa megowaa njike *da*sh yaawaat. mii*da*sh gonaa e kowaak maanda n*do* dibaadjimowin. aaniish, n*doo* gichi inendam gonaa gii bazindaw*a* yek.

anishinaabe gaa zhidebinaat mandaaminon

maanda sa dibaadjimowin e yaamaaN, anishinaabe nwii dibaadjimaa, m*a*n*d*aaminon gaa m*a*kawaat, gaa *o*shkim*a*kawaat go. maanda nikeyaa, makwa zhagishing, gaawiset gonaa maaba (*doo*) aawi anishinaabe, miidash gonaa maanda (*doo*) giiwiset, gibe giizhik gonaa (*doo*) bibaa ndendit, gaa*wiin* gaye gonaa gegoo gii nitoosiin. mii*da*sh gonaa e naakoshinik (*e*) bigiiwet owo, aapidji giiyeN go gii yekozi. miidash iidik e inendang iwi,

She was almost to the door of her home. It is not known how the doors looked back in the old days, but there was a door there of some kind. It may have been just the skin of some large animal that hung over the opening, covering the doorway. Then as the older sister got to the door, that is when her pursuer caught her, or so she thought. As she felt her pursuer clutching at her, she tripped and fell through the doorway of her home. Back then, the Anishinaabe people used to have their fires in the center of their lodges, and when this woman tripped through the door of her home, she fell right into the fire.

The people inside the lodge did not come to her aid right away, to help her out of the fire, as they were very startled by her sudden appearance and especially stunned by her falling into the fire, so they were sort of shocked by what they saw happen in front of them. However, they did jump up and help her out of the fire as soon as the initial shock wore off by her sudden appearance, and when they realized who it was, they quickly dragged her out of the fire. But, it was too late, as she had been severely burned by the fire.

The story I just finished telling you, this is what she related to the people while she was alive, and she only lived a short time after that. She only lived a little while after she fell into the fire. Well, she had been severely burned, although she was in the fire for a very short time. And the Anishinaabe people of old, especially the elders, always cautioned the people about this.

> "It is not a good to emulate what this woman had done. She married her brother-in-law much too soon after he lost his wife."

This is all that I know about this story. This really happened here in Wiikowedoowing, when the Anishinaabe people lived here alone, that is before the coming of the white man. So that is the end of my story. I am very elated that you listened to me tell my story.

How Corn Came to the Anishinaabe People

This one story I have is about the Anishinaabe man who first encountered the corn plant in this area. In the direction of the Sleeping Bear Dunes, there was this man out hunting in that area and he was out hunting all day and he did not see any animals so he did not kill any that day. So it was evening when he got home, he was very tired. So he thought, "ndaa kawe nibaa gonaa zhinda matashkamik e nshkwaandowe yaaN. baamaapii gonaa naagach ndaa zhitoon ge miiji yaaN."

miidash iidik gii weshing, niyiing e nshkwaandowet, mii gaye go iidik wewiip gii nibaat go. aaniish, (doo) yekozi, maanda go gibe giizhik bigiiwiset. miidash go gaa nibaat go iwi, mii gii aapowet, iwi gonaa giiwiseng gonaa. iwi gonaa giiwisewin, mii iwi gaa aabowaadang, iwi gonaa wiin (doo) giiwiset. miidash giiyeN go iwi (doo) giiwiset, aapidji giiyeN go maanaadakamigaanik bemizhizhaat. wesiiNon gonaa (doo) nandowaabimaat gonaa. miidash giiyeN gaa zhinoondawaat wiya baabaagonindjin, wodi gonaa gidaaki gonaa waasa. miidash iidik gaa inendang iwi,

"wiya iidik e wonishing.",

gii inendam. miidash iidik wodi nikeyaa gaa zhaat wodi, (doo) noondawaat newe (e) biibaagonit. gii naagozatawaan gonaa.

miidash giiyeN wodi gimaapiich go e nigidaakiiyet, mii giiyeN miinawaa (e) biibaagonit (e) noondawaadjin, ikwewon dash giiyeN newe. ikwewong gonaa (doo) nashkoziwon newe (e) noondawaadjin. e nigiizhidaakiiyet zhewe e nizhaat, nowonch giiyeN wodi waasa wodi (doo) danadwedamowin, miinawaa wodi bezhik pakokomigaa, mii wodi e tanawedang owo baabaagonit. naapowe maanda, gaawiin go (doo) goshkozisii. miidash iidik gii niisaakiiwet, gii nizhaat wodi nikeyaa wodi newe gii noondawaat baabaagonindjin. gii gidaakiiyet zhewe, zhago giiyeN go nji aaptadaaki e niyaat, mii giiyeN miinawaa (doo) noondawaat newe baabaagonindjin. (doo) nandowemo gonaa maaba baabaagomot. gimaapii sa iidik gii nigiizhidaakiiye, yaawaan dash giiyeN zhewe (e) naaniibowindjin, ikwewon. aapidji giiyeN (doo) gonaadjiwiwon ikwewizeNson, ikwe gonaa. miidash dash iidik e inaat newe,

"gdoo wonishin na.",

doo inaadigenon.

"kaawiin.",

(doo) kidawon dash giiyeN ninda ikwewizeNson.

"gaawiin ndoo wonishizii. mii go geniin zhinda e danakii yaaN zhinda gidaaki.",

"I will lay down to rest or even take a nap for a little while right here outside, at the front of my house. I will fix myself something to eat after I rest."

So he laid down outside of his front door and he quickly fell asleep. He had been very tired from hunting all day. As soon as he fell asleep, he started to dream about himself out on a hunting trip. And the area he was hunting in, the terrain was rough and hilly. He was hunting for animals. So as he went about, suddenly he heard somebody yelling out loud, and it seemed like the sound was coming from far beyond the next hill. He thought to himself,

"Somebody must be lost."

this is what he thought to himself. So he went in the direction he thought the sound was coming from. He tried to follow where the sound was coming from.

So, as he got to the top of this one hill, apparently he again heard that person shouting, and now he could make out the sound of the voice as belonging to a woman. The voice sounded like a woman's voice. As he got to the top of the hill, he realized that the voice of the person was coming from over the next hill further away. He was dreaming this, as he was asleep, resting. So he goes down this hill and up the next hill, going toward the voice he hears. As he is halfway up this hill, he hears the woman shouting again. The person who is shouting is calling for someone's attention. Eventually the hunter arrives at the top of this next hill, and he sees this woman standing right in front of him. This woman was so beautiful. So he asks the woman,

"Are you lost?"

he apparently says to her.

"No,"

he was told by this young woman.

"I am not lost. Here, on this hill, this is where I reside and work,"

doo igoon dash giiyeN. aaniish, maaba dash (e) giiwiset, (doo) ninaabit gonaa, gaawiin gegoo wiigwaam (doo) waabidaziin, wiya gonaa ge daapan gonaa. miinawaa giiyeN ninda ikwewon doo igoon,

"aapidji go ndoo gichitawaawiz.",

doo igoon giiyeN.

"giishpmaa wewena ganawenami yin, gga gichitawaawiz gegiin.",

gii igoon giiyeN. aaniish, gaawiin dash gegoo (doo) waabidaziin zhewe gidaaki ninda ikwewon naaniibowinit.

"mii zhinda e ndaa yaaN.",

doo igoon. gii aagonetawaan dash.

"anishaa maaba ndoo ik.",

gii inendam, aapowewin maanda debaadidamaaN. miidash giiyeN ndaawaach gii bigwekogaabowit, doo aagonetawaan ninda ikwewon e zhiwiindamaawigot. miidash iwi ji bibowaa go, kina go biniisaakiiyet zhewe pakokomigaak go dash yaat, miidash giiyeN ndaawaach gii inendang,

"ndaawaach gonaa ndaa giiwenaa maaba ikwe. daa naanaagodowendaan gaye gonaa e ndaa yaaN. ndaa naadimaak gonaa."

miidash giiyeN, ndaawaach miinawaa maaba gaawiset gii nigidaakiiyet, (doo) paskaabii wodi newe ikwewon naaniibowinit. miidash giiyeN wodi e nidagoshing, giyaabi sa giiyeN go zhewe naaniibowiwon.

"ndoo sadaawendam gonaa maanda gaa zhichige yaaN.",

doo inaadigenon dash.

"gaawiin gonaa ggii minodoodawasanoo maanda gii aagonewitawanaaN.", he was told by her. Well, this hunter looked around and he did not see any kind of dwelling anywhere, anything where a person may live in. Again this woman continued and said,

> "I am very well off,"

the woman said to him.

> "If you take good care of me, you, too, will be wealthy, and live a very good life,"

the man was told by the woman. Well, the man looked around and did not see any sign of a house where this woman could be living.

> "This is where I live,"

he was told by this woman. So of course, he did not believe her.

> "She is trying to pull a fast one over me,"

the man supposedly thought, and remember, he is dreaming this, I am talking about his dream. So, he then turned around to leave as he did not believe a word this woman was saying to him. So as he was coming down this hill, he was partway down, he had a change of heart and he decided,

> "I should take this woman home with me. She could take care of my house. She could help me a lot."

So, this hunter again went back up the hill, he went back to where the woman was standing at the top of the hill. So, when he arrived back at the top of the hill, this woman was still standing there.

> "I am displeased with myself for my behavior toward you,"

he must have said to the woman.

> "I did not treat you very kindly because I doubted what you were telling me,"

doo inaadigenon sa.

"eN, ggii gikenimin sa go gii aagonewitawa yin.",

doo igoodigenon dash newe ikwewon.

"ndaawaach sa gga maadjiinin.",

doo inaan dash iidik maaba gaawiset ninda.

"gga giiwenin, gga ganawenamin."
"aaniish, gga giiwewish sa.",

doo igoon giiyeN.

"bekaa.",

doo igoon dash giiyeN.

"gga wiindamawin gegoo. iwi go oonji gii aagonewitawa yin, nonggom go maanda naaniibowi ying, iwi go maanda aki go dekokaadaaming, maanda gaye go mitigowaaki, kina go maanda gdoo dibendaan nonggom, gaawiin dash wiyii go gibeying. bekaanizit wii dibendaan maanda, gwii wonaachitoon.",

gii igoon.

aaniish, mii sa giiyeN gii inaat ji biwiijiiwagot gaa shkwaa wiindamaawigot iwi. miidash go maanda zhigwekogaabowiwaat, wii biniisaakiiyet giiyeN gewiin maaba gaawiset, wii biwiidjiiwaat newe ikwewon, mii giiyeN gii goshkozit.

"geget sa gonaa ngii gichi aapowe.",

(doo) inendam dash iidik.

miidash maanda gaa waabaninik, miinawaa (doo) bibaa giiwiset,

"geget sa gonaa ngii gichi aapowe.",

(doo) inendam sa iidik, (doo) naanaagodowendang gonaa.

he further told the woman.

"Yes, I know you were doubting what I was telling you,"

the man must have been told by this woman.

"I decided that I will take you with me,"

this hunter must have said to this woman.

"I will take you home, and I will take care of you."
"Okay then, you will take me to your home"

the man was told by the woman.

"Wait,"

the woman added.

"I shall tell you something first. Because you doubted me, you will suffer the consequences, this land we are now standing on and the forests you see around us, these are yours right now but because you doubted me, you will not have this land for much longer to call your own. Someone else will occupy it as you will lose the land,"

he was told by this woman.

Well, he then told her to follow him after she had told him this ominous prediction. And as he turned around, and they were starting to come down this hill they were standing on, that is when he awoke from his nap.

"Wow, that was some dream I had,"

he must have thought to himself.

So the morning of the next day, he was again out hunting.

"Gee, that was some dream,"

he thought, as he kept thinking about it.

"wegonesh naa iwi iidik gaa aabowaadimaaN.",

gii inendam gonaa. miidash giiyeN baamaapii gonaa naagach, (doo) bibaa giiwiset, aapidji giiyeN go (doo) maanaadakamigaani bebaa zhaat. baamaa giiyeN go zhewe ngoding gonaa e nigiizhidaakiiyet, mii giiyeN go gegaa go beskowaat ninda mandaaminon, (doo) bidakoziwon. gaawiin gonaa mishi gonaa waabazosii maaba mandaamin. miinawaa gaye go mizaakoziiNak giiyeN, niizh goodjiniwon zhewe niyiing, (e) mitigooNsawit maaba yaawaa, mandaamin. miinawaa gaye (doo) wiindjisaa maaba mandaamin. mii giiyeN go ninda e naandenik maaba mandaamin (doo) wiindjisaawit gewiin, newe ikwewon gaa aapowaanaadjin.

"taaya, mii na gonaa maaba gaa aapowaanak iidik wii makawak.",

(doo) inendam dash giiyeN.

miidash giiyeN gii nisibanaat newe mandaaminon, niizhawaatik. gii bipaskaabiit miinawaa zhewe niyiing e njijiit gonaa, miidash miinawaa gii bigiiwet. gii bigiiwet zhewe gii waabidawaat anishinaaben, wiidji-anishinaaben,

"mii sa maanda gaa bowaadamaaN. miidash maanda gaa makamaaN,
mandaamin ngii makawaa."

miidash gwonda gichi-anishinaabek gii nisadowinawaawaan ninda mandaaminon. waasa giiyeN gonaa zhaawonong anishinaabek e yaadjik, mandaaminon gewiinawaa gii gitigaanaawaan. gwonda dash anishinaabek zhinda giiwedinong nikeyaa e yaadjik, gii inendamok gonaa ginimaa,

"gaawiin gonaa daa nitaagisii zhinda mandaamin, ozaam gonaa jina
niibin.",

gii inendam.

miidash giiyeN maaba anishinaabe gaawiset gaa zhichiget, gii gaakanaan giiyeN ninda mandaaminon. miidash bebezhigominak newe ensogamigak gonaa gii miinaat newe wiidji-anishinaaben, pii gonaa e zhaat gonaa. mandj gonaa minik gonaa gewe mandaaminon gonaa zhewe niizhawaatik gewe bizaagikiinit. miinawaa gii kinoomawaat waa zhichigenit wii gitigaanaanit, wii maadjiigininit gonaa ninda mandaaminon. gichi piitendaagozi dash go maaba mandaamin, kina maaba mandaamin gwodji nakaazam, banggii gonaa maaba doopawining mandaamin zhaa gonaa, gdoo mowaanaan gonaa ji kida yinggoban.

aaniish, ndoo gichi minowendam dash gonaa bazindawa yek. gichi miigwech.

"What does this dream mean, what is it that I dreamt about?"

he must have thought to himself. So as he went about hunting, he came across this area with rough terrain. As he walked about, he came up this one rise and he almost walked right into this tall corn plant standing at the top of the hill. The corn plant was not yet ripe. Also, he noticed that there were two ears of corn that had formed on the stalk of this plant. This plant also had hair growing from it. The hair of this plant was the same color as that of the woman whom he had dreamt about the previous day.

"Is this what I dreamt about, that I would find this plant?"

he thought to himself.

So he then proceeded to take the two ears of corn from the stem of the plant. He returned home to his village. He showed the two ears of corn to the people, to his fellow Anishinaabe people in the village.

"This is what I had dreamt about. I found this plant, and it is the corn plant that I found."

The elders of the community were the ones who recognized this to be the corn plant. The Anishinaabe people far to the south had always planted corn. But, the Anishinaabe people here in the North thought the following.

"The corn would not grow well in this area, as the summer season is much too short."

This is what they thought.

So this Anishinaabe hunter who had gotten this corn, he shelled the two ears of corn. He distributed one kernel of corn to each household in the village. It is not known exactly how many kernels were in those two ears of corn. This man taught the people how to grow and care for the corn plant. Corn is highly valued as it is used in many, many ways, as we can honestly say that today, people only eat a small portion of the corn that is grown, the rest has many other uses.

Well, I am grateful that you have listened to me. Thank you very much.

· PART 3 ·

HISTORICAL STORIES

zaagiinaa niniwok

aaniish, mii sa giiyeN, mii sa ji dibaadjimowi yaaN zhinda gaa zhiwebadagobaneN gichi zhaazhago. gaawiin wiya zhinda e waabshkiiyet gii yaasii, mii go eta anishinaabek gaa yaadjik zhinda, gaa oodetoodjik. miidash iwi, binoodjiiNik gonaa, gii baatiinawok gonaa, gichi yaawaaNsak gonaa, ginimaa gii niizhwaaswi nisabiboonigiziwidik owo gwiiwizeNs, (doo) bibaa daminowok dash giiyeN ooshti wodi nikeyaa maanda miikan e ninamok, zhinda gonaa oodenaang (doo) bibaa daminowaat. yaawaa dash maanda, zhinggobiiNsak zhinda kina gii bidakoziwok, yaawaak, giizkikaandigooNsak, (doo) bibaa daminowaat binoodjiiNik, gwiiwizeNsak. mii sa zhewe anishinaaben gii bidagoshininit. mii go eta nowonch owo zeziikoziiNwit, mii owo gaa binowodinind. gii binowodjibinind. gii maadjiibatoowaanaawaat, maanda gidaaki wodi gii nipatoowaat. miidash wodi gii gidjibowewaat, yeshkweying dash gii midjigonaawaan kaading newe, niizh, miidash gii mabatoowaanaawaat. gii gimoodiwaat newe binoodjiiNon, gwiiwizeNson.

miidash gwonda zhewe e yaapaniik, waadookawaapaniik newe, mii go weyiip gii bidibaadjimowaat zhinda dash gonaa oodenaweNsing, gii binowodjibinind wodi owo oshkiniigish.

miidash giiyeN gwonda anishinaabek kina gii maajaa, wewiip go gii maawondoobidowaat niyii, baashkoziganan gii nowodinamowaat. kina go iwi waa zhichigewaat go, baashkoziganan gii nowodjibidoowaat. miidash gii maadjiibatoowaat, gii naaginaawaan dash newe, newe sa gaa bigimoodinidjin binoodjiiNon. mii maanda dash go gweyek sa go maanda bezhik iwi nibisan wodi e ndigowogin, ooshti wodi waagwaaseNskaak. mii wodi iidik gii gibaawaat gewe anishinaabek, bigimoodiwaat dash binoodjiiNon. miidash wodi, maanpii eshkweying (doo) midjigonaawaat.

miidash gwonda gaye gii maadjiibatoowaat gaa gimoodimindjik binoodjiiNon, niniwok, niibana go, gaawiin go banggiisheN go, minik sa go e yaawaagobaneN zhewe. gii gidjibatoowaanaawaat newe binoodjiiNon. miidash gii ninaanoondaagoziwaat gewe sa nendonewaadjik newe gwiiwizeNson gaa bigimoodinid. (doo) naanoondaagoziwaat miinawaa gii nimadwezigewok, baashkoziganan gii baashkozigewok. (doo) naaginaawaan dash newe.

The Men of Zaagiinaa

Well, I shall talk about what supposedly happened in this area a very long time ago. The white people had not been here yet, there were just native people who lived here and had towns and villages throughout. There was this one village that had quite a few children and some were a little older and this one boy was about seven years old, and this group of children were playing along the trail that led through the town. There was this cedar bush just on the edge of the village, and that is where these young boys were playing around. That is when a man suddenly appeared in front of them. It was the oldest of the boys who was kidnapped by these strangers. They grabbed him and took him away. They ran away with the boy and they ran toward the hill away from the town. They each held on to one side, arms and legs, and they ran away with the boy. They were kidnapping that little boy.

And the ones who were playing with this boy, they quickly ran into the little village and told the people what had happened, that this one boy was being kidnapped.

So the men of this village quickly gathered together, they gathered their weapons. They gathered everything they were going to use. They started to run after the kidnappers and they followed the trail of those strange men. This is straight toward the lakes that are located over there where there are many birch trees. That is where those men had landed their canoes, as they came with the purpose of stealing a child. And they carried this young boy to where they had left their canoes.

So these men to whom the child belonged, they ran after these kidnappers, and there were many of them, practically all of the able-bodied men of that village. The kidnappers had a head start on them. So the men who were from the same village as the child, they made all kinds of noise as they ran after the strangers who had kidnapped one of their children. The yelled, whistled, banged on their drums, they made all kinds of noise. They were following the trail left by the kidnappers.

(*doo*) bowaashaagonigaade gaye maaba binoodjiiN. mii go eta go babagweyaaneNs e *a*gowad, maanda (*doo*) kowegodini. aapidji go gii nigaawaa*w*aan, mii go, gii baapaazigogaadeyaakodjin megowe datagaagomish*a*ki *o*wo binoodjiiN, gwiiwizeNs, (*doo*) mab*a*toowaanin*d*. mii*da*sh wodi gimaapii gonaa, mii (*doo*) noondawaawaat gewe gedjibowaadjik binoodjiiNon, binaanoondaagozinit, miinawaa (*doo*) bimadwezigenit. aapidji go (*doo*) binoowaatoowon, mii newe beminaashkaagowaadjin. mii sa wodi, besha sa go (*doo*) bidanowezigewon newe e baapaashk*o*zigendjin, wii nisaawok go. mandj go iidik waa naapininaandowaago*w*eN, miidash gii yaawaat, gii zegaziwok gewe gaa gimoodjik binoodjiiNon. mii go *n*iyiing gaa zhipaganaawaat megowe datagaagomish*a*ki, gii gagaandjiwebinaawaat, mii gii gidjibowewaat. wodi dash gii bigibaawaat waagwaaseNkaak, jiimaanawaa gii bitoowaat, mii wodi gaa powewaat.

mii*da*sh *n*iyii gwonda beminaashkaagedjik gii waabimaawaat zhewe newe binoodjiiNon *d*ash (*doo*) yaanit megowe datagaagomish*a*ki. aaniish, mii*da*sh go gii noogshkaawaat. (*doo*) g*a*gwedjimaawaat,

"aanipii*sh* dash gewe."

"gii gidjibowewok. miidash go zhinda gaa zhipag*a*zhiwaat megowe datagaagomish*a*ki."

aapidji giiyeN go miskowiiyaakogaade *o*shkiniigish, gii baapaazigogaadeyaakodjin, (*doo*) bowaashaagoniside gaye. miidash iwi, mii*da*sh go gii yaawaat zhewe gewe niniwok. gii gichi madwewezigewok e zhig*o*shkitoowaat go miinawaa (*doo*) naanoondaagoziwok. mii*da*sh go gwonda gii gidjibowewaat, mii wodi gaa powewaat jiimaanawaa gii nigadimowaat, gii bigimoodiwaat newe binoodjiiNon.

aaniish, mii*da*sh gii boonaabimindowaa. giishpin gegoo (*e*) doodawaawaapa*n* newe, ginimaa gaye (*e*) nisaawaapa*n*, mii go kina wodi wii naabiigomowaapa*n* gewe sa anishinaabek, wii oonisindawaa gewe gaa gimoodjik binoodjiiNon. gaa*wiin* dash gii zhichigesiiwok iwi, mii go bekaa gaa bizhipskaabiwinaawaat. gii bitakonaawaat newe binoodjiiNon, gii bigiiwewinaawaat. miidash gwonda gii gichi zegaziwaat, gwonda sa, zaagiinaa niniwok gewe gaa doodanggik iwi, zaagiinaang gaa binjibaadjik. mii*da*sh gii gichi zegaziwaat. gaa*wiin da*sh wiikaa miinawaa gii doodaziiwok iwi. pane go gii *n*indaziwok ji gimoodiwaat binoodjiiNon, *o*daawaan ji gimoodimaawaat binoodjiiNon. gii nishkenimaawaan newe odaawaan, gii pogodjiikowaawaan zaagiinaa niniwok. wegowendigenak gonaa gwonda zaagiinaa niniwok, gaawii*n* ngii gikenimaasiik. mii sa gii p*a*skaabiwinin maaba binoodjiiN, gii bigiiwewinin. gaa*wiin* ndoo gikenimaasii gaa zhinikaazat *o*wo e niidjaaniseNwit. mii sa gaa zhiweb*a*dagobaneN iwi.

The young boy was bare legged. All he must have had on was a small shirt that came down and covered his rear. They really mistreated this young boy as they ran through the blackberry bushes and the boy's legs got all scratched up from the thorns of those bushes. So these men could hear the people who were chasing them, and they must have been getting closer, at least it must have sounded like it. The villagers were making all kinds of racket as they chased after the kidnappers. Oh, the noisemakers seemed to be gaining on them, and they must have thought they would be killed when they got caught. The kidnappers did not know what fate would befall them if they should get caught, and this must have terrified them. So, in their fright, the kidnappers threw the boy into a blackberry patch, and they pushed him into the thorns, then they took off. They ran to where they made land with their canoes, at that lake with all those birch trees.

So the people who were chasing the kidnappers saw the boy in the blackberry patch. They then gave up the chase. The men from the village asked the boy,

"Where did they go?"

"They ran away. They deliberately threw me into this blackberry patch."

The boy's legs were all bloodied from being scratched by the little thorns of the blackberry bushes, as he had no leggings and he was unshod. So those men stayed there, where they found the boy, they did not go after those strange men. However, they made as much racket as they could, out of joy. So the kidnappers ran as fast as they could to where they left their canoes when they came to kidnap the child.

Thus, the villagers gave up on looking for them. If the kidnappers had killed the boy, these villagers were going to hunt these kidnappers until they were found and would have probably killed them for their evil deed. But they did not have to do that, as they found the child alive, and they all brought him back to their village. They carried the boy as they brought him home. So the men that tried to kidnap the boy were totally frightened, these were men from Zaagiinaa, as they came from the area called Zaagiinaang. They were very terrified as they narrowly escaped. So they never ever again did this to the people of this village. These men of Zaagiinaa were adept at kidnapping children from other villages. These men of Zaagiinaa disliked the Ottawas, and they always did things that provoked the Ottawas. Whoever these people were, these men of Zaagiinaa as I do not know any myself. Anyway, this boy was returned home safe and sound. I do not recall the names of the parents of this child. This is what had happened a long time ago.

mayegi anishinaabek gaa bigimoodjik *ikwewize*Nson

anishinaabek nwii dibaadjimaak. zhaazhago gonaa gwonda odaawaak zhinda njike gii yaawok. gii goziwok *dash* ko gwonda anishinaabek, odaawaak gwonda. zhaawonong gii zhaawaat *n*iyiing zhigaagoong nonggo*m* e ndigo*w*ok besha. zaagawaang gii zhinikaadaanaawaa zhewe gaa nji biboonishiwaat. gichi mookamaan ginimaa St. Joseph's doo zhinikaadaan iwi oodena nonggo*m*. mii gwonda anishinaabek zhewe gaa nji biboonishiwaat. miinawaa *dash* gonaa gwonda anishinaabek gii nan*a*kiiwok zhewe gaa dagoshiniwaadji zhewe, gii niigewok gaye gonaa wodi zhaawonong. miinawaa gonaa gii giiwisewok gonaa.

maaba *dash* go bezhik anishinaabe waa dibaadjimak, yaa*w*aan, maaba ikwewizeNson wodi gii gimoodimaaba*n* gonaa bibaa niiget gonaa, wodi *n*iyiing zhigaagoong nonggo*m* e ndigo*w*ok. gii waabshkokaa giiyeN niibana iwi. yaawaak dash gonaa gii yaawok zhewe, zhashkooNik, gii baatiin*a*wok giiyeN zhashkooNik. miidash gonaa gwonda odaawaak gaa nan*a*kiiwaat iwi biboong, *d*ash niigewaat zhewe. miidash *naa*nedaa maaba bezhik anishinaabe (*doo*) zhaat wodi, mii iidik gewii*n* gaa inendang,

"nga niige zhewe ziibiiweying.",

gii inendam. gaa*w*ii*n dash* gonaa gichi ziibi gii aawozinoo iwi, zhigaagoong nonggo*m*, gichi oodena megowaa. miidash iidik wodi gaa noodegozit, wii niiget go *dash* (*doo*) inendam. aaniish gii niige *dash* go zhewe.

miidash giiyeN ngoding (*e*) bigiiwet, (*e*) naakowenik, iwi gonaa wii wiisinit, mii giiyeN gaa*w*ii*n* gonaa nibiish gegoo doo *y*aaziin maaba jiibaakowenini, maaba sa gonaa nini wiidigemaaganon. mii*d*ash iidik ninda daaniseNon e inaat maaba *i*kwe,

"shkenaa ndaaniseN, nibiish naadin. gaa*w*ii*n* gosha nayiinawi*nd* gegoo."

ginimaa midaaswi *shi* niiwibiboonigizigoba*n* owo ikwewizeNs, ginimaa gaye gonaa midaaswi shi naanan. mii*d*ash giiyeN gii daapinang iwi *n*iyii, niimbaagan, gii m*a*daabiiset wodi *n*iyiing gichigomiing. gii nji ndendi giiyeN. gaa*w*ii*n* giiyeN go naash dagoshi*n*isii, gimaapii giiyeN gonaa gwonda gekaaNik zhewe baabiiwaa*w*aat, gii wiisiniwok ndaawaach gonaa. miidash iidik gaa shkwaa wiisiniwaat, mii gii kidawaat,

The Story of the Anishinaabe Girl Who Was Kidnapped by Strangers

I am going to talk about the Anishinaabe people. A long time ago, the Anishinaabe people were the only ones to live and settle in the area around here. The Anishinaabe people used to move to different locations occasionally, these people were the ones now known as the Ottawas. They used to travel south toward the area where the city of Chicago now stands. The Anishinaabe people called that place Zaagawaang, that is where they wintered. Today, the Americans call that area St. Joseph. This was the area where some Anishinaabe people usually wintered, and some even lived there year-round. The Anishinaabe people used to trap the animals that populated the area. This is one activity the people did during the winter. They also hunted bigger game for their subsistence.

So this one man in particular I will talk about, he had a daughter who was stolen from them while he was out checking his trapline, which was near the area where Chicago is now located. This area used to be a big marshy area. This area was plentiful with muskrats. So that is what the Anishinaabe people did during the winter, they trapped small game. So this man who had moved there, he decided to trap in the area as well.

> "I will set up a trapline along this river,"

thought this one Anishinaabe. That river was not really very big, the one that flows through where the city of Chicago now stands. So this man moved his family there and he was going to trap in that area. So that is what he did, he trapped in that area.

Supposedly, this one day shortly before it was the time for the man to come home for lunch, his wife, who was cooking, ran out of water. Apparently, the woman told her daughter,

> "Oh my daughter, go fetch some water. There happens to be none left for cooking."

The young girl may have been fourteen or even around fifteen years old. So she picked up the pail and walked toward the shore of the big lake. She was gone for a long, long time. She just did not return to the house, so eventually the man and the woman decided to start eating their lunch. When they finished eating, they must have said to one another, "aaniish gaye gonaa ndaawaach oonandowaabimaadaa owo. gaawiin go wiikaa go gwodji (doo) zhaasii owo."

miidash giiyeN gii zhaawaat wodi tibewe, yaawaan dash giiyeN gonaa eta zhewe niimbaaganon e zhibindjin maaba ikwewizeNs gaa nimaadjiipatoowaanaapaniin gonaa nibiish wii nibinaadit. gaawiin dash wiyii go wiya ikwewizeNs. aaniish, gii sadaawendam dash go maaba nini, aapidji maajaanit newe ikwewizeNson. naa-aash go giiyeN go gii dibikat go, gaawiin go ginigeN go gwodji go. mii go eta go zhewe gii madaabiit owo ikwewizeNs, mii gaye go zhewe e yekowaakowet go tibewe. ndaawaach gonaa maaba anishinaabe zhewe zaagawaang gii nipaskaabii, zhewe gonaa waa nji biboonishiwaat gonaa, gii bidibaadjimot iidik.

"ndo ikwewizeNsim ngii wonaachaa. dibi go iidik go. gaawiin ngii makawaasiinaan aanowi nandonewonggit."

miidash iwi, aazhoow ko gonaa e zhaadjik anishinaabek, maanda gaye gonaa niyiing, gichi mashkodeng gonaa gwonda gii bibaa zhaawok, yaawaak odaawaak. mii giiyeN gaa zhinakweshkowaat wodi newe ikwewizeNson, (doo) miwiidjiiwe maaba ikwewizeNs, (doo) bimiwinigoon giiyeN, niibana go niniwon. bezhik dash go maaba anishinaabe gii nisadowinawaan giiyeN ninda ikwewizeNson.

"n(doo) nisadowinawaa go owo ikwewizeNs.",

doo inaadigenon dash newe aanind wiichkiwezon.

"maanda maaba ikwewizeNs (doo) zhidibendaagozi niyiing, Oden Bay.",

ko dash (doo) kidawaat gonaa, anishinaabek gonaa. miidash iwi,

"aanipiish maaba gaa ndinaa yek ikwewizeNs.",

doo inaadigenon dash maaba newe odaawaa.

"gaawiin, ngii binoonigoomin sa maaba wii binaana yaanggit.",

doo igoodigenon dash newe mayegi anishinaaben.

"Let's go looking for her. She has never, ever gone anywhere before."

So the parents of the girl went along the shore of the big lake, and they found the water pail the girl had taken to get the water, the pail was laying on the shore. But, there was no girl in sight, nowhere to be found. The man was greatly saddened by the disappearance of his daughter. It was soon night, and the girl was nowhere in sight. All they found was that her tracks ended there on the shore of the big lake. So this man decided to go back to the place called zaagawaang, as this was the place where they would be wintering, so he went back there and told the people there what had happened to them.

"I lost our little girl. We just do not know where she went. We did not find her when we went searching for her."

And at that time, the Anishinaabe people traveled all over the area, and they even ventured out onto the prairies. And some of these Ottawa men who had been returning from the prairies had come across this girl as she was traveling with this group of men, the group was sizable. And one of these Anishinaabe men, this Ottawa, recognized this girl as being an Ottawa child.

"I know that girl,"

he must have said to his companions.

"This girl belongs to a family from Oden Bay."

That is what the Anishinaabe people referred to that area as. So then,

"Where did you get this girl from?"

this Ottawa man apparently asked.

"Oh, we were asked to come and get this girl,"

these strange Anishinaabe men replied to him.

"gaawiin go gegoo gdaa zhiniizaanendazii. aapidji go nayiinawi*nt* go maaba da minoyaa e zhaat ikwewizeNs. yaawaa wodi (*doo*) yaa ogimaa, anishinaabe ogimaa, niizhwaachiwon gwi*s*ison, wii wiidigemaagani *da*sh maaba zeziikozit oshkinowe. miidash gii noozho *yaa*nggit maaba anishinaabe ogimaa wii *na*ndowaabima*a yaa*nggit ikwewizeNs. miidash maaba newe zeziikozit oshkinowe, mii ninda waa wiidigemaadjin. mii sa maaba gaa oonji naana*a yaa*nggit iwi. giyegeti go ngii oogimoodinaa*n* maaba. gaa m*a*daabiit gonaa gichigomiing ngii waabimaanaa*n* *naa*nedaa, *naa*nedaa gonaa zhewe n*doo* biyaaminaaba*n*. aaniish, mii*da*sh go gii debinanggit, gii boozanggit jiimaaning. mii go gii bimaajaa *y*aang go wewiip."

aaniish, miidash go gwonda odaawaak wodi epanggishimok gaa bibaa zhaadjik mii gii bidibaadjimowaat zhewe goziwining, zaagawaang. gii bidibaadjimowaat,

"ngii waabimaanaa*n* owo ikwewizeNs bimiwinind."

miinawaa gaye gii kidawok gwonda anishinaabek, mayegi anishinaabek,

"gaawii*n* giiyeN ji zhisadaawendazi ying. miinawaa wii gichi minoyaa maaba ikwewizeNs gii wiidigemaat ninda ogimaa gwi*s*ison."

aaniish, gaa*wiin da*sh maaba e daaniseNwit ninda anishinaabe gii minowendazii.

"nga naanaa.",

gii kida iidik. miidash gii nandowaabimaat gonaa ge wiidjiiwigopaniin gonaa wodi ji zhaat epanggishimok gwonda sa anishinaabek gaa binjibaawaat, gaa bigimoodjik ninda ikwewizeNson. aaniish, mii*da*sh go iidik gii zhiitaawaat, wii mibigowok. megowaa gonaa bezhigogazhiin owo anishinaabe gonaa wodi, bezhigogazhiiNsak gonaa. mii*da*sh gonaa iwi gii maajaawaat gonaa iidik gaa denchiwaat, mii wii naanaawaat ikwewizeNson, (*doo*) nowaazowok gonaa. aaniish, gii gikenimaawaan go *zhaa*zhowaadj go ninda pii anishinaaben e danakiinit, (*doo*) oodetoowaat gonaa gewiinawaa gewe anishinaabek, mayegi anishinaabek.

gimaapii sa giiyeN wodi gii dagoshiniwok. aanii*sh* gii gichi minowaabimigoowaan giiyeN newe mayegi anishinaaben. aaniish, mii*da*sh go gii wiindamawaawaat iwi bebaanikaawaat wodi.

> "You all should have no worries as nothing untoward will befall her. This girl will have the best where she is going. She is going to be wed to the oldest son of our chief, our chief has seven sons. So our chief asked us to go looking for a suitable girl for his son to marry. So this is the girl that the oldest son of our chief will be wed to. That is why we went to get this girl. Yes, we did kidnap this girl. When she came down to the shore of the lake, we just happened to come by where she was on the shore. So we caught her and we put her in our canoe. And we left right away as soon as we got her."

Well, these Anishinaabe who were returning from out west came back and told about this girl at the village of Zaagawaang. They said that,

> "We saw a girl being escorted away from here."

And these strange Anishinaabe had said:

> "That we should not feel sadness. And that the girl will be living a very good life as she would be marrying one of the chief's sons."

However, the father of this girl was not comforted by this revelation.

> "I will go get her,"

this man supposedly uttered. Then he solicited the help of others to go with him to get his daughter back from the men of the prairies. So they prepared for the journey, and they would go on horseback. The Anishinaabe people already had horses then, they were ponies. So this group set out to get the girl who was kidnapped as this was their intention, and it was a sizable search party. They had a general idea where to go as they knew roughly where these strange Anishinaabe people lived.

After some time, they eventually arrived at a village where there were strange Anishinaabe people. The Anishinaabe search party was warmly welcomed into the village of these strange Anishinaabe people. They quickly told them what their purpose was, what they were doing there.

"eN*he*N, giyegeti sa go zhinda ikwewizeNson gii biinaawaan gewe niniwok.",

(*doo*) kidawon *da*sh giiyeN gonaa newe genoonagoowaadjin.

"gaa*wiin da*sh wiyii go nonggo*m* zhinda yaasii owo ogimaa, maanda nowonch waasa epanggishimok gii nizhaa."

ginimaa gonaa nowonch gonaa wodi gii gonaadjiwonidik gwodji gaa noodegozit maaba ogimaa. aaniish mii*da*sh go gwonda miinawaa odaawaak gii nimaajaawaat. (*doo*) maadjiibigowaat miinawaa m*a*shkodeng.

gimaapii sa giiyeN giyegeti wodi gii dagoshiniwok. *geget* sa gonaa (*doo*) baatiin*a*won *da*sh giiyeN go ninda. wewena go (*doo*) oodetoowok go zhewe iidik maaba ogimaa gaa zhaat. mii sa zhewe gii dagoshiniwaat, giyegeti giiyeN go (*doo*) minowaabimigoowaan ninda anishinaaben. miinawaa gaye go gii wiindamawaa*w*aan iidik zhewe e bibaa nikaawaat.

"n*doo* binaanaanaa*n* owo ndo ikwewizeNsiminaa*n*. zhinda ggii biinaawaa giinawaa owo.",

doo inaawaadigenon sa.

"gaawiin maamdaa ji maadjiin*a*diba*n*. ngwisi*s* sa newe wii wiidigemaan.",

doo igoon *da*sh giiyeN maaba odaawaa newe mayegi anishinaaben. ogimaa maaba mayegi anishinaabe, (*doo*) minoyaa gonaa. niizhwaachiwon *da*sh giiyeN maaba gwi*s*ison, maaba anishinaabe ogimaa. maaba *da*sh (*doo*) zeziikozit oshkinowe mii maaba waa wiidigemaad ninda odaawaa ikweNson.

mii*da*sh giiyeN go gwonda anishinaabek gii zhiitaawaat, iwi gonaa maaba go do ogimaawaan gii igoowaawaan ji wiisiniwaat giiyeN, ji gichi jiibaakowewaat. aaniish, gimaapii sa giiyeN gii minozekowewon. aapidji go niibana miijim, aaniish (*doo*) baatiinawok gewe anishinaabek, mayegi anishinaabek. mii*da*sh gaye gii zhisidjigaadek waa nji wiisiniwaat. aaniish, gaa*wiin* gaye gonaa doopawin gonaa owo anishinaabe pii gii yaaziin, m*a*tak*a*shkamik gonaa gii namadabi gonaa wiisinit. miinawaa gaye gwonda odaawaak waa nji wiisiniwaat gewiinawaa giiyeN gii zhitoowaawaak wii namadabiwaat. mii*da*sh giiyeN gii webiwiisiniwaat. aapidji giiyeN (*doo*) baatiinawon anishinaaben. wegowendigenak gonaa iidik, mayegi anishinaabek. miidash giiyeN gaa shkwaa wiisinit maaba odaawaa ninda debenimaat ikwewizeNson, mii giiyeN go gii nibot. mandj iidik gaa zhiweb*a*zigoweN. mii go gii nibot.

"The men you are looking for definitely did bring a girl with them when they came,"

the Anishinaabe men were told by one of these villagers who spoke to them.

"But the chief is not here now, as he went to another village farther west."

The village further west that the chief moved to may have been nicer or bigger. So these Ottawa left to go to the next village. They got on their ponies and rode further west on the plains.

Then they eventually arrived at the next village where the chief had moved. And this village had so many inhabitants. This was a sizable town they were living in that the chief had moved to. So when the Anishinaabe arrived there, these strangers welcomed them into their territory. Again, the Anishinaabe told these townspeople the purpose of their trip here.

"We have come to get our little girl. Your people brought her here,"

these Anishinaabe men must have said to these strangers.

"You cannot take her away with you. My son is going to marry her,"

this Ottawa man was told by this strange Anishinaabe. This was the chief of these strange Anishinaabe people, and he lived a good life. This chief had seven sons. And the chief's eldest son was to marry the Ottawa girl.

So these strange Anishinaabe people began to prepare a feast, as they were instructed to do this by their chief. Well, they finally got everything cooked. They had prepared so much food, as there were so many of these strange Anishinaabe people in the town. Then an area was prepared where they would all eat. At that time, the Anishinaabe people did not have tables like we do today, so they just spread some skins on the ground and that is where they sat to eat. A place was also prepared for the Ottawa men to eat at. So the feasting began. Oh, there were so many people at this feast. They were all strangers to the Ottawa men. So when they had finished eating their fill, the father of the girl suddenly died right there at the feast. It is not known what happened to him. He died instantly.

aaniish, mii sa go wodi gii bigidenimaawaat gwonda newe, gwonda sa aanind odaawaak. miinawaa newe bezhigogazhiimon maaba anishinaabe gaa nimibigowodjin, ogimaa giiyeN ninda gii daapinaan bezhigogazhiin. aaniish, mii sa go gwonda gii bipaskaabiiwaat niniwok, odaawaak, neyaap bipaskaabiiwok. aaniish gaawiin sa newe ikwewizeNson (doo) dibenimaasiiwaan. mii gaa dagoshiniwaat zhewe gozigoning, zaagawaang, mii gii dibaadjimowaat iidik gaa zhiwebaziwaat.

"gii nibow sa nayiinawint owo ndo ogimaanaan wodi gaa zhaa yaang. ngii gichi shamigoonaanik gwonda mayegi anishinaabek miidash go gaa shkwaa wiisinit maaba ndo ogimaanaan, mii go gii nibot. aaniish, mii sa go gaawiin niinawind ngii zhigashkitoosiimin wii zhichige yaang. mii go gii bipaskaabii yaang."

iwi dash iwi, zhaazhago gonaa zhinda gichi gindaasowin, eighteen-seventy, niyii ko gii nji maamaajaawok, yaawaak gonaa, odaawaaNsak gonaa nga kid, e ookinoomawandjik niyiing Haskell, Lawrence, Kansas. miidash giiyeN gwonda odaawaak ngoding wodi wiinawaa gonaa e nchiwaat gewiinawaa (doo) miyaawaat, mii giiyeN gii waabimaawaat ko zhewe mindimooyeNon (doo) bimosenit. miidash giiyeN e kidat maaba bezhik odaawaa, odaawaaNs,

"gegaa go nesadowinawak maaba. zhaazhowaadj go (doo) zhinaagozi maaba mindimooweN zhinda bemoset, bezhik gonaa maanda Oden Bay geniin negodenimak.",

(doo) kida sa giiyeN.

"mii go e zhinaagozit go iwi."
"gga ganoonaanaan miinawaa (doo) bimoset pii.",

(doo) kidawok dash iidik.

"gga nandogikenimaanaan endigoweN go giyegeti ji odaawaawit maaba mindimooweN.",

(doo) kidawok sa iidik.

aaniish, ngoding dash go giiyeN gonaa gii zhiwebaziwok iwi, miidash giiyeN go miinawaa owo mindimooyeN biidaasimoset. aaniish, maaba gii ooganoonaat,

"gdoo odaawaa na. gegaa go nesadowinawanaaN."

So then, these Anishinaabe men buried their fellow Ottawa out there on the prairies. And the horse that the father of the girl had ridden out there, this horse was claimed by the chief of the strange Anishinaabe people. So the remaining Anishinaabe search party returned home, they came back without the girl. The girl was not their daughter, so they came back without her. So when they got back to this community, Zaagawaang, these men told of what happened to them out west.

> "Our leader died out west where we went. Those strange Anishinaabe people put on a big feast for us and then when we finished eating, that is when our leader died. So we could not complete what we set out to do. That is why we came right back."

Now, around the year of 1870, the young people from around here were taken to a place down south for their schooling, the place was Haskell, in Lawrence, Kansas. And there was this one group of young Ottawa boys who happened to be at this school at that time, and they occasionally saw this old woman walk by the school. Then one of those young Ottawa boys said,

> "I almost recognize this old woman. She looks almost like someone I know who is from my community back in Oden Bay."

This is what this young boy told the others.

> "She looks exactly like that person I know back home."
> "We will speak to her the next time she walks by here,"

these Ottawa boys must have said to each other.

> "We will see if this old woman is really an Ottawa person,"

they must have stated further.

Well, it just so happened that the old woman came walking by the school on another day. So this Ottawa boy spoke to her in the Anishinaabe language.

> "Are you Ottawa by any chance? I almost recognize you,"

doo inaadigenon sa newe.

"eN*he*N, ndoo odaawaa go genii*n*.",

(*doo*) kidawon *da*sh giiyeN. mii giiyeN go maanda e nowenit newe mindimooyeNon.

"gii gimoodinaaban nwiiyaw awazh (*e*) ikwewizeNsiwi yaaN, wodi *n*iyiing zhigaagoong nonggo*m*, zhigaagoong e ndigowog. gaawii*n* oodena *i*wi pii zhewe gii tesinoo.",

(*doo*) kidawon *da*sh giiyeN ninda mi*n*dimooweNon.

"ngii maadjiinigook mayegi anishinaabek. maanda, zhinda nikeyaa ngii bizhiwinigowok, yaawaa giiyeN wii wiidigemak, ogimaa gwisison. gii niizhwaachiwon maaba gwisison ogimaa, miidash iidik *i*wi wii wiidigemak maaba zeziikozit oshkinowe, mii *i*wi gaa mi-*oo*nji gimooding maanda nwiiyaw.",

(*doo*) kidawon sa giiyeN.

"mii*da*sh *i*wi gii kidawaat iidik pii waa niibowitawak maaba ogimaa gwi*s*ison, mii gii gichi zhiitaawaat anishinaabek."

aapidji gaye go gii baatiinawok gaa dagoshinggik mayegi anishinaabek. naadowesiwok gonaa ginimaa.

"mii*da*sh go pii go wii niibowi yaang, wii niibowitawak maaba anishinaabeNs, mii gii nibot. mandj iidik gaa zhiweb*a*zigoweN. gii nibow go. aaniish, gaa*wiin* sa ngii wiidigemaasii, gii nibow sa. gimaapiich go miinawaa mii maaba gii izhid, bezhik miinawaa, e ko niizhowaat gwonda oshkinowek, mii miinawaa maaba waa wiidigemit. aaniish, mii sa miinawaa ogimaa gii zhiitaat. nahaaw, gichi zhichige go maanda wii niibowitawak maaba yaawaa oshkinoweNs, oshkinoweNs gonaa. mii gosha nayiinawi*n*t gaye go maaba gaa zhiwebazit go *i*wi, iwi zhago wii niibowi yaang, mii gii n*i*bot maaba gewii*n*. gimaapii go miinawaa bezhik go owo, e ko niswiwaat, mii zhago gewii*n* maaba iwi bi-igoo yaaN, mii giiyeN *i*wi owo, 'gwii niibowitaak giiyeN owo.' nwii wiidigemik giiyeN owo oshkinowe, mii e ko nis*w*iwaat. aaniish, mii sa go miinawaa ogimaa naasaap gaa zhichiget, gii gichi zhiitaa. miinawaa gaye wewena

he must have said to her.

> "Yes, I am an Ottawa person too,"

the old woman replied to him. And she sounded just like they did when she spoke to them in the language.

> "I was kidnapped when I was a young girl, near where the city of Chicago now stands. There was no town there back then,"

the old woman told them.

> "I was taken away by strange people. They brought me to this area, as I was supposed to marry the chief's son. The chief had seven sons, and I was supposed to marry his oldest son, that is why I was kidnapped and brought here."

The old woman continued.

> "And when the day approached when I was supposed to get married to the chief's son, these people made great preparations for our wedding."

Many strangers arrived from far away to attend the wedding. These may have been Siouan people.

> "Then the day we were to be married, when I was to marry this young man, he died. I do not know what happened to him. He just died. So, of course I did not get married, as the one I was to marry died. Then this other one says to me, the second oldest son of the chief's sons, he wanted to marry me. So then the chief again got his community prepared for the wedding. He made great preparations again for my upcoming marriage to his young son. Guess what, the same happened to this young man as happened to the first one, as the day neared when we were to be married, he died. Then, later on, the third son must have decided that he would marry me, and I was told, 'This young man wants to marry you.' This young man was going to marry me, he was the third one of the chief's sons. So, again the chief made great preparations for my wedding. They

> ngii biiskoniiyewigoo. mii gosha go miinawaa naasaap gaa zhiwebazit gewiin, e ko niswiwaat gewe, mii go gaa zhinibot go. mandj gonaa iidik gaa zhiwebadogoweN gonaa. jichkana gii nibow owo. aaniish, mii sa go gaawiin gii wiidigemaasiwak gewiin owo. aaniish, ngii yaa dash go zhewe go. aaniish mii zhewe gaa zhiwinigoo yaaN pii gemooding nwiiyaw. gimaapii, miidash go e ko niiwiwaat oshkinowek, mii iwi gewiin maaba nwii wiidigemik, e ko niiwiwaat gwonda oshkinowek. aaniish, 'ndaa wiidigemaa.', ngii inaa dash owo gichi ogimaa, do ogimaamowaan gonaa gewe anishinaabek. aaniish, mii sa miinawaa gii zhiitaawaat. geniin ngii zhiitaawigoo, aaniish, nwii wiidigemaa sa owo e ko niiwiwaat gewe. zhago go wii wiidigemak owo, wii niibowitawak owo, mii gewiin gii nibot owo. mandj gonaa gewiin gaa digigoweN, gii nibow go. aaniish, mii sa zhewe, miinawaa gaawiin gii niibowisii yaaN."

aaniish, gimaapiich go miinawaa, mii zhago e ko naananiwaat, gewiin owo,

> "aaniish, gaawiin niyii go ginimaa ndaa nibowisii. aaniish, niiwin gonaa gii nibowok gwonda nwiikaaneNik waa wiidigemaapaniik ninda ikwewon.",

gii kida gaye iidik maaba oshkinowe, e ko naananiwaat. aaniish, mii sa miinawaa gii zhiitaat ogimaa, wii niibowichige. zhago dash go ginimaa niizhogonigak go wii niibowit, wii niibowinit newe gwisison, mii gewiin gii nibot owo, e ko naananiwaat gewe oshkinowek. aaniish, mii sa go gii aanoowaakoset miinawaa maaba odaawaa ikweNs wii niibowitoowaat newe mayegi anishinaaben.

miidash e ko ngodwaachiwaat, mii iidik maaba gaa kidat giiyeN ji wiidigemaat newe. aaniish, mii sa go miinawaa gaa zhichigewaat, mii go miinawaa gii zhiitaawaawok go wewena go, ji niibowit maaba e ko ngodwaachiwaat gwonda oshkinowek. niizh eta giyaabi bimaadiziwok.

> "aaniish, mii sa go gewiin owo, gaa zhiwebazit iwi, iwi zhago wii niibowitawak go, mii gewiin gii nibot maaba, maaba nini."

miidash eta gii bezhigot giyaabi, e ko niizhwaachiwaat. mii gewiin go, miidash owo gaa gigetinaamendang,

> "giyegeti go nga niibowitawaa niin owo. gaawiin niiniin ganabach ndaa nibowisii.',

gii kida maaba e ko niizhwaachiwaat, miidash iwi kina.

> again dressed me in the finest clothing. The same thing happened to this third young man, he died also. Again, I do not know what happened to him. He just died suddenly. So, needless to say, I did not get married again. Well, I stayed in this community. This was where I was brought when I was taken from my family, when I was kidnapped. After a length of time, the fourth son wished to marry me. So I told the chief of these people, 'I would marry him.' Again this chief made grand preparations for my marriage to his fourth son. I, too, was prepared, dressed in the finest clothing for I would be marrying his son. Just as the day of our wedding was getting near, he too died. No one knew why he died, he just died. So then again, I did not get married."

Well, eventually, the fifth son of the chief figured he should marry the Anishinaabe woman.

> "Well, I do not think that I would die. Although, four of my older brothers died as they were about to get married to this woman,"

said this fifth son of the chief. So again the chief made all the usual preparations, he was going to see his son get married. So as happened before, just two days before the wedding, this young man dies. So the Ottawa girl, now a young woman, did not marry this young man.

So the sixth son of the chief spoke up and said he would marry the Ottawa girl. Again, great preparations were made, the dignitaries were invited again, everything befitting the great chief's son's wedding was done in a proper way so that the chief's sixth son would be married in grand fashion. There were just two sons of the chief still living.

> "Well, the same fate befell this sixth son of the chief, as the day neared when we were to marry, this young man died also."

Then there was only one son left, the seventh son of this great chief of these strange Anishinaabe people who lived in the prairies. And this one was really determined to marry the young Ottawa woman.

> "I will marry this woman. I do not think that I will die,"

this young man, the seventh son of the chief supposedly uttered, and he was the last of the chief's sons.

aaniish, mii sa go gii zhiitaawaat miinawaa, ogimaa gichi zhichige go miinawaa. (*doo*) nandomaan mayegi anishinaaben, wegowendigenon gonaa iidik, wii bizhaanit zhewe. aapidji go wii noowaatoowok. mii go shkwaach owo. eta (*doo*) baatiinawok anishinaabek degoshinggik. aaniish, mii sa miinawaa gii zhiitaat iidik maaba ogimaa, mii zhago wii niibowichiget, mii zhago maaba odaawaa ikweNs newe wii wiidigemaat niniwon, mii maaba shkwaach. aaniish, mii sa go maaba gii nibot, gewiin. maandj gonaa gewiin gaa digigoweN. zhago go wii wiidigemaaganit, mii gii nibot owo, mii sa kina.

gaawiin wiya gii wiidigemaasiin newe odaawaa ikwen. miidash maanda gaa inaadjimotaawigoowaat gwonda newe mindimoweNon zhewe kinoomaadiigamigoong gii waabimaawaat. mii iwi gaa zhiweb*a*ziwaat gwonda anishinaabek wodi gii ookinoomawandawaa. gii nisadowinawaan *dash* gwonda newe odaawaa ikweNson. aaniish, maanpii go gii ninjibaa maaba gaa gimooding. gaawii*n* go, wewena go maanda dibaadjimowin. gii zhiwebat go giyegeti maanda.

aaniish, mii*das*h gonaa e kowaak maanda n*do* dibaadjimowin. miigwech gonaa gaa bazindaw*a* yek.

odaawaak miinawaa mashkodeweNik

yaa*w*aak, mishiiminibaamikoong besha gii danakiiwok anishinaabek. mashkode*w*eNak gii zhinikaazawok. ngoding dash epanggishimok gii bibaa miigaazawok odaawaak, naadowesen gii miigaanaawaan. gii maazhaawok dash. beskaabiiwaat dash, nenggaach gonaa (*e*) bimishkaawaat mishiiminibaamikoong besha, mii iwi (*doo*) giisaadendamowaat, (*doo*) mindamitawaawaan wiidji anishinaaben gaa nisindjik wodi naadowesiiN*a*kiing. miinawaa yaawaak dash gii nisaakawaawaan, mashkode*w*eNik, e oshkiniigidjik gonaa, mii iwi bekish giiyeN gaye gii baam*a*siiniiwaawaan newe odaawaan. mii gii nishkaadiziwaat odaawaak. gaa bigii*w*ewaat dash, mii iwi gii giizhendamowaat ji mookiitawaawaat mashkode*w*eNon. gaa shkwaa *n*anaatoowaat makiziniwaan miinawaa gaye gii giizhiitaawaat, mii gii mookiitawaawaat, yaawaan mashkode*w*eNon. gichi aabiindji*w*aa*w*aan dash, gegaa go gii jaag*a*nanaawaan.

*n*iyiing dash, zooniyaang gii powewok gewe yaawaak, mashkode*w*eNak. miidash, gimaapiich go miinawaa ngoding, wiikaa gonaa, gii aandjimookiitawaa*w*aat odaawaak newe. miinawaa gii gichi miigaanaawaat. miidash epanggishimok nikeyaa gii nipowewaat yaawaak, mashkode*w*eNak.

mii iwi.

Again, they made grandiose plans for his son's wedding. Many dignitaries from the surrounding area were invited, all kinds of people were invited, all strangers to the Ottawa woman. This was to be a very big celebration. This was the last of the chief's sons. Oh, there were so many people who arrived for the wedding. The preparations for the wedding of this Ottawa woman and the chief's sole surviving son went well. Just before the wedding day arrived, he too died. It is not known what happened to him. So as the wedding day neared, he too dies, and he was the last of the chief's sons.

No one married the young Ottawa woman. This is the story that old woman told the young Ottawa boys in the anishinaabe language at the school where the boys were residing. This is what happened to those young Ottawa boys who were getting an education at the residential school. They recognized this old woman as someone they knew, and it was that young anishinaabe girl who had been kidnapped from near here many years before. Well, that girl was originally from here, as her family was from this area. This is a true story. This really happened.

Well, that is the end of my story. Thank you all for listening to me.

The Ottawa and the Mascoutens *(CONDENSED VERSION)*

There were these native people who had settled in an area near a place called Mishiiminibaamikoong. These people were called the MashkodeweNik. This one time, the anishinaabe people we now know as the Ottawa had gone out west to battle the Lakota. This group of Anishinaabe warriors had been repelled. When they were returning to their homes, they were slowly paddling their canoes by the area where the MashkodeweNik settled, the Ottawa were mourning their fellow Anishinaabe who had fallen in battle. They must have alerted the MashkodeweNik, and these were probably young MashkodeweNik, and they threw stones at the Ottawa as they paddled along the shore of the lake. The actions of these young MashkodeweNik infuriated the Anishinaabe. When they arrived at their homes, they held council and decided to attack the MashkodeweNik for their actions. So after they had fixed their moccasins and after they had finished preparing for battle, they attacked the MashkodeweNik. The Anishinaabe routed the MashkodeweNik and they almost annihilated them.

The remaining MashkodeweNik ran away to a place called Zooniyaang. After a long time, the Anishinaabe people attacked the MashkodeweNik again. They battled with the MashkodeweNik again. This time the remaining MashkodeweNik ran away toward the west, and they never returned.

That is it.

mashkodeNzhak gegaa gii jaaganinadawaa

yaawaa sa nwii dibaadjimaa, mashkodeNzh. mashkodeNzhak gewiin maanda gonaa gii wiidjinakiimaawaat odaawaan. mii gonaa gewiinawaa gonaa naasaap gonaa gaa zhibimaadiziwaat, odaawaa gonaa gaa zhibimaadizit. gii makadeke maaba odaawaa gonaa gegoo gewiin wii gikendang. aaniish, miidash go gaye maaba mashkodeNzh gaa zhichiget iwi. maaba dash go waa dibaadjimak mashkodeNzh, oshkiniigish maaba, mii gonaa maaba iidik gonaa dash piitizit gonaa wii makadeket, mii iidik newe niikigoon gaa igot,

"gdaa makadeke gegiin, gegoo gonaa ji wii gikendaman.",

gii igoodigenon gonaa newe niikigoon maaba mashkodeNzh oshkiniigish. aaniish, miidash go gii wewiiptaat iidik iwi (doo) makadeket. gwodji gonaa e ko biinnakamigaanik gaye gonaa gwonda gii nibeyaawok mekadekedjik gonaa. (doo) bagosendamowaat gonaa gegoo gonaa wii gikendamowaat. miidash giiyeN maaba mashkodeNzh zhewe zhinibaat ngoding, oshkiniigish sa gonaa, mii gii aapowet.

maanpii nibis gidaaki digowomigat niyiing, gweyek gonaa giiwedinong zhinda wiikowedoowing. waasa gonaa maanda digowomigat nibis. aaniish maanpii e ko nishwaaswi dibaganek pii gwonda noopiming mashkodeNzhak gii baatiinawok. gii oodetoowok sa gonaa zhewe, miidash iidik maaba oshkiniigish gaa njibaat, maaba sa waa dibaadjimak. miidash iidik e piichi makadeket maaba oshkiniigish, mii gii aapowet, (e) nibaat gonaa. gii anishkaat megowaa go nibaat, mii iidik gii nimaajaat, (doo) naamdam gonaa maanda. miidash wodi waawiyegomaa e daming, noopiming wodi nibis e ndigowok, mii iidik wodi gaa zhaat. gii nimadaabiit wodi, (doo) naabit giiyeN zhewe naawondj iwi, yaawaan dash giiyeN waabimaan, gichi binesiwon, yaawaan dash giiyeN maaba gichi binesi mendjigonaadjin, gichi ginebigoon. wii gindaagonigoon iidik maaba gichi binesi newe. gegaa dash giiyeN ko aanowi maaba migiziwaashk geshkiyaat newe wii mbiwinaat. aaniish, mii neyaap miinawaa (doo) banggishing nibiing. (doo) ganawaabidjige go maaba (doo) naamdam mashkodeNzh zhewe newe (doo) miigaadinit, ninda binesiwon miinawaa gichi ginebigoon.

miidash giiyeN e igot ninda gichi binesiwon maaba mashkodeNzh.

"shkenaa naadimawishin. aapidji go gga madjiyaawoshi giishpmaa bibowaa naadimawi yin.",

doo igoodigenon dash ninda yaawaan, migiziwaashon. gichi migiziwaashk go maaba. aaniish gewiin maaba ginebik, gewiin madjiyaawosh maaba go gewiin.

The Ottawa and the Mascoutens (*LONG VERSION*)

I am going to talk about the MashkodeNzh. The MashkodeNzhak lived alongside the Ottawa people a long time ago. They shared the culture of the Ottawa and lived like them. The Ottawa fasted so that they could learn things and know how to live. And so, the MashkodeNzh did likewise. But the one I am going to talk about, he was a young man who had come of age to go on his vision quest, as his parents had told him to do.

"You should go fast, so that you might learn something,"

this young man must have been told by his parents. So he quickly prepared to begin his fast. The ones who went on their vision quest, they were taken to an area that was considered sacred, and they were alone in the wilderness. There they would beseech the spirits for guidance and knowledge. Then this young MashkodeNzh man was on his fast, and one night as he was sleeping, he had a dream.

There is a lake located just over this hill, straight north from this place of wiikwedoowing. This lake is a long way from here. Roughly about seven miles north of here that is where many of the MashkodeNzhak resided. They had a village there and this young man I am talking about, this is the community he came from. And as he was fasting, he fell asleep and had this dream. He dreamt that he awoke from his sleep and he left the place he was at. And he went toward the place called waawiyegomaa, which is inland from here and this is where that lake is located, that is where he went to. He went down toward the lake, and when he got to the lake, he saw this great eagle out over the middle of the lake and this great eagle was holding a big snake in its talons. But the snake was fighting back and trying to drown the great eagle. They struggled, sometimes the great eagle almost could lift the big snake out of the water. And then he would fall back down into the water. This young man was watching this struggle between this great eagle and the big snake, he was dreaming this of course.

Then this great eagle spoke to the young man.

"Help me. If you do not help me, you will be a bad or evil person,"

he was told by the eagle. This was a great big eagle. And this snake, he too was an evil or a bad one.

"gegowa maaba debwetawaaken migiziwaashk e kidat. gaawiin maaba gegoo daa zhigashkigoosii ji naadimaak.",

doo igoodigenon sa newe. aaniish, mii sa giiyeN miinawaa wii mowaat newe yaawaan, newe sa binesiwon, maaba yaawaa mashkodeNzh, naamdam maanda.

"gegowa mowashiken.",

doo igoodigenon dash newe binesiwon.

"giishpmaa bibowa naadimawi yin, aapidji go gga madjiyaawosh."
"gegowa naadimawaaken maaba.",

(doo) kida sa giiyeN miinawaa maaba ginebik.

"gaawiin go gegoo maaba ge zhinaadimaagoban gichi binesi, waawaadj go wiin gaawiin (doo) gashkitoosiin wii naadimaadizat. aaniish giiyeN ge zhinaadimaak maaba.",

doo igoodigenon sa ninda ginebigoon maaba yaawaa mashkodeNzh. taaya, mii gosha giiyeN newe binesiwon maaba mashkodeNzh gaa zhimowaat.

"taaya, geget sa gonaa gdoo bimaazhiiyii.",

doo igoon dash sa giiyeN newe binesiwon.

"bekaa, gga wiindamawin. zhewe nonggom e danakii yek, aapidji go wiiba mii go ge zhimakamigaak zhewe. gaawiin go waawaadj go gdo biminaagaaNwaak ginigeN da gikendaagozisiiwok."

aaniish, mii sa maaba mashkodeNzh gaa waabang gagwedjimin endigoweN gegoo ji gii bowaadang iwi gii nibaat. mii sa giiyeN iidik gaa dibaadidang iwi sa gaa naamdang. wodi gii oomadaabiit waawiyegomaa, miinawaa gaye gii dibaadjimot iwi gii mowaat newe yaawaan, gichi binesiwon, aanowi nandomagot wii naadimawaat. miinawaa go gaa igot go iwi pii waa ninibonit. mii go kina go gii dibaadidaan iwi, miidash gwonda mashkodeNzhak gii gikendamawaat iidik,

"gegoo iidik waa zhiwebazi yaang.",

> "Don't listen to what this great eagle says. He cannot help you in any way at all,"

the young man was told by the big snake. Then in his dream, the young man saw that he was going to eat the great eagle.

> "Don't eat me,"

he was told by this eagle.

> "If you do not help me, you will be really wicked."
> "Do not help him,"

the big snake supposedly said to him.

> "There is no way this great eagle can help you, as you can see he cannot help himself. So, how can he be of help to you?"

the young man was told by the big snake. Oh my goodness, the young man did devour the great eagle.

> "Boy, you have done a great wrong,"

the young man was told by the great eagle.

> "Wait, I will now tell you something. Where your people now live, it will become barren and desolate. Your children will not be known, as they will disappear."

So the next day, when he awoke from his sleep, this young MashkodeNzh man was asked if he had a vision. So he related to the elders the dream that he had had that night. About how he had gone down to the lake at Waawiyegomaa, and how he had eaten the great eagle who had called to him for help. And what this great eagle had said to him as the great eagle was dying. He told them everything he could remember, and the elders of the MashkodeNzh knew that something would happen to them as a people.

> "I guess something will happen to us,"

gii inendamok iidik. gaawiin dash gii gikendaziinaawaa waa zhiwebaziwaat.

miidash gewiin maaba odaawaa nishkimagot iwi (doo) kakinootaawigot iwi, mii gii inaat ji kogaanit zhinda. maanda iidik gewiin gwonda odaawaak gaa zhaawaat epanggishimok, gichi mashkodeng, gii nisaawok dash iidik wodi. miidash maanda (e) bipaskaabiiwaat zhinda mishiiminibaamikoong, mii iwi zhewe gii waabimaawaat newe mashkodeNzhon. mandj gonaa gewiinawaa gonaa gaa binowewaagoweN gonaa (doo) dibaadjimawaat gonaa iidik gii nisindawaa. miidash giiyeN ninda mashkodeNzhon gii kakinootaawigoowaat. gaawiin dash maaba odaawaa gii minowendazii, gii nishkimagoon. miidash go gii inaat iwi iidik ji kogaanit zhinda. wiin gaye maaba odaawaa gii miinaan ninda mashkodeNzhon zhinda ji danakiinit, dibi gaye maaba mashkodeNzh gaa binjibaagoweN, iwi gonaa, degoshing gonaa zhinda. gaawiin giiyeN gwonda anishinaabek gwodji gii yaaziinaawaa waa danakiiwaat. miidash maaba odaawaa zhawenimaat newe, mii zhinda gii miinaat ji danakiinit.

gii gichi baatiinawok dash go gwonda mashkodeNzhak. gii baatiina maaba wii maadjiishkaat mashkodeNzh. miidash iwi owo odaawaa gii inaat iwi ji maajaanit, iwi gaa shkwaa kakinootaawigoowaat wodi mishiiminibaamikoong, aaniish (doo) baatiinawok dash gwonda mashkodeNzhak, gaawiin dash go gii maajaasiiwok. aaniish, miidash odaawaak gii miigaanaat, gii mikonaashkowaat go zhinda go gaa nidanakiinit go, maa go nikeyaa go tibewe gichigomi. zhaawonong nikeyaa wodi gii nitapinaan. shkwaach dash giiyeN wodi, aapidji giiyeN zhago (doo) banggiisheNgiziwok mashkodeNzhak, gii waanikewok gaye mashkodeNzhak gonaa wii gkizondamawaat gonaa, mii gaa oonji waanikaadimawaat iwi aki. miidash giiyeN wodi e zhinaagodinik iwi dash yaawaat, mii gwonda shkwaach, mii iwi zhago gegaa gonaa (doo) jaaganinaat maaba odaawaa newe, gichi mitig dash giiyeN zhewe gaye gwekozat. mii giiyeN wodi e zhigwekozat nikeyaa dash yaawaat gwonda mashkodeNzhak. aaniish waanikaade go iwi aki, ginoowaadik go maanda waanikaadek. aaniish, baatiinawok gonaa aanowi giyaabi gewe mashkodeNzhak.

aaniish, mii sa giiyeN gii wewiiptaawaat iwi niibaadibik gonaa, gowaawaat newe mitigoon. ngoding gaye gonaa de wepidawaan go maaba mitigoon wodi e zhaat jiigaatig, mii eta bikwaakoon zhewe bemiwewenik go. mii go naanigodinong zhewe e tapinin go bezhik owo. aaniish, (doo) baatiinawok dash gaye maaba gewiin odaawaa, (doo) baatiina sa. gimaapii sa giiyeN mii zhago maaba mitig (doo) madweweshkaat. aaniish, (doo) gogawewaagom. mii go wodi wii banggishing wodi maaba mitig dash yaanit mashkodeNzhon giishpmaa (e) goweset.

they must have surmised. But they did not know what was to befall them.

The Ottawa had been angered by the MashkodeNzh youngsters for mimicking them in their time of sorrow and the Ottawa decided that the MashkodeNzhak should leave this area. I guess the Ottawa had gone out west onto the prairies, and had some of their comrades slain in battle. And as they returned home, as they came by the area of Mishiiminibaamikoong, that is when they saw the MashkodeNzhak. It is not known what sounds they made as they came back mourning their fallen comrades. It was the MashkodeNzh youngsters who made fun of them by mimicking them. The Ottawa were not humored by this, in fact this angered the Ottawa. So this is the reason the Ottawa told the MashkodeNzhak to move away from here. It was the Ottawa who had given the MashkodeNzhak permission to settle in this area, and it is not known where these people, the MashkodeNzhak, originally came from. These people known as the MashkodeNzhak did not have any place to settle. So the Ottawa felt sorry for these people and allowed them to settle in their territory.

In a relatively short time, the MashkodeNzhak had become sizable in number. Their numbers grew quickly. So when the Ottawa told them to leave after the incident at Mishiiminibaamikoong, these people did not leave as they were large in number. That is when the Ottawa waged war on the MashkodeNzhak, and the Ottawa routed them and chased them all over the countryside and along the shore of the great lake. The Ottawa waged war upon them, wherever they went, even down to the south. Then toward the end there were only a few MashkodeNzhak left, and these remaining few dug a huge trench in the ground and used this as their last line of defense, and also, they could use it as a hiding place. At one end of this huge trench were the remaining few MashkodeNzhak, as the Ottawa had decimated their numbers, and there was this immense tree that was growing near the trench. This huge tree was slanted toward the trench that the MashkodeNzhak were using as their base of defense. This trench that was dug was long and deep. And the few MashkodeNzhak left, were much fewer than before, but they were still sizeable in number.

So the Ottawa began chopping at this great tree, and they did this at night, they began the process of chopping down this huge tree. One of them would make one stroke at the tree, and there were a shower of arrows that came toward the base of the tree and these arrows were unleashed by the MashkodeNzhak from their hiding place. Sometimes, the one who was chopping at the tree would be killed by the hail of arrows. However, there were many Ottawa warriors who were there, there were many of them. Eventually, the great tree began to make cracking sounds as it was nearly ready to topple into the trench where the MashkodeNzhak were making a stand. The tree was being felled. This great tree would soon fall into the trench where the MashkodeNzhak were gathered.

miidash gaye gwonda mashkodeNzhak iidik noondawaawaat ninda mitigoon madweshkaanit, mii sa giiyeN gii madwe mowinit. miidash giiyeN medwe kidanit,

> "giishpmaa gonaa wiya gonaa wiisinit gonaa, debisinii gonaa gimaapii.",

(doo) madwe kidawon giiyeN.

> "giishpmaa gaye gonaa ozaam gonaa niibana wiisinit, shagowe gonaa owo. ginigeN dash gonaa gdoo zhibagoseniminim gonaa dash odaawaawi yek.",

(doo) madwe kidawon sa giiyeN ninda mashkodeNzhon,

> "gdaa shagowaazhimin gonaa. ginigeN gonaa ji wiyii bimaadizi yaang gonaa.",

(doo) kidawon sa giiyeN. aaniish, miidash go maaba odaawaa gii boonenimaat, gii booninanaat. aaniish, miidash giiyeN gaa inaat ninda mashkodeNzhon iwi,

> "gga maajaam sa. gaawiin giyaabi zhinda gga yaasiim. ggii gichi minoyaam zhinda gii yaa yek. miidash iwi ji maajaa yek. gegowa wiikaa zhinda miinawaa bizhaakegon."

aaniish, miidash gonaa e kowaak maanda maaba (doo) dibaadjimak mashkodeNzhish. gichi miigwech gaa bazindawa yek.

So when these MashkodeNzhak heard this great tree begin to make the creaking and cracking noises of a tree that is about to fall, they began to cry out. And they said,

> "When someone eats, he eventually gets sated,"

the MashkodeNzhak supposedly said.

> "And if that someone eats too much, he may vomit. And we are beseeching you as Ottawa people to do likewise,"

the MashkodeNzhak were heard to say.

> "You should just puke on us and get it over with. At least, we beseech you to let us live,"

they, the MashkodeNzhak were heard saying. So, with that the Ottawa left them alone and stopped their fight with them. So then, the Ottawa told the MashkodeNzhak the following.

> "You all will have to leave this territory. You will no longer reside here. While you were here in our territory, you lived a good life. But, now you must leave. Never ever come back to our territory again."

Well, that is the end of my story about what happened to that darn MashkodeNzhak. Thank you very much for listening to me.

· PART 4 ·

CONTEMPORARY STORIES

odaawaa noozawinkewin

"ndoo gichi minowendam maanda noozawinkewin (doo) manaadjitoo yaaN. maaba gichimookamaanikwe, gichi waasa waabanoong e binjibaat, wii minozhiwebazi maaba. wii waawiiNzat dash (doo) inendaagozi. ndoo gichi minowendam dash wii waawiinak. waabanoo-ikwe dash da zhinikaaza. yaa aa yaa aa yaa ye aaya yaa aa yaa aa aa waabanoo-ikwe da zhinikaaza. yaa aa yaa aa yaa aa yaa aa yaa aa e yaa aa yaa aa waabanoo-ikwe, waabanoo-ikwe, waabanoo-ikwe, e e e e waabanoo-ikwe dash da zhinikaaza. oo oo oo oo oom oom.

anishinaabek gaa inaadjimowaat e piichi wiishkobimin*i*kewaat

yaawaa sa, anishinaabek nwii dibaadjimaak miinawaa. zhaazhago ko gonaa geniin megowaa gonaa, gaawiin gonaa aapidji geniin gegoo ngii gikendaziin gonaa, iwi gonaa bi-oshkibimaadizi yaaN gonaa. gwonda dash go nwii dibaadjimaak anishinaabek gaa zhiwaabimakgowaa. kina gaye gonaa anishinaabe pii iwi gii gitige, iwi gonaa maanda gonaa (doo) zhiitaawaat maanda wii biboonik miinawaa. miidash ko gwonda anishinaabek gii wiishkobiminikewaat, ngii ganawaabimaak ko gonaa. gaawiin gonaa gegoo ngii naabidazisii.

aapidji go ko gii minoyaawok maanda nidibikadinik iwi (doo) ziiskinaawaat ninda oshki mandaaminon, (e) giizhiinggowet gonaa owo, maaba mandaamin. miidash miinawaa ninda (doo) minozawaawaat, mitigooNsing gonaa maaba mizaakodj, (doo) niimaakodjiigaaza. miidash miinawaa maanda zhewe, nenggaach maanda (doo) zhitibaakonaawaat ninda, wii minozat gonaa maaba mizaakodj. miidash gaa minozanodji, aaniish, mii go miinawaa bezhigowaatik miinawaa (doo) saawaat zhewe gidjishkode. miinawaa gaa takishinindjin ninda mandaaminon, mii iwi (doo) gaakinaawaat. e panggidaatek gonaa mii wodi gwonda mandaaminak, gidji mazinigan gonaa, mii wodi (doo) nisawebinaawaat newe wii baasanit gonaa. miidash go gaa zhigikenimakgowaa iwi wiishkobiminikewaat, mii ko gii tibaadjimowaat gwonda akiweziiNik. gii nitaa tibaadjimowok aanind. aaniish, miidash gonaa aanind gonaa (doo) dibaadidaanaawaa gwonda, zhaazhago gonaa gaa bizhiwebaziwaat. aapidji gii minowaadjimowok aanind.

An Ottawa Naming Ceremony

"I am so very pleased and happy to be involved with and celebrating this naming ceremony. This white American woman hails far from the east, and she is to be honored and she will have this good event happen to her. She is to be given a native name. I am very, very happy to be the one to give her, her spiritual name. Her name will be 'Waabanoo-ikwe.' She will be called 'Waabanoo-ikwe.' 'Waabanoo-ikwe.' 'Waabanoo-ikwe.' 'Waabanoo-ikwe-e-e-e.' She will be called 'Waabanoo-ikwe.'"

Stories Told While the Anishinaabe Dried Corn

I am going to talk about the Anishinaabe people again. I do not know much about things of long ago, especially when I was younger. However, I will tell you about what I saw the men do back in my younger days. Back then, almost all the Anishinaabe people had a garden where they grew their food so they would prepare for the coming winter months. I used to watch these men who made dried corn, as I was very young and was not really useful in helping them with this activity.

They seemed to enjoy the work involved with shucking the corn as it got to be dark, this was done when the corn was ripe. They would roast the corn over the fire with a stick pushed into the cob of the corn. Then they would twirl this stick with the corn stuck to it over the fire, roasting the corn. As soon as one was finished, then they would put another ear of corn on the stick and begin roasting the corn. Then when the roasted corn cooled off enough, they would remove the corn kernels from the cob. They would spread the corn kernels on some paper that was on the ground and in direct sunlight, so the corn would continue to dry. And this is what I knew of these older men, they would tell stories to pass the time while they dried the corn. Some of these men were very good storytellers. Some would talk about what they did in the past and the things that happened to them. Some of them told very good stories.

ngoding *da*sh go iwi *da*sh naakoshik iwi (*doo*) dibaadjimowaat, mii maaba akiweziiN iwi gii dibaadjidizat gewii*n*, gii giiwise gonaa iidik pane gonaa. wesiiNon (*e*) *na*ndowaabimaat gonaa waa mowaadjin gonaa. miid*a*sh gaa kidat iwi, gaa*wiin* giiyeN wiikaa gwodji gii zegazisii iwi gonaa gewii*n* gii giiwiset gonaa, niiget gaye gonaa. nshike go maanda go (*doo*) maamaajaat go, neniiwigon (*doo*) ndendi go owo. nshike maanda go, waasa go bogodaakowaa (*doo*) bibaa danizi. gaa*wiin* giiyeN wiikaa gegoo gii zegagosiin. aaniish, gii shkwaaseni *da*sh gonaa iwi gaa inaadjimot gonaa, bekaanizit miinawaa (*doo*) *na*ndowenimaa wii dibaadjimot.

miidash maaba akiweziiN, gaa*wiin* gonaa gii akiweziiNwisii gonaa iwi pii aapidji, m*a*kwa nowii gii zhinikaaza maaba gaa mishoomisi yaaN. gaa*wiin* gaye gonaa iwi, iwi gonaa m*a*kwa nowii gaa oonji inin*d*, yaawaan gonaa maaba gii nitaa nisaan, makwan, pane giiyeN gii nisaan. mandj gonaa iidik minik (*e*) giiwiset gonaa gaa nisaagoweN ensa ngobiboon. miidash go gegopii go gii m*a*kwa nowiiwit go.

miidash wiin maaba miinawaa e inind wii dibaadjimot, newe sa bezhik gaa shkwaa dibaadjimonit. mii*da*sh gaa kidat maaba m*a*kwa nowiiba*n*.

> "genii*n* sa go pane ngii giiwise, megowaa gonaa b*a*zhisigosing gonaa maanda *a*ki.",

gii kida.

> "gichimookamaanak gonaa aapidji ji bibowaa yaawaat. gaa*wiin* sa gonaa gichimookamaan gonaa gii yaasii.",

(*doo*) kida.

> "ngoding *da*sh go maanda giiwise yaaN, mii gii gikendamaaN giyegeti genii*n* iidik e zhiwebak zegazing. aaniish, gaa*wiin* gonaa ndaa debwesii gonaa (*e*) kida yaaN iwi, 'gaa*wiin* wiikaa n*doo* zegazisii.', ji kida yaaNmbaa. ngii gikendaan dash iwi e zhiwebak iidik zegazing, gwotaadjing gonaa ji kida *y*inggoba*n*. megowaa maanda anishinaabe ziibiing *da*sh niige yaaN, digwaagik, mii go zhago go iwi go gichi gonaa kisinaak, mii iwi gii naadisoonaagane yaaN. mii go wii boonitaa yaaN go *da*sh niige yaaN. aaniish, wii biboon gonaa. maanda pii maaba gonaa shkwaagimin*d* gonaa maaba yaawaa November. miidash iwi (*e*) bimaajaa yaaN wodi, ninda n*do* nasoonaagaaNan kina gaa gezibinimaaN, mii iwi (*e*) bikodamaaN iwi anishinaabe ziibi, miidash go zhewe zaagada zhewe (*e*) bidagoshinaaN, mii iwi (*doo*) gikendamaaN iwi gichi waawayewaanimok, epanggishimok miinawaa giiwedinong, zhiibaayiing ndaanimot, zhewe

This one evening they continued to tell stories, then this one older man began to talk about himself and he talked about his hunting prowess and how he always hunted. He looked for animals that he would eat. And he stated that wherever he went to hunt or to trap, he never got scared or was afraid of anything, no matter where he went. He told of going out by himself, alone into the woods, and he would be gone sometimes for up to four days at a time. He would be alone deep in the woods. He was never frightened of or by anything in all those years. So this man finished talking about his hunting prowess, and someone else was expected to tell another story.

Then this old man, well he was not really an old man then, but he got up to speak, and this man's name was Makwa Nowii, and this was my grandfather. The reason he was named Makwa Nowii was he had always been able to kill bears, and lots of them. He had the ability to kill bears and he did it regularly. It is not known how many bears he had killed in a single year, but it was quite a few. And so, he became known as Makwa Nowii.

Now it was Makwa Nowii's turn to tell a story, after the other man had finished telling about his hunting and trapping prowess. And Makwa Nowii began this way.

> "I, too, have always hunted this land before the coming of the Euro-descendant to our lands,"

he said.

> "Before there were many white people here. Well, there were really no white people here then,"

he continued.

> "Then this one time while I was out hunting, that is when I found out what it means to be afraid of something. Well, I would not be truthful if I were to say, 'I was never afraid of anything.' I know what it is like to be afraid, to be frightened of something, so to speak. This was in the fall while I was maintaining a trapline down along Indian River, and it was getting colder so I collected my traps. I was going to stop trapping for a little while. Well, winter was setting in soon. This was late in the fall, on toward the end of November. After I had collected my traps, and I was paddling upstream on Indian River, there was a swirling wind that came up as I was approaching the area where the Indian River narrows a little, it seemed that the wind was from the west and then from the north and it seemed to swirl all around. And the settlement of the Anishinaabe people

> dash go iwi anishinaabe ziibi e ko nji maadjii digoweyaak. miinawaa zhewe gewe anishinaabek zhewe *n*iyiing, zhaabowiganing nibising gaa danakiiwaat, ngodwaaswi dibagan ginimaa piichaadik zhewe. gichi waasa gaamigaam gonaa iwi. miinawaa gaye gichi noodin. zhewe dash go iwi e nji maadjii digoweyaak anishinaabe ziibi, *n*iyii zhewe tibewe anishinaabek gii zhitoonaawaaba*n*, zhaazhago gonaa aapidji iwi, mitig*o*gamigooN, wiya gonaa (*e*) ganisanigot gonaa, zhewe ginigeN gonaa ji yaapa*n* gonaa, gibedibik gonaa inendang. ngii nigaashkaa *da*sh gonaa naanigodinong genii*n* zhewe, gaa zhitoowaat aanishinaabek gonaa. gimiwong gaye gonaa, mii gonaa zhewe gii nibaa yaaN ko. iwi *da*sh go pii nonggo*m* (*e*) dibaadjimo yaaN, wodi niisaadjiwon anishinaabe ziibiing gii binjibaa yaaN, aapidji go digwaagi, mii gonaa zhago gonaa wii biboong. mii zhewe gii bidagoshinaaN genii*n* zhewe iwi sa mitig*o*gamik *d*ash tek debaadidamaaN. mii zhewe (*e*) maadjii digoweyaak iwi *n*iyii anishinaabe ziibi. taahaa, gaa*wiin da*sh maamdaa wii takamii yaaN, aaniish, waaw*a*yeyaanimot, aapidji gaye gichi noodin. aapidji go (*doo*) maanggaashkaa. ndaawaach dash gonaa ngii inendam gonaa ji gibeshi yaaNmbaa*n*.",

(*doo*) kida sa maaba m*a*kwa nowii iwi (*e*) dibaadjimot.

miidash giiyeN gonaa ninda adikowaaNan gonaa benaasininggin iidik gaa zhi-aaw*a*doot, iwi gonaa shkode wii yaang gonaa niibaadibik zhewe wii yaa. aaniish, kisinaamigat miinawaa gichi noodin. aa*n*iish, wiiba dash maanda digwaagik dibikat, wiiba gonaa, ginimaa niswidibaganek gaye gonaa ginimaa gaye niiwidibaganek, mii gonaa giinawi*nt* dibikak zhinda, aapidji go digwaagik. aaniish, gii de nchinidigenan *d*ash go newe migitooNan gaa aawadjinigaadanggin maaba sa makwa nowii.

> "aaniish, mii*da*sh gonaa iwi gii boonitaa yaaN gonaa debikak, gaa*wiin* gonaa miinawaa nwii aaw*a*djinigaad*a*ziinan newe adikowaaNan benaasinggin.",

gii kida sa.

> "mii*da*sh gii zhiitaa yaaN zhewe wii boodowe yaaN jiigigamik iwi mitig*o*gamigooN *d*ash tek. miinawaa gonaa ngii dibinoow*a*ge gonaa zhewe, aapidji gonaa wii bibowaa *o*zaamaanimok gonaa zhewe e nshkwaandowe yaaN.",

(*doo*) kida sa.

known as Zhaabowiganing was about six miles away. The width of the river was still fairly wide. The wind was really getting strong. And there at the mouth of the Indian River where it begins to narrow a little, along the river's edge somewhere, the Anishinaabe people had built a shelter a long time ago, and this house was used by many as a shelter whenever a storm overtook them so they had a place to wait out the storm overnight if necessary. I occasionally made use of that shelter from time to time, that shelter made by the Anishinaabe people. If it was raining, I would spend the night there. And the time I am now talking about, when I was coming up Indian River and this was in the fall and it was getting colder as it would soon be winter. I was arriving near that old wooden structure that I have been talking about. That is the area where the Indian River starts to narrow. As I was making my way across, that is when a swirling wind came up, and it was very windy, so I was not able to cross. The waters were very rough, that is the waves were very big. So I decided that I would stay at the old shelter overnight,"

said this man called Makwa Nowii as he told his story.

So he then gathered some twigs and branches that had fallen from the trees, as he would need this dry wood to build a fire as he was going to stay there that night. It was already getting colder and it was also very windy. Well, in the late fall, it gets dark early, shortly after three or four o'clock, at least in our area, it gets dark early in the late fall. Well, he had gathered and hauled quite a lot of twigs and branches to the old shelter for his fire.

"Well, when it was dark I quit gathering and hauling the twigs and branches, as I had enough for the night,"

he said.

"So I prepared to build my fire near the old wooden shelter. I also tried to make a wind break to block some of the wind from the fire and also from the doorway of the old shelter,"

he continued.

"miinawaa gii jiibaakodaadiza yaaN, wii wiisini yaaN gonaa. miinawaa gaa shkwaa wiisini yaaN, mii miinawaa iwi, yaawaa gaye ko ngii bimiwinaa,",

gii kida maaba makwa nowii, makwa nowiiban.

"gichi makwaweyaan niyii gonaa maaba gaa mipishimowi yaaN gonaa, (doo) minibaa yaaN gonaa.",

gii kida.

"ngii bimiwinaa gonaa maaba, wiigwaasijiimaaneNing gonaa maaba ngii bimiwinaa maaba makwaweyaan waa mipishimowi yaaN.",

gii kida sa.

"miidash go maanda iwi gaa nidibikak, mii gii webi bigotaadji yaaN. gaawiin geniin wiikaa ndoo gotaadjisii maanda gonaa (e) bibimaadizi yaaN.",

gii inaadjimo sa maaba makwa nowii.

"mii go maanda nishpidedibikak, eshkam gosha nayiinawind ndoo gotaadj go. wiya gaye go ndaa ganawaabimik go. mandj iidik gaye e nigonigoweN owo wesiiN genawaabimit iwi gotaadji yaaN, ngii inendam.",

(doo) kida.

"miidash gonaa e kowaatek gonaa zhewe gaataawigamik ndaa nibibaa naaniibow.",

(doo) kida sa.

"gaawiin dash wiyii gaye wiya ngii waabimaasii. mii go eta pashigiishibikak.",

(doo) kida owo.

"aapidji gaye gichi noodin. gaawiin go ginigeN go ndaa waabimaasii go. ndaawaach dash go miinawaa ngii paskaabii zhewe niyiing, wiigwaameNing.",

> "Then I cooked myself my evening meal. And after I ate, I went to get this thing. I always traveled with it,"

this Makwa Nowii said, the late Makwa Nowii.

> "A rather large bear skin, and this was my mattress and blanket that I used when I went to sleep,"

he added.

> "I took this bear skin with me in my canoe as this was my bedding and also I used it as a cushion,"

he said.

> "Then when it was nighttime, that is when I began to feel frightened. Never before in my life have I ever been afraid,"

this man called Makwa Nowii said.

> "As it got darker, the more afraid I became. I also sensed that someone was watching me. I did not know how big the animal was that was watching me or looking at me, I thought to myself,"

he said.

> "So then, I walked around the area to where the light from the fire reached,"

he continued.

> "And I did not see anyone or anything. It was just darkness of night that I saw,"

said he.

> "It was also very windy. There was no way and no how that I would see anyone or anything. Therefore, I went back to the little shelter,"

(*doo*) kida.

> "mitigogamigooNing, ngii oowenab miinawaa wodi, miinawaa gaye gonaa maaba ndo pwaagan gonaa ngii z*a*kowaa gonaa. ngii nashkaniyaa sa gonaa miinawaa ngii z*a*kowaa, (*e*) baabiindaakowe yaaN zhewe. taaya, gaaw*iin* gosha nayiinaw*int* maamdaa.",

(*doo*) kida.

> "eshkam go n*doo* gotaadj go zhewe (*doo*) namadabi yaaN nshike."

miid*a*sh giiyeN e inendang,

> "togowa nga *na*ndowaabimaa wegowendik maaba gowesaagoweN miinawaa.",

(*doo*) indendam *da*sh iidik. miid*a*sh giiyeN baashkozigan gii daapinang, (*e*) nashkanideni iwi baashkozigan. gii bibaa zhaat wodi e kowaatenik miinawaa. aanowi bibaa (*doo*) *na*ndowaabimaat wiya, gaaw*iin* sa giiyeN gaye wiya gii waabimaasiin.

> "miinawaa wodi gii p*a*skaabii yaaN mitigogamigooNing. gaaw*iin* go maamdaa zhewe wii yaa yaaN.",

gii kida. miidash iwi iidik gaa inendang,

> "ndaawaach gonaa ndaa maajaa zhinda.",

gii inendam *da*sh iidik.

> "wodi gonaa niyiing gaaming wodi, gaamiziibi wodi ndaa oozhewoshkose wodi megowe miishkooN. mii zhewe ge zazaabi yaaN. nga koowaabidaan maanda wiigwaameN.",

gaa inendang sa iidik.

aa*n*iish, miid*a*sh go gii boozitoot gonaa gewii*n* gonaa bemiwidoot neyaap jiimaaning, gii oozhewoshkoset wodi niyiing megowe miishkooN, gaaminggoninik gonaa iwi ziibi. miid*a*sh giiyeN gaa zazaabidang iwi mitigogamik gaa binjigidjibowet. aapidji giiyeN go minowaateni wodi iwi shkode p*a*skanenik, (*doo*) naam*a*dabit iidik zhewe (*doo*) ganawaabidang iwi mitigogamigooN.

he added.

> "I went to the house and sat down, then I decided to light my pipe. I loaded my pipe, then I lit it and then I smoked it. Still, I could not shake this sense of foreboding or fear,"

he said.

> "I was even more afraid than before as I sat there all alone."

So he then thought,

> "Well now, I will go look for whoever this is that is causing me to be fearful,"

he must have thought, I guess. So he picked up his weapon, as it was already loaded. He again went to where the light from his fire reached. He was looking around, peering into the night trying to see whatever or whoever might be out there, and again he did not see anyone or anything.

> "Again I went back to the old wooden house. I just could not stay there any longer,"

he said. I guess he must have thought,

> "I think I should leave this place,"

he must have decided.

> "I will get in my canoe and go to the other side of the river and sit among the reeds and rushes. I will watch this old shelter from there. I will keep an eye on this shelter from there,"

he must have thought.

Well, he then loaded his belongings back into the canoe, and he paddled his canoe across to the other side of the river and he backed the canoe in among the reeds and rushes that grew along the shore of the river. It was from this hidden vantage point that he kept an eye on the old wooden shelter that he had run away from. The fire he had built lit up the area in front of the shelter, and he watched the house.

"mandj iidik waa bizhinaagozigoweN *owo* waa bizaagewet zhewe (*e*) gowesak.",

(*doo*) inendam giiyeN. gaa*wiin dash* giiyeN go naazh zhewe go iidik gaa zaagewesik. gaawii*n* go wiya gii waabimaasiin. gimaapii go iidik gaa gowiingkoshid, gii nibaa gonaa zhewe, jiimaaning go maanda (*doo*) nibaa bonowodibik. aa*n*iish (*e*) koowaabit go, mandj gonaa e piitaadibik*a*dinik, mandj gonaa gaa piitaadibik*a*dinigoweN gonaa *i*wi pii, mii*da*sh giiyeN gonaa iidik gii gichi nibaat. zhaazhago giiyeN gonaa (*doo*) waabaninigoba*n* (*e*) goweshkozit.

"taaya, gege*t* sa gonaa ndoo zazaamiz.",

(*doo*) inendam *da*sh iidik.

"ndoo koowaabinaaba*n*. mbe sa nga zhaa wodi gaa binjigidjibowe yaaN.",

(*doo*) inendam *da*sh iidik maaba m*a*kwa nowii.

aa*n*iish, mii sa wodi gii nit*a*kamowot ziibiing. neyaap wodi gii nizhewoshkoset gaaming. gii nizhaat wodi iwi mitigogamigooN nikeyaa *d*ash tenik. aa*n*iish giiyeN gonaa, yaawaan iidik gaa baatiinawaat zhewe niniwok gaa miyaadjik. aapidji giiyeN go (*doo*) midjinametoowon iidik zhewe gaataawigamik iidik gii dizhigaabowiwaat gewe. gaa*wiin* gii gikenimigoosiin dibi iidik gaa zhaagoweN. wodi gaye jiigaakowaa gii zhaat, gii aaw*a*djiniget, mii gaye iidik wodi aanowi (*doo*) zhaawaat, aanowi (*doo*) bibaa *n*andowaabimigot. aaniish, mii*da*sh go pane gii p*a*skaabikowet zhewe wiigwaameNing, mitigogamigooNing. gaawii*n* gii m*a*kaakgoosiin.

gegoo *d*ash go maaba akiweziiN, maaba makwa nowii gii naadizi. maanda gonaa anishinaabek gonaa gii m*a*kadekewaat, mii iidik gaye maaba makwa nowii gii makadekewet gonaa, oshkiniigishiwit gonaa. ginimaa gonaa midaaswi shi niizh sabiboonigizigoba*n*. ngoding gonaa gii dibaadjimo gonaa *i*wi (*e*) dibaadjimot gonaa. miidash genii*n* (*doo*) g*a*gwedjimak iwi, aaniish ngii mishoomisonon maaba m*a*kwa nowii gaa inin*d*.

"aaniish gonaa gegii*n* gaa naamdama *y*in iwi gii m*a*kadeke yin.",

ngii zhigagwedjimaa dash.

"ngii gichi naamdam sa n*a*yiinawi*nd*.",

ngii ik dash. miidash gaa kidat,

"I have no idea what the one I was fearful of would look like if and when he or it showed up,"

he supposedly thought. While he was watching the shelter, no one showed up. He did not see anyone or anything. Eventually he fell asleep as he was waiting, as this was already very late into night. He fell asleep while he was watching the shelter, and he did not know at what time of the night it was, and he finally succumbed to sleep, and he went into a deep sleep. When he finally awoke, it was already morning.

"Oh I am so foolish,"

he then thought to himself.

"I was watching out for something or someone. I better go there and check that area out, the place I ran away from,"

this man called Makwa Nowii must have thought.

So, he paddled back across the river to the other shore. He landed the canoe back across the river. He went to where the old wooden shelter was located . And to his surprise he noticed that there were many, many tracks made by men all around the wooden shelter. The entire area around the house, the grass was trodden smooth by the many men who must have walked around and stood around looking for him. But they did not know where he had gone. He noticed that they followed his tracks he had made when he went around gathering wood for his fire, they must have followed his trail looking for him. However, his tracks always returned to the shelter. These people never found him.

There was something strange about this old man called Makwa Nowii. As was the custom back then, when he became of age, he fasted, the ritual of going without food and water for several days and meditating, praying for a vision that would give the individual some direction in his or her life. He may have been around twelve years of age when he went on his fast. He spoke about that, his fasting, at another time. Well, I had asked him about it, as he was my grandfather.

"What was your vision when you fasted?"

I had asked him.

"Oh, I had a very great vision,"

he said to me. And he also said,

"*n*iyii sa gaa bowaadimaaN genii*n* gii m*a*kadeke yaaN, bimaadiziwin.",

gii kida.

"iwi go maanda (*e*) nibaa yaaN, (*doo*) aapowe yaaN, ngii waabidiz (*e*) gikaa yaaN iidik ge zhinaagozi yaaN.",

gii kida.

"ngii bowaanaa akiweziiN (*e*) waabimak, aapidji go (*doo*) gikaa.",

gii kida.

"aapidji go (*doo*) waabshkindibe, miinawaa gaye, aapidji go (*doo*) ziigiinggowe. miinawaa gaye (*doo*) waagoshkaa maaba akiweziiN (*e*) bimoset. miinawaa gaye (*doo*) nanggabizo. mii*da*sh maanda (*doo*) bizhiganawaabimit wewena, taaya, n*doo* zhoobiinggowetaak gosha nayiinawi*nt* maaba akiweziiN. taaya, ngii nisadowinaadiz, niin. taaya, geget sa gonaa, niin sa nayiinawi*nd* maaba, nd*oo* inendam maanda (*doo*) nibaa yaaN ganawaabidiza yaaN. aapidji go akiweziiN genawaabimak. aa*n*iish, miidash iwi gaa waabang, gii gagwedjimigoo yaaN mandj iidik gaa naapowe *y*aaneN. ngii wiindamawaak dash gwonda gonaa genii*n* gonaa gaa bikoginidjik gonaa gaa naamdamaaN."

miidash maaba bezhik gichi *a*nishinaabe zhewe gii yaa, gaaw*iin* gonaa giyaabi genii*n* ngii gikenimaasii gonaa gaa zhinikaanaat maaba m*a*kwa nowii ninda anishinaaben, miidash giiyeN gaa igot iwi.

"gichi gibeying sa gwii bimaadiz.",

gii igoon giiyeN.

"gwii gibe gikaa."

aaniish, giyegeti *da*sh go maaba m*a*kwa nowii gaa inin*d*, gichi gibeying gii bimaadizi. aapidji go giyegeti gii gikaa. aaniish, mii*da*sh gonaa maanda e kowaak maanda (*doo*) dibaadjimak maaba m*a*kwa nowii gaa inind.

gichi miigwech gaa bazindawa yek.

> "I had a vision about life, that is what I saw when I fasted,"

he said.

> "As I was sleeping, or so it seemed, I had this dream, I saw myself as how I would look like in the future,"

he said.

> "I saw this very, very old man in my dream, I mean he was aged,"

he added.

> "This old man's hair was all gray and his face was very wrinkled. And this old man was bent over when he ambled about. He also shook from his frailty. And in my dream, I saw him take a good look at me and this old man smiled at me. Oh my, I recognized myself, the old man was me. Oh my, 'This is me,' I thought to myself as I looked at myself in my dream. This was a very old, old man I was looking at. So, the next day, when my fast was over, I was asked to talk about what I had seen. And I told the elders and my parents who had raised me about the vision I had during my fast."

Then there was this one respected elder who was there at the time, and I forgot the name Makwa Nowii had called this old man, anyway this old man was the one who told Makwa Nowii the following.

> "You will have a very long life,"

Makwa Nowii was told by him.

> "You will live to be very old."

Well, this man called Makwa Nowii did live to be a very old man. He was definitely very old. Well, that is the length of my story about the one called Makwa Nowii.

Thank you very much for listening to me.

danezhiiN gaa zhinikaazat iidik gaa zhimadjizhichigegobaneN

yaawaa sa nwii dibaadjimaa, anishinaabe. zhaazhago gonaa zhinda gii danakiiba*n* gonaa *o*wo anishinaabe. gii nibowiba*n* gaye gonaa *o*wo. mii gonaa zhinda gaa *t*apinet niyiing nikeyaa makwa ziibiing, biidaasage nonggo*m* (*e*) zhinikaadek. yaawaa dash maaba gii zhinikaaza anishinaabe, danezhiiN.

miid*a*sh gonaa gii bi-oshkibimaadizit gonaa, banggii gonaa nwii dibaadjimaa. gaa*wiin* gonaa niibana gonaa ngii gikenimaasii gonaa ge naadjimakgoba*n*. miid*a*sh go maanda waa dibaadidamaaN, zhaazhago gonaa gwonda anishinaabek gonaa, gii waawiikondiwok gonaa, (*e*) niwaa-oodetoowaat gonaa. miid*a*sh iidik gaye maaba danezhiiN gaa inind, niyiing *naa*nedaa gonaa ginimaa (*doo*) zhaagoba*n* wodi mishiiminibaamikoong nonggo*m* d*a*sh daming. anishinaabek gonaa zhewe gii danakiiwok, *o*daawaak gonaa.

miid*a*sh maaba iidik danezhiiN wodi gaa bibaa zhaat. (*doo*) gichi wiisiniwaat iidik wodi, (*doo*) magoshewaat gonaa gwonda anishinaabek. mii iidik gaye maaba gii wiidoopangget wodi danezhiiNba*n*. aa*n*iish, giigaanggok d*a*sh gonaa iidik bemiiwizidjik gonaa, (*doo*) bimiikowaawaat gonaa waasinindjin. mii iidik maaba danezhiiN gaa zhimisowinawaat ninda bezhik ikwewizeNson. mii go iidik go (*doo*) inendang ji wiidigemaapa*n* go. mii gaye gonaa bidjiinak gonaa zhewe (*doo*) waabimaat gonaa newe. wiikaa d*a*sh giiyeN gonaa iidik gii jichaan gonaa wii ganoonaat. miid*a*sh iidik e inaat iwi, aa*n*iish, (*doo*) inendang iidik, ji wiidigemaapa*n*. gaa*wiin* d*a*sh wiyii giiyeN gewii*n* ninda wii wiidigemigoosiin.

> "gaawii*n* gonaa nd*oo* inendazii*n* iwi ji wiidigeminaaNmbaa*n*.",

gii igoon iidik.

aa*n*iish, aanowi (*doo*) gigetinaamizi dash go maaba go danezhiiN gaa inin*d*. gaa*wiin* go maamdaa go, aaniish, gaa*wiin* sa go wii wiidigemigoosiin.

> "baamaampii miinawaa nga bizhaa.",

gii inaan d*a*sh giiyeN ninda ikwewizeNson.

> "gdaa bizhaa, gaawii*n* gonaa gegoo daa naabidasinoo gaye go aanowi (*doo*) bizhaa yin.",

gii igoon d*a*sh giiyeN, gii igoodigenon.

The Evil Deed that the Man Called DanezhiiN Supposedly Did

Now I am going to talk about a man. This particular man lived in this region many years ago. This man has long since departed this world and gone on into the spirit world. This man died in the area of Bear River, the place that is now called Petoskey. And this man's name was DanezhiiN.

I am going to tell you a little about him, something that happened during his younger years. I really do not know much else to tell about him. I am going to talk about how the Anishinaabe of long ago used to hold gatherings at their villages, and others from the other villages in the area would be invited to come to a feast at a particular village. And this man called DanezhiiN just happened to be going to a village that was located in the area that was called mishiiminibaamikoong. All these villages were settled by Anishinaabe people, the Ottawa people.

So this DanezhiiN apparently went to that area. The Anishinaabe people there were hosting a huge feast for some occasion, maybe a ceremony of some kind. So this DanezhiiN joined in on the feasting and partook of the food. As was customary, the young girls, teenagers, were the ones who served the patrons at the feast. And this DanezhiiN was very attracted to one of these young girls. He decided that he was going to marry her. And this was the first time he had ever laid eyes on her. And it took him a long time to build up the courage to speak to her. Then he told her that he wanted to marry her. But, she did not want to marry him.

"I do not want to marry you,"

DanezhiiN was told by her, I suppose.

Well, DanezhiiN pestered her and he persisted in telling her of his wish to marry her. But, it was to no avail, as she steadfastly refused to marry him.

"I will come back again later on,"

he supposedly told this young girl.

"You can come back if you want, but it will be of no use,"

he was told, he was probably told.

gimaapiich dash go iidik miinawaa gaa *pa*skaabiit wodi mishiiminibaamikoong. naanedaa iidik miinawaa gaa zhiwaabimaat ninda ikwewizeNson wodi. aa*n*iish, ginimaa gaye gonaa gii gikenimaadigenon gonaa e ndaanit. aa*n*iish, mii sa go miinawaa gii gagwedjimaat,

> "mii go iwi (*e*) binjizhaa yaaN zhinda (*doo*) bigagwedjiminaaN miinawaa iwi gaa zhigagwedjiminaaN nitam gii waabiminaaNmbaa*n*.",

d*oo* inaadigenon newe.

> "aaniish, ggii wiindamawin sa go, gaa*wiin* gwii wiidigemisinoo.
> mii go gii debisek gonaa iwi gii wiindamawinaaN wodi gii oshki waabiminaaNmbaa*n*.",

d*oo* ig*oo*digenon sa ninda ikwe*wi*zeNson. mii*da*sh maaba danezhiiNba*n* iwi iidik e inaat ninda yaa*w*aan ikwe*wi*zeNson.

> "giishpmaa bibowaa wiidigemi yin, gga giim*a*nanin.",

gii inaan iidik.

> "aaniish, mii sa go nonggo*m* ji giim*a*nani yimba*n*.",

gii igoon *da*sh iidik.

> "gaawii*n*, gaawii*n* gonaa memowech gonaa gwodji gonaa gdaa giim*a*nanisii, mii gonaa nonggo*m* ji giim*a*nani yimba*n*.",

gii igoon iidik.

> "gaawii*n* gwii wiidigemisinoo.",

gii igoon giiyeN. aaniish, mii*da*sh go *i*wi minik go zhewe gaa waabimaat. aaniish, (*doo*) giyetinaamendam go iidik maaba danezhiiN wii wiidigemaat newe.

So apparently DanezhiiN returned to Mishiiminibaamikoong later on. And, as luck would have it, he happened to see this young girl. Well, maybe he knew where she lived. So, again he asked her to marry him.

> "The only reason I came here is to ask you again what I had asked you the first time I saw you,"

he must have said to this girl.

> "Well, I told you already, I do not want to marry you. That should have sufficed the first time I told you that when I first saw you,"

he was probably told by this teenage girl. So then this man called DanezhiiN supposedly said to this girl.

> "If you do not marry me, I will kill you,"

he supposedly said to this girl.

> "Well, now is your chance to kill me,"

he supposedly was told by the girl.

> "You do not have to kill me anywhere else, you could kill me here right now,"

he supposedly was told.

> "I will not marry you,"

he was further told by her. Well, that was the end of that encounter, as they parted ways. But, he was determined, still very determined, to marry this girl.

gimaapii go iidik gaa *pa*skaabiit miinawaa wodi mishiiminibaamikoong. mii*da*sh iidik iwi pii iwi (*doo*) gitigewaat anishinaabek. mii*da*sh iidik gaye maaba *i*kwewizeNs wodi niikigoon gonaa gitigaaning *da*sh (*doo*) nakiinit, mii iidik gewii*n* gii wiidjiiwaat. (*doo*) naadimawaat gonaa (*doo*) kitigenit gonaa, (*doo*) ganawendamonit gonaa iwi gitigaaneNwaa gonaa ji kida yinggoba*n*. mii*da*sh giiyeN e naakoshinik mii wii bimaajaawaat, wegodigowendik *da*sh gaye iwi gaa biniikewaagoweN wodi gitigaanigamigooNing. baamaa*mpii* gonaa zhewe gonaa daashti gaa biyaawaat gonaa, mii gii bimesinamowaat iwi. ge gichi nakaazawaagobane gaye go iidik, wegodigowenidik iwi. mii*da*sh giiyeN maaba iwi giigaang e kidat,

> "ndaa naadin sa gonaa. gga ni*y*aapiitisem *da*sh gonaa. aaniish, gga bidaminewinim. waasa nanggaye gitigaanigamigooN temigat.",

(*doo*) kidawidik sa maaba giigaang. mii*da*sh go gii *pa*skaabiit. aabidek go iidik gewii*n* wii naadin iwi wegodigowenidik gaa biniikewaagoweN.

miidash maanda (*doo*) bi*pa*skaabiit iidik, mii ninda gii *na*kweshkawaat zhewe miikaaNsing newe yaawaan, danezhiiNon. aaniish, mii*da*sh maaba danezhiiN gaa zhiwaawiindamawaat iwi, giishpmaa bibowaa (*doo*) wiidigemigot, wii nisaan.

> "aaniish, mii sa go ji nisi yimba*n*.",

gii igoodigenon dash ninda giigaanggooNson. mii*da*sh iidik gii miigaadiwaat. aapidji go iidik gaa gichi miigaadiwaat. aaniish, nini dash nowonch (*doo*) mashkowazi, ikwe dash. miinawaa gaye maaba danezhiiN, mookamaan iidik bemiwidoogobane, mii iidik ninda giigaanggooNson iwi gaa wepidawaat iwi mookamaan. gegaa go iidik aanowi gaa maazhawigot.

miidash iwi iidik gonaa gwonda e niikigodjik gonaa newe, (*e*) gowiinabiiwaa*w*aat gonaa ninda daaniseNwaan.

> "gdaa *pa*skaabiimi*nd* gonaa, ginimaa gegoo (*doo*) zhiwebazidik *o*wo.",

gii inendamodigenak gonaa. miidash iidik neyaap gii *pa*skaabiiwaat, kitigaaning miinawaa *da*sh (*e*) zhaawaat. aaniish, gimaapii *da*sh giiyeN wodi e niyaawaat, mii giiyeN gii waabimaawaat newe daaniseNwaan wodi (*doo*) zhabinit miikaaNsing. zhaazhigo gii nichigaazawon. mii *o*wo danezhiiN iwi gaa zhichiget iwi.

Apparently he went back to Mishiiminibaamikoong again later on. This was during the spring as that is when the Anishinaabe people began planting in their gardens. So this young girl went with and helped her parents with the planting of their garden. It could be said that she assisted with the planting and the other things in taking care of the garden. Then when it was getting late in the day, they left for home, but apparently they forgot something at the garden. After they had walked a fair distance, that is when the parents of this girl realized that they forgot something in the shed at the garden. I guess they had made great use of it, whatever the item was. So the young teenage girl said,

> "I could go back to get it. While I am going back, you two will keep on walking toward home. Of course I will catch up to you. The shed in the garden is not really that far away,"

this teenage girl must have said. So, she went back. I guess she too realized that they needed this thing they forgot, whatever it was, and she had to go back to get it.

So, as she was returning on the trail from the garden, that is when she met DanezhiiN. And, as DanezhiiN had promised her in their previous encounters, if she did not marry him, he would kill her.

> "Well, you should kill me now,"

he must have been told by this young teenage girl. Then they fought and struggled hard. It must have been a great struggle. Well, a man is usually physically much stronger than a woman. Also, DanezhiiN had a knife with him, and he stabbed this teenage girl with the knife. The girl had put up a great struggle, and she apparently almost overcame DanezhiiN.

Then the parents of this teenage girl began to wonder where their daughter was, as she should have caught up to them by now as the garden was not that far.

> "We should go back, maybe something happened to her,"

they probably thought. So they quickly went back to the garden. Then, after a while as they made their way back to the garden, they saw their daughter lying on the trail, she was already dead. She had already been killed by her assailant. It was the one called DanezhiiN that did that evil deed.

aaniish, gaa*wiin* *da*sh go zhewe gii yaasii, gii gidjibowe. aaniish, maanda gonaa nonggo*m* zhinda aki e waabiminaagok, kina go maanda gii mitigowaagkaa. aaniish, gaa*wiin* *da*sh go wiya gii m*a*kaagoosiin, aano*wi* (*doo*) *n*andonewewaawaat gaye, dibi gonaa iidik gaa zhaagoweN. maanda dash maaba nikeyaa danezhiiN iidik gaa zhaat, gaa shkwaa nisaat ninda *i*kwewizeNson, waashedinong ko *da*sh daming. niibana giiyeN go wodi nisabiboon maaba gii danakii. gimaapii gonaa gekaat, mii iwi gii bip*a*skaabiit zhinda niyiing makwa ziibiing dash gii damiwaat anishinaabek. gichimookamaan wiyii nonggo*m* biidaasage d*oo* zhinikaadaan iwi. mii gii bigiiwet.

"mii gonaa ginimaa (*doo*) booninenimigoo yaaN.",

gii inendamodik.

aaniish giyegeti *da*sh gonaa, gaa*wiin* gonaa wiya gii bibaamenimigoosiin. aaniish (*doo*) gikaa sa. gaa*wiin* gonaa aapidji gonaa gibeying gii bimaadizisii zhinda gaa p*a*skaabiit. mii maaba gaa zhinoondamaaN (*e*) zhinaadjimigozit maaba danezhiiN gaa inind. aaniish, mii*da*sh gonaa *i*wi minik gonaa eta e zhigikendamaaN genii*n* da naadjima*k*goba*n* gonaa maaba, maaba sa danezhiiN gaa inind.

miigwech gaa bazindawa yek.

makwa nowii gii gidaakiiyepan wodi makwa zhagishing

yaawaak sa miinawaa nwii dibaadjimaak anishinaabek, zhinda gonaa e danakii ying, zhaazhago sa ko gwonda anishinaabek, gaawii*n* giiyeN zhinda gii nji biboonishisiiwok zhinda go nonggo*m* go *da*sh (*doo*) yaa ying go. maanda ko gwonda gii zhaawok, niyiing zaagawaang gii zhinikaadaan *o*wo odaawaa iwi gaa nji biboonishiwaat. St. Joseph wiyii nonggo*m* zhinikaade iwi oodena, gichimookamaan gonaa gewii*n* d*oo* zhinikaadaan.

mii*da*sh ko gwonda anishinaabek ensa digwaagik gaa zagakanagewaadji gonaa, mii (*doo*) maajaawaat. maanda nitibewewaat maanda gichigomi, zhaawonong dash (*doo*) zhaawaat. maanda dash go iwi waa dibaadidamaaN, bezhik go maaba anishinaabe nwii dibaadjimaa. mii *o*wo makwa nowii gaa inind. yaawaan *da*shmaaba gii koginigoon, ookomison. gaa*wiin* giiyeN maamdaa newe yaawaan gashiwon e ndaanit wii yaat, maaba gonaa gewii*n* m*a*kwa nowii gaa gashidjin. gii nibowonigoba*n* gonaa gaye maaba gaa wiidigemaadjin. mii*da*sh miinawaa gii wiidigemaaganinit. gii zhiinggenimigoon dash maaba m*a*kwa nowii newe, miinawaa gonaa gaa oosodjin gonaa ji kida *y*inggoba*n*. miidash gaawii*n* maamdaa zhewe newe gashiwon wii ganawenimigot. miidash newe ookomison maaba m*a*kwa nowii ndaawaach gaa zhidaapinigot, gii koginigot dash.

Well, of course, he did not stick around, he ran away from the area. Well, as you look at the land around here, this was all forest at that time. So the people looked for him, and they did not find him anywhere, no one knew where he had gone. I guess this DanezhiiN went to a place called Waashedinong after he had killed the young teenage girl. He lived and worked in that area for many years. Then when he was very old, that is when he returned to the area of Bear River as this is what the Anishinaabe people used to call that area. The white people, the Americans, now call that place Petoskey. So, he came home then.

"They must have forgotten about me and my actions,"

he probably thought.

And that is what happened, no one really bothered him when he came back here to live. Well, for one thing, he was very old. He did not live much longer after he came back here. This is a story I had heard about this one man called DanezhiiN. Well, that is all I know about the story about this man, the one called DanezhiiN.

Thank you for listening to me.

When Makwa Nowii Climbed Sleeping Bear Dunes

Well, I am going to tell another story about the Anishinaabe people. Long ago, the Anishinaabe people did not spend the winter here where we are living now. The Ottawa used to go south of here for the winter, to a place they called Zaagawaang. Today, the white people, or Americans, call this place St. Joseph.

So every fall, after they had taken in and stored their crops, they left. They would follow the shoreline of this big lake as they went south in their canoes. And the story I am going to tell you, I am going to talk about this one man. This is the one who was called Makwa Nowii. This man was raised by his grandmother. He could not stay with his mother at his mother's place. His mother's first husband, his father, had died. Then his mother remarried. Makwa Nowii was not liked by this man, we could say that this is his father. So his mother could not take care of him at her home. So that is how Makwa Nowii was adopted by his grandmother, and this is the one who raised him.

miidash ko gwonda gaa zhichigewaat ensa digwaagik iwi, maanda dash (doo) zhaawaat anishinaabek, gozining. miidash giiyeN ngoding maanda (doo) zhaawaat niyiing, gozining, mii giiyeN gaa zhinoonde gichi bigomaandimodinik. daashti go makwa zhagishing dash (doo) daming gwodji, mii giiyeN zhewe gii nibigomaanimok. aaniindi giiyeN gonaa gaa zhi-aanimiziwaat. aapidji giiyeN gichi noodinini, boweyaanimodinik gonaa. mii go aapidji giiyeN go gii maanggaashkaani. aanowi giiyeN go debiwaabiminaagot go iwi makwa zhagishing.

anishinaabek dash gonaa zhewe gii nigibeshiwok ko, gii gichi piitendaanaawaa iwi makwa zhagishing dash (doo) daming. gii manidookenaawaa gwonda anishinaabek zhaazhago iwi. gii gichi ishpidanaamigat iwi. miidash ko gaa nanakaadimowaat anishinaabek zhaazhago iwi, gii gagidaakiiyewaat zhewe, wii gikendamowaat giiyeN, mandj giiyeN iidik minik waa bimaadiziwaagoweN. miidash iwi, miidash go iwi gaa zhimashkowendamowaat giishpmaa giiyeN wiya (doo) giizhidaakiiyewaat zhewe, wii gaagiye bimaadizi giiyeN. mii gaa zhibagosendamowaat.

iwi dash go maanda dibaadjimak maaba makwa nowii, gii niginasinigowaat, mii giiyeN zhewe naawondj gegaa dibishkoo (doo) niyaawaat, aapidji giiyeN go (doo) maanggaashkaani zhewe boweyaanimodinik. mii giiyeN newe ookomison, gaa ookomisodjin e igot, naanigodinong gonaa maanda (doo) zhigowiidjiwebowigoowaat gonaa, mii iwi debiwaabidamowaat maanda aki. aapidji giiyeN (doo) baatiinawon anishinaaben zhewe e yaanidjin makwa zhagishing. miidash giiyeN e igot newe gaa ookomisodjin,

> "gdoo waabimaak na gewe. ggii waabimaak na gewe anishinaabek gii naabi yin akiing.",

doo igoodigenon sa.

> "eN (heN), ngii waabimaak sa."
> "mii sa go wodi gegiin nonggom ji minaaniibowi yin wiiba go.",

gii igoon dash giiyeN.

> "aapidji go ndoo aanimizimind.",

(doo) kida.

And so every fall the Anishinaabe people would move to their residences in the south. So this one fall, as they were heading to their southern residences, while they were on the lake in their canoes, a strong wind came up and a storm blew in off the lake. This was just this side of what is now called Sleeping Bear Dunes, where they ran into this strong wind. Oh, they had so much difficulty because of the storm. The wind was so strong and also, the wind seemed to come at them from several directions. Also, the waves on the lake were increasing in size. And from where they were, they could see the Sleeping Bear Dunes off in the distance.

The Anishinaabe people used to stop at this place, they even camped there, and they had great respect for this area, and also it was considered a sacred place. The Anishinaabe people used it as a place for ceremonies, such as the vision quest ritual. The dunes were very high, it was a high sandy hill. One of the things they used to do, was they would climb up the dunes and learn how long they were to live. One of the things they believed was that if one was able to make it to the top, that person would have a long life. This is what they may have wished for.

As I was talking about Makwa Nowii and being caught in the storm on the lake in the area of the Sleeping Bear Dunes, the waves were getting bigger and the wind was getting stronger. One of the times, as the canoe would rise to the top of the swell, they could see the land and the shoreline. There were many people already camped at the base of the dunes. So his grandmother said this to him.

> "Do you see them? Did you see those people when you looked toward the shore?"

she must have said to him.

> "Yes, I saw them."
> "Well, soon you will be standing among them also,"

he was told by her.

> "We were in dire straits."

he said.

miidash iwi maaba mindimooyeN, maaba makwa nowii gaa ookomisodjin, gaawiin wiikaa maaba gii kinoomawaasii. aapidji dash go gii naabindokowe. mii go maanda niibaadibik gaye go (doo) ganawaabimaat ananggoon, mii go (doo) gikendang go iwi waa zhigiizhigadinik gonaa ji kida yinggoban. miinawaa waabang, mii go miinawaa maanda (e) biwaabananik dash (doo) naabit waabanong, mii go (e) nisadowinang go waa zhigiizhigadinik iwi. ginimaa gaye ji bigomaanimok, ginimaa gaye ji minogiizhigak. aapidji go maaba mindimooweN gii nibwaakaa.

miidash miinawaa wodi ji nidibaadjimakgowaa, mii zhago giiyeN zhewe dibishkoo makwa zhagishing (e) niyaawaat. aaniish, newe ookomison gii igoon,

"mii go gegiin nonggom wodi ji minaaniibowi yin.",

gii igoon. aaniish, gii debwetawaan dash go. miidash iwi, miidash giiyeN ninda e zhiwaabimaat ookomison, mashkimodeNs giiyeN doo yaani zhewe, gegoo dash go zhewe gii godinaan zhewe mashkimodeNsing.

"gii kawe danaandigidoon dash go.",

(doo) kida sa.

"miidash nibiing gii bagidinang iwi. ndoo biminiiwimint dash zhewe bibamaashi yaang wiigwaasijiimaaning.",

gii kida. miinawaa iwi gonaa (doo) danakaazawinawaa gonaa gegoo (doo) bimiwidoonaawaa, (doo) de mooshkinedik go maanda gichi wiigwaasijiimaan.

"miidash maaba mindimooweN ninda digowon gii koowaabimaat.",

(doo) kida.

"miidash iwi (e) waabimaat gichi digowon (doo) biidjibizonit, mii gweyek wodi gii inaat ninda e daakendjin wii nakowegenit akiing. aaniish, mii sa go maaba gaa zhichiget iwi. wiin go maaba mindimooweN go ninaabikowaani ogimaawi go ji kida yinggoban gonaa. aaniish, gii gikendaan maanda tibewe gichigomi e nizhizhinaagodinik. pane gonaa zhaazhago gonaa gii bigoziwok gewe anishinaabek, aazhoow sa gonaa gii zhaawok gonaa maanda tibewe gichigomi. aaniish, miidash go gaa zhichiget maaba e daaket iwi, (e) waabimaat newe gichi digowon (doo) biidjibizonit, mii gii nakoweget gweyek wodi akiing. maanda

And this old woman, the grandmother of Makwa Nowii, she had never been schooled in anything. However, she could tell what the weather was going to be like. She could read the stars and be able to tell what the next few days would be like. And also, in the morning, she would look to the east and she would be able to sense what the day would be like. She would know if the wind would come up or if it would be a good day weather-wise. This old woman was wise in those ways.

And back to the story, now they were getting near Sleeping Bear Dunes. Well, his grandmother had already told him that he too would be there soon.

> "You will be standing there among them soon,"

he had been told by her. And of course, he believed her. He had noticed his grandmother had this little pouch, and she would take something out of it now and then.

> "She would then say a few words,"

he said.

> "Then she would put it in the water. There were four of us in this canoe as we were cruising,"

he said. Also, in this canoe, which was rather large, they carried some of their belongings with them, in fact it was quite full with their belongings.

> "Then this old woman would watch the waves rolling toward us,"

he added.

> "Then when she saw a huge swell coming, she told the man who was sitting at the back steering the canoe, to steer the canoe toward land. And this is what the man did. It could be said that this old woman was the skipper of the canoe. Well, she knew what the shoreline of this great lake looked like. The Anishinaabe people had always traveled back and forth along the shoreline of this great lake. So that is what the helmsman did, as he saw a big wave coming, he would steer the canoe toward the

> (doo) zhigichi gowiidjiwebigoowi yaang mii waabimanggidowaa anishinaabek wodi tibewe (doo) niibinegaabowiwaat, aapidji go (doo) baatiinawok. wiigwaameNsan gaye gonaa (doo) nitenoon. niyiin gonaa waagonagaaneNsan, wenibik gonaa wii gibeshid gonaa e zhinaagok wiigwaaman. mii gosha nayiinawi giyegeti zhewe maaba gichi digow (doo) bibigomibizot, ndo jiimaananaan (doo) miwebang, miidash go gidjiyiing gaa nidanizi yaang, gidjidigow go. gii dibaabidaan go maaba mindimooweN go iwi go pii waa nakowegaadenik sa gonaa iwi wiigwaasijiimaan akiing. mii gosha nayiinawind maaba gaye e daaket maanda (doo) zhinakoweget akiing nikeyaa, mii gii bookobidoot iwi niyii, do abwint. aaniish, mii sa go nibiing gii banggishing. aaniish, gaawiin sa wiyii go nonggom e zhiyaa ying go gwonda anishinaabek gii zhiyaasiiwok. mii go maanda (doo) gikendang nibiing (doo) banggishing mii go baabagiye miinawaa iwi jiimaan gii debibidoot. miidash go zhewe gii nigoodjing go owo, aaniish, (doo) gwetaanibizo maaba digow, gweyek akiing dash (doo) pizot. miidash iwi wodi pii (doo) baashkiiwaat, aaniish ndoo maadjiiyaashimind go, gwetaanaanimot go, e nidanizi yaang go wodi e ko baashkiiwaat go, mii eta (e) waabshkaaminaagot nibiish. mii go zhewe gaa nipizo yaang go. miinawaa wodi maanda wiigwaasijiimaan pii (e) zhewoshkosek niyiing tibewe, mii go zhewe gewe anishinaabek gii bipaagomosewaat. aapidji go niibana, mii go gaa zhimichawe (doo) gowiidanimowaat go iwi wiigwaasijiimaan, gii oobigidinamowaat dash wodi e ko benggokamigaanik, (doo) benggokamigaak iwi aki. aa sa gonaa geniin n(doo) minowendam (doo) bimaadizi yaaN.",

gii kida dash maaba makwa nowii.

> "gwetaanaashkaa naawondj. wiigwaaman go e zhishpaak, mii go e ishpiziwaat gewe digowok. aapidji go ngii aanimizimint. miidash nonggom mii zhewe gonaa (doo) minaaniibowi yaaN zhewe akiing, aapidji gonaa ngii minowendam."

iwi dash anishinaabek, nitam gaye go ngii dibaadjim go iwi gii gagidaakiiyewaat sa zhewe makwa zhagishing. miidash maaba makwa nowii gaa ookomisodjin, mii giiyeN gaa igot iwi,

> "gdaa gidaakiiye gegiin zhinda, maanda gichi ishpakamigaak, maanda makwa zhagishing e daming. ji wiyii gikendamayin gonaa aabidek endigoweN ji wiyii gibe bimaadizi yin.",

> shore. Then when we were riding on the crest of the big wave, we could see many Anishinaabe people standing along the shore of the lake. There were shelters dotting the coastline. These were not permanent structures, but temporary shelters erected by the Anishinaabe people when they were just camping overnight. And when this big wave would roll in to the shore, we would ride on top of the wave. The old woman would direct the man which way to steer the canoe. Then this one time when the man was steering the canoe toward the shore, the oar he was using broke in half. As it broke he fell out of the canoe and into the water. The Anishinaabe people back then were not like us today. As soon as he knew he was falling into the water, he quickly grabbed at the canoe. He hung on to the side of the canoe as we raced to the shore. And where the waves broke onto the shore, that is where we were going toward, and the water was just white where the waves broke onto the shore. We traveled right to the shore where the waves were crashing. And when this canoe landed on the shore, there were many men who arrived there to meet our canoe. As soon as the canoe landed on the shore, there were many men there who grabbed on to the canoe and literally lifted the canoe with us still in it, and placed it farther up on the shore. Oh, I was so happy to be alive,"

Makwa Nowii said.

> "The waves in the middle of the lake were really rough. It seemed that some of the waves were as high as houses. Oh, we had a very difficult canoe trip. And now, here I was standing among the people on land, and I was elated."

And I already talked about what the Anishinaabe people used this area for, it was sacred grounds to them, and they would climb the dunes. And Makwa Nowii's grandmother told him the following.

> "You should climb up this very high sand dune, this place called Sleeping Bear Dunes. Just to find out if you will have a long life and gain some knowledge,"

gii kidawidigenon sa ninda ookomison. wii gidaakiiyewok go.

"gaawiin kina wiya bemaadizit zhinda gashkitoosiin wii gidaakiiyet.",

gii igoodigenon dash newe ookomison.

aaniish, maaba gewiin makwa nowii nitaagi gonaa zhago, oshkininiiwi gonaa.

"aaniish, ndaa gidaakiiye sa zhinda, nookomis.",

gii inaan dash giiyeN.

aaniish, gii gichi zhichigewok dash go, gii kawe gaagiigidowok go gwonda iidik go pii wii gidaakiiyewaat e oshkibimaadizidjik. noomak go gwonda go gii ganoodjigewok zhewe anishinaabek. aaniish, mii sa giiyeN gewiin makwa nowii gii wewebigidaakiiyet. mandj gonaa gaa ninchiwaagoweN, gii de nchiwok go.

aapta giiyeN aanind gii de dagoshiniwok, aanind giiyeN gonaa ooshame. aaniish, makwa nowii, maanoo go.

"giyegeti (doo) zanagat.",

(doo) kida.

"ndoo zhazhaashibooz gaye aanowi takokii yaaN. aaniish, maanoo sa go, maanoo go ngii wiikodjitoon wii gidaakiiye yaaN. gimaapii gosha nayiinawind wodi zhago besha. aapidji go aanowi (doo) beshawaabiminaagot, mii go iwi nwii aanowitoo go, ngii inendam.",

(doo) kida.

"maanoo dash go ndoo wiikodjitoon go. miidash go gewe mitigooNsak jiigiyiing gonaa gwodji jiigidaaki (doo) bidakiziwok gonaa (doo) ninaabiigimowok go, mii gosha nayiinawint bezhik gaa zhidebinak owo mitigooNs.",

gii kida.

his grandmother must have said. There were people who were going to attempt to climb the high dunes.

> "Not everyone who climbs up, makes it all the way,"

he must have been told by his grandmother.

Well, this youngster, Makwa Nowii, is already of age, he will soon be a young man.

> "Well grandmother, I guess I could climb this dune,"

he must have said to her.

As it was customary, the elders prepared those who would attempt the climb, and the young people talked about why they climbed. And the elders prayed for and spoke to the young people for a long time, those young people who were attempting to climb the dunes. When they made their way up, Makwa Nowii went steadily up the dunes, and he was determined to make it. I do not know how many there were, but there were quite few.

Some of the young people who were climbing made it halfway up and they quit, and others went more than halfway and then they would quit. But Makwa Nowii persevered and went up.

> "Oh, it was so difficult,"

he said.

> "I would slip in the sand with each step I took. But I just kept on trying to go up the dune. It seemed after a long time, I was very close to the top. It looked so close, and I was running out of stamina, as I was ready to give up too, I thought,"

he added.

> "But, I just kept on trying. And sometimes you see these little shrubs that grow along the edge of a hilltop, I was able to grasp one of those little shrubs,"

he said.

"miidash gonaa gaa zhiwiikonimaakowii yaaN gonaa. miinawaa wodi pii wii giizhidaakiiye yaaN, nwii kodoodowe miinawaa wodi. (doo) de nishpaa go gewiin iwi. mii sa miinawaa zhewe gii zanagak. wiya dash naanetaa shkweyaang (doo) biyaaban, miidash gonaa iwi gaa oonji gashkitoo yaaN gonaa geniin wii gidaakiiye yaaN. miinawaa gaye maaba nookomis ngii ganamaak.",

gii kida maaba makwa nowii.

"aapidji go wodi (doo) gonaadjiwonoon asiniiNsan gidaaki e tegin zhewe makwa zhagishing, gegowa newe bibaamendangge newe.",

gii igoon giiyeN.

"nowonch go (doo) zhinaagodoon asiniiNsan wiikaa go yaabidazawonan. giyegeti dash go gaa giizhidaakiiye yaaN, ngii waabidaanan newe asiniiNsan.",

gii kida maaba makwa nowii.

"gaawiin dash wiyii ngii bibaamendaziinan. noomak dash go wodi ngii yaa gaa giizhidaakiiye yaaN, gii bibaa ninaabi yaaN gonaa.",

gii inaadjimo.

"miidash iwi wii bipaskaabii yaaN, mii iwi, togowa nga nandogikendaan maanda mandj iidik e zhishpadanaagoweN maanda makwa zhagishing.",

(doo) inendam dash iidik.

aaniish, mitigowaabiin (doo) bimiwinaan miinawaa bikwak, miidash giiyeN wodi gaa binda bimod wodi.

"geget sa gonaa waasa (doo) nidebiwaabiminaagot naawondj iwi bikwak, ndoo inendam.",

(doo) kida.

"taaya, aapta daawong gosha nayiinawind gii banggisin. miidash gii biniisaakiiye yaaN, gii bimakamaaN gonaa zhewe (doo) zaagodaanggising iwi nbikwak.",

> "So I pulled myself toward the top of the dune using this little shrub for assistance. And at the very top, when I got there, I still had to crawl over a small ledge to get to the very top. This little ledge was kind of high also. And this was another hardship, to get to the top, the very top of the dune. I guess there was someone else coming up behind me and this person helped me over the very top of the dune. Before I had gone up there, my grandmother had warned me about certain things,"

Makwa Nowii continued.

> "There are many beautiful-looking stones at the top of the dunes, do not bother with them,"

he was told by her.

> "There are many different kinds of stones, most of which you have never seen before. And as I got to the top of the dunes, I saw those pretty-looking stones,"

Makwa Nowii said.

> "And I did not bother with the stones. I stayed up on top for some time, and I went looking around at the things up there,"

he said.

> "Then when it was time to come down, I decided to find out how high the Sleeping Bear Dunes was,"

he must have thought to himself.

Well, he had his bow and arrows with him, so he shot an arrow into the sky from atop the dunes out toward the lake.

> "Oh wow, the arrow looked like it was going out into the middle of the lake, at least that is what it looked like to me,"

he said.

> "Oh wow, it only made it halfway down the dune. Then I came down and I found my arrow sticking out of the sand halfway down the dunes,"

gii kida.

"miidash miinawaa gii bi-aandjibimodaakowe yaaN. miidash gonaa zhewe e ko zhagadaanggaak gonaa gii banggising iwi nbikwak."

gii kida.

"mii iwi gaa kokamigaak iwi. gaawiin gonaa ngii gikendaziin gonaa iwi ji dibaadidamaaNmbaan iwi e ishpakamigaak iwi."

gii kida.

"miidash gonaa gaa zhichige yaaN iwi gii dibage yaaN iwi.",

gii kida.

aaniish, pane dash gonaa anishinaabek zhewe bemiyaadjik gonaa gii gidaakiiyewok, gii manidookenaawaa iwi makwa zhagishing. mii gonaa gaa zhibagosendamowaat iwi, wegoweN giiyeN gaye ge giizhidaakiiyegoweN zhewe, mii giiyeN owo ge gaagiye bimaadizit, gii zhibagosendamowok.

aaniish, miidash gonaa maanda e kowaak ndo dibaadjimowin miinawaa. miigwech gonaa gaa bazindawa yek.

anishinaabek ko gaa zhidibaakonigewaat

yaawaa sa nwii dibaadjimaak miinawaa, odaawaak. megowaa gonaa iwi (doo) goziwaat ko gonaa, zhaawonong gii zhaawaat nidigwaagik. iwi dash go iwi waa oonji dibaadjimakgowaa, maaba makwa nowii gaa inind anishinaabe, aaniish, mii gonaa gewiin zhinda gaa nji nitaaginind owo. miidash gonaa ngoding (e) niwiidjiiwet maanda digwaaganinik wodi (doo) zhaawaat zaagawaang, degoshiniwaat dash giiyeN wodi, mii gii noondamowaat iidik owo anishinaabe wii dibaakoniget. yaawaa gonaa zhewe wiya gonaa anishinaabe zhewe gonaa e yaat gii nisaan wiidji anishinaaben. gaawiin gaye gonaa iwi wii nisaasiigoban gonaa newe, anishaa gonaa iwi mookamaan gonaa gii wepidawaagoban, gii ozaamiganaamaan dash ninda. miidash go maaba iwi anishinaabe iwi gaa nijinet.

he added.

> "Then I again shot my arrow toward the lake. And this time, it landed where the dune starts to flatten out at the shore,"

he said.

> "That is how high that dune was. I do not know how else to describe the height of the dune to you,"

he said.

> "Anyway, that is how I measured the height of the dune, using my bow and arrow,"

he said.

Well, the Anishinaabe people who traveled back and forth through the area always stopped at the Sleeping Bear Dunes and they climbed it as this was one of their sacred areas. And that is one of the things they believed in and wished for, if they were to get to the top, they would have a long life.

And so, this is the end of my story. Thank you for listening to me.

How the Anishinaabe Used to Conduct Trials

I am now going to talk about the Ottawa people. This is during the time they used to move to their southern wintering grounds in the fall. The reason I am going to talk about the Anishinaabe, this man, Makwa Nowii was raised in this area during that era. So this one fall as they were moving to the south for the winter, when they got there, they found out that there was going to be a trial. Apparently, a man from that area had taken the life of another man. He had not meant to kill the man, he was just threatening him with his knife, and he struck him with a fatal blow. And this man died from the wound he suffered from being stabbed with a knife.

aaniish, miidash go iwi gii takonind maaba anishinaabe gaa nisaat newe wiidji anishinaaben. miidash gewiin gwonda wodi odaawaak iwi pii (e) nidagoshiniwaat, mii iwi iidik iwi wii dibaakonigewaat gwonda wodi anishinaabek gonaa giizhaa e yaadjik. aaniish, bidjiinak gewiin gwonda zhinda odaawaak nikeyaa e ninjibaadjik (doo) nidagoshiniwok zhewe gozining.

zhewe dash go waa nji dibaakonigewaat, ozaam giiyeN gii gaachikamigaa iwi aki zhewe. miidash giiyeN gaa zhi-inindawaa gonaa iwi ji mizhiiwaakonamowaat niibana go iwi aki, ji wiyii debabiwaat gonaa waa bazindaagedjik gonaa wii, iwi sa gonaa, wii dibaakonigewaat zhewe. wii dibaakonaawaat ninda gaa nitaagendjin anishinaaben. aaniish, noomak dash go gii dazhiikaanaawaa iwi, iwi zhewe gii mizhiiwaakonagewaat wii denigokamigaak gonaa wii debibiwaat gonaa waa bazindaagedjik.

miidash iwi gaa giizhitoowaat iwi, mii gwonda yaawaak, mizhonowek gaa inindjik, mii bebezhik wiigwaasan gii miinadowaa zhibiigaadek iidik pii iwi waa jitisek wii dibaakonind maaba gaa nitaaget. aaniish, mii sa go gwonda gii maadjiibatoowaat bebaa dibaadjimodjik.

geget sa giiyeN gonaa gii gichi dagoshiniwok anishinaabek. waasa gaye go iidik go aanind gaa binjibaawaat gwonda, wegowendigenak gonaa anishinaabek. aaniish, anishinaabe dash go aanowi go, mii iwi (doo) bibazindaagewaat. aaniish, giyegeti sa giiyeN gimaapii gii jitise iwi giizhigat iidik wii dibaakonigewaat, wewena go maanda go gii waakaawigonikaade maanda zhewe waa nji dibaakonigewaat. mii giiyeN gaye go eta bezhigong shkwaandem e nji biindigeng. ishpaabii go maanda michikan.

aaniish, mii sa gii bibiindigewaat anishinaabek. aapidji giiyeN go gii baatiinawok. miinawaa gaye gii zhichigaadeni gwonda, maaba sa anishinaabe gaa nitaaget, e nowemaadjin wii namadabinit. miinawaa gewiin maaba anishinaabe gaa nisind, gewiin maaba gii zhitoowaawaan e nowemaadjin wii namadabinit, aapidji giiyeN go gwonda baabaatiinawok gewiinawaa. gwonda dash anishinaabek e nowemaadjik ninda gaa nitaagendjin, kina gonaa gegoo gii biidoonaawaa gonaa niyii gonaa agowin gaye gonaa, miijim gaye gonaa, kina sa gonaa gegoo gonaa e nakaazang gonaa. bezhigonong dash giiyeN maanda gii temigat.

"aapidji go gii ishpisin iwi.",

gii kida maaba makwa nowii gaa inind.

miidash iwi gewiinawaa gwonda ogimaak gii zhitoowindowaa wii namadabiwaat. gii de nchiwok go iidik gewiinawaa gwonda ogimaak. miidash gaye gonaa gewiin maaba makwa nowii gii biindige gonaa gimaapii zhewe biindji waakaawigan. aapidji dash giiyeN go (doo) baatiinawon newe anishinaaben zhewe gewiin pii baandiget. miidash giiyeN gii madwe giigidat wodi owo megowe ogimaa, owo sa gonaa iidik naagaanizit ogimaa.

So this man who committed the crime was placed under arrest. And when the Ottawa from here arrived there, they heard that the people who lived there were going to have a trial. The Ottawa from here were just getting there as they had just moved there.

And the area where they were going to have the trial, the area was determined to be too small. So the people were told that they should clear more ground, that is, make the area bigger so they could accommodate a bigger crowd who would come to listen to the proceedings and to witness the event. They were going to conduct a murder trial. Well, it took them some time to make an area that would be large enough to accommodate many people who would come to listen to the proceedings.

So when the people had finished the meeting area, the messengers, or runners, were each given a birch bark scroll with a message on it telling of the upcoming trial of the man for murder. So these men left, they ran to other communities, spreading the message.

Oh, so many Anishinaabe people began arriving. Many were from far away, whoever they were. But they were Anishinaabe people, and they had come to witness the event. Finally the day arrived when the trial would begin, and there was a well-made structure where the proceedings would be held. This building had only one doorway. The surrounding wall of the structure was quite high.

So the people began filing into the building. There were so many people who had come to listen to the trial. A special place had been set aside for the family members of the one who committed the crime. Also a special place had been set aside for the relatives of the man who had been slain, and this man had so many relatives. The relatives of the man who killed his fellow man, these people brought so many things with them, food items, items of clothing and tools, many items that the people used. And all these things were piled in this one area of the building.

"These items were piled very high,"

said this man who was called Makwa Nowii.

Also, those who were chiefs from the various communities, they had a special place made for them to sit. There was quite a number of chiefs who were in attendance. Then Makwa Nowii entered the structure later on. There were already many Anishinaabe people inside this building by the time he went inside. Then, the head chief spoke from the chief's area just as Makwa Nowii entered.

> "bezhik giyaabi ogimaa zhinda (doo) nandowendaagozi.",

gii madwe kida giiyeN. miidash giiyeN maaba makwa nowii gaa inind, mii giiyeN maaba gaa madwe waawiinind.

miidash giiyeN e kidat owo ogimaa.

> "giishpmaa e yaagoweN zhinda biindik owo makwa nowii e inind, niigaan zhinda da bizhaa, da binamadabi gaye zhinda megowe ogimaa.",

gii madwe kida sa giiyeN owo. aaniish, mii sa maaba makwa nowii wodi niigaan gii nizhaat, gii oowenabit. naanetaa dash giiyeN newe gaa mishoomisodjin gii oowiidabimaan, aaniish, ogimaa gewiin maaba akiweziiN.

miidash go maanda (e) waabimigowaa gwonda baandaakowedjik gonaa, mii giiyeN maaba gichi pwaagan gii biidjigaazat. noomak go maaba gii danaandigidoon iidik ninda pwaaganon dekonaat. miinawaa gii dibaadidaan e naabadazit iidik maaba pwaagan, e inaadjimigaazat sa gonaa. miinawaa gaa shkwaa danaandigidoong, mii miinawaa bezhik akiweziiN gii gagiigidat. gaawiin dash gonaa aapidji gonaa wii bibowaa nishkendiwaat gonaa anishinaabek, mii iidik maaba aanowi (doo) kidat akiweziiN. mandj gonaa.

> "gaawiin gonaa daa nishizinoo gonaa ji maanaadendi yinggoban gonaa e zhi-anishinaabewi ying.",

gii kida sa iidik maaba. miinawaa gaye maaba gaa nitaaget, gaawiin giiyeN maaba gegiibaadizit gii aawisii. bekaa gonaa bemaadizit gonaa gii zhi-aawi. miidash maaba iwi anishinaabe gaa nitaaget, (doo) mibaabiindaakoweban giiyeN, miidash maaba bezhik iidik gaa bizhigidiskabinaat newe do pwaaganeNon. aaniish, gii nishkigoon dash, miidash iwi mookamaan gaa oonji wepidawaat. gaawiin gaye gonaa wii nisaasiigoban. anishaa gonaa iwi gonaa banggii eta nga naganaamaa gaa inendamagoweN, gii ozaamiganaamaan dash. miidash owo gaa nijinet iwi.

miinawaa bezhik gii bizagowii gii giigidat. gii dibaadjimaan dash ninda gaa nisindji, ginimaa dash go ko gonaa maaba menakwedjik gonaa ginimaa gonaa gii pogodizowidik gonaa, ngii zhinisastawaa sa maaba makwa nowii newe gii dibaadjimaat. aaniish, mii sa gwonda gii danaandigidooniwaat, gwonda niizh gaa dibaadjimaadjik ninda, gonaa e oonji dibaakonigewaat gonaa. miidash miinawaa maaba pwaagan gii inaawok dash gonaa gwonda anishinaabek ji daapinaawaat ninda pwaaganon, ji boonendiwaat gonaa.

miidash giiyeN iwi gewiin maaba newe makwa nowii mishomison gaa igot giimooch gonaa,

> "We still need one more chief to sit up here with us,"

this head chief was heard to say. And this one called Makwa Nowii, this is the one who was named to come to the front.

This is what the head chief said.

> "If the one called Makwa Nowii is inside this building, he is to come up front and sit with the chiefs,"

the head chief said. So, this man called Makwa Nowii, he went and sat in the front with the chiefs. Fortunately, his grandfather, who was also a chief, was sitting there, and that is the person Makwa Nowii sat beside.

And as I personally usually saw the ones who smoked pipes, there was this very large pipe that was brought into the building. The pipe keeper spoke at length about the importance of the pipe in these proceedings. He spoke of its usage and the many stories about the pipe. After this pipe keeper had finished speaking, another old man, an elder, got up to speak. He encouraged the people that they should let go of their anger they had for each other. I am not really sure of what he said.

> "We as Anishinaabe people, it will not do us any good if we harbor hatred in our hearts for one another,"

this elder had said. Also, he told them that this man who committed this evil deed was really not an evil man. This man lived a good decent life. And this man who killed his fellow man, he was smoking his pipe, praying, and this other man came by and disconnected his pipe. Well, he was angered by this prank, so he stabbed at the man with a knife. He had not meant to kill him. He thought he would just wound him a little, but he wounded him fatally. The other man died from this wound.

Then another man got up to speak. He talked about the man who was killed, and I understood Makwa Nowii saying that this man may have been involved in imbibing and probably was intoxicated and he was a nuisance when he drank. Then these two spokespersons talked about why the people were having this trial. Then when these two had finished speaking, they encouraged the people to accept and smoke the pipe, and to let go of their anger and hatred.

Makwa Nowii was secretly told by his grandfather this:

"giishpmaa owo pwaagan (*doo*) bininamaagoo yin, gegowa daapinaaken."

gii igoon giiyeN newe mishoomison.

zhaazhago dash gonaa (*doo*) bizhiwebat iwi, kakowaach gonaa pii gonaa (*doo*) bidibaakonigewaat iidik gwonda anishinaabek, (*doo*) gichi zagoni giiyeN nini gii daapinaan newe pwaaganon, iwi gonaa pwaaganon gonaa gaa daapinaadjik, mindimooweNik gaye gonaa, ikwewok gaye gonaa gii daapinaawaan. aaniish, mii sa go aanowi gonaa iwi gii biindaakowewaat gonaa. gii boonendiwaat.

nonggom dash go iwi (*doo*) dibaadjimowi yaaN, aanowi go gii inaawok ji minodaapinaawaat newe pwaaganon, ji biindaakowewaat. aaniish, gaawiin dash niniwok (*doo*) inendaziiwok. gegoo ginimaa gonaa gii zhimaanaadendidigenak gonaa banggii gonaa gwonda. gwonda gaye aanind e nowemaadjin maaba nini gaa nisind, (*doo*) gagibaashkoziganiwebiwok giiyeN go gewiinawaa gwonda. mii go eta go wii miigaazawaat go. gaawiin go (*doo*) minonendaziiwok go, (*doo*) nishkaadiziwok gonaa ji kida yinggoban gonaa.

miidash maaba anishinaabe ninda pwaaganon, mii giiyeN gii maajaat, (*doo*) mabanit newe ogimaan, gii inaat ji daapinaanit newe pwaaganon. gaawiin dash wiyii giiyeN gaye maaba gewiin ogimaa newe, naagaan nemadabit, gaawiin giiyeN gewiin gii daapinaasiin pwaaganon. mii gonaa gwodji gonaa gii zhigowekabi (*doo*) bininamawint newe. mii giiyeN go gewe mizawe go, kina go gewe ogimaak, gaawiin giiyeN wiya. zhago giiyeN gewiin makwa nowii pwaaganon bininamawind.

"shkenaa, giin maaba daapin pwaagan.",

(*doo*) inaadik sa.

"gga boonendamint gonaa maanda (*doo*) nishkendi ying zhinda. gaawiin gonaa daa zhinaagosinoo gonaa iwi ji bibowaa daapinek maaba pwaagan. aaniish gonaa iidik ge nizhibimaadizi ying.",

gii kidawidik sa maaba ninda pwaaganon bemitakonaadjin. aaniish, gii inaa dash maaba makwa nowii, gii igoon newe mishoomison,

"gegowa daapinaaken maaba pwaagan.",

gii igoon. giimoodj gonaa maanda gii igoon. gaawiin go wiya go wii noondaawigot gegoo owo akiweziiN gii inendazii. aaniish, mii sa giyegeti owo makwa nowii newe pwaaganon (*doo*) biniimanamawind, taaya, endigoweN go gwodji gewiin (*doo*) nizhigowekabi. aaniish, mii sa gii aanowewizit zhewe maaba anishinaabe waa biindaakowewet.

> "If the pipe is offered to you, do not accept it,"

he supposedly was told by his grandfather.

And as it used to happen in the old days, when they had the occasional trial, a man would take the pipe with difficulty and weigh the facts, as would a woman, since they too could accept the pipe on these special occasions. So once the pipe was accepted by someone, everyone would have to accept it. Then they would stop hating and being angry with one another.

And in this story I am telling you now, they were told to accept the pipe in a good way and smoke it. But the men did not agree with this. They must have harbored some grudges against each other. The relatives of the man who had been killed sat with their weapons inside the building. They were ready to do battle. They were not a happy bunch, in fact they were very angry.

So the pipe carrier began to make his rounds, he went to the chiefs first, and asked them to smoke the pipe. The head chief did not accept the pipe from the pipe carrier. He practically turned his back on the pipe carrier when he tried to offer the pipe to the head chief. Every single chief followed the head chief's example, they all refused to smoke the pipe. Now the pipe carrier was offering the pipe to Makwa Nowii.

> "Oh please, won't you please accept the pipe?"

he was probably asked by the pipe carrier.

> "We will stop being angry and hating one another. It is not right that you do not accept this pipe. How will we continue to live in harmony as Anishinaabe people?"

the pipe carrier must have said. Well, Makwa Nowii was told by his grandfather the following.

> "Do not accept the pipe when it is offered to you,"

he was told by his grandfather. He was told this secretly. The old man did not want others to hear what he said. So, of course Makwa Nowii followed the wishes of his grandfather, and when the pipe was offered to him, he too turned his back to the pipe carrier. So the pipe carrier was not able to get any of the chiefs to accept the pipe and smoke it.

miidash bemaadizidjik wodi bem*a*dabidjik, mii giiyeN wodi minaaniibowit, mi-aanowi migaakiizomaat newe. gaa*wiin* sa giiyeN go wiya go, aapidji go giiyeN go (*doo*) jaagshkowaan zhewe ngoding maanda e nizhigiiwitaabanit newe. gaa*wiin* sa go wiya go. zhago go giiyeN go wodi aapta (*doo*) midebiwaabiminaagozi. gaa*wiin* go ginigeN go wiya, gaa*wiin* go wiya go waa daapinaat pwaaganon. gaa*wiin* giiyeN gaye go wiya waa giigidat zhewe biindji waakaawigan, kina go (*doo*) nishkaadiziwok go gewe anishinaabek. taaya, zhago go*sha* nayiinawi*nd* giiyeN go wodi shkweyaang go wodi waasa (*doo*) nidebiwaabiminaagozi *owo*. gaawii*n* go nigika go maanda, (*doo*) mimowi, (*doo*) mimowi giiyeN go maaba newe pwaaganon bemit*a*konaadjin, gii gikendaan waa zhiweb*a*ziwaat giishpmaa wiya pwaaganon bibowaa daapinaat.

"taaya, zhago go*sha* go wodi ngoding giyaabi eta bimabiwok.",

gii kida maaba m*a*kwa nowii. mii go eta e naakodabiwaat go. gaa*wiin* go ginigeN waa giigidat wiya. zhago gewe shkwaach (*doo*) mabiwaat zhago go aapta (*doo*) miyaa,

"gaawii*n* gaye wiya waa daapinaat pwaaganon.",

(*doo*) kida.

"aangowaamish gonaa gegoo zhinda da zhiwebat iwi giishpmaa gwonda bibowaa daapinaawaat newe pwaaganon.",

(*doo*) inendam sa iidik maaba m*a*kwa nowii gewii*n*. mii sa iidik zhago gewii*n* (*doo*) makowit gonaa ji kida *y*inggoba*n*. gaawii*n* gonaa yeshkawot gonaa gii gikendazii*n* iidik iwi e inaadji*m*igaazanit ninda pwaaganon.

"zhago go*sha* nayiinawi*nd* wodi, ginimaa gaye giyaabi niswi (*doo*) namadabidigenak.",

(*doo*) kida.

"aanowi go maaba newe (*e*) bimit*a*konaat pwaaganon, daa nigaakiizomaan newe. gaa*wiin* *dash* go newe (*doo*) bazindaagosiin ginigeN. zhago eta giyaabi (*doo*) bezhigoowaakodabi. miidash iwi pii ikwe gii bibiindiget.",

(*doo*) kida.

Then this man went walking in front of the assembled people, asking them, beseeching them to accept the pipe. No one would accept the pipe as he finished walking in front of the first row of people. There was not one person who would accept the pipe. He was soon seen to have gone halfway through the assembled crowd of people. There still was no one who would accept the pipe. No one would dare speak while this man was beseeching people to accept the pipe, as all of the people were angry. Oh wow, he was now seen walking in front of the people sitting at the back of the building. This was not an easy task for the pipe carrier, he was crying the whole time as he beseeched each person to accept the pipe, for he knew something unhealthy would happen to the community if no one accepted the pipe.

> "Wow, there was only one row left,"

said Makwa Nowii. And the people just sat still. Not one person would dare say anything. Now the pipe carrier was halfway through the last row of people.

> "There was not one person who was willing to accept the pipe,"

he said.

> "Something terrible might happen right in here if no one accepts the pipe,"

Makwa Nowii must have thought to himself. I guess we could say that he was just becoming aware of the possible dire consequences. I guess he did not really have a clear understanding about the pipe and its teachings.

> "Now, there may be only three left sitting who were yet to be approached by the pipe carrier,"

he said.

> "The pipe carrier tried his best to urge and to coax someone to accept the pipe. But, no one would listen to him. Now, there was only one person left to be asked to accept the pipe. And just then a woman came into the building,"

he said.

> "gaaNwaaN go gii gashkitoon gii bibiindiget shkwaandeming, binoodjiiNson (*e*) bitakonaadjin. aaniish, maaba gewiin (*doo*) bezhigoowaakodabi giyaabi wodi newe gonaa pwaaganon waa inind wii daapinaat, endigo gewiin gwodji (*doo*) nizhigowekabi owo.",

(*doo*) kida.

> "taaya, mii eta giyaabi bezhik. mii owo ikwe shkwaach gaa bibiindiget."

aaniish, (*doo*) zhiwebat dash gonaa iwi, binoodjiiN wiya gonaa, gegoo gonaa (*doo*) niimanamawind gonaa, baabagiye go (*doo*) nowodinaan, mii sa maaba owo ikwe gaa zhiwebazit iwi. gaawiin go maaba ikwe newe gii daapinaasiin, maaba sa binoodjiiN, maanda maaba anishinaabe besha wodi dash (*doo*) yaanit (*doo*) nidigogaabowit, (*doo*) niniimanaat newe pwaaganon, mii maaba binoodjiiN gii nowodinaat newe.

> "aaniish, mii sa go aanowi gii daapinigaazat owo pwaagan.",

(*doo*) kida.

> "miidash gaa kidat owo yaawaa, ogimaa naagaanizit,",

gii inaadjimo maaba makwa nowii,

> "mii giiyeN go eta ngoding maaba shkodekaan wii wepidawin, wii paskaneganaamind, mii go eta ngoding."

mii iwi e inaadjimigaazat iidik gewiin maaba iwi pwaagan wii dibaakonigeng, iwi gonaa gewiin anishinaabe gii dibaakoniget. gii yaa dash giiyeN go zhewe naanedaa owo iidik netoot iwi shkode, shkode dash zhitoot. aaniish, mii sa gewiin maaba gii nandondjigaazat wodi niigaan, kina go wegowendik go wiya wii waabimaat go gii zhichige maaba ogimaa. aaniish, mii sa gii miinind newe shkodekaanon. taaya, mii go eta ngoding gii wepidawaat,

> "mii eta shkode.",

(*doo*) kida.

> "She could barely make her way through the doorway as she was carrying a child in her arms. There was that last person who was sitting yet to be offered the pipe, and he too, practically turned his back on the pipe carrier,"

he said.

> "Now, there was just one more person, and it was the woman who was the last one to come in."

As it so often happens, when someone holds something in front of a child, the child will oftentimes quickly grab at it, and that is what happened to this woman who was carrying her child. She did not accept the pipe when it was offered to her, it was her child who took hold of it, as the pipe carrier offered the pipe to the woman, the child was the one who grabbed it.

> "Well, someone finally accepted the pipe,"

he said.

> "And the head chief gave these instructions,"

said Makwa Nowii.

> "The flint can only be struck one time, to make a spark, only once."

This is the teaching about the pipe when it is used in a trial, the way the Anishinaabe people conducted their trials. And there happened to be a person in the crowd who had the task of being a fire keeper, and he was the one who made fire. So this man was summoned up to the front of the building, as the head chief did things properly, and he wanted everyone to witness what was going on. And the head chief was given the flint. He struck the flint just the one time.

> "There were a lot of sparks,"

he said.

"mii gaye go gii paskanet maaba semaa. mii go gii pakowaapasat go wewena go. aaniish, mii sa gii boonendiwaat aanowi. gwonda dash e nowemaadjik ninda gaa nisindjin, mii maanda nakaadjigan zhewe niibana gaa biidjigaadek, mii gwonda gaa maatoowondjik iwi.",

gii kida maaba makwa nowii gii dibaadjimot. miinawaa gonaa gaa shkwaa maatoowondowaa maanda nakaadjigan gonaa, gii gaakiizomaawok gegoo gonaa wii bibowaa zhinishkendiwaat gonaa. aaniish, miidash go gaa zhichigewaat iwi, gaawiin gonaa wiya gii nishkendazii gonaa iwi gaa shkwaa dibaakonigewaat, mii gonaa gaa zhiminowaabidiwaat miinawaa. mii maaba gewiin anishinaabe iwi gaa zhichiget gii dibaakoniget.

iwi dash go gii kida maaba makwa nowiiban,

"nowonch (doo) zanagat anishinaabe (doo) dibaakoniget, yaabshkiiyet dash, gichimookamaan e inind. aabidek go gwii debwe giishpmaa gegoo (e) kida yin iwi anishinaabe (doo) dibaakoniget. gaawiin gwii giiniwishkisii."

nonggom wiyii debaakonigedjik, mii go e zhimashkowagiizhiwed wiya giiniwishkid. gaawiin dash wiyii maamdaa iwi anishinaabe gii inendazii wiya wii giiniwishkit.

miidash go pane gaa kidat maaba makwa nowii gaa inind,

"ge giiniwishkit nonggom debaakonind, mii owo bekanaaget.",

gii kida ko.

"maaba dash gewiin anishinaabe dibaakoniget, giyegeti gii zanagat.",

gii kida.

"aapidji go."

miinawaa gaye newe gii dibaadjimaan newe gaa nitaagendjin, iwi go iwi gaa piichi bimiwinind maaba pwaagan,

"aapidji go maaba gii zegazi anishinaabe.",

gii kida.

"And the tobacco began to smolder as it lit. The smoke began to rise from the burning tobacco. So the people now had to release their anger they had for each other. And the relatives of the slain man, these were the ones who received the gifts that were piled at the front of the building, the gifts were divided amongst them,"

Makwa Nowii said as he told this story. After the gifts were divided among the relatives of the slain man, they were counseled and advised that it is unhealthy to carry the anger they have or had, and that they should let it go. And, that is what they did, they accepted the others in friendship and brotherhood after the trial was over. This is the way the Anishinaabe people conducted their trials in the past.

And Makwa Nowii always maintained the following.

"It was much more difficult to go through a trial using the Anishinaabe custom than it is to go to trial in the white man's court. When you are in an Anishinaabe trial, you must speak the truth. You cannot lie."

Today, when people go to court, they sit up there with a straight face and lie. This was not the case when the Anishinaabe held a trial, you could not tell a lie.

The one called Makwa Nowii always said that.

"Now, the one who lies in a court of law, that is the one who usually wins,"

he used to say.

"But the way the Anishinaabe conducted a trial, it was very difficult,"

he said.

"Very much so."

And he also talked about the one who was on trial, and how he looked while the pipe carrier was making his rounds with the pipe inside the building.

"This man was very scared,"

he said.

> "niigaan go gaye wodi gii zhichigaadeni wii namadabit. *n*iyii gaye zhewe (*doo*) teni (*doo*) namadabit, mookamaan. aapidji go gii waabanaagozi gaa piichi zegazit.",

gii kida.

> "mii go baamaampii gonaa gewii*n* gii minonaagozit gonaa *o*wo, maaba pwaagan gaa daapinigaazat.",

gii inaadjimo, gii inaadjimoba*n* maaba m*a*kwa nowii gaa inind.

aaniish, mii*da*sh gonaa iwi e kowaak maanda n*do* dibaadjimowin. mii gonaa iwi ji boonaadjimow yaaN. gichi miigwech gaa bazindaw*a* yek.

> "He sat in the front, in an area that had been set aside for him. The knife was right there near him. This man was pale, that is how frightened he was,"

he said.

> "He did not relax or regain his composure or his regular complexion until the pipe was accepted,"

the one called Makwa Nowii, the late Makwa Nowii, said as he told this story.

Well that is the end of my story. I will stop talking now. Thank you very much for listening to me.